backstage pass

OLIVIA CUNNING

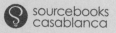

sourcebooks
casablanca

Published by Sourcebooks Casablanca, an imprint of Sourcebooks, Inc.
P.O. Box 4410, Naperville, Illinois 60567-4410
(630) 961-3900
Fax: (630) 961-2168
www.sourcebooks.com

Printed and bound in Canada.
MBP 10 9 8 7 6 5 4 3 2 1

Dedicated to
"Dimebag" Darrell Abbott,
master of the metal guitar riff
and cowboy from hell,
who burned up his fret board
with magic fingers.
He was a gifted musician,
taken from us much too soon,
but he lives on in his music
and in the strings of the guitarists
he continues to inspire.
I still hear you, Dimebag.
Rock on.

\m/

Chapter 1

A STACK OF HANDOUTS TUMBLED FROM MYRNA'S laptop case to the floral-patterned carpet. Un-freakin'-believable. She'd forgotten to zip the compartment in her haste to flee the seminar room. With a loud sigh, she bent to gather the scattered papers. Could this day suck a little more, please?

A chorus of "chug, chug, chug, chug," followed by enthusiastic cheers came from across the lobby near the elevators. Well, someone was having a good time tonight. It certainly wasn't her.

She crammed the papers inside her bag and jerked the zipper closed before continuing through the over-done hotel lobby on her way to her sixth-floor room. A long, hot bath sounded like heaven. How had she let her associate dean talk her into presenting at this stupid conference in the first place? What a total waste of time. The other professors in her field wouldn't know an innovative idea if it stood on its head and sang "The Star-Spangled Banner." And why did she care what her colleagues thought of her methods anyway? Students loved her classes. They were always full. She had wait-ing lists for—

Steps echoed hers. The hairs on the back of her neck stood on end. She paused—her heart racing, palms damp.

Whoever followed stopped several steps behind her. She could hear him breathing.

Jeremy?

No. It couldn't be her ex-husband. He didn't know how to find her. Right? Tell that to the cold sweat trickling between her breasts.

She clutched the handle of her laptop case, prepared to clobber whoever was dumb enough to sneak up on her.

"You gave a great seminar, Dr. Evans," an unfamiliar voice said to her back.

Not Jeremy. Thank God. She took a deep, shaky breath and glanced over her shoulder.

A lanky, fortyish man extended his hand in her direction. "Who would ever think to use guitar riffs in discussions of human psychology? Not me. I mean, I'm sold on the method. I'm just not sure I can pull it off with your level of, uh..." He cleared his throat. "...*enthusiasm*." He grinned, gaze dropping to the neckline of her tailored gray suit.

Her heart still hammering in her chest, Myrna suppressed the urge to throttle him and extended her free hand to accept his handshake. "Thank you, Mister uh..."

When his fingers wrapped around hers, his smile spread ear to ear. "Doctor. Doctor Frank Elroy from Stanford. Abnormal psych. Head of the department, actually."

Ah, Doctor Ass. Doctor Pompous Ass. I've met you before. Thousands of times.

She nodded and plastered a weary smile to her face. "Nice to meet you, Doctor Elroy."

"Say, would you like to have a drink with me?" He nodded toward the cocktail lounge to her left, his thumb stroking the back of her hand.

Myrna cringed inwardly while maintaining her smile. This guy was the antithesis of her type. Boring. No, thanks. Her present aversion to boring existed at a visceral level. "I'm sorry, but I'll have to pass. I was heading up to my room to crash. Maybe some other time."

He deflated like a punctured balloon. "Sure. I understand. You must be exhausted after that lively…" He grinned again. "…discussion."

Discussion? Had he been there? "Bloodbath" seemed a more fitting description, and she felt particularly anemic at the moment.

"Yeah," she muttered, eyes narrowing. She yanked her hand from his, spun on her heel, and continued toward the elevator, walking around the edge of the hotel's bar and skirting several bushy potted plants.

A loud round of laughter drew her attention to the cocktail lounge. Four men sat in a semicircular booth, laughing at a fifth man who was lying on his back in the center of their table. The table, covered with glasses containing various amounts of amber liquid, tilted precariously under the man's weight as he leaned to one side. His companions scrambled to rescue their beers from certain demise.

"Tell the room to stop spinning," the lounging man shouted at the knock-off Tiffany lamp above the table.

"No more beer for you, Brian," one of his friends said.

Brian held up a finger. "One more." He lifted another finger. "Or two." Another finger. "Mmmmmaybe four."

Myrna grinned. The five of them didn't exactly "blend" with the conference attendees, mostly professors, scattered throughout the lounge and lobby. The unconventional crew in the booth drew more than their fair share of animosity and stares. Was it the tattoos? The various piercings and spiked jewelry? The dyed hair, strange haircuts, and black clothing? Whatever. They were just guys being guys. And not a boring one in the bunch, she'd wager.

Myrna took a hesitant step toward the elevator. She'd love to go hang out with them for a while. She could use a little fun—something other than stimulating conversation with an intellectual. She got enough of that at work.

Brian, still lounging in the center of the table, vocalized a riff while playing masterful air guitar on his back. Myrna recognized the series of notes at once. She used it in her class discussion on male sensuality, because no one on earth played a guitar more sensually than Master Sinclair. Hold the phone! Could that be...? Nah, what would the rock group Sinners be doing at a college teaching conference? They were probably just fans of the band, though the name Brian made her lead guitarist senses tingle. Wasn't Sinners' lead guitarist named Brian Sinclair?

One of the men seated in the booth turned his head to scratch his chin with his shoulder. Despite his mirrored sunglasses, she instantly recognized vocalist Sedric Lionheart. Her heart rate kicked up a couple notches. It *was* Sinners.

"I am so fucking drunk!" Brian yelled. He rolled off the table, knocking over several empty beer glasses, and landed on the laps of two of his companions. They dumped him unceremoniously on the floor.

Myrna snorted and then glanced around to make sure no one had witnessed her produce such an unladylike sound. She *had* to go talk to them. She could pretend she wanted to meet them because of her seminar. In truth, she loved their music. They weren't too hard on the eyes either. The definition of exactly her type. Wild. Yes, please. Guaranteed to give her exactly what she needed after the day she'd had.

Abandoning her plan to hide in her room, Myrna skirted the low wall that separated the lounge area from the corridor. She paused in front of Brian, who was struggling to crawl to his hands and knees. She set her lumpy laptop case on the floor and bent to help him to his feet. The instant she touched his arm, her heart skipped a beat and then began to race.

Animal magnetism. He had it. *Hello, Mr. Welcome Diversion.*

His gaze drifted up her legs and body, his face slowly tilting into view. He had features a sculptor would love: strong jaw, pointed chin, high cheekbones. Would it be presumptuous of her to examine the contours of his face with her fingertips? Her lips? She forced her attention to her hand, which gripped his well-muscled upper arm.

"Be careful with this arm," she said. "So few guitarists have your skill."

He used her support to stagger to his feet. When he stumbled against her, she caught his scent and inhaled deeply, her eyes drifting closed. Primal desire bombarded her senses. Did she just growl aloud?

His strong hands gripped her shoulders as he steadied himself. Every nerve ending in her body shifted into high alert. She couldn't remember the last time she'd been instantaneously attracted to a man.

Brian released her and leaned against the back of the booth for support. He blinked hard, as if trying to focus his intense, brown eyes on her face. "You know who I am?" he asked, his voice slurred.

She smiled and nodded eagerly. "Who doesn't?"

He waved a hand around theatrically, which set him even further off balance. "Every stuffed-shirt geek in the whole damned place, that's who."

He snarled at a gray-haired woman in a heavy cardigan who sat openly gaping at him. The woman gasped and turned her attention to her ocean-blue cocktail, slurping the blended beverage through a tiny red straw as nonchalantly as possible.

"Brian, don't start shit," Sed, the group's lead singer, said.

The acidic look Brian shot at Sed could peel paint. "What? I'm not starting anything. These people all have *fuck*-king staring problems!"

True. They were staring. Most of them at Myrna now. Probably wondering how to best rescue her from *enemy* territory.

"Do you mind if I sit with you for a while?" Myrna asked, hoping to become less noticeable by sitting. She tucked the lock of hair that had escaped her hair clip behind her ear and smiled at Brian hopefully. He stroked his eyebrow with his index finger as he contemplated her request. She knew what he must be thinking. Why would a stuffy-looking chick in a business suit request to sit with five rock stars?

Sed scooted over in the booth and patted the empty expanse of forest-green vinyl beside him. She tugged her gaze from Brian to look at Sed. Sed's boy-next-door good looks contrasted his bad-boy, womanizing reputation. She didn't follow the personal lives of the bands she admired, but even she knew Sed's rep. His smile, complete with dimples, could ice a cake, which was likely why he covered it so rapidly with a scowl. A quick veil of indifference returned his cool status. Those darling dimples didn't quite fit his image.

Myrna slid into the booth next to Sed, wiping her sweaty palms on her skirt as she settled beside him. *Okay, I'm in. Now what?*

"Are you some kind of businesswoman or something?" Sed leaned back to examine her professional attire.

Myrna didn't mind his twice-over. "Or something. Actually, I'm a stuffed-shirt geek. A college professor here at the conference."

"No shit?" She recognized the speaker, who sat across from her, as Eric Sticks, the band's drummer. "If I'd have known college professors were hot, I might have considered an education."

Myrna laughed. She glanced up at Brian, who was still leaning against the booth next to Eric's right shoulder. Her heart gave a painful throb. God, he was gorgeous. "Would you like to sit down, Brian?"

Myrna scooted closer to Sed, her knee settling against his beneath the table. Brian collapsed on the seat beside her, lodging her between two of the sexiest and most talented musicians in the business. She'd died and gone to heaven. *Play it cool, Myrna. If you start spazzing out like a fangirl, they'll tell you to get lost.* And she certainly didn't want that.

Brian leaned forward and rested his forehead on the table with a groan. It took all of Myrna's concentration not to offer a soothing touch. She knew who he was, but he didn't know her from Adam. Well, hopefully, he could tell her from *Adam*, but, uh…

She took a deep breath to collect her scattered

thoughts and forced her attention to Eric. She could look at him without getting all giddy but found she couldn't stop staring at his insane hairstyle—half-long, a center strip of short spikes, the rest various lengths and just plain strange. A crimson, finger-thick lock curled around the side of his neck. *Rock star hair*. She stifled an excited giggle.

"So what do you teach?" Eric took a sip of his beer, his pale-blue eyes never leaving her face. Well, maybe he checked out her chest a little, but he mostly kept his gaze above her neck.

Myrna winced at his question and lowered her eyes to the table. Any chance of her earning their respect would evaporate the moment she revealed what subject she taught. "Do I have to say?"

"Come on."

She sighed heavily. "Human sexuality."

Eric sputtered in his beer. He wiped his mouth with the back of his hand. "Fuck me."

"Well, yeah, I guess that is my subject matter," Myrna said with a crooked grin.

The guys laughed. Except for Brian. Unmoving, his head still rested on the table in front of him. Had he lost consciousness? *Wasted* didn't come close to describing his current condition.

"Is he okay?" Myrna asked.

"Yeah, he's just a little fucked up," Eric said.

"He's a lot fucked up," said Trey Mills, the band's rhythm guitarist, who lounged in the booth next to Eric.

"Shut up," Brian murmured. He turned his head to look up at Myrna. He held one eye closed as he tried to focus on her. She had an inexplicable urge to straighten his tousled, jet-black hair, which fell just below collar length and stuck out at odd angles all over his head. "What's your name, Professor Sex?"

She smiled. Maybe he was interested. "Myrna."

He chuckled. "That's an old lady's name."

Or…maybe he wasn't. She hoped she hid her disappointment well.

Sed reached behind Myrna and slapped Brian on the back for his insult. Brian didn't even flinch. He most certainly wasn't feeling any pain.

Myrna shrugged. "He's right. I was named after my great-grandmother. She qualifies as an old lady."

Brian turned his head so his forehead rested against the table again. He swallowed several times. "I think I'm gonna be sick."

"Eric, take him to the bathroom," Sed said. "The last thing we need is a table covered in Sinclair puke."

Eric groaned. "I want to stay and talk to the pretty lady. Nothing but the same boring dudes at this table all night." Despite his protests, Eric slid from his end of the bench and hauled Brian to his feet.

"I'll still be here when you get back," Myrna promised.

"Buy her a drink, Sed. Or, since they're all on you tonight, buy her two." Eric looped Brian's arm around his shoulders and walked his staggering friend toward the bathroom.

Myrna watched them go, her appreciative eyes on Brian's perfect, black-denim-encased ass.

"Don't hold it against him, Myr. He's not usually like this. He just…uh…got out of a relationship," Sed said.

Trey rolled his eyes and shook his head. "Yeah, you might say that."

"Not sure why this keeps happening to him." Jace Seymour, the bassist, massaged the silver hoop earring in his earlobe. He was the only blond in the group—bleached, if his dark brows and beard stubble were any indication. The smallest member of the band, he had a James Dean tough-guy thing going on. Probably trying to understate his natural cuteness. Myrna just wanted to squeeze him.

"Dude gets dumped more than any guy I know." Trey just looked damned sexy. Whenever his sultry bedroom eyes met Myrna's, a tingle settled at the base of her spine.

"That's because he's a fucking retard when it comes to women." Sed ran a hand over his shorn black hair. "He falls for these bimbos one right after another. He'll never learn."

"Or maybe his problem is that *someone* keeps fucking things up for him," Trey said. "Just a thought."

"That bitch wasn't worth his time. Brian's way too good for her," Sed growled.

Myrna looked from one man to the next. There was something more to this story than they were saying aloud. Or maybe… "Brian's a hopeless romantic, isn't he?"

Sed leaned close to her ear. "Shhh. That's a secret."

A thrill raced up the side of her neck. She turned her head and found Sed's nose less than an inch from hers. She could see the fringes of his lashes just behind the mirrored surfaces of his shades. Finding it disconcerting to be stared down by a guy in sunglasses, she reached up and slid his eyewear down his nose. She'd like to think it was better to look him in the eye, but his probing blue-eyed gaze made her heart go pitter-pat. He grinned, undoubtedly aware of the effect he had on women.

Sed lifted his arm in the air to signal the cocktail waitress. "What's your poison, Myrna?"

"Just water for me."

"Don't you need something stronger to loosen up a little?" Cocking an eyebrow at her, his eyes scanned her conservative suit.

"Totally unnecessary. I'm always loose."

"You don't look loose." He fingered the top button of her jacket. It just happened to be situated directly between her breasts. This guy was trouble with a capital T.

Must. Avoid. Hot. Vocalist.

"Looks can be deceiving." She twisted away from him to look up at the waitress and break the contact between their knees.

Sed chuckled. "Somehow, I believe that in your case." To the waitress, he said, "Two waters, please."

"Oh, I just need one."

"The other one is for Brian."

Myrna flushed. "Of course."

The waitress set a glass of water before her. Myrna gazed toward the men's restroom and hoped Brian would be okay. He hadn't looked well at all. And she'd much rather concentrate on him instead of Mr. Player here, who was currently rubbing his knuckles against the side of her knee. When his fingers found their way under the hem of her skirt, her eyes widened and she shifted sideways a few more inches. Trey looked safe lounging across from her, sucking on a red lollipop. Maybe she should move to the other side of the table. She lifted her glass of water to her mouth.

Sed squeezed her knee. Myrna choked and reached beneath the table to remove his hand from her leg.

Undeterred, he leaned closer. She got the feeling this guy wasn't used to being rejected.

"Would you like to go upstairs with me?" Sed whispered into her ear, his nose brushing against the side of her neck as he lowered his head.

"Uh…"

Chapter 2

BRIAN FLUSHED THE TOILET AND LEANED AGAINST THE stall door. He pressed the back of his wrist against his mouth and swallowed several times to fight his nausea.

No good.

He rushed forward and vomited into the toilet again. One day he would learn the limit of his alcohol tolerance. Apparently, today wasn't the day.

"Dude, do you need me to hold your hair for you?" Eric called from outside the stall. He snickered.

"Fuck you," Brian gasped, and threw up again.

"That's a lot of perfectly good beer you're wasting."

"If you want it, come get it."

Brian leaned against the cool metal partition and flushed the toilet with his foot. He stood there for a moment and finally decided he felt well enough to come out of the stall.

Eric looked at him hopefully. "Better?"

Brian nodded slightly.

"You've gotta stop letting chicks get to you."

Tell him something he didn't know.

Brian moved to the sink and rinsed his mouth with water several times before glancing in the mirror. Bloodshot eyes. Pale and waxy skin. He ran a hand over his slack face. "God, I look like shit."

"I don't notice any difference."

Brian held up the three centermost fingers of his right hand. "Read between the lines, asshole."

Eric looked more puzzled than usual. "I never learned to read."

"Here, let me help you." Brian bent his ring finger and index finger down, leaving his middle finger extended. "Do you know sign language?"

"Nope. Sorry." Eric punched him in the arm, thumbed his nose, and punched him again. Brian knew he'd feel those in the morning. Eric never held back in his blows. "You ready to go back? You sure made an ass of yourself in front of that classy babe."

"Thanks for the reminder." Luckily, Brian probably wouldn't remember any of it tomorrow.

"Come on. Let's go."

"What's your rush?" Brian asked.

"How often do you get to hang out with a sophisticated sexpot like her?"

"Besides last night when I boned your mom?"

"Dude, if I had a mom, I might take offense."

Brian scowled. Why had he said that? Being drunk was no excuse. "Sorry, man. I didn't mean..." He rubbed his face vigorously with both hands. "Fuck."

"If we don't hurry back, Sed will be all over that sweet piece of ass."

Brian splashed some cool water on his face. "Yeah, so what's new?" Sed was all over *every* sweet piece of ass.

"It's totally unfair. Sed gets all the pussy."

All of them did fine with that. Couldn't complain. Actually, it would do Brian good to lay off the pussy for a while. "We all get plenty."

"But Sed gets all the *good* pussy. This is Certified Grade A pussy we're talking about, Be-Rye. He's probably already got her on her back with her ankles around his neck." He tilted his head back and did his best chick-getting-laid-by-Sed impression. "Oh, Sed. Yes. Yes. Sed. Ohhhh!"

Brian rolled his eyes and shook his head. "You're an ass, Eric. You know that?"

"I'd like a piece of ass. I do know that. Hurry the fuck up or I'm going back without you."

Brian dried his face on a paper towel and headed for the bathroom exit. "All right then, let's go get you some Certified Grade A pussy." He clapped Eric on the back, walking without any assistance now. Eric had no chance with Myrna if Sed had his sights on her. But hey, a guy could dream.

When they reached the table, Brian found Myrna sitting demurely next to Sed. All her clothes were still in place. Sed's hand wasn't up her skirt. They weren't even making out. In fact, they were talking and laughing. Even Jace, who said fewer than five words in the average day, chatted quietly with the Certified Grade A Sex Professor. When Brian's shadow crossed her face, Myrna glanced up at him and smiled brightly. She had a great smile, flashing perfect, white teeth between soft, kissable lips.

"Are you feeling better?" She looked him over with genuine concern.

Don't do that, he thought. *I'm still trying to get over what's-her-face. Angie. Yeah. I'm trying to get over Angie.*

Brian glanced at Sed, who avoided his accusatory glare by finding Jace uncommonly interesting.

Angie… Brian's heart panged unpleasantly and he clenched his fist.

That fucking slut.

"Yeah, I feel a little better," he said to Myrna.

"He blew chunks," Eric found necessary to inform everyone.

Myrna patted the seat next to her, which apparently signaled Eric to shove Brian out of the way so he could sit next to her. She laughed and hugged Eric's arm. "Thanks for taking care of Brian."

Eric beamed. "Hey, no problem. That's what friends are for."

Fuckhead.

Brian took a seat next to Trey, who lounged on the bench across from Myrna with the lollipop stick protruding from his mouth. Trey had to be the only guy on earth who could make sucking on a lollipop look cool. He'd given up smoking a few months ago but still needed something in his mouth at all times. His dentist made a killing.

"So are you really a fan of ours?" Eric asked Myrna.

"Yeah, for years. Even before you made it really big. I use snippets of your guitar music in my classes to discuss male sensu…" She glanced at Brian, her eyes widening as if she'd been caught doing something wrong.

She never finished the thought, because Jace decided now was a good time to break his regular silence. "She even knows all of our names."

Looking relieved about the subject change, she pointed to each of them in turn. "Eric Sticks—drums. Three bass drums, fourteen cymbals. He does it with perfect rhythm."

"Every time," he said, tapping the table with his palms.

"Sedric Lionheart. Lead vocals. The sound of his voice makes the ladies cream their panties."

Sed leaned closer to her and said in his signature, baritone growl, "Yours included? I could sing a few bars, if you like."

"That's entirely unnecessary."

"Ah, you're killing me, Myr."

She grinned deviously. Brian wondered what he'd missed while he'd been worshipping the porcelain god. Just like Sed to move in for the kill immediately.

She continued, "Jace Seymour. Bassist." She paused, contemplating the newest member of their band.

"Hey, don't I get a byline?" Jace complained.

Myrna leaned across Sed and beckoned Jace closer. She whispered something in his ear and he flushed to the roots of his bleached hair. "Seriously?" he sputtered.

She stared into his eyes and nodded. "Seriously."

Now that was just wrong. What had she told him?

"Trey Mills. Rhythm guitarist. Dreamy green eyes to melt hearts. Nimble fingers to, well, get a lady's thoughts going in all sorts of inappropriate directions."

Trey winked and wriggled his fingers at her.

Her eyes moved to Brian. "Brian Sinclair." She paused. Brian's gaze focused on her pouty, pink lips. He wondered how many of her male students sat through her class with wood in their pants. Captivated, he waited for her words. A slow smile spread across her lovely face. "A musical genius."

No way! He didn't get something sexy said about him? He might melt under the heat of her gaze, however. She wanted him. He'd been around enough women to know that look. Why had he drunk so much? He was in no condition to pull off any level of seduction.

"I guess she does know who we are," Eric said.

"Did you think I was lying?" Myrna's gaze moved to Eric.

"You just don't look like a rocker. Like, at all."

"What does a rocker look like?"

"More makeup. Fewer clothes. Piercings. Tattoos."

"Who says I don't have any piercings?"

Sed traced the edge of her ear with his fingertip, drawing attention to a pair of small diamond studs in her earlobe. "Ear piercings don't count."

"I wasn't talking about my ears."

Sed's eyes searched her face. "Then where? I don't see any oth— Oh…"

Brian shifted uncomfortably in his seat.

"So where is it?" Eric asked excitedly. "Navel? Nipple?"

"Clit?" Jace asked, his eyes downcast as he grinned crookedly.

That's what Brian expected, too. Her clit. *Fuck me.* He found it challenging enough to stay upright with his head swimming from the booze. He sure didn't need blood vacating his brain to engorge more attentive pieces of his anatomy. He clutched the table as the room tilted.

Myrna grinned, her hazel eyes moving to Brian's face. "I'll never tell," she said, but her eyes said *I'll show you, Brian.* She was toying with him. She *had* to be. He practically had "drunk loser" tattooed on his forehead at the moment.

Sed leaned closer to her and whispered something in her ear. She shook her head.

"You're killing me, Myr."

"Do you have any tattoos?" Eric asked.

"Not as many as you do." Myrna's eyes widened. She

pulled Eric's hand above the surface of the table and released it. "You do not have permission to touch me."

Brian bit his lip to hold back his laughter and lowered his gaze. *Harsh!* Surprisingly, none of the guys ripped on Eric for Myrna's blatant dismissal. This chick was as intimidating as hell. Brian couldn't remember the last time a woman had rattled his self-confidence. High school?

"I assume your body art isn't visible either." Sed tugged the collar of her suit to one side to reveal an unmarked collarbone. Her elbow in his ribs convinced him to cease his inspection.

"I am a college professor. I have to maintain a certain level of propriety."

"And you hang out with us in public?" Trey snorted and chuckled.

She glanced at her companions, considering each individually. "Good point." She laughed. Delightful. Warm. Brian bet there were other things about her that were delightful and warm. "I need to head up to bed. It's been a long day."

"Don't go yet," Eric protested.

Brian's eyebrows shot up in surprise. Hadn't she just publicly rejected him? And he wanted her to stay?

"Are you coming to our concert tomorrow night?" Trey asked.

Myrna's jaw dropped. "You're playing live? Oh my God. I'd absolutely love to go!"

"It's sold out," Sed said.

She scowled. "That sucks. Well, I mean, it's great for you, but it really sucks for me."

"We'll put you on the guest list. Come to the back

door and give them the name Myrna Suxsed," Sed said. "They'll hook you up with a backstage pass."

Eric snorted with laughter.

"That would be fantastic," she said.

Brian found it hard to believe she hadn't caught Sed's connotation. Or maybe she had.

She hugged Sed's arm and somehow managed to avoid his questing lips. "Okay, scoot, Eric. I'm going up to my room now."

"If I refuse to move, you can't go anywhere," Eric said smugly.

"Oh really?"

"Really."

"I'll just take a page from Brian's book."

Brian couldn't, for the life of him, figure out what she meant until she crawled up onto the table. She rolled off the table onto his and Trey's laps. She smelled fantastic– coconut, vanilla, and something uniquely Myrna. His mouth went dry, his palms damp. My God, he was a glutton for punishment. He'd already had his heart broken once this week.

Myrna leaned close to his ear and whispered, "I've got something for you up in my room if you'd like a little help with your condition."

His *condition*? He'd love her to help him with his *condition*. She'd gotten him in this condition after all. His self-confidence restored, Brian smiled. His hand wrapped around her narrow waist.

"Room 615," she whispered, her breath tickling his ear. "Don't wait too long to come up. I want to get to bed soon."

"Room 615."

"That's right." She climbed from his lap and straightened her skirt before glancing over her shoulder at Eric. He was banging his head repeatedly on the table.

"You'll stick around after the concert tomorrow, won't you?" Sed asked.

"Of course."

Trey saluted her with two fingers to his brow. "Good night, Professor."

"Good night, Trey, Jace, Sed, Eric." She nodded to each of them in turn. "I had fun talking to you. Thanks for indulging me."

She picked up her laptop case and left the lounge, the eyes of every man in the room following the gentle sway of her hips.

"And thank you for en-bulging me," Sed muttered.

"She wears garters under that suit," Eric groaned.

"I saw that," Sed murmured. "When she climbed up on the table."

"I felt that…when I slid my hand up her skirt." Eric banged his head on the table again.

"You didn't make much progress, did you?" Sed said. "She's good at throwing off a guy's advances without making it obvious."

"Or in Eric's case, making it totally obvious." Jace laughed and ducked to avoid Eric's wild swing across the table.

"None of that here, Eric," Sed said. "You'll end up getting arrested again."

"Why didn't she say good night to you, Brian?" Trey, ever perceptive, asked.

"She wants me to come up to her room."

"You lucky bastard." Eric reached across the table to grab Brian by the shirt. Brian slapped his hands away.

He sat there for a moment, fighting the urge to put his head down on the table again. He massaged his face, but it was entirely numb. "I just wish I wasn't so drunk. Christ!"

"You're still going, aren't you?" Trey crunched his sucker between his teeth and tossed the empty stick into an ashtray. "Rebound pussy?"

Brian glanced at his best friend and fellow guitarist. "What do you think?"

"I think we should tie you up and hide you in the tour bus," Eric said. "She'll think you stood her up. Then I'll go console her and move in for the kill." He opened his mouth and tapped the tips of his index and middle finger on his tongue.

"Dream on, Sticks." Brian chugged half his glass of water and checked his breath by blowing into the palm of his hand. He winced. He pulled a sucker out of Trey's jacket pocket, unwrapped it, and stuck it in his mouth. Too sweet. Bleh. He started to toss it in the ashtray, but Trey rescued it.

"I was gonna eat that."

"Anyone have breath spray?" Brian asked. "My mouth tastes like roadkill."

Sed dug various tubes of spray, a tin of breath mints, and some gum out of his pocket.

"Sed's make-out arsenal," Eric said.

Brian spritzed some peppermint spray in his mouth, hurled the tube at Sed, the *jerk,* and then hauled himself to his feet by grabbing the edge of the table. He stumbled sideways into the bench's back, but quickly regained his footing. *Get it together, man. There is a seriously hot chick waiting upstairs to help you with your condition.*

"Twenty bucks says he passes out before he can get his dick out of his pants," Sed said.

"I'll take that bet," Eric said. "There ain't a man alive who'd pass out before sliding into that Certified Grade A pussy."

"He'll get it out of his pants, but he'll pass out before he does anything with it," Jace said.

"He won't even find her room." Trey entered his bet and polished off his beer in three gulps. He stuck the cherry sucker he'd rescued from Brian in his mouth.

Brian shook his head. The company he kept. Sheezus!

He concentrated on walking a straight line to the elevator and, once inside, pushed the button to the sixth floor. He leaned against the wall as the car rose, his stomach settling in his boots. What was her room number again? Six something teen. Fifteen. Sixteen. Fourteen? He should have written it down. His eyes drifted closed as he thought about the feel of Myrna's breath against his ear. Her soft voice played through his head.

Six fifteen. He remembered now. He knew he wasn't at his best. Why had she picked him? What could she possibly find attractive about him at the moment? Not that he was complaining. He just didn't get it. And she'd been sitting next to Sed. The guy drew chicks like moths to a flame. Even unavailable chicks. Like Angie.

That sucking flut.

He needed another beer. Or three. Maybe he could raid Myrna's minibar. Or maybe she could use those pouty lips of hers to wipe the image of Angie sucking

Sed's dick from his memory. Yeah, he liked that plan better. What had Trey called it? Rebound pussy. Exactly what he needed. He just had to keep his head together and not fall for this one.

Once off the elevator, he followed a sign to the correct corridor, stopped at the door labeled 615, and knocked.

"Just a second," Myrna called from inside. A small victory. Trey lost the bet.

Brian leaned his forearm against the doorframe to keep himself on his feet and rested his forehead against his arm. He really needed to sleep this off. He hoped she wasn't hard to satisfy. He wasn't even sure if he could maintain an erection in his condition.

She finally opened the door and smiled when he lifted his head to look at her. She'd removed her suit jacket, revealing a silky white camisole and all sorts of creamy white flesh begging for his touch. God, she was fucking hot. *Score!*

"You really aren't feeling well, are you?" she asked, her brow furrowed with concern.

He didn't want to lie, so he said nothing.

She stepped aside. "Come in."

He pushed off the doorframe and entered her room. She closed the door behind him, and he knew he had to move quickly or Sed would win the bet. Or worse, Jace would win and he'd pass out with his pants around his knees. He turned Myrna to face him and pressed her up against the door with his body. She gasped in surprise just before his mouth claimed hers in a passionate kiss.

She wrenched her head to the side, breathing hard. "What are you doing?"

"Kissing you."

"I never kiss on the first date."

"This is our second date."

She hesitated, her expression thoughtful. "Good point."

Her fingers slid up his back and tangled in the longish hair at his nape. She closed her eyes and leaned closer. He rested his forearms on the door on either side of her head and tested her eagerness with a gentle brush of his lips against hers. Though his body told him to devour her, his partially functioning brain wanted to treasure the feel of her soft lips against his for the first time. His hands curled into tight fists over her head so they wouldn't rip off her clothes.

He watched her through half-closed eyes as his lips caressed hers. She responded with total submission — mouth open, body limp, fingers digging into his scalp as if she were trying to control herself. It drove him crazy. And that wasn't the only thing driving him crazy. The taste of her mouth, her scent, her warm, soft body against his, the barely perceptible sound of longing she made in the back of her throat. Her tongue brushed his lip. His body tensed as if he'd been struck by lightning. She withdrew her tongue, coaxing his into her mouth with gentle strokes. He eagerly followed, caressing her lips with the tip of his tongue, and then touched her tongue with his. When her tongue tentatively caressed his in return, his eyes drifted closed.

After several moments, he pulled away and gazed down at her in the low light coming from the bathroom.

"I didn't ask you to come to my room for this," she murmured.

"You didn't?"

She shook her head. "No, but you're such a good kisser." Her gaze dropped to his mouth.

He grinned and lowered his head to kiss her again. He pushed off the door and pulled her against him, his hands sliding down over the swell of her ass as he molded their lower bodies together. When was the last time a woman had worked him into a frenzy so quickly? Uh, never. He moved backward, toward the bed, drawing her along with him. She dug her heels into the carpet and wrenched her head to the side.

"I never have sex on a second date," she said firmly.

"This is our third date."

She wagged a finger at him. "That only works once, Master Sinclair."

Her use of his stage name cooled him off significantly, but he still wanted her. Desperately. What was it about her that made his blood boil? She was so different from the girls he usually dated. So...*proper*? But no, not proper at all.

"How about I step into the hall for a couple of minutes and then return?" he suggested.

She laughed. "Brian, you're drunk. I don't sleep with drunks."

He scowled. "But I'll be sober in the morning."

Her hands slid down his back to his ass. She pulled him closer, crushing his partially engorged cock against her pubic bone. "Promise?"

He gazed down at her, a lazy smile on his lips. "Oh, I get it. You're a cock tease."

She grinned. "Cocks were made to be teased." She rotated her hips, rubbing against him.

He groaned, growing harder. More distracted.

"Besides…you like it," she said.

Her naughty streak was showing, twinkling in her green-flecked, hazel eyes. And yeah, he liked it. He liked it a hell of a lot. "Are you sure?"

"Positive. I have a PhD in cock-tease-ology."

"Was that an honorary degree?"

She laughed. "I've studied it for years. I'm something of an expert."

He sighed. "Okay. So if I'm not going to get laid, why did you ask me to come to your room?"

"I already told you. I want to help you with your condition."

"So you said. And that's why I hurried up here, instead of passing out under the table in the lounge."

"Sit down."

He didn't want to let her go, her soft curves fit against him so perfectly, but she wriggled out of his arms and disappeared into the bathroom. He sat on the edge of the bed to stop the room from spinning.

She returned a moment later and pressed two pills into his hand. "Ecstasy?" He tossed the pills in his mouth without looking at them. She handed him a sports drink and he swallowed the pills.

"Actually, that was Vitamin B and Vitamin C," she said. "Drink that entire bottle."

"You're giving me vitamins?" He cocked an eyebrow at her and took another drink from the bottle.

"They'll prevent a hangover." She went over to a side cabinet and returned with a banana.

He eyed the piece of fruit warily. "I'm not that kinky, Professor Sex."

She grinned. "I was hoping you are."

"Okay, I am." His cock throbbed. Fully erect now, it tried desperately to break free of the fly of his jeans. Was she really going to leave him in this condition? She'd said she would help him with it. And this wasn't helping. At all.

She stood close to him, his knee between hers. The hem of her skirt brushed his thigh. He wanted to put more under that skirt than his knee. The silk of her top pulled against her breasts when she moved. Such nice breasts. So soft against his chest. The only thing keeping his hands off them was the orange-flavored sports drink he gripped with both hands. Well that, and the fear she'd tell him he did *not* have permission to touch her.

She peeled the banana, broke off a chunk, and slid it in his mouth. "Eat it. It will settle your stomach and also help prevent a hangover."

He chewed the piece of banana and swallowed. "You're taking care of me?"

"Trying to. Are you resisting?"

Taking her hand, he kissed the inside of her wrist gently. "I like it. Can I do something for you?" He flicked his tongue against the inside of her wrist suggestively while looking up at her.

Her fingers curled involuntarily and her nipples hardened beneath her thin, white top. He found himself completely immersed in her. Her scent. The sound of her soft voice. The taste of her skin. And her body? Perfect. How much resistance would she offer if he tossed her down on the bed and tried to have his way with her?

"Grrrr." Uh... Did he just growl? He hoped he'd imagined it.

She tugged her hand from his and took a step away.

She seemed to realize he wasn't as harmless as she'd first gauged. "Sleep it off, Brian. And I *might* let you make it up to me tomorrow."

She broke off another piece of banana and pressed it into his mouth. He chewed, swallowed, and chased the banana with the rest of his sports drink. He set the empty bottle on the side table and placed a hand on the back of her leg, just above her knee. She emitted an excited little gasp.

He grinned up at her. "You'd better get some rest then. You'll need your stamina."

"So will you." She fed him more banana and shifted sideways out of his grasp. "Do you need me to help you get back to your room?"

He frowned. "I can't stay here?" If he returned to the band's hotel suite tonight, he'd never hear the end of it from the guys.

It made his head swim to look up at her, but he did it anyway. He liked to look at her. Gorgeous. Feminine. Mature. No girl, she was all woman. She maintained an outer appearance of propriety, but he sensed an undercurrent of blazing-hot sexuality. He'd never been with a woman like her. Sophisticated sensuality. What would she be like in bed? Reserved? Kinky? Passionate? Placid? Dominant? Submissive? He had to know.

She touched his lips with her fingertip. "If I let you stay, do you promise to behave?"

"Absolutely not."

Her finger moved from his lips to trace his eyebrow. "In that case, I insist."

He moaned and fell back on the bed, pressing the heels of his hands into his eyes. "Why did I have to get so drunk?"

"Take off your boots and climb into bed."

"Do I get a good-night kiss, at least?" he murmured. His eyes refused to open. His body went limp as he lost awareness.

———∽∿∿∽———

Myrna leaned over Brian and pressed a good-night kiss to his forehead. The poor guy had passed out cold. She bent to remove his black leather boots, took the spiked bracelet off his wrist, and removed a long, silver chain from his belt loop. She rolled him onto his side, in case he threw up in the middle of the night, and covered him with a blanket.

She watched him sleep for a moment.

Brian Sinclair.

Brian Sinclair, the renowned guitarist.

Brian "Master" Sinclair, guitar hero, rock god, perfect specimen of a man, was passed out in her hotel room! He'd kissed her. God, how he'd kissed her. If she didn't have rules about when she allowed herself to have sex with a new acquaintance, he'd probably be making love to her right now. She seriously needed to amend her rules. Her body ached with wanting him. The man was too sexy for his own good.

She gnawed her lower lip as she watched him sleep. Would he still be interested in her when he wasn't looking at her through beer goggles? Their age difference weighed heavily on her mind. She was at least seven years his senior, but she looked younger than thirty-five. Everyone said so. Maybe he wouldn't realize... He'd probably figure it out tomorrow, though. She didn't have the body of an eighteen-year-old anymore. She'd just have to show him that being with an older woman had certain advantages. Assuming he was interested. The way he looked at her had made her bones melt. And his strong, yet gentle, touch? Her legs had almost given out on her when he'd placed a hand on the back of her thigh. It had been way too long since she'd last had sex. That had to be the explanation for the lustful creature he'd awakened in her. She'd just get him out of her system and send him on his way.

Myrna drew away from the bed to get ready to sleep with him. Heat rose to the surface of her skin. No, not sleep *with* him, sleep *next* to him. The ache between her thighs intensified. As she changed into her nightgown and hung her suit in the closet, she wondered if she'd ever get to sleep tonight. If she had any sense at all, she would have made him go back to his room, but he'd kissed her entirely senseless. She went through her nightly routine and then climbed into bed next to Brian, suddenly grateful that she'd taken a suite with a single king-sized bed, instead of one with two queens. With only one available bed, she had a perfectly good reason to share it with him. Right?

And with him passed out, he'd never know what she did to him while he slept.

She reached across the bed and took his hand, tracing his fingers in awe. She hadn't just been making small talk in the lounge. The man really was a musical genius. These fingers worked magic on a fret board. She didn't doubt they'd work magic on her skin. She gently kissed each fingertip of his left hand, and cradled it between her breasts. She closed her eyes and tried to clear her head enough to sleep. When Brian shifted and buried her under his hard body, she decided sleep was highly overrated.

Chapter 3

MOIST HEAT TRAILED UP THE SIDE OF MYRNA'S neck. She sighed, more asleep than awake. A gentle suction just under her ear drew a shudder from her body. She gave herself over to the feel of his mouth against her skin and the warm strength of his hard body behind her. The backs of his fingers brushed over the bare skin just beneath her navel. Her body tensed with need. His fingers slid beneath the waistband of her panties, teasing curls of hair as he sought her clit. She was so hot and swollen. How had he gotten her so worked up so quickly? His fingers stroked her with the speed, pressure, and rhythm required to bring her to orgasm in seconds.

"Oh God!" she cried as her body convulsed with release. She'd never climaxed so quickly in her life.

She turned her head to seek his mouth with hers. She reached for him, her hand finding the warm skin of his arm. He'd removed his shirt while she'd been sleeping. A little more exploring found he still wore his jeans. Damn.

He kissed her, and then shifted her back against his chest with one hand splayed over her bare belly. His other hand cupped her breast through her nightgown. He rested his chin on her shoulder and sighed.

"How do you feel?" she asked.

"Horny."

She chuckled. "I meant your hangover."

"What hangover?"

She smiled and her hand slid between their bodies, cupping his erection through his pants. She'd suspected it last night when he'd pressed his bulge against her mound, but her fondling confirmed it. Oh yes, huge. Her entire body throbbed. Brian caught her hand to prevent her from stroking him but didn't move it away.

"Hold on," he said. "You left me in quite a state last night. I'm about to explode already."

"Do you even remember last night?"

"Every moment, Myrna."

She was surprised he remembered anything, much less her name. "There is something warm and wet between my thighs that wants to be filled with this." She squeezed his cock gently, her hand still trapped in his.

He groaned and moved to climb from the bed.

"Where are you going?"

"I gotta go to the bathroom and jerk one out or I won't last five seconds."

"Oh no you're not." She clung to his waist to prevent him from climbing from the bed. "I'll take care of that for you."

She unfastened his belt buckle and unbuttoned his fly before freeing his cock from the confines of his boxers.

At the sight of his thick erection, her pussy twitched with longing. "Beautiful," she murmured.

"Beautiful?"

She supposed guys didn't want their cocks referred to as beautiful. She hadn't called it cute at least. It wasn't cute though; it was at least ten inches of smooth, gorgeous man flesh. Veins strained against the darkened skin. She couldn't wait to taste him, to run her tongue along the rim of the enlarged head. She tore her gaze from his cock to look at him.

"It's a fucking beast, Brian. You're going to tear me in half with that thing!"

He looked stunned at first, but then laughed. "The only way to save yourself from my beast is to put it in your mouth."

She kissed the tip, sucking one side gently, and then moved away to peel his pants, boxers and socks off in one sweep.

"Just lie back and relax," she said. Her ex-husband's accusatory voice filtered through her thoughts, *Go ahead, Myrna. Suck his cock. Prove me right again, you whore.*

She paused, glancing up at Brian uncertainly. He propped a pillow against the headboard and leaned back, spreading his legs, trusting her with his most sensitive areas without hesitation. He'd think she was a whore, too, wouldn't he?

"What's the matter?" Brian touched her hair gently. "If you don't want to…"

But she did want to. She ran her hands up the insides of his thighs and spread his legs farther apart. She cupped his balls in one hand, finding them full and tight, the skin cool to the touch. He gasped. She gently raked her fingernails over his scrotum, and then lowered her head to draw the loose skin into her mouth, sucking and licking his flesh until his entire body tensed. She nipped the wrinkled skin with her teeth. He jerked.

"What the—?"

Go ahead, Brian, call me a whore.

When his body relaxed again, she lifted her head and took his cock in her mouth, sucking him deep into her throat. She swallowed. He groaned. She sucked hard as she pulled back and rubbed the rim of the head with her tongue before drawing away completely. He grunted in protest when he fell free of her mouth. She blew a breath of cool air over the moistened tip. He sucked a breath through his teeth.

"Mmm," she murmured, and then lowered her head to suck on the skin of his scrotum again.

"Myr, you're killing me," he whispered.

She sucked a testicle into her mouth.

"Whoa!" He clutched the bedclothes in both fists and banged his head back against the headboard.

She released his flesh from her mouth and touched his cock with her fingertips. It jumped in response.

"Please," he begged. "Suck me. God. Please."

She lowered her head farther, tonguing the crease of skin between his balls and her ultimate goal. When her tongue danced over the puckered flesh of his anus, he squirmed, panting as she tested the limits of his self-control. After a moment, he relaxed and she pressed the tip of her tongue inside him. He twitched.

He hadn't called her a whore yet, but she knew he must have been thinking it.

She withdrew her tongue and placed a sucking kiss around his puckered flesh before moving to take his cock in her mouth.

"Yes," he gasped. "Thank you."

She cupped his balls in one hand, massaging gently as she drew his cock in and out of her mouth, applying the most suction at its head as she let it fall from her lips, and then she'd take it within again. By the hitch in his breathing, she could tell he was close. She wanted him to come in her mouth. Wanted to taste him. Swallow him. Make his body spasm with release.

Only whores like to swallow, Jeremy's voice assured her.

She squeezed her eyes closed and took Brian's cock deep into her throat.

"Mmmmmm…" she purred loudly.

"God!"

She drew back and bobbed her head up and down rapidly as she sucked. Her lips bumped over the sensitive rim faster and faster. One hand held the base of his cock firmly so she could concentrate on her technique, the other continued to massage his balls gently. His groans of pleasure encouraged her to suck harder, move faster. *Come, Brian. Come on. Give me what I want.*

She knew he was holding back on her, selfishly trying to prolong his pleasure. She didn't mind. She loved a challenge. She wriggled her tongue against the underside of his cock as she sucked him deep. When he was buried deep in her throat again, she hummed and dipped the tip of a finger into his ass.

"Fuck, woman!" He grabbed her hair as his hips bucked off the mattress and he bathed the back of her throat with his juices.

She smiled, sucking him and swallowing his offering until he stopped spurting. When his body went limp, she released his cock from her mouth and collapsed beside him, breathing hard to catch her breath.

"You're amazing," he whispered, still panting. "Amazing."

Why don't you tell me what you really think of me? Jeremy had never had a problem expressing himself.

Brian reached for her and drew her against him. She buried her face in his side, inhaling his scent. Sexual excitement had strengthened his unique, musky aroma. She loved the smell of his body. There was probably something wrong with that, too. She struggled to free herself from his embrace, but he held her fast.

"I need to take a shower," she said, her hand pressing against the skull tattoo on his abdomen. "I have several sessions I'm supposed to attend this morning."

"The only sessions you're attending will be right here." He pointed at his softening cock. "As soon as I can move, that is."

She didn't disgust him? She looked up at him, expecting him to be staring her down with accusation, but he just grinned as if he was half stoned.

"Don't you have things to do today?" she asked.

"Lots," he said. "And they all involve your body."

Her heart kicked. She smiled. Maybe he was okay with her uninhibited side. "You rock stars have such hard lives."

He was quiet for a long moment. "Did you just suck me off like a maniac because I'm a rock star or because you like me?"

She cringed. "Does it matter?"

"Yeah."

"I like you." She paused. "I also like that you're a rock star. I'm especially drawn to those magical fingers of yours." She took his hand in hers and kissed his fingertips.

"But if I wasn't famous, you wouldn't have anything to do with me."

"If you weren't famous, I probably would have been

too shy to introduce myself to you last night. I would have wanted to suck you off like a maniac, regardless. You're irresistibly sexy, Brian."

He grinned. "I guess that's good enough for me."

She reached up and touched his handsome face. "Does it bother you that women respond to your fame?"

"Not usually." He shrugged. "Sometimes."

He wanted something real, not the fantasy. She could see it in his soft, brown eyes as he gazed at her. She was sorry to disappoint him, but she was all about the fantasy. He'd just have to find a way to cope when her few hours in fantasyland came to an end. And so what if that made her a whore. She was tired of pretending to be a good girl. *I always saw the real you and I loved you anyway,* Jeremy's voice intruded in her thoughts again. She shook her head slightly.

"Can you move yet?" she asked, hoping Brian could exorcise the demon of Jeremy from her thoughts.

"Let me try." His free hand covered her breast and squeezed. "Almost."

She gazed down his body. Her hand slid down his belly toward his slack cock. It twitched in response. She grinned. "Almost."

"So where is this piercing you told us about last night?"

She flushed. "I was only teasing. I don't really have a body piercing. Or a tattoo."

"I don't believe you. I'll need to look you over for myself."

He stripped her nightgown off over her head and pressed her down flat on her back.

"Hmm. I don't see any here," he said, gazing at her breasts. "Just let me make sure." He stroked her nipple with his fingertips, drawing it to a hardened bud. He lowered his head, flicked the taut tip with his tongue, and then sucked it into his mouth.

Myrna gasped. He sucked hard, stroking the underside of her nipple and breast with his tongue.

"Nope, definitely no piercing," he said. "Better check the other one."

He repeated the treatment on her other breast. Her fingers stole into the soft strands of his longish hair, holding him there. He lifted his head and blew a cool breath over her moist nipple. Her body jerked.

He didn't move for a moment and she gazed down at him. He was watching her as if waiting for something.

"If you let go of my hair, I can continue my inspection."

She flushed and released his hair. His mouth left a trail of wet kisses along the underside of her breast, across her ribs to the center of her stomach, and then down to her navel. He dipped his tongue into her belly button rhythmically, causing a flood of heat to rush between her thighs. She throbbed with need, craving that thrusting rhythm within. *Ah God, fuck me, Brian.* She bit her lip so she didn't make the mistake of saying it aloud.

"No navel ring," he murmured.

He continued down her body, sucking a trail over her lower belly. A spasm shook her body and she giggled.

"Ticklish?"

"A little."

He blew a cool breath over the moist trail he'd left behind and she moaned. He used the distraction to slide her panties from her body.

"One more place I need to check." He wrapped a

hand around each leg, just above her knees, and spread her thighs wide.

"You already checked there." Her body tensed. She wasn't a fan of having her clit licked. So few men did it right.

His fingers combed through the nest of curls at the apex of her thighs. "You don't shave this off regularly?"

She flushed. She knew the trends among younger women. She kept her pubic hair trimmed but didn't shave it into unusual shapes or thin strips.

"It's there for a reason." She slipped into sex professor mode. "It maintains the sexual scents. Also, each hair is associated with a nerve ending, so increases sensory input to the brain during copulation."

He quirked an eyebrow at her. "Copulation?"

Oh God. Had she turned him off with her cerebral discussion of a primitive urge? "Fucking?"

"I prefer making love." He grinned. "And you're right about the scent." He inhaled her essence deeply through his nose. "Definitely a turn-on."

His callused fingertips found the hood of skin covering her clit. He exposed the swollen nub buried within and, using a second finger, stroked her to climax in seconds. She cried out, her thighs quivering as the sensation rippled through her body. How did he do that?

"You come so easily." He kissed the inside of her thigh. "Definitely a turn-on." She couldn't lift her head to look at him but could hear the smile in his voice.

She didn't usually come so quickly. Usually when a man was in control, she never reached climax. Brian was a genius with those fingers of his. And not just as a guitarist.

"You're amazing," she gasped.

"All those solos." His finger stroked her again and she shuddered.

"Feel free to practice on me any time."

He chuckled. "I'm not sure you want to offer that."

She was one hundred and one percent sure that she did.

His hair brushed the insides of her thighs as he lowered his head. She tensed again. He sucked her clit into his mouth and stroked it with the tip of his tongue.

"Oh God," she groaned. He was good at this, too?

Brian continued sucking and stroking her with his tongue. Her pussy throbbed in protest of its neglect. She wanted him inside her so bad. His big, beautiful cock pounding her fast and hard. She couldn't take any more. She had to have him.

She grabbed a handful of his hair and pulled him away from the glorious things he was doing to her clit. "Take me, Brian," she said. "Now."

"Not yet."

If demands didn't work, perhaps begging would earn his mercy. "Please. Please, Brian. I ache with wanting you inside me."

His fingers traced the slippery rim of her eager opening. "You want me in here?"

She shifted her hips, willing to accept even his fingers inside her. Anything to fill that aching emptiness.

He drew his hand away, leaving her wanting. "You're dripping wet, baby. Has it been a while since you've been fucked properly?"

She wasn't sure if she'd ever been fucked properly. She knew she'd never been this turned on in her life. "You're cruel." She pouted.

"If I was being cruel, you'd know it. Let go of my hair and trust me to satisfy you."

She released his hair, lifted her head, and looked down at him. "I'm sorry."

"Don't apologize. My cock is calling me every sort of a son of a bitch right now. He wants to be inside you twice as much as you want him there."

"Impossible."

He grinned. "He'll wait for a few more minutes though. Can you handle that?"

"Just a few?"

He nodded.

"I'll try." Some of her building excitement had dissipated. She wished she hadn't stopped him now. She relaxed onto the bed and gripped handfuls of the sheets to prevent herself from pulling his hair again.

He doesn't want you, Myrna. Who'd want a cheating whore?

Shut up, Jeremy.

Brian lowered his head and drew his tongue along the inside of her labia, flicked it across her anus, and then trailed it back up the other side.

"Nnggnn," she groaned.

He sucked her clit back into his mouth and her hips bucked involuntarily. While he sucked her and stroked her with his tongue, his fingers traced the rim of her vaginal opening, never dipping inside, just teasing her to the point of tears. He kept her at the brink of orgasm. Whenever her breath would hitch as she approached release, he'd pause in his torment until she settled down again. Her need for him intensified with each increasing peak.

When she was convinced she was going to die, he slid two fingers inside her.

She cried out, her back arching. He curled his fingers and pressed up inside her, slowly withdrawing until she screamed with release. He rubbed that perfect spot inside until her legs trembled and her thighs clamped together over his hand. He knew how to find a G-spot? Ah, God. Gifted. The man was sexually gifted. Myrna forced herself to relax her leg lock on his hand. When her body stopped quaking, he removed his fingers and slid from the end of the bed.

"Don't get up," he said.

He left her lying there, dazed. He was done? He didn't want her? Fighting tears of rejection, she watched him search the floor for his clothes. His hard cock jutted before him, thickly veined and straining. Did he find her so repulsive that he'd just leave while still in that condition?

Brian bent to retrieve his pants—giving Myrna a spectacular view of his perfect, bare ass—and fished a condom out of his pocket. Her breath caught. He tore the package open with his teeth and unrolled the condom over his cock. Such a shame to cover its perfection from her view, but it meant…

He climbed back onto the bed and settled his narrow hips between her thighs.

"You want me?" she whispered around the knot in her throat.

"Did you seriously just ask me that?" He brushed her hair from her damp cheeks and kissed her tenderly. His lips tasted and smelled like her. So intimate. He lifted his head to stare into her eyes. "I think the question is do you still want *me*, or did I overdo it a little?"

"I still want you. So much," she whispered. "I'm not sure I can move though."

He grinned crookedly. "I'll do all the moving at first."

He rocked his hips forward, probing for her opening without using his hands for guidance. When he found her, he slid into her slowly, holding her shoulders as he burrowed deeper and deeper.

"Mmmmm," he murmured and buried his face in her neck. "Certified Grade A."

Her brow creased. "What?"

"Nothing."

His strokes were slow and deep. Slow and deep. Slow and deep. Stretching her wide, withdrawing. He more than filled her. She'd never been with a man as well-endowed as he was. Perhaps it was his size that thrilled her. Nope, definitely the way he used it. She groaned— her excitement building again. His quiet gasps in her ear sent her lust spiraling out of control. Her hands moved to his ass, digging into his flesh as she bucked her hips against him. His gasps grew shaky and punctuated. His strokes faster and harder. And harder. And harder. Harder. God yes, harder. *Make me feel you, Brian. Drive everything away but you.*

Myrna's head banged into the headboard. "Ow."

"Sorry," he whispered, rubbing her head with the palm of his hand. "Too hard?"

She shook her head vigorously. "I like it."

He dragged her sideways across the bed, turning her partially on her side, so that he straddled one of her legs. He wrapped her other leg around his waist.

"Oh," she gasped at the change in stimulation. She liked that, too.

He thrust into her, biting his lip as he pounded against her. Soon his hard thrusts pushed her beyond the edge of the bed. She caught herself with her hand to keep from tumbling to the floor.

"Damn it," he growled, and pulled her back up onto the bed. "I can't seem to get deep enough. I want... I need..." He gasped and ground his hips as he pushed into her. His fingers dug into her hips and held her steady, seeking to possess her fully.

"Let me try." She pushed him onto his back and sighed in frustration when he slid out of her. Emptiness replaced the perfect way he filled her. She hurried to straddle his hips and sank down on his thick cock, taking him as deep as he would go, stretched to her limits. Her head tilted back in ecstasy.

His hands wrapped around her waist, pulling her down, urging her body to take more of him. "Deeper," he groaned.

She bounced against him, taking him a centimeter at a time until, at last, she had accepted all of him.

"Now you have all of me," he whispered, looking up at her through heavy eyelids. His fingers traced paths up and down her spine, making her shudder. "Ride me, baby. Show me how you like it."

He cared how she liked it? She didn't understand why that turned her on so much, but she rode him. Lifting her hips and grinding downward, gyrating to stimulate her clit against his pubic bone, she used him for her pleasure, ignoring his needs. She just wanted to get off. An orgasm rippled through her. She cried out but didn't stop. Again. She wanted to come again with him inside her. She took him faster, rotating slightly with each downward stroke. She wasn't sure when she'd started chanting his name. "Brian. Brian." After her second orgasm? "Oh, Brian." Her third? "God, Brian. Yes."

His hips rose off the bed to meet her strokes. He bit his lip, his head tossed back. She'd never seen anything sexier in her life. Watching his expression was almost better than the waves of pleasure coursing through her own body.

"Oh fuck, fuck," he shouted, and grabbed her firmly by the hips to stop her gyrating thrusts. "Stop, stop. Give me a minute."

She slapped him hard on the chest. "Don't hold back on me, goddammit. I wanna make you come."

"No, no. Not yet. Not yet. Damn." He pulled her off him and tossed her onto her back in the center of the bed. "Shit, shit, I'm going to lose it."

Lose what? His erection? Not bloody likely. He was as hard as granite.

He rolled on top of her and slid inside her again. Her eyes drifted closed. Her back arched, rubbing her belly against his. The fingers of his left hand tapped rhythmically against her shoulder. His strokes were different this time, a three-quarter time beat, if she wasn't mistaken, and he was humming under his breath.

"What are you doing?" she asked.

"Shh. Shh. I've almost got it."

She watched him for a moment, trying to figure out the sudden change in him. "Are you hearing music in your head?"

"Shh, sweetheart. Please."

She fell silent. Whatever he was doing was obviously important. She closed her eyes and concentrated on the perfect rhythm of his deep strokes. The riff he hummed in her ear was outstanding. Sensual. Even more sensual than his usual work. She'd never heard anything like it before, and she was a collector of excellent guitar segments.

He paused and looked down at her. "I need something to write on."

Her eyes widened. "You're kidding me, right?"

"Baby, I haven't written a new riff in months. You are beyond awesome." He grinned down at her, pumping into her hard and steady. "Making love to this perfect body stimulates more than my cock."

"Thanks." She quirked an eyebrow at him. "I guess."

He reached for a pen on the side table and uncapped it. He wiped the sweat from her body with the sheet and drew a straight line across her chest. He then added a series of dots on, above, and below the line. Scribbled letters appeared here and there. E. C. C#. She just watched him, too surprised to protest. The line of musical notes continued across her breasts, under her breasts, several lines along her belly.

He paused, his eyes drifting closed. "God, you feel good, Myrna. So good." She planted her feet on the bed, lifted her hips, and gyrated. "Yeah." He rose up on his knees slightly and thrust forward, grinding deep. "Perfect," he murmured. "Take me. All of me. Inside." He began to pump into her again, withdrawing only slightly as if he didn't want to move at all. "I hear you," he whispered.

Her brow furrowed. Her panting? Is that what he meant?

He pulled out unexpectedly, leaving her empty. She groaned in protest.

"Turn over," he demanded breathlessly.

"What?"

"I'm out of space and this solo you've inspired…" He shook his ink pen at her.

She laughed. "You're crazy."

"All geniuses are."

She smiled and rolled onto her stomach. She'd thought he'd just start writing on her back, but he eased her onto her knees and slid his cock inside her again. He thrust into her with the same rhythm as before, drawing notes across the skin of her back while she groaned. This man would be her downfall. She knew it with a certainty. She rocked back against him, loving the way his balls slapped against her with each steady stroke.

"Hold still," he complained.

"Then stop screwing me so well."

"I need the rhythm to get the spacing of the notes right. I could call Sticks for a tempo, if you'd like."

"I prefer this method." She concentrated on holding still for him so he could write and maintain his rhythm at the same time.

"God, me too. But I need to come soon. I'm about to explode. Do you have any idea how fucking amazing you are?"

He scattered line upon line of notes across her back and then tossed the pen across the room. He leaned forward to squeeze her breasts and pinch her nipples as he deserted his music-writing tempo for quick, shallow strokes. His moans grew louder and louder as he gave himself over to pleasure.

With one final deep thrust, he cried out, "Myrna. Oh God. Oh God, yes."

She felt him shudder violently behind her and regretted

that she couldn't see his face. He grasped her hips and held her still, grinding deeply until his spasms calmed.

He pulled out and collapsed on the bed beside her, eyes closed, breathing hard. "That was fantastic." He drew her down beside him and placed a tender kiss on her shoulder. "I'd cuddle with you, but I don't want to sweat off my riff and solo."

She laughed. "That must be the first time *that* excuse has ever been used to avoid after-sex cuddling."

He took her face between both hands and kissed her reverently. Never had she been kissed reverently before.

"It's the truth, though. I'd love to hold you close for hours."

She smiled. A sweet sex god. What more could a girl want? He kissed her again.

"Ah, Myrna," he murmured. "I think my muse resides deep, deep inside you."

"You sure know how to use her in exactly the right way."

Chapter 4

WALKING THROUGH A HOTEL IN NOTHING BUT A bathrobe and panties… Only Brian Sinclair could talk Myrna into doing something that bold. He'd actually tried to convince her to go naked, but she'd reminded him that her stuffed-shirt colleagues would likely be roaming the halls at this hour. She and Brian took the elevator to the top floor. While the car rose, he wrapped an arm around her shoulders and kissed her temple.

"I'm sorry to make you miss your conference."

"No, you aren't." And she wasn't either.

He grinned deviously. "You're right. I'm not."

"At least I don't have to present a session today. How would I look walking up to the stage bowlegged and limping?"

"You'd look sexy," he said. "Especially since I'd know why you were walking funny." He tapped her nose with his fingertip.

She tried to ignore the little thrill of happiness that fluttered through her heart. She was glad they'd be saying their good-byes tonight. The last thing she needed in her life was a distraction as monumental as Brian Sinclair. And he had her entirely distracted.

There were only two rooms located on the top floor. Brian fished his keycard out of his wallet and opened the door to one of the suites.

"After you, gorgeous."

She stepped into the marble entryway of the suite, impressed by its expanse.

"Is that you, Brian?" Trey stepped out of the bathroom, shirtless and in baggy black jeans, drying his hair with a towel. His best feature was undoubtedly his sultry green eyes, and hiding one of them behind long bangs made him sexier for some reason.

"And guest," Brian said.

Trey tossed the towel aside. "Oh, hey, pretty lady."

"Hi, Trey." She waved self-consciously.

"I guess he found you last night," Trey said.

"Barcly," Brian admitted.

"Is that Lucky Von Shithead I hear?" Eric's voice came from a room off to the right. "Goes out and gets himself some Certified Grade A pussy while leaving us high and…" He paused in the doorway, his eyes racking over Myrna's disheveled hair, bathrobe, and bare feet. "Shit. Sorry, Myrna. I figured you'd have dumped him by now."

She flushed. "Not yet."

"So we have this little bet," Eric began.

"Shut up, numbnuts." Brian turned to Trey. "Did someone bring my guitar upstairs last night?"

"It's in the dining room." Trey nodded down the hall.

Brian headed in that direction. Myrna followed him, but Eric darted into her path. She looked up at him. His pale blue eyes seemed to penetrate her robe, skin, flesh, and peer right into her soul. She shivered and crossed her arms over her chest.

"Wait, wait, wait," he said. "We need to know who won our bet."

"I lost," Trey said. "He found her room." He stuck a cherry sucker in his mouth and brushed past Eric and Myrna to follow Brian. "Hey, what's going on? Why do you want your guitar? Did you finally come up with a new riff?"

"When did he pass out last night?" Eric asked Myrna.

"After he swallowed my banana and I forced him to consume my fluids." She winked at him.

His mouth fell open. "What?"

"Excuse me." She brushed Eric aside and followed the sound of a guitar being plugged into an amp.

A second guitar hummed with feedback.

"Myrna, hurry," Brian called.

She entered the dining room and paused. Brian "Master" Sinclair, his signature black and white Schecter guitar slung low. Trey Mills, sucker stick jutting out of his mouth beside him, adjusting one of the leads on his yellow and black guitar. *Nice!* Brian beckoned Myrna closer by flicking two fingers at her. He shifted her in front of himself and Trey, and then untied the sash of her bathrobe. He tossed the fabric aside, revealing his score, and the vast majority of Myrna's naked body. Under the robe, she wore only pink bikinis. Heat flooded her face, but she stood still.

"Nice tits, Myr," Trey said around his cherry sucker. His gaze moved from her bare breasts to the string of notes written above and below a single line. "There's no staff, Brian. What in the hell am I looking at?"

Brian pointed to the start of the line, near Myrna's right shoulder. "Middle C. The first chord."

Brian showed Trey his fingering and struck the strings with his pick.

Trey moved his hand along his guitar strings, glanced back at the score on Myrna's skin, and nodded. "Okay. I see. Harmony or concert?"

"Let's try harmony first."

"Gotcha." Trey shifted his sucker to the other side of his mouth, and then struck the first chord.

"Grungier," Brian said.

Trey adjusted a knob on his guitar, tilted his wrist slightly, and struck the chord again.

"Yeah, like that."

"Okay, let's go."

Myrna's eyes widened as they played one of the most amazing riffs she'd ever heard. The idea that she had something to do with its creation thrilled her.

Eric entered the dining room. "Sounds great."

Trey missed a beat and his guitar rang with a discordant note. Brian paused and glanced at him. "Something wrong?"

"I can't concentrate with those…" He lifted his hands in front of Myrna's chest and flexed his fingers inches from her breasts. "…in my field of view."

"Oh, come on, Trey. How many pairs of tits do you see in an average week?" Brian asked.

"Doesn't matter. I've never seen hers." Trey nodded toward Myrna.

Myrna's face flamed as she closed the robe over her exposed chest.

"Hey, I didn't get to see them yet," Eric complained.

"Go bang on a drum in the other room." Brian pulled the robe sash free from its loops and handed it to her. "Here. Hold this over your tits so Trey doesn't knock his guitar out of tune with his hard-on."

She laughed and glanced sidelong at Trey, her face burning even hotter.

Trey nodded, pulling his sucker out of his mouth with a slurp. "Seriously."

"All right," she said.

Brian pulled her robe off her shoulders and she held the sash across her breasts. It covered her nipples but little else.

"That's almost worse," Trey murmured. "Uhn. She's so goddamned sexy. I just want to lick her all over." He drew his tongue over his bottom lip, his gaze drifting over her skin.

Myrna's eyes widened.

"Get your game face on, Trey." Brian thumped him on the head.

Trey stuck his sucker back in his mouth and nodded. He struck the first chord and Brian joined him. The riff got better as their eyes moved over her chest, under her breasts, along her belly. A few times through the sequence and they could play it without reading the notes. Myrna was so drawn up in the music, she didn't notice Sed until he sat on the edge of the dining table beside her.

"Are you responsible for that?" he said into her ear.

She gasped and closed her robe. "I don't know."

"Well, I thank you for getting Sinclair out of his funk, whatever it was you did."

The two of them watched Brian and Trey play the riff repeatedly until they'd perfected it. Trey started altering parts slightly to fit his rapidly strumming, shredding style. Brian added more triplets, his fingers flying over the strings. It sounded…perfect and, as always, sensual. The two guitarists, Brian right-handed and Trey left-handed, leaned back-to-back and closed their eyes, letting the music carry them away.

She'd never seen anything sexier in her life. Well,

maybe Brian's face when he made love to her, but he almost had the same expression as he leaned against Trey's back and fingered his guitar.

Jace entered the room rubbing his face sleepily. "What's all this racket? It's ten o'clock in the fucking morning."

With a start of surprise, Jace noticed Myrna and his gaze drifted down his naked body. His eyes darted back to her. "Aw, shit. Excuse me." He left the room. When he returned a few minutes later in a pair of shorts, he took his bass out of its case and plugged it in to a third amp.

Jace stood in the corner with his eyes closed and soon found a bass groove to complement the new guitar riff.

"You guys are awesome," Myrna murmured under her breath.

Brian watched her as he played. He smiled. "It's all because of you, baby."

She grinned, her heart fluttering stupidly.

Brian stilled his guitar strings with his hand and reached for Myrna, turning her to face the opposite direction. He tugged her robe down to her waist and brushed her long, auburn hair aside. Myrna glanced over her shoulder at him, clutching the robe to her breasts.

"My solo."

Trey leaned closer, his brow furrowed. Not even a line for direction here. Just notes and a few letters scrawled here and there. "Well, let's hear it."

When Brian began to play, excitement raced down Myrna's spine.

"Wow," Sed murmured.

Brian's fingers flew over the fret board, drawing

sounds from his instrument that few guitarists could emulate. He finished the solo with one final, long screech on the whammy bar. The entire band whistled in appreciation. He flipped his guitar over his shoulder so it hung upside down over his back. He spooned up against Myrna and drew her against him.

"Now I'm all horny again," he murmured into her ear, his hands splayed over her belly. "I'll never be able to play that solo without getting hard for the feel of you around me."

"It sounded awesome."

"Let Trey copy that down before you go bone her again," Sed said. "We don't want to lose it."

Brian dropped a kiss behind her ear and backed away reluctantly.

"Or I could take a picture of it." Eric fished his camera phone out of his pocket.

"If you do, I'll break your fingers," Brian said.

"You're no fun, Be-rye."

"You just want jerk-off material."

Trey located some music score paper and a pencil in a guitar case. He started copying Brian's guitar solo off Myrna's back, asking Brian for clarification now and again. Very ticklish, Myrna giggled and squirmed as their fingers trailed over her bare skin.

"What's this note?" Trey asked.

"I think that's a mole." Brian leaned forward and licked a spot in the center of Myrna's lower back. She shuddered. Brian rubbed the spot with his thumb. "Yeah, it's a mole. It doesn't come off."

"I'm adding it in for the hell of it." Trey chuckled.

"Myr, your mole is interrupting my solo."

She snorted. "You guys are too funny."

"I think it's a great addition," Trey said. "You can never have too many high C's in a solo."

"I like Hi-C," Eric quipped. When no one laughed, he murmured, "The orange kind."

"Turn around so we can get the riff," Brian said.

Myrna turned. Holding the robe's sash over her breasts, she watched them transfer the dots scattered across her body to paper.

"Sixteenth notes there," Brian said, watching over Trey's shoulder. He pointed to the page.

"Sixteenth? You're giving me arthritis, man."

"Don't be a douche."

Trey took the sucker out of his mouth and tapped it on Brian's nose. Myrna stole it from him and stuck it in her mouth. Trey glanced up at her, pinning her with his sexy, green eyes. "That's my sucker." That was the look that turned female legs to rubber. Myrna was no exception. She leaned against the table for support.

She pulled his sucker out of her mouth and offered it back to him. "My apologies."

Trey took it from her and returned it to his mouth, turning his attention to the score sheets. Brian wiped at the sticky spot on his nose with his knuckles. Myrna's gaze moved to Brian's soft brown eyes. He was watching her, his lips slightly parted.

She wondered what he was thinking.

"Are you hungry?" he asked.

Obviously not what she was thinking, but now that he mentioned it, she was hungry. "Yeah."

"I'm starving. I'm gonna go call room service." He poked Trey in the arm. "Can you finish this on your own?"

"Yeah, I got it. I played it ten times already."

Brian kissed Myrna on the temple and lifted his guitar strap over his head. He set the instrument on a stand and left the room. Sed and Eric followed him. Jace still thumbed a quiet bass groove in the corner, switching it out several times as he sought the perfect sound to complement Brian's new riff.

When the group was out of earshot, Trey said, "Don't destroy him, Myrna. Brian falls fast and hard. Chicks can't handle his intensity and he ends up getting hurt."

"No worries. We're just having a good time."

He took her chin in between his thumb and forefinger. "I mean it, Myrna. If you're not serious about him, you have to get out now."

"How can I be serious about someone I just met?"

He closed his eyes and shook his head. "Every time." He opened his eyes and pinned her with a heavy stare. "We told you he was a romantic retard last night. Did you hear any of it?"

She pushed his hand away. "I won't hurt him, Trey. Okay?"

"I hope you mean that."

He stared her down until she had to look away. And he thought Brian was intense? Jeez!

"Leave her alone, Trey," Jace said.

"Am I wrong?" Trey said over his shoulder.

"No, but that's not her fault."

Trey looked at her again. He sighed. "I'm sorry. It's none of my business."

"He's lucky to have someone who cares so much about him."

Trey cocked an eyebrow at her and laughed. "Yeah, I

guess. One or the other of us always has our nose in his business. Just forget I said anything."

Trey finished scribing the last few lines of music. Myrna closed her robe and tied it with the sash. She sat in one of the dining chairs and listened to Jace play, her foot tapping in time. Trey spread the score sheets across the table and started playing again, pausing every few measures to add a second set of rapid notes above Brian's sustained notes. Trey's signature shred complemented Brian's wail. It's what made them sound so good when they played together. Moments later Brian returned, picked up his guitar, and joined his bandmates. The new composition already sounded like a song. It amazed Myrna how quickly each guitarist had adapted a single riff to fit their particular styles and strengths.

Sed entered the room and sat in the center of the dining room table with his eyes closed. Puzzled, Myrna watched him. He seemed to be in some sort of trance.

When the guitarists returned to the beginning of the riff, Sed sang, or more like screamed, "It came to me in a dream."

"You could call her that," Brian yelled.

Trey laughed and shoved him.

Was this how they always wrote songs? The privilege of witnessing their process sent shivers of excitement racing down Myrna's spine.

"Okay, okay," Sed said. "That sucked even for my first attempt."

That *sucked*? It had sounded great to her. Sed's voice was low, with an edgy rasp that made various parts of her anatomy swell in response.

Sed continued, "Maybe if I bone Myrna, the lyrics will come to me. What did you just call it, Brian? Magically."

"Shut up," Brian said, working on a bridge to the solo with Trey now.

"Magically delicious," Myrna murmured, watching Brian play and wanting his fingers on her body instead of his guitar.

Sed burst out laughing. He fell back on the table, covering his eyes with the palms of his hands as tears of mirth streamed down his cheeks. "I wonder if we can use that in a song without getting sued by a leprechaun."

"Fucking Myrna," he sang in his signature growl, "is magically delicious. Wooooaahhhh. Ohh. Ohhh. Yeaaahh eahh eahhh."

Myrna covered her mouth, trying not to laugh. She slapped Sed on his bare belly. "Don't sing that."

He leaned off the edge of the table and grabbed her around the waist, digging his fingers into her ribs. She laughed and wriggled from side to side, trying to throw him off. Brian's guitar protested loudly as he leaned across the table and grabbed Sed by one leg.

"Knock it off, Sed. I'm not playing," Brian said.

Sed released Myrna, who tumbled to the floor. "I'm just teasing her. I'm not after your chick, dude."

"Bullshit," Brian said. "You're after every guy's chick. Especially mine."

Sed sat up and shoved Brian. "Get off me."

Brian let go of Sed's leg and lifted his fist to pound him. Myrna jumped to her feet and stepped between them, cringing as she waited for the blow of Brian's fist to connect. It never did.

"Please, don't fight," she said. She laid the palms

of her hands on Brian's chest. He lowered his fist, and she smiled up at him in relief. "Thank you." She leaned close, his guitar digging into her belly. "I only want you, Brian." She kissed the spot just beneath his ear, her fingers curling into his hard chest. "Only you. Trust me, okay?"

His hands stole around her back to draw her closer. She caught Trey's grin of approval out of the corner of her eye.

"Breakfast!" Eric called.

A hotel worker, looking frazzled and overwhelmed, pushed a cart into the room. Eric moved around him and sat at the table with a drumstick in each hand. He pounded his fists on the table. "Let's eat. Let's eat."

Sed rolled off the table and sat in a chair. A muscle in his jaw flexed, but he didn't say anything. The hotel worker began to unload the cart, spreading a veritable feast across the table.

Eric lifted lids off plates of food and tossed the covers back on the cart. About half of them hit his target, the rest clattered across the floor. "Mine!" he declared when he found a fluffy omelet smothered in jalapeño peppers.

Sed reached for his plate of eggs over medium and ham. The three guitarists removed their instruments before joining the rest of the band at the table. Myrna wasn't sure what to do. They hadn't asked her what she wanted, so she didn't want to steal someone else's food. Not that there was a shortage. They'd ordered more than enough for fifteen people.

"I didn't know what you'd want," Brian explained, "so I ordered a bunch of stuff."

She smiled. Sweet sex god. Yep, that was Brian. He

handed the now doubly frazzled hotel worker a tip and then sat at the head of the table, pulling Myrna onto his lap.

"Oh puke," Trey said, grinning. "Don't get all lovey-dovey in front of us."

Brian flipped him off and then tugged a bowl of fruit, a plate of scrambled eggs, pancakes, biscuits, and bacon toward them.

"What's your pleasure?" he asked.

Being this close to him had stolen her appetite for food. A different sort of appetite had awakened. She leaned close to his ear. "Your cock."

His hand slid under her robe and up her thigh. She tensed.

"That's the second course," he whispered.

"I guess I can wait a few minutes. So long as you promise me dessert, too."

His fingers slid under the elastic band of her panties and brushed one swollen labium. Her body shuddered.

"That's a promise."

When he moved his hand above the table to start eating, she relaxed.

She settled for nibbling on chunks of melon while Brian polished off a plate of scrambled eggs drenched with ketchup and several pieces of bacon, also drenched with ketchup. She poured him a glass of orange juice and insisted he drink it all.

"Sickening," Trey said, still grinning. "Will you look at them? All domestic-y."

"He needs his strength," Myrna said, glancing at Trey, who sat to her right eating his pancakes smothered in syrup and sausage, also smothered in syrup. She popped a piece of melon in Brian's mouth. "I'm horny."

Eric proceeded to bang his head repeatedly on the table.

Sed laughed. "And you're wasting your time with Sinclair?"

"Trust me, he's no waste of time. Guitar isn't his only talent."

Brian squeezed her thigh in appreciation. She wondered how much shit he took from these guys for being a romantic.

His nose brushed against her neck. "I'm full now."

Her belly tightened with need. "Good, because my panties can't get any more saturated."

"Fuck. Fuck. Fuck." Eric punctuated his head banging against the table with curses.

"Bath?" Brian asked, looking up at her.

She cupped his cheek and leaned her forehead against his. "It'll wash off your song."

"We've got that one on paper. I'm hoping I'll need a blank slate to write a new one."

She smiled. "I didn't think of that."

She slid from his lap and secured her robe before heading toward the bathroom. As she walked past Sed, she heard him say, "I hope the groupies are ready for a good, hard fuck tonight. Goddamn, the pheromones are thick in here. I've got a proximity hard-on."

"Brian gets all the good pussy," Eric moped.

Brian laughed and slapped Eric on the back as he followed Myrna to the bathroom. She entered the large room, delighted by the Jacuzzi tub in the corner. "Nice."

Brian closed the door and pulled her back against his belly. He released the sash of her robe and pushed the fabric aside. Her breasts ached as he massaged them with the palms of his hands and her breath quickened as he suckled the side of her neck.

"Are you really horny or did you just want to get away from the guys?" he asked.

She drew his hand to the moist heat between her thighs. "What do you think?"

His fingers stroked her through pink lace. He turned her body to face the wall. Her eyes flipped open lazily and she caught her reflection in the mirror. Their eyes met over her shoulder in the reflective glass. So he wanted to watch her when he made her come. He didn't have to wait long. His fingers stroked faster. Faster. Faster. Her eyes slid closed, her mouth fell open, and she leaned her head back against his shoulder as ripples of pleasure shook her core. She cried out, clutching his thighs for support.

He rubbed the tip of his nose against the rim of her ear. "You're so sexy, Myr. This time I'm going to hold you first. I don't want to get carried away and miss out again."

He released her and moved to the bathtub, turning the taps and testing the water with his fingers. His wonderful, mesmerizing fingers. Watching him play had worked her up more than she'd realized. She moved behind him and wrapped her arms around his waist, unfastening his belt and the fly of his jeans. She rearranged his boxers until his half-hard cock sprang free. She took it in her hand, stroking its smooth length gently.

He caught her hand. "Wait. I don't even have my boots off yet."

"Your point?"

His point is you're being a whore again, Myrna.

Jeremy's voice sent delight spiraling out of reach. She closed her eyes and shook her head slightly.

Brian turned and peeled her robe from her shoulders, leaving it in a puddle on the tile floor. She crossed her arms over her chest.

"Something wrong?" His thumb brushed her cheek, and she opened her eyes to look at him.

"No." She forced a smile and put her hands on her hips, eyeing his state of dress with disdain. "How is this fair?" she asked.

He stripped himself naked in seconds. His gaze slowly drifted down to her pink lace panties. "How is this fair?" he countered.

She peeled her panties down her thighs and removed them. She looped a finger in the elastic band and shot them at his face like a slingshot. He caught them, drew them to his nose, and inhaled deeply. "Can I keep these?"

"If you like."

He bent and tucked her panties into his pants pocket. He then climbed the stairs to the tub, stepped into the water, and extended a hand in her direction. She took his hand and climbed into the tub with him, standing before him. Staring up at him, she traced the angled contours of his face with her gaze—strong jaw, pointed chin, sharp cheekbones. Eventually, her eyes settled on the upper curve of his beguiling lips. He lowered his head and kissed her passionately—lips, tongue, and teeth all caressing her mouth. The water rose up their calves as his kiss continued. When he drew away, he gazed down at her.

"You'd better turn off the water," she said.

He turned off the taps and sank into the water's warm depths, holding his arms out in invitation. She sat between his thighs, leaning back against his chest. The Jacuzzi jets startled her.

"Feels good." He leaned his head back against the edge of the deep tub and sighed.

Myrna hadn't joined him here to relax, but she couldn't argue. It did feel good. It felt even better when he began to rub a tiny bar of soap over her chest and belly. Though his touch wasn't meant to entice, she was panting with need in moments.

"So do you live nearby?" he asked nonchalantly.

"Um..." She didn't really want to share personal information with him. This was a quick affair. Nothing more. "No, I'm just here for the conference. Which I'm missing, by the way."

"If you'd rather go—"

"I didn't say that."

He set the soap aside, wrapped his arms around her waist, and leaned the side of his head against hers. "Quiet is nice sometimes."

She supposed his life would be consistently loud. So he wanted to talk quietly and cuddle. She shouldn't complain. She could wait a of couple minutes.

"Do any of your tattoos mean anything special?" She trailed a finger down his hard-muscled arm and the intricate, colorful artwork there.

"Some of them." He lifted his left arm out of the water and showed her an elaborate display of bloody roses around the name Kara on the inside of his forearm.

"Old girlfriend?" she asked, tracing the letter K with her fingertip.

"My little sister. She died in a car accident when she was sixteen."

Myrna glanced up at him, noting the raw pain on his face. "I'm sorry, Brian. That's horrible."

"It happened almost ten years ago. You'd think I'd be able to bury it by now."

"She was your little sister. You thought you could always protect her."

He smiled slightly. "How did you know that?"

She shrugged, not wanting to slip back into psychology professor mode again.

"Do you have siblings?" he asked.

"Two younger sisters. Both pains in my ass."

"Kara was a pain in the ass, too." He chuckled. "I still miss her."

Did he always wear his heart on his sleeve? He must. Even when naked.

"So if you're not from Chicago," he said, "where are you from?"

"Missouri."

"Saint Louis?"

"Does it matter?"

"You have no interest in getting to know me, do you?"

She'd promised Trey she wouldn't hurt him. She just wished it were harder to do. She knew this relationship could never resemble something significant. He was a rock star on tour. She was a professor with a demanding career. They just didn't…fit.

"Country girl, originally. I went to college in Columbia, Missouri. Grad school in Saint Louis. I'm in Kansas City now."

"So you're not too far from home."

"Where did you grow up?"

"L.A."

She grinned. "Cliché."

"They warned you that I'm a romantic retard, didn't they?"

She turned her head to glance up at him. "Huh?"

"Don't play dumb. You don't have to walk on eggshells, Myr. If I'm stupid enough to fall in love with you in twelve hours, I deserve to have my heart broken."

"I don't intend to break anyone's heart."

"I don't think anyone intends to break hearts." He paused. "Well, Sed, maybe. I'd just like a few minutes with something a little more permanent than a fucking tour bus, you know?"

"I understand, but—"

"Even if I'm just pretending."

"Brian, if I'm not careful, the person who is going to get their heart broken is me."

"We could always try to make something out of this."

"It's just not pos—" He covered her mouth with one hand.

"Okay, don't say it. Just let me pretend then." He kissed her temple and moved his hand from her mouth to her breast. "I'll get really drunk tomorrow to try to forget you."

"Brian."

"I'm kidding. If you want no strings, no strings you'll get."

She didn't know if she believed him, but she felt a measure of relief. Her career was complicated enough. She didn't have time for a serious relationship. Especially a long-distance one that had no chance of success. And after Jeremy… She forced thoughts of her ex-husband out of her mind.

Brian lifted her from her comfortable position against his chest and set her in the middle of the tub. "I'll scrub the ink off your back." He reached for the tiny bar of soap.

She sat quietly, her knees drawn up to her chest, while he washed her back. The silence between them hung uncomfortably. She wondered how she could break the ice again. Was he mad at her? It was better to be honest with him, wasn't it? But he said he wanted to pretend, so maybe he didn't want honesty at all.

She glanced over her shoulder to find him smiling to himself. He didn't look mad, more like amused.

"I wonder if I can get another twenty solos or so out of our time together," he said.

"Twenty?" Her eyes widened. "But I'm leaving after your concert tonight."

"So am I."

She grinned. "We'd better get busy then."

He laughed and placed an open-mouthed kiss on her shoulder. "I don't think you've got it in you."

She splashed water in his face. "Hey! You're the one who wanted to cuddle."

He chuckled. The cruelty behind his laugh caused a shiver to run down her spine.

"I'm done cuddling."

He slid her body in front of the Jacuzzi jet and lifted her slightly so the water gushed down the crack of her ass and between her legs. She shuddered. She leaned back against the edge of the tub, her bent elbows resting on the rim to hold herself over the pulsating water. Brian moved between her legs and took his cock in one hand. He rubbed its swollen head over her clit and then gently probed her aching opening. She squirmed, wanting him to thrust into her quickly. The stimulation of the water and his gentle probing were more than she could take.

She opened her eyes and found him watching her. "Are you going to fuck me or not?"

He lunged forward, filling her in one deep thrust. "Is that what you want?"

She moaned, her head falling back. "Yes, yes, that's what I want."

He backed away and then thrust into her again, lifting her out of the water jet. She gasped when he withdrew slightly and her ass sank back into the pulsating water. Her body jerked.

He kissed her gently, his cruelty evaporating. "Do you like that?"

"I like everything you do to me, Brian." She rubbed her nose against his.

He smiled lovingly.

"Everything except how you make me wait," she added.

His lips brushed hers. "I won't make you wait any longer."

He buried himself inside of her and withdrew rhythmically now. His little gasps of pleasure gave her goose bumps. She looked up at him. His eyes were closed, his mouth open, as he lost himself in the feel of her body and the constant shift of the Jacuzzi jet over their combined genitals. God, he was sexy.

The bathroom door opened. Myrna stiffened. Brian paused and looked over his shoulder.

"Don't mind me." Eric entered the room and closed the door. "I've gotta take a piss."

Brian shrugged and thrust into Myrna again. As she was no longer relaxed, his cock rammed into her cervix. "Ow," she gasped.

He paused and looked down at her. "Did I hurt you?" He kissed her tenderly. "I'm sorry."

She forced herself to relax, trying to ignore Eric who was standing at the toilet, flooding it with a steady stream of urine. Eric didn't bother to pretend he wasn't watching them. He openly gawked.

She looked into Brian's eyes and smiled. "I'm fine."

"Should I stop?"

"No."

She expected him to wait until Eric had left, but he immediately started thrusting into her again, grinding into her now. She cried out as an orgasm caught her unexpectedly.

"Oh God, Brian. Yes!"

"I hear it again," he whispered, thrusting harder and deeper. He hummed a new riff.

Was he really hearing music? She was seeing stars. He was so good.

"Eric," he said. "Eric."

She opened her eyes, surprised he was calling out the name of his drummer while he made love to her.

Eric moved to stand beside the tub, holding his crotch as if in pain. "Threesome, dude?" he asked hopefully.

Brian shook his head. "I need you to hold her. I've got to get deeper."

"Deeper? Are you trying to bruise her liver?"

Myrna laughed.

"Just hold her, okay?"

"My pleasure."

Eric sat on the edge of the tub behind Myrna with his feet in the water. With one leg on each side of her body, he used his knees to hold her hips still in the water. She gripped his shins and leaned back against his chest as Brian rammed into her deeper and deeper. The water slapped against her lower belly with each thrust.

"Awesome view," Eric murmured into her ear.

She looked down. Beyond the peaks of her breasts, she could see Brian's cock thrusting into her. Hard. Thick. Glistening with moisture. In view one moment. Buried within her the next. Her mouth fell open. Something about Eric watching Brian's cock pounding into her made this more exciting. Shameful, but exciting. *Whore*.

"Damn, Brian, you are tearing it up," Eric growled.

"Shut up, I'm trying to concentrate."

Eric's hardening cock prodded Myrna in the back between her shoulder blades. Brian's rhythm was apparently getting to him, too. Eric rocked against her back slightly with each of Brian's thrusts. After a moment, Eric's hands moved to cup her breasts. He plucked at her nipples to Brian's tempo until she thought she'd go insane.

Eric bent his head to whisper in her ear, probably afraid to interrupt Brian's guitar solo writing. "Trey was right. You do have perfect tits." He stroked the outer edge of her ear with his tongue, again using the same rhythm.

The beat consumed her. Brian's deep thrusts. His hands squeezing her ass rhythmically. Eric plucking at her nipples, stroking her ear with his tongue. The water sloshing against her belly and thighs. God, she was going to explode.

Her fingers dug into the wet jeans covering Eric's shins and her head fell back against his shoulder as the first ripples of orgasm gripped her. "Oh."

Eric reached down between her body and Brian's. When his fingers found her aching clit and flicked it, she exploded with a scream of ecstasy.

"God damn, this chick is hot," Eric said.

"I've gotta come," Brian murmured

He pulled out and climbed to his feet, circling his cock with his hand. Why had he pulled out? She noticed he wasn't wearing a condom. She wasn't going to let him waste his load though. She pulled away from Eric's grasp, knelt before Brian, and looked up at him.

"Let me suck you off," she said. "Please."

He smiled down at her. "Like I'm going to say no to that request."

His hand stopped stroking his flesh and gently cupped her face. She leaned forward and took him deep into her throat, and then pulled back, sucking hard. His fingers clenched in her hair. If she hadn't been so turned on by him, she might have protested, but the pain was stimulating. She wanted him to hurt her. He jerked her head back by her hair until just the head of his cock was in her mouth. She understood what he wanted and began to bob her head rapidly to stimulate the head. She was careful to keep her lips over her teeth so she didn't scrape him while she sucked him vigorously, her lips bumping over the rim.

"Yeah, baby," he gasped. "That's it."

The sound of Eric jerking off behind her distracted

her for a moment. She paused. Brian yanked her hair again. Her nipples grew taut in response. *Yeah, treat me like your dirty whore*.

She moved her hand between her thighs and slid two fingers inside herself, withdrawing them slick with her juices. She then reached between Brian's legs and slid two lubricated fingers up his ass.

He gasped in surprise, his body jerking. He didn't ask her to stop. Instead, he widened his stance so her fingers could slide deeper. Most guys freaked out when she tried this. Jeremy had berated her for days—*Where did you learn that? Who have you been fucking?*—but Brian seemed to trust her. Or maybe he was kinkier than most. She searched for her target. He was close to coming. It shouldn't be hard to locate.

She continued to give him head while her fingers probed inside him. Eric was still jerking off behind her, his rhythm matching hers. She twisted her fingers inside Brian and found what she was looking for. The little gland that secreted semen was swollen to bursting. When she pressed against it, Brian cried out as his seed spurted into her mouth unexpectedly. Well, unexpectedly to him. She'd known exactly what would happen. She swallowed his offering greedily, loving the salty taste of him.

"What the fuck?" Brian yelled. "God. Myrna. God."

Even after he'd spent his load, she continued to rub the little gland. It pulsated against her fingers, prolonging his orgasm for more than a minute. His entire body shuddered and trembled.

"Oh God, Myrna, what are you doing to me? I can't stop coming." He put a hand on the wall for support.

She smiled around his cock and removed her fingers from his ass, letting his orgasm dissipate.

Eric cried out behind her as he came over her back. Correction. Into her hair.

She released Brian's cock from her mouth and glared up at Eric. "Did you just come in my hair?"

"I'm sorry," Eric said. "You're just so hot, Myrna. I had to come on you. I couldn't help it."

"Do you know how hard it is to get cum out of long hair?" She found the sticky mess on the side of her head with her hand. "Eww. Damn it, Eric."

Brian cupped her face, and when she looked up at him, he kissed her with loving reverence. "I've never had an orgasm that intense in my entire life, Myrna. You're amazing."

She smiled. "I'm glad you enjoyed it."

"That's an understatement. I've never met a woman as uninhibited as you are." She wasn't usually like this. His lack of inhibition brought out something primal in her. He kissed her again and leaned away to stroke the tip of her nose with one finger. "I hate to leave you right now, but I've got to get this new solo down on paper. I hope you understand."

"I think it's awesome." She meant it.

He stared at her for a moment, contemplating her with a serious expression. "Wanna go to Vegas and get married?"

Her heart stuttered to a stop and then started to race. *Married?* "Uh, no, actually. Not at all."

He shrugged. "I had to ask." He kissed her forehead.

Brian climbed from the tub and reached for a towel. He wrapped it around his slim hips, collected his pants from the floor, and headed toward the door. He paused in the doorway, his gaze shifting to Eric, who was still in the tub with Myrna.

"Hey, numbnuts. Keep your pants on around her or I'll castrate you in your sleep. And wash your cum out of her hair, you ass."

Eric grinned. "My pleasure."

Brian hesitated, and then left her alone in the bathroom. Naked. With Eric Sticks.

Chapter 5

MYRNA WATCHED ERIC TUCK HIS SLACK COCK INTO his pants and button his fly. He sat in the water in his jeans and beckoned her closer. She didn't trust him and, now that she was no longer delirious with pleasure, she was embarrassed that he'd seen her with Brian. She covered her breasts with her hands and sank deeper into the water.

"I can wash it out," she said, avoiding his self-satisfied grin by focusing on the edge of the tub.

The sound of Brian's guitar throbbed through the wall. Wow. This solo rocked more than the last one he'd composed while in her company.

"I'm not going to molest you, Myrna." Eric chuckled. "Unless you want me to."

She knew he'd just watched her get fucked, suck cock, and ram her fingers up his friend's ass, but she couldn't relax.

"I'll just wash your hair. I promise. Besides, I'm not even horny anymore. You're perfectly safe."

She did like to have her hair washed. A simple, soothing pleasure. One of her favorite luxuries. But Eric? She wasn't sure she wanted him to indulge her.

Eric reached for a tiny bottle and dumped a healthy amount of shampoo in his outstretched palm.

Myrna leaned back in the tub, wetting her hair thoroughly, and then sat up. Not waiting for her to come closer to him, Eric moved behind her and massaged the shampoo into her scalp. His strong fingers worked the fragrant lather into her hair. She closed her eyes and relaxed, keeping her breasts covered with her hands. Eric's hands felt fantastic. She stifled a groan of contentment.

The distant sounds of Brian's sporadic solo drew her thoughts to their lovemaking session. Had she really allowed Eric to fondle her without protest? She hadn't even considered stopping him. What had she been thinking?

It had felt good. That's all she'd been thinking. And this felt really good, too. His thumbs kneaded the muscles at the base of her skull, while his fingers massaged the top and sides of her head and his pinkies rubbed her temples. His large, strong hands and thin fingers hit her in all the right places.

"Mmmm," she murmured.

Her hands drifted away from her breasts, down her belly to her clit. She wasn't sure how she could be horny again, but Eric's fingers on her scalp and Brian's music had her in a state again. She stroked her clit persistently, thinking of Brian's fingers moving over his fret board in the other room.

Her breath caught in the back of her throat as the first ripples of pleasure gripped her.

"You know I like to watch, don't you?" Eric said into her ear.

She sat up with an awkward splash. Had she really been leaning against Eric and masturbating? What was wrong with her? These guys. These rock stars had her behaving in a totally uncharacteristic manner. *No sale,*

Myrna. You were born a whore. You live as a whore and you'll die a whore.

She ducked her head under water to rinse the shampoo out of her hair and drown Jeremy's words. When she emerged, she moved to the far side of the tub, avoiding Eric's heavy gaze.

"I shouldn't have said anything," he said. "I didn't mean to interrupt. Please, continue."

"I'm ashamed."

"Why?"

Unwilling to share her turmoil, she shook her head. "Do you really like to watch?"

"I'd rather watch than fuck." He rinsed the shampoo from his hands in the water. "Sed lets me watch him do chicks all the time. That's the first time Brian's let me watch. I never realized what a stud he is. I mean… Damn."

Myrna flushed, but nodded.

"Is Sed a stud, too?" she asked. Why had she asked that? She didn't want to know. Okay, she kinda wanted to know.

Eric laughed. "Is Sed a stud?" He scratched his head. "I've seen him do four girls at once and have them all begging for more."

"Four girls? How is that even possible?"

"One on each hand. One on his face. One riding him like a mechanical bull."

Myrna's eyes widened. "And you just watched? Didn't participate?"

"I wore a blister on my hand from stroking myself."

"Seriously?"

"No, not seriously. They invited me in after Sed passed out."

"So you got his leftovers?"

"I guess you could call it that, but I honestly had more fun watching Sed make them scream."

"Interesting. And Brian never let you watch before today?"

Eric shook his head. "He's a very private person."

Myrna nodded slightly. She could see that. "What about the other guys?"

Eric grinned. "Why do you want to know?"

She shrugged. "Research."

"Research?"

"I'm a human sexuality professor. Remember?"

"That would explain your knowledge. What did your fingers do in Brian's ass? I thought he was going to blow off the back of your head when he came. And came. And came. I didn't think it was possible for a guy to come that long. That wasn't some regular ass probe. You did something in there, didn't you?"

She winked at him. "That's my secret." And yes, that did explain her knowledge. Eric understood and she scarcely knew him. She'd been married to Jeremy for three years, and anytime she wanted to try something new, he'd been certain she was cheating on him.

"Will you show me your secret?" He leaned forward in the tub.

She laughed. "You wish."

"Damn straight."

"I can't, Eric. I promised not to hurt Brian."

Eric scowled. "You did what?"

"Trey made me promise not to hurt him."

"Well, you'll never be able to keep that promise, Myr, so you might as well break it with me right now."

She shook her head at him, smiling. "I'm not going to stick my fingers up your ass."

He sighed. "That figures. Will you let me watch you masturbate though?"

"I'm not really in the mood."

"Even with the sound of Brian's solo coming through the wall? He wrote that when he was ramming his cock into you. I saw it."

She squeezed her thighs together at the memory. Eric was right. Brian had written that wonderful, poetic solo while he'd been making love to her. She leaned back against the far edge of the tub, the warm Jacuzzi jets against her back. She closed her eyes and listened to the sounds of Brian's guitar as if he played just for her. Someday soon, thousands of fans would hear, and love, that beautiful string of notes and have no idea how it had been created. She let the music carry her back to his lovemaking as he played the same string of notes over and over and over again. With each repeat, the piece sounded more masterful. As his fingers found each note, she imagined his cock inside her, filling her, withdrawing, filling her. Her hand moved between her legs. She sighed. How could she want him again already?

But want him she did.

She stood, water pouring from her body as she stepped from the tub. Eric banged the side of his head against the wall repeatedly as he watched her leave the bathroom. Naked.

Dripping water through the hotel room, she sought Brian. Caught up in his music, he didn't notice her at first, but his band members, who sat around the dining table watching him play, did.

Trey pulled the sucker out of his mouth. "Um, Myrna," he said. "You seem to be naked."

"Everybody get out," she demanded.

Brian's guitar screeched as he quit playing mid-solo. His eyes widened in surprise.

"Except you," she said to Brian. "You stay."

The other three men grumbled but obeyed her and left the room.

"Why are you walking around in front of my band naked?" Brian asked, his jaw tense with anger.

"I was listening to you play," she said, "and it made me want you so badly. I considered getting myself off, but I'd rather—"

He grinned. "My playing made you touch yourself?"

She lowered her gaze. "Will you play for me?"

"If you show me what my playing does to you."

Myrna pushed the remaining breakfast dishes to the far end of the table. She then sat on the edge of the table in front of Brian, turned a chair sideways, and rested her feet on the seat. "If you promise to make love to me when you're done playing."

He didn't promise, but he did strike the first note of his guitar solo. She spread her thighs wide, knowing he had an unfettered view of everything between her legs. It made her hotter for him. She wanted him to see. She leaned back on one elbow and slid three fingers inside herself, her fluids dripping over the back of her hand as she plunged them deep and withdrew them, plunged them inside. She withdrew them again and shifted one finger to her ass, filling both holes with a groan. She fell back on the table, freeing her other hand to rub her clit. Brian's solo was building, his fingers moving over the notes faster and faster as she stroked herself toward orgasm.

"Brian," she gasped. "Brian!"

His solo stopped and his guitar landed somewhere on the floor with a clang. He tossed the chair aside and struggled with the fly of his pants. When his cock sprang free, he pushed her hands aside and plunged into her.

She lifted her head to look at him and then dropped it back onto the table with a bang as her back arched in pleasure.

"Good God, woman. What are you doing to me?" he groaned. He fucked her harder than ever, cursing under his breath as if she'd made him angry. He shifted her hips off the table slightly, which gave him the leverage to slam into her even harder. It hurt so good. His balls slapped against her ass with each penetrating thrust, teasing her into wanting something a little dirtier.

"We eat on that table, you know," someone yelled from the other room.

Brian paused in mid-thrust. She looked up at him. His face was red with exertion. Hair sticking to his sweaty forehead. Mmm. Gorgeous man.

"Trey has a point," he said.

He pulled out and Myrna groaned in protest. He dropped to his knees between her legs and plunged his tongue inside her. He gripped her thighs as he ate her out. Sucking, biting, licking, probing her cunt, her ass, her cunt again with his tongue. She couldn't keep track of his chaotic motions, could only focus on the excitement and pleasure it drew from her trembling body. When his mouth shifted to her clit, she cried out with release. "God, yes, Brian. Yes! Yes!" Her juices dripped down the crack of her ass. He lapped up every drop.

"What are you doing to her?" someone called from the other room.

"He's eating," Myrna yelled. "Don't bother him."

There was a smattering of laughter from beyond the dining room. Brian stood up and smiled down at her crookedly. His lips were wet and swollen. She rose up to kiss him. The taste of her fluids on his lips made her belly quiver. She grabbed his cock and guided it inside her body, shifting forward to force him deeper. He thrust into her gently but not deeply enough to do anything but drive her mad with anticipation. He kissed her deeply though, his tongue mingling with hers.

He pulled away and looked down at her, his eyes glazed with passion.

"Brian," she whispered. "Will you do something for me?"

"Anything."

"Fuck me in the ass."

"You like anal? I'm not very good at—"

She covered his lips with her fingertips. "I've never tried it. I want to try different things with you. Is that okay?"

He made a sound of amusement against her fingertips. "I'm game for anything, sweetheart."

Her mind began to flip through all the dirty fantasies she had but had never been able to fulfill. "Anything?"

"Anything."

"Just this for now. Will it hurt?"

"It might. I'm not really built for it, you know?"

"You are huge." She trailed her fingers over his bare chest. She'd been craving pleasurable pain from him all day. Why hesitate? "But I don't want you to be gentle. I want you to hurt me."

His eyes widened in surprise. "Seriously?"

"Yes." She pushed him away, her heart pounding with excitement and a little fear. She turned around and bent over the table, using her hands to spread her ass cheeks. He lowered his head and licked her hole, wetting it with as much saliva as he could. When he stopped, she looked at him over her shoulder. He tore open a condom from his pants pocket, applied it, and stood behind her. She forced herself to relax, waiting in anticipation for his huge cock to fill her forbidden hole. He rubbed the head of his cock over the puckered flesh and gently pressed forward. She bit her lip to stop herself from crying out. Surely his penis had enlarged three times its normal size. She grunted as he pressed deeper. She released her ass cheeks and reached her arms in front of her, her fingertips digging into the hard, smooth table surface.

"Ow," she gasped.

"I'll stop," he said.

"No, don't stop. We just need—"

A tube slid across the table toward her and she caught it. "Lubrication," she said gratefully.

"Dude, so not cool. Lube is always needed for back-door entry." Trey stuck his sucker back in his mouth and left the room.

"Thank you, Trey," Myrna called.

She handed the tube to Brian and waited while he applied it to his cock and used his fingers to spread it inside her. "Does it bother you that they're out there listening to everything we're doing?" Brian asked.

Them being there made her feel that much dirtier. She didn't want to pretend to be pure. Jeremy had always expected that of her, and she hated everything about that man. "If it bothered me, I'd have taken you into a room with a door."

He chuckled. "I do think I'm in love with you."

She tensed. *No, don't say that*. He pressed deeper. "Ah, God," she gasped, squeezing her eyes tightly closed. She couldn't take any more. It burned. Deeper. She bit her lip, tears streaming down her face, the pressure inside her painful and thrilling at the same time.

"Are you sure about this?" Brian asked.

She wasn't. It hurt pretty badly, even with the lube, but she nodded, several tears splashing down onto the table in front of her. He started to withdraw and the pain was instantly replaced by blinding pleasure. "Mmmmm," she purred.

He pressed forward again. Even deeper this time. The pain receded to a heavy fullness. Not pleasurable exactly. Strange. He backed away. A feeling of relief. Definitely pleasurable.

"It feels so good when you pull out," she gasped. But to pull out, he had to slide in.

He pressed forward again. The pain of his penetration blended with the pleasure of his withdraw. She gasped and shifted her legs farther apart to give him better access.

"That's it, baby." He took her slowly for a few more strokes, allowing her body to adjust to his size, and when she was able to take him completely without whimpering, he leaned over her and rested his fists on the table. His strokes increased in speed and her pussy ached for its neglect as his balls bounced against her throbbing labia and clit. He fucked her harder now, the pain intense, but the pleasure ten times sweeter. She sobbed from the excitement of it.

"Are you crying?" He paused and leaned over her shoulder to look at her.

She hid her face in her hands. "Don't stop now," she pleaded, her voice hitching.

"You are crying."

"I like it, Brian. Don't stop. Do it hard. Please. Hurt me. I'm so dirty. I'm so fucking dirty. Punish me."

He dropped a tender kiss on her shoulder. "You're not dirty, sweetheart. You're beautiful. Tell me when you've had enough."

He slowed his strokes, not backing off on how deep he took her, just how quickly. Her thighs quivered. Slow was better. She could take this languid pain without sobbing.

"This feels nice, Myr, but I don't hear music." He reached around her and stroked her clit until she sputtered with an orgasm that left her entirely disoriented. He pulled out. "I know you crave pain because I made you feel like a whore."

How did he know that? She lifted her body from the table and turned to look at him. She opened her mouth to protest. He covered her lips with his fingers.

"That voyeuristic stuff was hot, Myrna, but I'd rather treasure you. I don't think you understand how beautiful you are. How amazing your lack of inhibition is. How wonderful…" He seemed to realize he'd said too much.

Her heart twanged. Sweet sex god. "Thank you," she whispered.

He kissed her cheek, and stripped himself of the condom before forcing his hard cock back into his pants. He handed her the towel he'd worn out of the bathroom.

"And it might not bother you to run around naked in front of my bandmates, but I don't like it."

She nodded and wrapped the towel around her body.

"Let's go find a room with a door. And we'll try something different, if you like."

"I would like that, if you're willing to indulge me."

"I'm the one who's being indulged here." He grinned, took her hand, and led her from the dining room toward one of the two bedrooms in the suite.

Sed glanced up from the TV to watch them pass. "You two done so soon?"

"Just getting started," Brian said.

Chapter 6

BRIAN LED MYRNA TO THE BEDROOM AND CLOSED the door. She looked up at him expectantly in the limited light spilling between the heavy drapes. He smiled, cupping her cheek and running his thumb over her cheekbone. This woman. This beautiful, intelligent, witty, fun, sexy woman. How could he not fall for her? He knew she'd crush his heart like a bug and didn't care. He wondered if she had marathon sex with every lover she'd taken. She was certainly eager and skilled. He didn't dare ask her. He didn't want to know that he wasn't special. Wanted to believe that he was the first, the only man with whom she'd experienced this level of passion. He could pretend. And he could indulge. If new experiences were what she wanted, he'd do his damnedest to give them to her.

She laid a gentle hand on his bare belly and he tensed. He was still rock hard, but he wanted to go slow with her this time, not lose himself in mindless fucking. Not that mindless fucking was bad. It was spectacular, and she was so open to it. It blew his mind. She deserved to be treasured though, and he would take the time to make her feel beautiful, as he'd promised.

He should have never let Eric watch. He knew that's why she was feeling dirty. When that solo had come to him, he hadn't been thinking about how his total disregard for her feelings would affect her.

He bent his head to kiss her eyelids. Her cheeks. The tip of her nose. Even though she offered her beguiling mouth, he refused her lips. Not yet. But her jaw, yes, he kissed her there, and her neck just beneath her ear. Her pulse drummed just beneath his lips.

She sighed and buried her fingers in his hair, tilting her head to the side to allow him easy access. Her skin was damp and cool. He used his mouth to warm a trail down the side of her neck.

She shuddered.

"Are you cold?" he whispered, drawing her toward the bed and warm covers.

"I'm on fire."

He grinned. She was always on fire. And he willingly dove in, knowing he'd get burned. Perhaps that was part of the attraction.

He lifted her and laid her down on the bed, leaving her most beguiling parts covered with the towel. He'd get to those parts eventually, but he wanted to start where she wouldn't expect it. He knelt on the end of the bed, lifted her leg, and took her dainty foot in his hands, massaging the instep with his thumbs. He rested her heel against his shoulder and kissed her ankle, her calf, and the back of her knee. She sighed. His tongue darted over the sensitive skin there, tracing chaotic patterns behind her knee.

He could almost see the sweet well between her thighs. The shadow of the towel was the only thing keeping her secrets from view. His cock throbbed with need. His balls ached. He'd already exploded several times today. How could his body crave more already? He wasn't usually this randy. Why her?

Why not?

He brushed the towel aside. He just wanted a peek. A mistake. He didn't want to start rutting on her like a horny teen, but the lovely vision of her slightly parted pink lips, opening to parts that begged to be filled, had him reaching for the fly of his jeans. He released the buttons and freed The Beast from his pants, grabbing it firmly with one hand to try to keep it under control.

She chuckled and he glanced up at her, his tongue still darting over the skin behind her knee. She was watching him. He lifted his head. "What's funny?"

"Nothing. I know what you're thinking, is all."

"What am I thinking?"

"That there's a silky hole in your line of sight that needs filling, but you promised to make me feel beautiful, so you're going to hold off as long as possible."

He smiled and released his cock to slide a finger inside her. Her slick flesh swallowed his finger in liquid heat. "This silky hole?"

He loved the look of his finger buried inside her and was unwilling to remove it.

"That's the hole I was thinking of. Is that the one you were thinking of?"

He moved his other hand from her foot and probed her ass with another finger. "There's this one, too."

She squirmed. "Do you prefer that one?"

"I greatly prefer the former, actually."

"So do I. And now I know for sure, thanks to you."

He removed the tip of his finger from her ass and slid a second finger into her pussy. Yeah, that looked even better. His thumb rubbed over the hood of her clit. Her body jerked.

"I'm sorry to be so predictable," he murmured. "I really did bring you in here to smother you with affection."

"I'd rather you submit to what you really want to do."

Withdrawing his fingers slightly, he pressed them inside her again, absorbed by the appeal of watching. Deciding he'd much rather watch his cock ramming into her, he glanced around the well-decorated room. The long dresser was about hip high. He slid from the end of the bed, stood up, and applied the last condom from his pocket. Waiting was no longer an option. He leaned over the bed, gripped her soft ass, and dragged her toward him.

She gasped in surprise when he picked her up and turned to sit her on top of the dresser.

"Here?" she asked.

"I want to watch," he murmured. "Have you ever done it like this?"

She shook her head, kissed his forehead, and perched on the edge of the dresser, spreading her legs wide to give him an unfettered view. He had to possess her. Right then. No more waiting.

He grabbed his cock and inserted it into her beckoning warmth. He sighed as he slid deep, his eyes focused on the action between their bodies. The vision of his cock buried inside her, matched with the feel of her warmth gripping him, caused his stomach to clench with need. Her forehead rested on his shoulder so she could watch, too.

He let the urgency carry his rhythm, sliding in and out of her faster and faster. Watching the ebb and flow of her flesh as it accepted his so perfectly. He rocked on the balls of his feet so he could take her hard. Ground his cock deep so she'd make that pleading, mewing sound in the back of her throat. He didn't know if she even realized she made it, but it drove him crazy.

And then, he heard it again.

The music.

He tried to ignore it, only wanting to concentrate on the sight of his cock disappearing into Myrna's tight body. Feel her warmth around him and the slightly painful dig of her fingertips into his upper arms. Smell her skin, her sweat, her sex. Hear nothing but those maddening little sounds she made. Taste her lips. He placed a finger under her chin and claimed her mouth, plunging his tongue into her mouth. So sweet.

The series of chords repeated in his head.

He tore his mouth from hers and looked down into her eyes. "Say my name," he whispered.

"Brian."

He could still hear the music. "Louder."

"Brian."

Not loud enough. He'd make her scream it. Her cries would drown out the music.

He picked her up off the dresser, still impaled by his cock, and carried her to the bed. He tumbled onto the bed with her, driving himself deep. Her back arched and she made that sound that grabbed him by the balls. He pounded into her, ground against her clit, and then withdrew completely. She cried out in protest.

"What do you want, baby?" he whispered into her ear. "Tell me."

"Your cock. Take me hard, Brian. Please."

"I'm sorry. I can't hear you. What do you want me to do?"

"Hard! Fuck me hard, Brian!"

Yeah, that's it. He could barely hear the riff now. He slid into her body slowly. "Like this?"

"Harder!"

He slid out slowly. "You want me to pull out?"

She slapped him hard across the face. He flinched, his cheek stinging. He was too stunned to respond at first. She grabbed a handful of his hair.

"I said to fuck me! Did you hear that?"

Oh, he'd heard her. He'd fuck her until she begged him to stop.

He took her hard, fast, and deep. She was screaming his name now, "Yes, Brian. Yes!" but it was no use. The music consumed him. Her body convulsed beneath him, the muscles inside her tightening around his cock in hard spasms. He leaned away from her enough to find her clit with his fingertips. He stroked her persistently as she came, her pussy sucking at his cock in a maddening fashion. The chords playing through his mind sucked at him almost as maddeningly.

"Brian, you've got to stop," she panted. "Please, I can't take any more."

He moved his hand away and she relaxed slightly. He grinned wickedly and stroked her clit again. Harder and faster this time, as he continued to drive his cock into her. Her entire body shook uncontrollably.

"Oh God. Oh God!"

"Yes?" He bit her earlobe. "I'm going to keep you here, coming repeatedly, until I let go. Is that okay with you?"

He stopped moving his fingers so she could think well enough to respond.

"Please, stop," she gasped. "Oh. Oh. Don't stop. Never stop. Never." She shuddered violently again. "Oh God, you have to stop."

He paused, letting her catch her breath.

"There's got to be a compromise in there somewhere." His fingers stroked her mercilessly again.

The solo struck him as her pussy clenched around him in another orgasm and she writhed beneath him in ecstasy. Damn. He couldn't pretend to ignore the music anymore.

"You're not going to believe this," he murmured.

She blinked at him as if he'd asked her to define the meaning of life, and then she seemed to drift back to her senses. "You're hearing music again?"

"Yeah. And…it's a ballad."

"You need to slow down?"

"Unfortunately."

"I think I can tolerate it, if you can." She chuckled tiredly, her body limp beneath him.

He sighed and pulled out before collecting a pad of hotel stationery and a pen from a round table near the window. He climbed back on top of her. He set the paper on her shoulder, uncapped the pen with his teeth, and jotted the first few notes down. He couldn't hear the music when he wasn't inside his lovely Myrna, so he slid into her body and concentrated on the sounds in his head while he filled her body with slow, steady strokes.

He was scarcely aware of her soft sighs, as the notes seemed to appear by magic, just like before. It turned out he was writing a series of connected solos. By the time he finished scribbling them down, he'd exhausted himself entirely. The pen tumbled from his fingertips, and he looked down at Myrna.

She smiled up at him. "All finished?"

How many women would let him drift off like that in the middle of sex without busting his balls over it? How many women evoked that response in him in the first place? Only one.

He smiled sleepily. "I think I'm too tired to finish."

"You've been at it for over an hour," she whispered. "Do you want me to take over and help you out?"

Over an hour? That would explain why he was drenched in sweat and weak with exhaustion. "I'd appreciate it."

He rolled onto his back. Cold air bathed his crotch. He shivered. She straddled his hips and eased him inside her heavenly warmth. Myrna must have realized he needed to find release quickly. He'd built himself up beyond his usual peak without realizing it. He ached. She rode him fast, increasing his urgency.

Ah, she felt good. Tight. Warm. Soft. Smooth. Slick. Tight. Ah, God. So warm.

He had to come. Had to let it go. Couldn't stop it. Had to. Had…

He erupted with a hoarse cry, spurting into her with glorious release, wishing he wasn't wearing a condom. Wanting his seed inside her. Confused about those feelings. She collapsed on top of him and he wrapped his arms around her to hold her close. He drifted to sleep with her soft cheek pressed to his chest, his achingly full heart throbbing within. At last. He'd found her. His one.

Chapter 7

MYRNA KNOCKED AT THE "STAFF ONLY" DOOR behind the stadium. A large man pulled the door ajar, blocking its opening with his broad body.

"Can I help you, ma'am?"

She'd had nothing to wear but professional attire, but being called ma'am smacked of elderly lady and set her teeth on edge.

"I'm a guest of Sinners."

He gave her a "yeah, right" look and consulted a paper attached to his clipboard. "Name?"

"Myrna." She coughed. "Myrna Suxsed."

He grinned at her. "You must have a lot of sisters. There are half a dozen girls with that same last name on my list."

She cleared her throat. "Indeed."

He stepped aside, handed her a backstage pass with her fake name on it, and pointed her down a corridor. People stood outside doors marked with the names of the opening bands. Most of the hall-dwellers were young women who looked as expected. Wearing a black bra as a shirt seemed to be the norm. Myrna pretended to fit in, but she stuck out like a sore thumb. Every person she passed stopped talking in mid-sentence to gawk at her. Perhaps she should have bought some blue jeans. She hadn't thought wearing a suit would be a big deal. Uh, wrong.

When she spotted the dressing room marked Sinners, she smiled. She'd be safe from the glares of rabid fans once safely inside. Right?

She knocked on the door and someone pulled it open. Expecting to see only the band members, she found the dressing room filled wall-to-wall with people and didn't recognize anyone. She slipped inside and closed the door. As she made her way across the room, looking for anyone who looked remotely familiar, she got a lot of double takes.

"Myrna!" Eric called. "You made it."

She cringed as he sprinted across the room and lifted her off the floor, her arms trapped at her sides. His height threw her off guard, six-four maybe, but rail thin. She hadn't realized how damned tall he was until her feet rose nearly a foot off the ground.

"Put me down."

Eric spun her around, kissed her loudly on the temple, and set her on her feet.

A young woman wearing black lipstick grabbed Eric's arm. "Who's she?"

He smacked the girl on the ass. "None of your business. Go get me a beer."

And off she went without protest.

"Where's Brian?" Myrna asked.

"He's getting all dolled up for the stage. I can look like crap. I sit behind the drum kit. But he's front and center so he needs to look beautiful. Do you want a beer?"

"No, thanks. And you don't look like crap." She smoothed the lock of crimson hair that rested against his neck.

"Does Myrna have a crush on me?" He wrapped

an arm around her shoulders and pulled her against his side.

Someone snapped a picture.

"Hey," Myrna called after the guy with the camera and squirmed out of Eric's grasp. "Hey, I didn't say you could take my picture. Hey!"

A black T-shirt over a hard-muscled chest appeared before her. She paused. Too tall to be Brian. She glanced up and her knees went weak.

"Sed?"

His lips curled into a self-satisfied smile, but she couldn't see his eyes beneath his dark, mirrored sunglasses.

He fingered the backstage pass she had clipped to her suit lapel. "Hello, Miss Suxsed. Good to see you here."

"Y-you look…different." Hot was what she meant, but she didn't want to turn into one of those blubbering fans prostrating themselves at his feet. He had half a dozen of them in tow as it was.

"I can't believe you wore a business suit to a metal concert, Professor. I think your balls are bigger than mine."

"Not possible," the blonde to his left said and snorted at her own joke.

"Master Sinclair is in the bathroom." Sed jerked his head in the direction of a door toward the back of the room. "He needs the quiet before a gig, but I'm sure he wouldn't mind seeing his muse for a few moments."

"Thanks, Sed."

"Who was that?" the blonde asked Sed.

"None of your business. Go get me a beer." And off she went without protest. A brunette took the empty place at Sed's side.

Myrna picked her way across the room. She spotted

Jace in the far corner getting his hair fashioned into spikes by a roadie with a huge tub of green hair gel. Trey had two suckers in his mouth and a girl on his knee. The incredibly attractive young man sitting next to him had his hand on Trey's thigh, but Trey didn't seem to notice. He waved at Myrna when he saw her. She waved back, stopped in front of the bathroom door, and knocked.

"Occupied," Brian's voice came from the other side.

"It's Myrna. Can I come in?"

The door opened. A hand in a fingerless leather glove grabbed her forearm and tugged her inside. Brian wrapped her in a tight embrace. She buried her nose in his leather jacket at his shoulder. God, he smelled good. In the three hours since she'd last seen him, she'd actually missed him. Not good. She had to say good-bye to him in a couple of hours.

"I'm glad you made it," he murmured.

His hard body trembled against her. She leaned back to look at him, and she couldn't help but gape. Heavy black eyeliner surrounded his eyes.

"You're wearing more makeup than I am."

"Do I look like a pussy?" Staring into the mirror above the sink, he bared his teeth at his reflection to make himself look mean.

Myrna hugged him from behind. "No. As always, you look sexier than should be allowed by law."

"Are you going to arrest me?"

Her hand slid down to cup his package through his pants. "No, but I might have to punish you."

Brian caught her hand. "Don't get me worked up now," he said. "I've got to be onstage in thirty minutes, and I can barely walk as it is."

She chuckled. Her hips and legs had gotten quite a workout today as well. "I know the feeling. Is that why you're trembling?"

He shook his head. "Typical preshow jitters. I'll be fine once I'm onstage."

He tugged her around his body so that she faced him. She leaned back against the sink and accepted his tender kiss.

"I'm glad you came," he said. "I had it in my head that I'd never see you again."

"I wouldn't miss this show for anything. I might not look it, but I'm your biggest fan."

"I like this suit." He fingered the top button of her blouse. "Do you have your garters on underneath?"

"If I decide you're worthy, you might find out after the show."

"Now there's an incentive. I better get warmed up. My fingers are stiff."

"Will you kiss me first?"

He rested his hands on the sink on either side of her hips and leaned forward to claim her mouth. Like a struck match, she ignited with need. She wrapped her arms around his neck, her fingers intertwined with the hair at the nape of his neck. Normally soft, it was now stiff and sticky with hair spray and gel. She felt she had access to two undeniably sexy men in one. The real Brian she'd spent the day with—a ten out of ten. And this rock star version, Master Sinclair—another ten out of ten. They were the same person, and yet totally different.

Pulling away slowly, he opened his eyes to pin her with a sultry look. "I'll play something for you onstage."

"What?" she asked breathlessly.

"You'll know."

Leaving Myrna leaning against the sink, Brian opened the bathroom door. Some girl with black and purple hair was instantly in his face. "Master Sinclair! Finally. I've been waiting to see you for-like-ever!" She grabbed his arm and hopped up and down. "Oh my God, I loooooove you. Can I have your autograph? Pleeeeeease."

He scarcely glanced at her as he signed the insert to a Sinners CD that she'd handed him.

The girl looked over his shoulder into the bathroom. "Who's that?"

"None of your business." He handed her pen and CD insert back to her. "Go get me a beer."

And off she went without protest.

Myrna laughed. Brian glanced at her over his shoulder, an eyebrow quirked at her. She shook her head at him, still grinning. How easy would it be to get a superiority complex with these fans racing around to fulfill his every request?

Chapter 8

STANDING ON THE FLOOR LOOKING UP AT THE STAGE with a couple of the roadies and several girls from the dressing room, Myrna waited for Sinners to make their entrance. Her heart thudded with anticipation.

"Who are you, anyway?" one of the dressing room girls asked.

"None of your business. Go get me a beer," Myrna said.

The girl scowled at her, creasing her heavy blue and black eye makeup. Myrna wondered if she thought that much glitter was really necessary. It detracted from her looks rather than adding to them.

"Uh. That was a joke," Myrna said. "I'm a friend of Brian's."

"Did you babysit him when he was in elementary school or something?"

Ouch.

"No, actually, I'm fucking him."

"Heh, I thought so." The girl grinned. "How'd he hook up with a stuffy chick like you?"

Myrna shrugged. "Who are you here with?"

"Sed or Trey. I was hoping Brian, since Angie split, but he's a one-chick kind of guy."

"Sed *or* Trey?"

"Maybe both. Depends on their mood and how tired they are after the show."

"Not Eric or Jace?"

"Eric will probably watch. He can bang me when Sed's done if he feels like it. And Jace… He's way too extreme for me."

"Jace is?" Cute and quiet little Jace?

Another girl nodded, joining their conversation. "Jace is a lunatic. First, he asked me to hit him with this whip thing to get him all in the mood, and then when we were doing it, I thought he was going to kill me. I mean literally. I almost suffocated."

"Huh." Myrna never expected that kind of thing from Jace. "And what are your names?"

"I'm Darlene," the girl in heavy eye makeup said.

"Joyce," said the near fatality.

"I'm Myrna. Myrna Suxsed."

The girls laughed. "We're related. Sisters, I guess."

"So you sucked Sed off before you hooked up with Brian?" Joyce asked. "I'm surprised Brian tolerated that."

"Uh, no."

"Then how'd you get a backstage pass from Sed?"

Myrna flushed. She supposed since Sed's fake last name branded her pass, everyone thought she'd sucked his cock to get backstage. "Let me get this straight. Sed makes young ladies suck him to get backstage?"

"Minimum," Darlene said.

"That ass!" Myrna sputtered.

"Yes, it's a very nice ass," Joyce said. The two girls giggled and hugged each other.

"So you're okay with being treated like that?" Myrna asked. "Do you let all men treat you that way?"

"Of course not. But this is Sed Lionheart we're talk-ing about here. *The* Sed Lionheart. You know? If he stepped in dog shit, I'd lick it off his boot if he asked me to," Darlene said.

"Not if I did it first," Joyce said.

"Un-fucking-believable," Myrna murmured under her breath.

The stadium lights went off, and a blue light illuminated just the floor of the stage. Four sets of feet moved through the blue glow. The roar of the crowd was deafening. Myrna's heart thundered. One of those sets of feet belonged to Brian.

The thud of a bass drum vibrated through her body. Jace's bass groove joined Eric's beat, throbbing deep in Myrna's chest. Trey's rhythm guitar was added, and then Brian's unmistakable solo intro. The crowd roared. A bright light flashed and the lights came up. Center stage, Sed entered the song with a low growl into the microphone. The girls beside her screamed and thrust their fists in the air.

Myrna couldn't take her eyes off Brian, not even to blink. She watched him stalk the stage, playing his guitar as if it were an extension of his fingers. It was almost as if he were making love to it. And she wasn't jealous of the attention he paid to the strings. It excited her in a primitive way she couldn't describe. Perhaps it was the ten thousand other people he engaged with his wickedly seductive fingers. When they reached the guitar solo in the middle of the song, Brian took center stage and Sed moved to the back next to Jace. The crowd roared, bodies undulating against each other in a sea of flesh and sweat before the stage.

"You're a fucking genius, Master Sinclair," one of the roadies hollered. The dude must see this show almost every night, and he was still caught up in it. Myrna just watched, every nerve in her body responsive. She felt…alive.

"Fuck yeah! Play it, baby!" Myrna yelled.

Darlene laughed and patted her on the back enthusiastically. "Excellent score, Myrna. Master Sinclair is smoking hot."

Trey's dueling solo entered into harmony with Brian's, and he stepped beside him center stage. They strummed each other's guitars while fingering their own fret boards in synchrony. There was something highly erotic about watching them play together. An unexpected intimacy flowed between the two men. An intimacy she'd like to share. Simultaneously. Heat flooded her face and the swelling folds between her thighs. Oh my. *What* was she thinking? Brian *and* Trey. Together. With her? Just the thought sent her into sensory overload. She fanned her face with one hand.

Another roar from the crowd erupted as the guitarists finished and spun away from each other. Trey did this heel stomping thing that was entirely adorable. It was as if his body couldn't help but respond to the music. He rocked forward on his toes in rhythm with each chord he strummed. Myrna hadn't realized how irresistibly sexy Trey was until that moment. Hell, Jace and even Eric excited her, and she couldn't see anything of Eric but his flailing drumsticks behind the drum kit.

Sed entered the song again, singing his heart out at the far end of the stage. Fans surfed the crowd, eventually landing in the space between the low barrier fence and the stage. Security guards pulled them to safety and the fans rushed past where Myrna was standing, screaming excitedly as they raced to rejoin the crowd from the back. Myrna scarcely noticed anything but the five men onstage and one in particular. Brian had moved into the background again. He faced Eric's drum kit and bobbed his head to the beat as he played. When the song ended, the stage went dark and the crowd roared their approval. Myrna was no exception. These musicians were beyond awesome. And she *knew* them. This was all so un-fucking-believable. She cheered with the rest of their fans, hungry for more.

A spotlight lit the stage front and center, showing Sed standing on a platform at its front. "How are you tonight, Chicago?" he yelled and pointed his microphone at the audience.

The crowd roared. He put a hand to his ear and they screamed louder.

Sed spoke into the mic again. "We started working on our new album today. What do you think about that?"

More excited screams. Myrna's entire body grew hot. She'd had a little something to do with that. Not much, but she'd been there.

"Master Sinclair will be treating you to a new solo in a little while, but right now we're going to climb…the gates…of hell."

The crowd roared when Brian's intro to "Gates of Hell" poured from the speakers. The rest of the band joined him on the fifth measure. The crowd went insane. Electrified by the energy of ten thousand young adults, Myrna eagerly joined the insanity. Brian crossed the stage in her direction. She doubted he could see her standing in the dark on the floor beside the stage, but he looked right at her and winked. Myrna's breath caught. He headed across the stage in the other direction, still playing. Sed dropped his mic during the long musical outro and jumped into the crowd. Myrna's heart thudded with apprehension, hoping he wasn't hurt. Not a chance. The crowd tossed him back toward the stage until the security guards rescued him from their eager clutches and set him to his feet on the floor. The entire barrier fence buckled as the crowd surged forward in his wake. A roadie darted across the stage, picked up Sed's mic, and tossed it down to him. Brian, Trey, and Jace were having a guitar-playing orgy center stage.

Sed sang the rest of the song on the floor before the barrier fence. He allowed the crowd to touch his shoulder, arm, and free hand as he paced back and forth. When the song ended, he ran toward the side of the stage where Myrna was standing.

"Hey, Myrna," he said breathlessly as he passed her. "Are you enjoying the show?"

"Y-yeah," she sputtered stupidly.

"Sed!" Darlene screamed.

But he had already trotted up the steps and returned to the stage.

"This audience fucking rocks!" Sed yelled to the crowd. They responded with another roar of excitement. "What do you think, Master Sinclair?"

"I don't know, Sed. I can barely hear them." The sound of Brian's voice over the sound system made Myrna's knees wobbly. That same voice had brought her to screams only hours before, and now ten thousand people responded to him with deafening shouts of approval. Brian held up his guitar pick. "Who wants it?"

Arms extended over the barrier, straining for the proffered prize. He tossed the pick into the audience, causing a wave of bodies to sink in pursuit. He removed his guitar and a roadie dashed across the stage with a silver acoustic. Brian exchanged instruments, and the roadie returned to the side of the stage with the electric guitar. After Brian had settled the instrument in place, he plucked a new pick from the tape attached to his mic stand. He glanced at it, as if looking for flaws, and then moved toward Myrna. He didn't look at her this time. Instead, he sat on a platform, facing the audience at an angle. She'd have to settle for looking at his back and imagine the feel of his hair between her fingers.

"Should we slow this down a little?" Sed asked the crowd. The lights lowered except for a soft glow coming from behind the band. Brian sat on a platform on one end of the stage and Trey sat on the other end. They strummed the gentle chords of their most famous ballad on acoustic guitars.

"Let me see your mood lighting," Sed said.

Lighters flicked on. Cell phones flipped open. The sea of small lights shone brightly in the darkness of the crowd. The music of this song wasn't as loud as the previous, so Myrna could hear the crowd singing along with Sed. He had a satin-smooth voice when he wasn't screaming. She had forgotten how beautifully he sang. He sat on the front edge of the stage and gave every word a piece of his soul. Myrna could totally see Sed's allure, but Brian was the one she wanted.

After the first six songs, the rest of the band left the stage for a short break, leaving Brian by himself. He took the mic in the center of the stage. "Sed promised you a taste of my new solo. Don't laugh if I fuck it up. I wrote it today." He paused for effect and then started to play.

The notes of "Twinkle Twinkle Little Star," with Trey's signature shred, emitted from the amplified speakers. Brian hit the whammy bar on the last note. If anyone could make "Twinkle Twinkle Little Star" rock, it was Master Sinclair. "Awesome, huh?" He grinned. Myrna's heart melted. "I guess that's more Trey's speed."

The crowd cheered and laughed.

"If you wanna hear this thing for real, you're gonna have to yell louder than that."

The crowd yelled so loud that Myrna covered her ears with her hands. When they quieted, she pulled her hands away. She didn't want to miss a word of what Brian was saying.

"Myr, this is for you."

Darlene and Joyce shoved her excitedly but stopped as soon as Brian started his solo. The entire stadium fell silent, stunned by the skill and speed of his fingers. He executed the notes in perfect succession. When he reached the end, Trey appeared at his side.

"Was that fucking awesome or what?" Trey said into the microphone.

The crowd cheered.

"We've got a new riff, too. Brian's been consumed by his muse." Trey shoved him in the back, a huge grin on his face. Brian stumbled sideways and laughed. "What do you say, Chicago? Do you want to hear it?" Trey asked.

More cheering. The two guitarists segued into the riff they'd practiced in the dining room that morning. Myrna no longer felt like she was standing in a jam-packed stadium. Brian was making love to her and recording notes on her body with a pen. Onstage, Brian had his eyes closed while he played. He leaned heavily against Trey's back. Myrna felt a connection between herself and the man onstage. She wondered if he was thinking of her while he played for all these people.

Sed stepped back onto the stage. "Are these mother-fuckers talented or what?"

Eric drummed. Jace strummed. The crowd cheered.

"I guess I'll need to come up with some good lyrics now. I can't take the pressure!" He gripped both sides of his head in distress. Myrna chuckled.

Sinners moved into the next song. By the time the show ended, every person in the room was drenched in sweat. A fog of condensation hung over the crowd. When the band left the stage, they looked both pumped up and fatigued. Eric, the last to leave the stage and by far the sweatiest person in the room, tossed drumsticks into the crowd like one-way boomerangs.

The crowd chanted, "Sinners, Sinners, Sinners," for several minutes until the stadium lights came up. Myrna made a beeline to the backstage area. She spotted Brian going through the door behind the stage area that led to the dressing rooms. She flashed her backstage pass at a security guard and dashed after him.

"Brian."

He paused and turned in her direction. His smile, meant only for her, dazzled. She ran to him and wrapped him in an enthusiastic embrace. Her ears were numb from the loud music, but every other sense was height-ened. The scent of his sweat made her tremble.

"You are amazing," she sputtered.

He popped the earplugs out of his ears. "Don't get all fangirl on me now."

He wrapped an arm around her shoulders and walked her past the dressing room. As they passed, Myrna caught a glimpse of Sed, minus his shirt, surrounded by several girls.

"Where are we going?" Myrna asked.

"Trust me, you don't want to go anywhere near Sed for a while. He's in one of his moods. We're going to the bus. Is that okay?"

She nodded. If he asked her to walk on hot coals, she would have eagerly complied. And why was that? She didn't understand her own psychology at the moment.

He kissed her temple. "Did you like your solo?"

"How could I not? All I could think about was you making love to me when you wrote it."

He chuckled. "I was thinking the same thing."

"You were?"

"What else would I be thinking about?"

"Five thousand girls screaming your name?"

"There were five thousand dudes screaming my name, too. Not exactly a turn-on. Besides, I only care about one woman screaming my name."

Her heart warmed as he squeezed her closer. They exited the building to a crowd milling outside the tour buses. The fans cheered when they recognized Brian, but the security guards kept them at bay until he could get Myrna safely up the steps and on the tour bus.

"I need a shower," he said. "But I think I'll lie down for a bit first."

Her body thrummed, pumped full of adrenaline. She didn't know why he needed to lie down. Unless…

"Yeah, I think you should lie down. Can I join you?"

"What do you think?" He looked down at her. "I'm getting sweat all over your dry-clean-only suit."

"It's disposable as far as I'm concerned."

He grinned. "Seeing me onstage really worked you up, didn't it?"

"What do you think?"

She unfastened the buttons of her suit jacket and shrugged it off her shoulders. She tossed it on a random pile of jeans and black clothes before working on the small buttons of her silver satin blouse.

Brian took her hand. "Come on. No telling when a roadie or Eric will show up."

He led her to the back of the bus and through a door at the end of a narrow passage. They entered a small bedroom, its space dominated by a queen-sized bed.

"I'm not sure how clean the sheets are," he murmured, helping her with her buttons now. "We're slobs."

"Wonderful. All of you."

He paused, looking into her eyes in the dim interior of the room. The only light came from the streetlamps outside, filtering through the metal blinds. "Oh God, you aren't lusting after Sed now, are you?" he asked. "I lose more women that way. They see him onstage and—"

She covered his lips with her fingers. "I'm lusting after you, Master Sinclair."

"Don't call me that here," he said against her fingers.

"Brian." She replaced her fingers with her lips, kissing him hungrily.

Her shirt fluttered to the floor. His fingers moved to the fastening of her skirt. He unzipped it and it dropped to the floor around her feet. He glanced down her body with a sexy smile on his lips. "I'm glad you decided I was worthy to see what was under that suit. Very nice." Collapsing face down on the bed, he belly-crawled to the pillows and sighed in exhaustion. "I need a nap."

She climbed up on the bed with him and straddled his body. She tugged his shirt off and sat back on his thighs, massaging his shoulders and back.

Brian sighed contentedly. "Exactly what I need, Myr. Thank you."

She leaned forward to kiss the skin along his shoulders, her tongue darting out to collect the salt of his sweat.

"I can use some of that, too," he murmured drowsily.

"Do you want me to leave you alone? I can tell you're tired."

"No, I like your company. This is nice. I don't have the energy to devour you. You're probably disappointed in me."

"Never." She took his hand in hers and massaged the base of his fingers and his palm.

"Mmmmmm."

She lowered her head to kiss his fingers. "These are magical."

"We both know there's only one magical body part in this bed. I think the fans liked your solo, Myr."

"Your solo."

"That's all you, baby. I just play it."

She smiled. She knew she didn't deserve any credit. "You're sweet."

"Shhhh. Don't tell anyone…"

He slept. So much for an hour of amazing sex before they had to go their separate ways. Myrna stretched out beside him, her hand tracing lazy paths up and down his back. Was she really here? This had undoubtedly been the most amazing day of her life. And even if she never saw this remarkable man again, she'd never forget him.

A short time later, there was a commotion outside the bus. Loud chattering and laughter moved closer — a mix of masculine and feminine voices.

Myrna climbed from the bed, separated the metal blinds with her fingers, and looked through the small window facing the stadium. The rest of the band had emerged from the building. They moved toward the periphery of the blocked-off lane and mingled with their excited fans. Separated from the crowd by the metal barrier, band members passed out hugs and autographs and posed for photographs with enthusiastic admirers.

Myrna glanced over her shoulder at Brian, lost in dreamland. She wondered if he always kept to himself or if he indulged the fans on occasion. She returned her attention to outside. Sed lifted a scantily clad young woman over the barrier and added her to his entourage of females. When his attention turned to signing an autograph, the girl did a happy dance behind him and then pulled her skirt down to cover the tops of her thighs.

Myrna wondered about the girl. Myrna doubted she knew Sed. Doubted Sed knew her. Would she sleep with him without hesitation? Myrna was pretty sure the answer to that question was yes, but did the young woman hop into bed with any guy, or was it Sed's fame that seduced her? Myrna had to ask herself the same question. Why was she so willing to sleep with Brian? Typically, she felt the need to get to know a man personally before she got to know him physically. And honestly, she hadn't known many men well enough to sleep with them. So why did she act differently with Brian?

Brian sighed in his sleep, his hand stretching across the bed to the location she'd been when he'd drifted off. He took a deep, startled breath as he regained consciousness and lifted his head. When he saw her standing near the window, he smiled and dropped his head back to the bed, stretching his arms above his head, then out to the sides.

"That was a quick nap," Myrna said.

"I was dreaming about you."

"Was it a good dream?" She stepped away from the window and sat on the edge of the bed next to him.

"Not really. I was chasing you and you wouldn't stop running from me."

"I'm not running now."

His hand moved to squeeze her thigh. "I guess you're not."

She wiped at a black smudge under his eye. "Your eyeliner is running, however."

"I fell asleep on my face again."

There was a sharp knock on the door. Brian groaned. He climbed from the bed and opened the door. "Yeah?"

One of the roadies said, "We're heading out in an hour."

"All right. Thanks for the heads-up." He closed the door and turned to look at Myrna. "An hour."

"I've got to go anyway." Why did she suddenly feel so lonely? "I have to drive back to Kansas City, and I need to get a head start tonight so I can make it home tomorrow."

He glanced at the ceiling, his expression thoughtful. "How far is it from Des Moines to Kansas City?"

"Des Moines? We're in Chicago, sweetie." She smiled. "Have you lost track of where you are?"

"No, tonight we're driving to Des Moines for tomorrow's show. Maybe you'd like to stay the night with me on the bus and leave from Des Moines in the morning."

Her heart thudded with excitement. In three short hours, she could drive from Des Moines to Kansas City. When she realized it wasn't actually feasible, her heart sank. "I can't. I need my car."

"One of the roadies can follow the buses with your car. They're used to driving all night."

"I suppose that would work." She smiled, her loneliness evaporating instantly. "I'd very much like to stay the night with you, Brian."

He moved toward her, where she sat on the edge of the bed, and eased her to her feet. He drew her body against his and kissed her deeply. She shuddered, still excited by his stage performance.

There was another knock at the door. Brian stiffened and broke the contact between his lips and Myrna's.

"Sheezus," Brian muttered under his breath. "What?" he yelled at the door.

The door opened and Sed ducked his head in. "You busy?"

"I was about to get that way."

"I think you've hogged the bedroom for long enough."

"The other bus—"

"Trey's occupied over there. Besides, you promised."

"Yeah, I know." He looked down at Myrna. "Let's go get your car."

She nodded, positioning her partially naked body behind Brian so that he blocked her from Sed's view. "Just let me get dressed."

"Two minutes." Brian held up two fingers in Sed's direction.

Sed closed the door. Brian pecked her on the cheek and retrieved her blouse from the floor.

"Sorry about that," he said. "I promised him he could have the bedroom tonight. Of course, that was before I knew you'd be staying. Ah...shit."

"It's okay. We can just hang out. I'm fine with that."

He smiled broadly. "Really? That sounds nice, actually."

She slid into her blouse and skirt, buttoning and tucking as fast as she could. Brian pulled his T-shirt over his head. He reached for her hand and led her to the door. Exiting the room, they continued down the narrow hall, flanked on either side by bunks concealed behind curtains, and into the main room. Myrna counted eight people. Sed, three girls, Eric, and a few roadies.

"All yours, Sed," Brian said.

Sed picked up the nearest girl, tossed her over his shoulder, and headed down the hall toward the bedroom. The attractive young woman squealed in delight as he burst through the door and tossed her on the bed. The other two girls and Eric followed in their wake, excitement emanating from their bodies.

Myrna must have looked as stunned as she felt. Brian laughed at her expression.

"He's always like that," Brian said. "I'm surprised

he didn't just burst in on us earlier. It's not like Sed to knock."

"Sed's reputation precedes him for a reason," one of the roadies said. He could have passed as a member of the band himself. Tattooed. Dark hair. Sunglasses at night. Chains, piercings, and muscular.

"Who's driving tonight, Travis?" Brian asked.

"I've got the truck. Matt the other bus. I think Dave's driving this one." He nodded at the normal-looking blond guy to his left. Dave gave a curt nod.

Brian turned toward a third roadie, who was without a driving assignment. "Jake, would you do me a favor?"

"Anything," he said without batting an eyelash.

"Myrna needs someone to drive her car to Des Moines."

Jake smiled slyly. "I see. Sure, no problem." Tall and slim, sporting a short Mohawk hairstyle, he looked down at Myrna. "Where's your car?"

"It's out in the parking lot. I'll go get it," she said. "Should I just park it outside the bus and give you the keys?"

"That would be perfect. It isn't some lame minivan, is it?"

"Erm… '57 Ford Thunderbird convertible. I just had her restored to mint. You'll be gentle, won't you? I'm sort of protective of her."

"Sweet," Dave said. "I'll trade you, Jake. You can drive the bus. I'll take the Thunderbird!"

"Hell no," Jake said. "Brian asked me."

"I must warn you that it's pink," Myrna interrupted.

"Pink? Aw, how could you do that to a classic car?" Jake said, running a hand over his forehead and Mohawk.

She laughed. "I *am* a girl, you know."

"I'm pretty sure everyone here recognizes that," Brian said into her ear. Her entire body throbbed in response to his low voice.

"I've got no problem with pink," Dave said, his blue eyes wide with eagerness. Dave looked like a clean-cut kid. Myrna wondered how long he'd been working with the band. Jake, on the other hand, looked wild. Based on looks alone, Myrna would prefer Dave drove her car, but she knew that wasn't fair. The roadies all worked hard, and the band trusted them with expensive equipment and their lives. "Trade me, Jake. Come on, dude. You like to drive the bus and you know I hate it."

"You two fight this out," Brian said. "We need to go get the car before it's time to leave. Is the truck loaded?"

"I suppose we should get to work," Dave said.

"Whoever gets their equipment loaded first gets to drive the T-bird," Jake said. He pushed open the bus door and headed down the stairs.

"Hey, that's no fair," Dave called after him. "I'm in charge of the drums! There are, like, a million of them!"

Jake's voice grew more distant as he walked away from the bus, calling over his shoulder, "Yeah, but I've got amps in addition to Trey's guitars. Quit complaining."

"Let's go," Brian said.

"Wait," she said. "I need my suit jacket. My keys are in it."

He waited for her to put on her jacket, then took her hand in his and helped her climb down the steep steps to the pavement.

The crowd outside the barriers was thinner than earlier, but when Brian stepped off the bus, they emitted a loud cheer.

"Shit," Brian said. "Um… Hold on a minute, okay?"

He kissed her on the temple. Several camera flashes went off. She wished people would stop snapping pictures of her with Sinners' band members without her consent.

Brian headed for the crowd, starting at one end of the barrier fence and working his way down. He signed autographs, shook hands, offered the occasional hug, allowed his picture to be taken dozens of times, and put up with a heck of a lot of groping from female fans. Myrna waited patiently, trying to curtail her jealousy. She knew this was important. His fans made his entire career possible. Still, she didn't like all the touchy-feely young women rubbing up against him while he was distracted with signing an autograph or answering a question.

After about fifteen minutes, he offered a salute to the crowd and returned to Myrna's side.

"I'll have to go around the front of the bus and then sneak along the back side. Otherwise, they'll see me again and we'll never catch a break. You go between the buses and meet me on the other side. Pretend like we're saying good-bye now."

"Okay."

He hugged her with the same kind detachment he hugged enthusiastic fans, and waved at her slightly before turning in the opposite direction. She walked along the side of the bus facing the venue, watching the roadies pushing equipment out a door toward the large moving van parked next to the second tour bus. She glanced over her shoulder and then slipped between the two buses. Shouts of passion and pleasure came from the bedroom at the back of the bus as she walked behind it. She paused, glancing up at the window above her.

Sed must be really working one of those girls over. She screamed Sed's name at the top of her lungs. Myrna flushed, wondering how much of her earlier vocalizations had been overheard.

A hard body pressed her against the back of the bus. A hand groped her breast in the darkness. Her heart hammered in her chest. She struggled against the man, trying to twist away.

Jeremy. Oh God, he's found me. How?

The man grabbed her wrist before she could connect a blow, and slammed the back of her hand against the bus next to her head. She opened her mouth to scream but found a tongue shoved in her mouth. She knew this taste. Brian?

He'd scared her. Really scared her.

She shoved him away.

"What are you doing?" she said. "I thought I was being attacked."

"You are," he growled and crushed her body between his and the back of the bus.

When he tried to kiss her, she punched him in the stomach. "Stop it."

"Ow. No one can see us." Shadows completely obscured them.

He held her up against the bus with his body and released her wrist so he could push her skirt up around her waist. Though she knew he wouldn't hurt her, her heart drummed faster and harder in her chest. She hit him as hard as she could in the arm. He paused. She couldn't see his expression in the darkness, so didn't know if he was getting the message.

"Do you really want me to stop, Myrna? I thought we

could get in a quickie back here, since Sed has seized the bedroom."

"Don't sneak up on me like that. You scared the hell out of me."

He pressed his fingertips to the center of her chest. "Your heart is really pounding, sweetheart. You knew it was me, didn't you?"

"No," she whispered. "I thought… I thought he…" She fought tears, feeling stupid. "It doesn't matter what I thought. Just don't ever do it again."

He hugged her gently. "I'm really sorry, Myr. Forgive me?"

How could she stay mad at him? She knew she'd overreacted. Jeremy was out of her life for good. Sure, he was out of prison now, but he didn't know where she was. Hell, he didn't even know her name anymore. And this…this was Brian, not Jeremy. She liked Brian. Perhaps a bit too much, considering their short acquaintance.

Once she tackled her fear, she sought Brian's mouth in the darkness and kissed him gently, a soft smile on her lips. "You're wasting time. The buses will be leaving soon."

"You're game for this?" he asked incredulously.

"You promise not to sneak up on me, again, right?"

"Yeah, I promise." He drew her closer and whispered in her ear, "Take your panties off."

Her hand moved to his crotch to find his cock hard as granite. He drew a pained breath through his teeth. She pushed her panties down her thighs and allowed them to fall to her ankles. She stepped out of them with one foot. Cold air bathed the hot flesh between her thighs as Brian forced his knee between her legs to part them.

"That's good," he murmured. "Don't move now. I've got to warn you, I never last long after a show." He pinned her against the bus with his body.

She heard his pants unzip. He leaned his hips away from hers as he applied a condom. His hard cock brushed against the inside of her thigh as he relaxed against her, sighing in anticipation. He grabbed her thigh in his hand and lifted her leg to his hip. As he filled her body with his, he gasped brokenly as if he were already near orgasm.

Her head fell back in ecstasy. "That feels so good, Brian."

"Yeah," he said, resting his head against the side of her face. "Uh, God." He thrust into her gently, rotating his hips to intensify their pleasure. "Feels fantastic."

Several people walked past the side of the bus, talking amongst themselves about packing the truck. Roadies, she assumed. They kept right on walking though, and Brian didn't even pause in his slow, easy thrusts. She sought his mouth with hers, kissing him deeply. His strokes increased in tempo. He groaned into her mouth. She answered him with a moan. His thrusts grew faster now. He'd completely lost control. She grabbed his hair, fingers digging into his scalp as her excitement began to build. He tore his mouth away from hers.

"Are you close?" he asked. "God, please tell me you're close."

"You're done?" She couldn't believe it. He typically lasted, like, forever.

"Mmmm," he murmured. "Almost. Yeah, yeah. I

can't hold it." His hands tugged at her suit jacket desperately. "Ah, God." He thrust into her harder. Harder. Harder and he shuddered against her with a hoarse cry. His hands moved to splay against the back of the bus on either side of her head, as his body trembled with satisfaction. He went limp, crushing her into hard steel.

"Sorry, baby. I didn't mean to come that fast," he whispered.

"It's okay. You did warn me."

"That's not a good excuse."

Sliding out of her body, he dropped to his knees, looping her leg over his shoulder. He probed between her legs until he found what he sought in the darkness. He sucked her clit into his mouth, and she shuddered. Two fingers slid inside her, curling forward to stimulate her in that perfect spot he'd discovered that morning. His fingers plunged deep and slowly withdrew before plunging deep again. She burrowed her fingers into his hair and leaned heavily against the back of the tour bus, mewing in pleasure with each stroke of his fingers, each flick of his tongue.

A bright light hit Myrna in the face. She squinted, blinded by the beam of a flashlight. She lifted her arm to shield her eyes.

"Whoops, sorry," a masculine voice said. The light switched off.

Myrna's body tensed. She lost concentration and her excitement waned. Brian didn't let off her though. He started to build her up again with his mouth and fingers. Before long, she forgot where she was.

From inside the bus came Sed's animal-like groans and the answering cries of three girls. Three? How could one guy do three girls? Maybe Eric was participating now. Their excitement lent to her own, and soon her body shuddered with release. She cried out as pleasure rippled through her body. Her legs went limp. Brian caught her with his free arm as she slid down the back of the bus. As her shudders subsided, he removed his fingers from her body, cradled her in his arms, and kissed her tenderly.

"We've got to stop getting so carried away," she murmured.

He chuckled. "Where's the fun in that?"

She snuggled up against him. "They're going to leave for Des Moines without us."

"They'll wait. Sed hasn't even kicked those girls out of his bed yet." That was obvious. The girls continued to scream Sed's name as if involved in some World's Loudest Vocalizer contest. She could hear Sed swearing loudly, and the bus rocked slightly with each curse he shouted.

Myrna frowned, remembering a light shining in her face moments ago. "Someone saw us."

"One of the roadies, I think. They're used to seeing things like that, sweetheart. Don't worry. No one will say anything."

She pouted. "They've seen you eating out a woman pinned to the back of the bus?"

"Yeah."

"What do you mean, yeah?" Why was she jealous? He probably did this sort of thing all the time. New experiences for her, but same shit different day for him.

He laughed. "Yeah, just now."

She slapped his chest halfheartedly. He always made her feel better about herself. Made her feel special, even though she knew she wasn't. Not really. "Let's go get my car now."

He helped her to her feet. She located her panties around one ankle and put them on before rearranging her clothes. Her legs were still trembling. Wow! This guy. This guy was so good for her, and oh, so very bad.

Brian rearranged his clothes as well, tossing his expended condom on the ground, and then took her hand in his. "Lead the way, pretty lady."

"You're not afraid some rabid fan will pick that up and try to impregnate herself with it?" Myrna asked, nodding toward his litter.

"Myrna, that's disgusting."

"And tossing it on the ground isn't?"

"Nope."

"Pick it up."

He sighed loudly. "Fine." He retrieved the condom and held it out to her. "Here, put it in your pocket."

"Ewww. No."

"You'll put it in your body, but not your pocket?"

"That's different."

"If you say so."

She fished her keys out of her jacket. "Just throw it away."

They walked behind the second bus and into the mostly empty parking lot, complete with a handy garbage can for easy disposal. It was dark enough that no one recognized Brian as they headed for the distinctive pink car in the distance.

"What a beautiful car," Brian said, peering into the driver's side window. "Can I drive it?"

She hesitated. She really was overprotective of this

car. The thought of a roadie driving it over three hundred miles made her quite nervous. Spending extra time with Brian was a powerful motivator though. She handed him the keys.

He unlocked the door and opened it. "Wow," he whispered. "It *has* been fully restored. Get in."

She moved around him and entered on the driver's side before sliding over the white leather bench seat to the passenger side. He climbed in, closed the door and started the engine. It roared to life with a low-pitched purr. He revved the engine. "She has some kick."

"You bet your sweet ass she does," Myrna said.

"V-8 engine?"

"Yeah. A 312 with dual Holley carburetors."

"Fuckin' sweet." Brian put the car in gear and peeled out of the parking space. He cranked the wheel to one side and drifted sideways before settling into a straight path toward the buses. He decided to drive around the parking lot several times. Myrna cringed every time the tires barked, but Brian was enjoying himself so much, she couldn't dampen his spirits.

Myrna caught sight of Jake, the roadie with the blond Mohawk, waving at them wildly. "I think they're ready to leave."

"Yeah, I suppose." Brian drove up behind the bus and stopped abruptly. "That was fun."

He drew her across the bench seat and kissed her. "Let's go to bed."

"Again?"

"I could use some sleep."

"Oh, we're going to sleep." She smiled, ducking her head.

"For a few minutes, at least. You've worn me out today, woman. And I'm not used to getting up early. It's usually party all night, sleep all day around here."

The car door opened. "Ha," said Jake. He tipped his head into the car. "I get to drive the Thunderbird."

"Not if you drive like Brian, you don't," Myrna said.

"I'll be sweet to her."

Brian climbed out of the car. "I'm not a bad driver. You can't put a big engine in a little car and expect me not to see what she's capable of."

Brian helped Myrna out of the car.

"Sweet!" Jake said. He climbed into the driver's seat. "See you in Des Moines." The door slammed. The tires squealed as the car shot backward.

"Great!" Myrna said. "A maniac is driving my car."

"He won't hurt it. If he does, I'll buy you a brand-new Porsche."

"I don't want a Porsche. I love that car! It belonged to my grandparents."

"It will be fine. I promise."

She watched the round taillights of the Thunderbird brighten at a stop sign. The tires squealed again as the car shot forward. It fishtailed before gripping the road and speeding into the night.

She stomped her foot in frustration. She grabbed the front of Brian's T-shirt and pulled him toward the bus. "Let's get moving. The faster we get to Des Moines, the faster I can kick that guy's ass."

"Ooooo. Can I watch?"

"Oh yes. You can definitely watch. You are going to hold him down for me."

Myrna started up the bus stairs, but a body hurled

from the bus's interior halted her progress. She caught the young woman and if Brian hadn't steadied her, she'd have toppled to the asphalt.

"What part of 'get the *fuck* out of here' don't you understand?" Sed bellowed at the young woman from the top of the stairs.

Myrna recognized the girl as the one Sed had lifted over the barrier about an hour before.

"Sed," the young woman sobbed, clutching her hands together in front of her chest. "Please let me stay with you. Please!"

"I'm finished with you. Get lost."

Sed, looking highly annoyed, turned and moved farther into the bus. The young woman started up the steps, but Brian grabbed her arm. Enraged, she yanked on her arm and slapped at Brian's chest repeatedly. Her eyes widened when she recognized who she was beating the hell out of.

"Oh God, I'm sorry, M-Master Sinclair." She covered her mouth with a trembling hand. Tears poured from her eyes. "Talk to him for me. Please! T-tell him I love him." Mascara ran down her face in black-tinged rivulets. "Tell him I'll kill myself if he doesn't love me back."

Brian took her shoulders in his hands and shook her slightly. "Hey. Hey. What's your name, sweetie?"

She looked up at Brian, and Myrna was struck by how vulnerable she appeared. She couldn't have been much over twenty.

"My name?"

"Yeah."

"K-K-K-Karen." She threw herself against Brian, clinging to him desperately.

He spread his arms wide and gave Myrna an "I'm not touching her" look over Karen's shoulder.

Brian spoke in a soothing tone to the girl. "Karen, you have to understand something about Sed. He's not looking for a relationship with anyone. He just wants to get laid. You know? There's nothing wrong with you. You're a beautiful girl. He wouldn't have picked you if you weren't."

Myrna smiled. So sweet of him to try to console her.

"I just thought…" She took a deep, gasping breath. "I thought…" She rubbed her face against his shoulder, smearing tears and makeup over his shirt.

"What did you think?" He patted her shoulder lamely.

"I thought if I showed him how much I loved him, that he'd…" Her voice lowered to a whisper. "…love me back."

Brian pulled her away and looked into her watery eyes. Myrna had never seen him look so serious. "Sed can't love anyone, Karen. Not since Jessica."

Jessica?

Karen's eyes narrowed. "I'd kill that bitch if I could."

"Not if I got to her first," Brian murmured. He gave Karen a gentle hug and released her. "Now, walk away with your head high, sweetheart. You survived sex with Sedric Lionheart. I'd wager you even enjoyed it."

The girl grinned and kissed Brian on the cheek. "Thank you for making me feel better, Master Sinclair." She glanced at Myrna as she passed but quickly averted her gaze.

Myrna would love to talk to her to learn more about her psychology. Did she really think she was in love with Sed? The *real* Sed? Or the rock star version who paraded up onstage? And who was the real Sed? Myrna honestly couldn't say she'd met him.

Brian ran up the stairs of the bus. There was a loud crack, followed by a thud. Myrna dashed after him. She paused in the stairwell, eyes wide. Sed lay sprawled across the bus's floor with Brian standing over him, his fist balled. Sed rolled over to lean on his elbow and wiped at the blood at the corner of his mouth with his thumb.

"Can you be any more of an ass?" Brian yelled. "I'm so fucking sick of being your damage control."

"Why do you care so much about my whores, Brian?"

They're just like you, darling, Jeremy's voice intruded. Myrna's eyes widened.

"Because they're not whores," Brian said. "Whores don't cry when you tell them to get out of your bed."

"They sure do act like whores."

Sed climbed to his feet. He grabbed Brian by the back of the head, and Myrna winced, thinking her lover was about to get pounded. Brian was much smaller than Sed, who was several inches over six feet and could no doubt bench-press twice his own weight. Sed didn't hit Brian though. He kissed him on the side of the head.

Sed's gaze was on Myrna when he said, "I don't think you realize how lucky you are, my friend."

He turned, shuffled down the hallway, and closed himself in the empty bedroom.

Eric leaned out of one of the curtained bunks along the side of the cabin. "You shouldn't have hit him, Brian. You know why he's like that."

"Yeah, I know." Brian slid into a leather-upholstered booth surrounding the dining table and rubbed his face with both hands.

"Who's Jessica?" Myrna asked.

Brian glanced up at her. "The woman who ripped Sed's heart out and fed it to sharks."

Myrna lowered her eyes. She could identify. Her heart had been fed to sharks long ago, and she'd never retrieve it.

Chapter 9

MYRNA ROLLED OVER IN THE NARROW BUNK AND snuggled up against Brian's warm body. He sighed in his sleep, his arm tightening around her before relaxing again.

The bus hummed loudly as it climbed a hill, temporarily drowning out Trey's soft snores coming from the bunk beneath them. They hadn't reached Des Moines, so what had awoken her?

She opened her eyes to darkness. The bed was comfortable enough, but was twin sized, so there wasn't much room to move. Fine with her. It gave her a good excuse to press up against the wonderful man beside her. She burrowed her nose in his neck and inhaled deeply.

From the nearby dining area, a can clinked against the table. So that's what had pulled her from sleep. Who'd be awake at this hour? She crawled over Brian's body and peeked through the curtain. Sed sat at the dining table with his back to her. He took a sip of his beer while he gazed down at something in the palm of his hand. She wondered if he'd mind some company. He seemed lonely.

Myrna climbed from the bunk, tugging Brian's T-shirt down over her panties. Her luggage was still in her car, so she hadn't had anything to wear to bed, and Brian hadn't wanted her to sleep nude this close to the guys.

When her feet hit the floor, Sed turned his head to look at her. He smiled slightly and slid whatever was in his hand into his pocket. She stood next to the bench across the table from him and waited for him to acknowledge her.

"I couldn't sleep," he said.

"Can I join you?"

"Yeah, of course. Do you want a beer?"

She shook her head. "I don't drink. My ex-husband was an alcoholic and I can't stomach the taste of it." *Or the smell*.

Sed pushed three empty beer cans aside. "I…didn't realize you'd been married before."

She shrugged. "It was a long time ago." She brushed her hair behind her ears and changed the subject. "I think Brian's really sorry he hit you."

"Yeah, I know. But I deserved it. Sinclair doesn't clobber someone unless he deserves it. Brian's a good guy. Not like the rest of us."

"I think you're all good guys."

He grinned at her, his blue eyes sparkling in the low-luminosity cabin lamps. "Even Eric?"

She chuckled. "Yeah, even Eric."

"You're right. They are good guys. I'm the asshole of the bunch."

She reached across the table and took his hand. "That's not true, Sed. I know something's bothering you. You can talk to me, you know."

Sed lowered his gaze. "You shouldn't touch me, Myrna. Brian wouldn't take it well."

She wanted to ask him something that she'd wondered since meeting them two nights before. "The last girl who dumped him. The one he got drunk over. Did you…?" She tilted her head to one side in question.

"Yeah, I banged her. And his previous girlfriend, too. I told you I was an asshole. He should hit me more often."

Myrna squeezed his hand. "I won't let you bang me. Okay?"

He glanced up at her and smiled. "You sure?"

Her heart thudded. She blew a breath through her lips. The man was mesmeric. Enigmatic. Virile. She'd never met anyone like him before. "Yeah, I'm sure."

"You had to think about it though." He chuckled. "Women are all alike. Whores."

She stiffened, even though she knew he was just trying to get a rise out of her. That word bothered her. It had been flung at her too many times in her past. "Yeah, we're all wh-whores. Especially around the rock stars we admire. Why do you think that is?"

"Huh?"

"Why do you think women are so promiscuous when they're near you? Or Brian? Or Trey? Any of you?"

"Hell if I know."

"Yeah, me neither. It would be fascinating to study it though." Maybe she could get a research grant funded on the topic. Were groupies always loose, or did their behavior change when around the band? She knew Sinners' fame affected her. The excitement of screwing a man whom thousands of women lusted after. A strange psychology. Not that she had time to research something fun like groupie promiscuity. Her current project wasn't going well at all. She had to concentrate all her efforts on keeping her grant funding or she might as well kiss her academic career good-bye.

Sed squeezed her hand, drawing Myrna's thoughts from her worries. Funny how none of the things that usually weighed her down had even crossed her mind since she'd met Brian.

"I don't really think you're a whore, Myrna," he said. "I don't even want to bang you."

She chuckled. "Wow, that hurt."

"You misunderstand. I respect you. You're the type of woman who I could…who maybe I could…" He shook his head.

"Tell me about Jessica."

His eyes narrowed dangerously. "Don't even say her name."

Bodies shifted in the bunks.

"Weren't you just staring at her picture?" She was guessing. Turned out she was right.

He took a deep breath and bit his lip. After a moment, he said, "I should have burned it with the others. I just can't let her go. Not entirely. It's like the pain keeps her close to me somehow."

She squeezed his hand. "That's pretty twisted, Sed."

He pulled his hand out of hers and rubbed it over his buzzed black hair. "Yeah, I know." He slid out of the booth. "I'm going to bed. I think I can sleep now."

She was sorry she'd chased him off with her prying. "Good night, Sed."

"Good night, Professor."

Myrna left the table and used the tiny bathroom before climbing back into bed with Brian.

"Did you have a nice talk with Sed?" he asked.

"Oh, you're awake?"

"Did you have a nice talk with Sed?"

"Yeah. He's feeling pretty low."

Brian sighed. "I shouldn't have hit him. I know why he is the way he is. That's why I can't hate him no matter how much heartache he causes. I know he's hurting ten times more than those he hurts."

She cupped his face between her hands, wishing she could see his expression in the darkness. "You're wonderful. Do you know that?"

He kissed her gently. "I'm horny again. I do know that."

"I'll never walk properly again." She laughed.

"I figure if you can't walk, you can't leave my bed." He kissed her jaw. The side of her neck. "Not ever."

The sun rose entirely too early. He'd touched her, kissed her, stroked and suckled her skin, tasted her lips, embraced her, for hours, and he'd yet to take possession of her body. At least not in the way she wanted him to. He did possess her though, in a way she'd never meant to happen.

Chapter 10

MYRNA STOOD NEXT TO HER STILL-IN-ONE-PIECE car, which had reached Des Moines a full hour before the buses. Brian stood before her, plucking absently at a button on her blouse. She stared over his shoulder, finding it difficult to look at him. Every time she did, her heart constricted with anguish.

She hated good-byes. Especially permanent ones.

She slid a hand into her suit pocket and fingered her business card in indecision. She knew continuing this was a mistake. It would just lead to heartache for both of them. They'd both suffered enough in the past, she decided. She pulled her empty hand from her pocket. No strings. For the best.

They started to speak at the same time. "I—"

"We—"

They laughed. Their eyes met. Brian drew her into his arms and kissed her deeply, his embrace tight. Her throat was also tight. *Don't cry, Myrna. Wait until…*

She pulled away. "I had a great time with you." She hoped she sounded impersonal, not emotional.

"This doesn't have to be the end."

She ducked her head and swallowed her tears. "Yeah. It does."

"Myrna…"

She kissed his cheek and turned to open the car door. Locked. She struggled with the handle for a moment before realizing the keys were in her hand. Brian stepped closer and took her shoulders in his hands.

"Myrna…"

She unlocked the door with trembling fingers. *Don't cry. Don't cry.*

She got the door open, but Brian didn't step away. He hugged her from behind, his arms circling her waist, his chin resting on her shoulder. "Stay," he whispered. "Please."

"I can't."

"Then tell me when I can see you again."

She shook her head vigorously. "Good-bye, Brian."

She pulled away from him and climbed into the car. Its familiarity comforted her. She closed the door and started the engine, forcing herself not to look up at him outside her window. She drove off, making sure her face was out of sight before she let the tears fall in hot trails down her face. From her rearview mirror, she glimpsed Brian, hands crammed into the front pockets of his jeans as he stared down at his feet. He took a deep breath, glanced up at her retreating car, and then returned to the tour bus alone.

Chapter 11

TREY POUNDED BRIAN ON THE BACK. "YOU FUCKING loser, get off the bus. You aren't doing anyone any good sitting here drinking by yourself again."

Brian tossed back the rest of his beer. "Shut up."

"You know what you need? You need to get laid."

Trey was probably right. It had been two weeks since his weekend of bliss. It was time to forget about the amazing sex professor and move on.

"Yeah," Brian said. "I guess so."

"Sed's getting a circle suck together. Maybe you should join us."

Brian rolled his eyes at Trey. "Is that why you came over here?"

"Well, you always beat him. And he bet Eric that if he didn't win, he'd give up sex for a month."

Brian laughed. Sed didn't even bother denying his sex addiction. A month? The man would spontaneously combust. "Yeah, I'd like to see that."

"We'd all like to see that. He figured since you weren't participating, he'd win for sure."

"I'm in." Brian climbed to his feet, staggering slightly.

Trey wrapped Brian's arm around his shoulders to help him walk. "You've got to quit drinking so much."

"I know." But it dulled the pain so nicely.

His alcohol-induced buzz had started to dissipate by the time they entered the other bus.

"Brian's in," Trey announced.

Eric leapt from his chair and hugged both guitarists. "Yes!" He glanced over his shoulder at their vocalist. "You're going down, Sed."

"I thought we were going down," one of six women murmured, looking confused.

"No one invited Brian," Sed protested.

A bombshell blonde in red lipstick shot her hand into the air. "I call Master Sinclair."

"Are you chicken, Sed?" Brian asked. "Afraid you'll lose?"

Sed grabbed the nearest girl and urged her to her knees in front of his chair. She reached for his belt buckle. "I'm ready. Are you?"

Brian sat in the captain's chair next to Sed. The eager blonde knelt before him. She reached for his fly, but he caught her hand.

"Who else is in?" Brian asked.

Eric, Trey, and Jace sat next to each other on the leather sofa across from the two captain's chairs. Two girls got in a scuffle over the privilege to suck off Trey. He put his hand on top of the winner's head and gave the loser his sucker. She went to sulk in the corner, licking her consolation prize.

"I'll fuck you later, babe. Okay?" Trey called to her.

Beaming, she nodded.

"The first girl to make her guy come gets a backstage pass," Sed said. "And the last guy to spend his load gets bragging rights."

"And you can't have sex for a month," Eric reminded him.

"That's only if I lose."

Zippers released, hard cocks revealed, flavored condoms rolled in place.

The blonde kneeling before Brian pulled her hand free of his and opened his pants. She soon discovered that he wasn't hard at all. His bandmates were waiting for him so they could get started. Just the idea of a suck circle usually had him busting the zipper out of his pants, but the thought of this blonde chick with her candy-red lips around his dick held no appeal. Maybe a different girl? He glanced around the interior of the bus, but none of the congregated women was Myrna. His heart constricted.

"I guess I'm too drunk," he said. He zipped his pants and shoved the stunned blonde out of his way before leaving the bus.

"Brian?" Trey called after him.

"Brian's out," Sed said as Brian stepped off the bottom step. "Start."

Brian walked between the buses and leaned against the back bumper. He didn't know how long he stood there just breathing. Ten minutes, maybe. He knew the guys would rib him for not being able to get it up, but that wasn't what was really bothering him. That woman. Myrna. He couldn't get her out of his head.

Trey wandered out of the bus a few minutes later. He walked past where Brian was standing, turned around and came to lean against the bus bumper beside him.

"I guess you lost," Brian said.

"I don't even try to win. The real prize is having a girl working her damnedest to make you come. Who am I to deny her a backstage pass?"

Brian grinned. "My poor girl didn't even get the chance to try."

"You've got to call her," Trey said.

"Huh?"

Trey punched him in the arm. "Myrna, you retard. Call her."

"I don't have her number. Besides, she doesn't want to see me." He ducked his head to stare at his boots.

"I don't believe that for a second," Trey said. "And you could get her number if you really wanted to."

He laughed. "I don't even know her last name."

"Where is she from?"

"Kansas City," he said automatically, but Trey already knew that. Brian couldn't stop talking about her, so Trey knew more about Myrna than he could possibly want to know.

"And she's a professor, so she has to work at a college around there."

"So?"

"And there are only so many human sexuality professors at those colleges. Maybe one or two at each, right?"

He shrugged. "I guess."

"Myrna isn't a very common name. And even if every human sexuality professor in the Kansas City area were named Myrna, you could still call them all until you found her."

"She'll be majorly pissed if I call her," Brian said, though hope fluttered through his aching heart.

"So what? If she tells you off, then maybe you'll get her out of your system, and if she doesn't, then we'll get to see you happy again. Shit, the whole band is suffering

because of this funk you're in. We need you, you know.
You're our glue."

Brian sighed loudly. "All right, I get it. I'll try to
find her."

Trey rubbed his hand vigorously over Brian's hair
until Brian leaned away, his scalp tingling.

"No need. I already have." Trey handed Brian a piece
of paper with a phone number scrawled on it. Lefties
and their scarcely legible handwriting. "Here's her work
number. Her home phone is apparently unlisted."

"How'd you get this?"

"Internet. Her last name is Evans, by the way. Her
picture was in the faculty directory."

Picture? He'd have to check it out later. See if she
was as beautiful as he remembered. "When did you
do this?"

"About a week ago."

Brian scowled. "And you waited until now?"

"I thought maybe you'd get over her."

Brian stared down at the slip of paper. "Now I just
have to get up the nerve to have my heart shredded again."

"Don't take too long," Trey said. "I mean seriously.
I've never seen you like this. Not for this long."

"Myrna's different."

Trey snorted and laughed as if they were back in the
fifth grade. "You've got it bad, Sinclair."

Chapter 12

Myrna answered her office phone on its second ring. "Doctor Myrna Evans, psychology department."

"Myrna. Ah. It's really you."

All the blood drained from her face. "Brian?"

"It's so good to hear your voice."

"How did you find me?"

"Trey looked you up on the Internet by checking the faculty lists of the universities around Kansas City. You aren't hard to find." He fell silent for a moment. "Are you mad that I called?"

She couldn't lie and pretend she was anything but delighted to hear from him. She was disturbed that she was so easy to find. She wasn't hiding from Brian, but there was another man she didn't want to find her. Ever.

"No," she said. "I'm not mad."

"Will you meet me somewhere?"

"What? Now? Are you in Kansas City?"

He chuckled. Her breath caught and her nipples tightened. How could the simple sound of his laugh turn her on?

"No, I'm in Oregon for the entire weekend. More tour dates. I'll send you a plane ticket."

"I can't just drop everything and get on a plane to Oregon."

"Why not?"

"I'm busy. I have this job, you see." This job that

was quickly going down the tubes. She reached for the letter from the National Science Foundation and slid it into her top desk drawer. She didn't want to be bothered with thoughts of losing her grant funding. Not when she had Brian Sinclair's deep voice in her ear.

"You don't get weekends off?"

"Most of the time."

"Are you working this weekend?"

"Not necessarily."

"Then what's the problem?"

She hesitated. *Eh, why not?* She could really use a short break from this place. Maybe a couple of days away would clear her head and she could figure out what to do about her current predicament. "You haven't sent me a ticket yet."

"Fuck," he murmured.

Disappointment made her heart drop to her toes. "What's wrong?"

"Oh, nothing. I'm just standing outside the stadium to get better phone reception and have been recognized by a group of fans. Bad timing. I have a raging hard-on, thanks to you, and can't run very fast."

"As long as it's thanks to me," she said, laughing.

Some chick squealed in the background, "Oh my God! Oh my God! It's Master Sinclair!"

Myrna laughed.

"Could you hold on just a minute? I'm on the phone," he said to someone.

"Oh my God! Will you sign my tits? Please. Please. You're soooo hot! Where's Sed?"

"They always want Sed," Brian said to Myrna. "Let

me get away from these girls and I'll call you back with your flight information."

"Okay."

"Great."

"And Brian?"

"Yeah, baby?"

"Hey," a whiny girl said in the background. "Who are you calling 'baby'? Do you have a girlfriend?"

Myrna shook her head. She didn't know how he put up with it. "It's great to hear your voice, too."

"I'm glad," he said quietly. "I'll call you back."

He disconnected, and she sat back in her office chair, listening to dead air until the phone began to beep at her. She hung up. It had been almost a month since they'd parted in Des Moines. She missed him and regretted not staying in contact with him, though she hadn't realized how much until that moment. When the phone rang almost an hour later, she was still staring off into space with a stupid grin on her face.

"Can you be on a plane in four hours?" Brian asked.

"Four hours? I'm still at work."

"Well, I realize that. I did call your work number."

She laughed. She hadn't laughed this much in…a month. "It's Thursday. I have to work tomorrow."

"Call in sick."

"Call in sick?" She never called in sick. Not even when she *was* sick.

"I'm not worth a sick day?"

"I don't know. Are you?"

He chuckled. "You sure don't make this easy on a guy. Our concert isn't until Saturday night, so I thought we could spend all day tomorrow getting reacquainted."

Reacquainted? Yeah, they'd need at least a day. Her gaze drifted to the huge stack of her students' final papers. She'd been grading them when Brian had called. One sick day wouldn't hurt. She could finish her grading by Tuesday, when final grades were due. "Where am I flying?"

"Portland." She could hear the smile in his voice.

"What's the flight number?"

"Fuck."

"What's wrong now?"

"I thought I had that hard-on under control. Turns out I was wrong."

She laughed.

"God, I want you," he whispered. "Laugh again."

"I can't laugh when I try." She did laugh though, because she was incredibly happy.

"Do you have something to write on?"

She reached for a pen. "Yeah." She wrote down the e-ticket information he read to her. After she hung up, she shut down her computer and locked her office. She walked out of the office suite and stopped at the department secretary's desk.

"Gladys, I'm going home early. I don't feel well."

Gladys's eyebrows shot up in surprise. "You're sick?"

"Yeah. I probably won't be in tomorrow either."

"That's too bad. I hope you feel better."

"Thanks."

"Oh, here's your mail." Gladys handed her a stack of mail.

Myrna tucked it into her purse and headed to the airport. She didn't bother packing any luggage. She didn't have time. Besides, it wasn't like she would need clothes.

Chapter 13

INSIDE THE CRAMPED BATHROOM OF THE TOUR BUS, Brian hurried through his shower. He couldn't wait to see Myrna. Couldn't believe she'd agreed to come visit him. Couldn't think of anything but drawing her into his arms. Holding her. Touching her. Looking at her. *God, I'm a fucking moron.* He knew she would break his heart, but he didn't care. After his shower, he hurried to the bedroom in search of clothes.

"You could knock," Trey said.

Brian paused in the bedroom's doorway holding his towel around his waist. Standing before the long dresser, Trey wrapped his arms around the thin young man in front of him and plastered his body to the guy's back. Trey's hand slid up under the hem of his new friend's T-shirt.

The guy's eyes widened and he caught Trey's hands in his. "H-hey, Master Sinclair, erm, Brian. Can I call you Brian?" Brian shrugged and the guy flushed. "This isn't what it looks like. I don't like guys or anything." He shook his head vigorously.

"You will," Trey murmured, inching the guy's shirt farther up his belly.

"Trey, are you molesting virgins again?" Brian grinned at his best friend's delight with his latest conquest.

"This one is named Mark. And you know how much I like cherries."

Brian chuckled. He supposed that didn't only apply to lollipops.

Trey slowly ran his tongue up Mark's neck. Mark shuddered and turned his head to look at Trey over his shoulder.

"You know this bedroom is mine as soon as I collect Myrna from the airport."

"Yeah, yeah," Trey murmured. "This won't take more than a couple of hours."

Mark tensed.

Brian rolled his eyes. "I need to get dressed. I'll be gone before you know it, and then you two can continue doing whatever it was you were about to do."

"Um, wait. I…" Mark untangled himself from Trey's embrace and pulled a piece of paper from his back pocket. He spread it across the dresser. It was a drawing of Brian's and Trey's guitars crossed at the necks with Sinners' band logo above the V-shape. "I'm going to have this tattooed across my back, and I wanted to include your signatures under the guitars. A tribute to my favorite guitarists." He glanced at Trey nervously and quickly averted his gaze to settle on Brian. "You guys rock. I absolutely idolize you. I want to *be* you."

"I want to *do* you," Trey said, toying with the hair at the nape of Mark's neck.

Brian scratched his head behind his ear, deliberately staring down at the drawing to avoid watching Trey's actions. "Nice design," Brian said. "Sure, I'll sign it. Do you want my real name or my stage name?"

Mark smiled brightly and handed him a black fine-point pen. "Just Sinclair would be awesome." Mark glanced at Trey, who leaned up against his back to stare over his shoulder at the drawing. "And Mills." Mark swallowed. "Please."

Brian scrawled his last name under the black guitar with white flecks. "After you get this done, you should send a picture of your tattoo to the webmaster on the Sinners website. There's a fan tat page on there. Sinners Ink."

"I'm the webmaster," Trey murmured. "So make sure it's a naked picture."

Mark laughed nervously.

Brian handed the pen to Trey, but he set it on the dresser and covered his pretty fanboy's belly with both hands. His pinkies dipped into the waistband of Mark's jeans. "I'll sign it later."

While Brian got dressed, he tried to ignore Trey and his entertainment for the afternoon. It turned out to be as easy as ignoring an air horn.

"You're so sexy," Trey murmured as he suckled and licked Mark's neck and ear.

"No…"

"Shhh. You are."

A black T-shirt landed at Brian's feet. Brian dressed faster. His zipper went up; someone else's zipper went down.

"Don't like guys, huh?" Trey murmured. "Is this a rabbit in your pocket?"

"Wait," Mark gasped. "Ohhhh."

"Yes," Brian yelled. "Wait until I'm gone. Please!"

Trey chuckled. Mark's breath caught in his throat and he groaned in pleasure.

Brian grabbed his boots, socks, and shirt and headed for the door, keeping his eyes off Trey's defilement of Mark. And then he remembered his lucky hat.

"Shit," Brian muttered under his breath. He'd put it in the dresser. In the drawer right in front of where Trey was stroking that guy's cock. And rubbing. And stroking. Slightly twisting his wrist at the tip. And...

Why was watching Trey give a hand job turning Brian on? He seriously needed to get laid. It had been almost a month since he'd seen Myrna, and he wasn't used to this length of abstinence. He hoped she was as sexually uninhibited as he remembered.

Trey glanced at Brian, grinning wickedly. The green eye not obscured by his overlong black bangs twinkled with more mischief than usual. "Need something, bro?"

"I need to get in that drawer." He pointed at it, his nose wrinkled.

"What's wrong? Afraid Mark's going to come on you?"

Actually, yes. The guy looked about ready to blow his load as Trey worked him over with practiced ease. Mark glanced down at Trey's hand, gasped brokenly, and then dropped his head back on Trey's shoulder, his eyes squeezed shut. "Ah, God. I am gonna come. I am."

Trey chuckled and released Mark's cock. He then shifted his lover back against his body so Brian could get into the drawer.

"Feel how hard I am for you?" Trey said in Mark's ear. "That's going in your ass as soon as Brian clears out of here."

Mark gasped and tried to pull away. "No, I don't want... It will hurt. Won't it hurt?" He glanced over his shoulder at Trey uncertainly. Brian noticed he wasn't protesting very hard.

"Not the way I do it."

"Change the sheets when you're done." Brian

retrieved his hat from the dresser and hurried out of the room. He finished dressing in the hall, pretending he couldn't hear Trey's newest lover crying out in ecstasy on the other side of the thin door. Brian tipped his lucky hat—a floppy leather fedora—on his head. He didn't want to waste time fixing his shoulder-length hair in its usual messy, spiked style. What he wanted to do was make Myrna's flight arrive sooner.

"So is she on her way?" Eric asked.

Brian checked his watch. "She should be here in a couple of hours. Will you do me a huge favor?"

"Depends on what it is."

"Clean this place up. It's a fucking embarrassment."

Eric glanced around as if seeing their living conditions for the first time. "You're right. God, how do we live like this?"

"We're slobs, but I doubt Myrna will appreciate having to stay here in our filth. Do you know where Jace is? I want to borrow his bike."

"No idea."

Brian went in search of Jace, checking his watch excessively. He didn't want to be late picking her up. If necessary, he'd drive the fucking bus to the airport.

Chapter 14

THE FIRST HOUR OF HER PLANE RIDE, MYRNA COULD think of nothing but Brian and all the things she wanted to do to him when she saw him. The plane could not get to Portland fast enough. Eventually, she grew tired of checking her wristwatch every thirty seconds and sorted through her mail. Among the textbook advertisements and interdepartmental memos, she found a letter from a funding agency. Her last-ditch grant! She'd almost missed the submission deadline and knew it wasn't her best work, but without research funding, the university wouldn't let her keep her job for long. She didn't have tenure yet.

Myrna hesitated, afraid to open the letter. She'd applied on a whim the day after she'd left Brian in Des Moines. She had the groupies to thank for the inspiration. And now that she knew for sure her government-sponsored grant would not be renewed for the following year, she didn't just want to work on this project as a fun summer side project. She needed this project to keep a roof over her head. But would it make good research? Did anyone care why women became promiscuous in the company of rock stars?

Heart hammering, she tore open the letter and scanned its contents. Score! Full funding. Enough to get her through the summer, in any case, and hopefully secure her faculty position for one more year.

"Yes!" she said, startling the man in the seat next to her. He snorted and fell back to sleep.

She could use the summer months to do her field work. That would give her the time she needed to collect data without her added teaching responsibilities. She just needed a famous rock band to follow around for three months. Would Sinners be willing to let her tour with them? It wouldn't hurt to ask. It probably would hurt if the band refused her request. She cared about them. As friends. But if she spent every moment of the next three months with Brian, how would she keep him at arm's length? Did she even want to? The joy his call had incited indicated she was more attached to the man than she'd like to think. Here she was on an airplane to Oregon to visit him, after all.

She took a deep breath. The only reason she wanted to see Brian so badly was because he was so good in bed. So open to suggestion. So accommodating. He never tried to make her feel like a whore. She could be herself with him. Yeah, *that* was the reason her heart rate hadn't returned to normal since he'd called. Holding him at arm's length would be no problem. No problem at all.

But what if he didn't want her to tour with his band? How would she feel if he said no?

Maybe she should ask another band. She couldn't put her heart on the line again. She'd barely survived her marriage and divorce. Emotionally. Mentally. Physically. It had literally almost killed her. She slid her hand under her hair and absently fingered the thick scar on the back of her head. No, she never wanted to open herself to that kind of devastation again. Not even with a great guy like Brian. Jeremy had been great in the beginning. She couldn't let herself forget that.

Myrna tucked the grant letter into her purse. This news was too good to dwell on negative possibilities. She would decide if she wanted to ask Sinners to participate in her study at the end of the weekend. For now, she'd just enjoy her moments with Brian and not think about real life. Or her ex-husband.

Near the end of the plane ride, she went to the bathroom and removed her panties. She tucked them into her suit jacket pocket. A little present to get Brian in the mood and set this rendezvous on the right track from the start. Not that Brian ever needed help to get in the mood, but she was competing with young girls begging him to autograph their perky tits. If she wanted to keep him interested in her body, she'd have to surprise him occasionally. With all that young, available pussy around him, he was sure to get bored with her in no time.

When the plane circled Mount Adams and landed in Portland, Myrna felt a surge of nervousness. What if his opinion of her had changed since she'd last seen him? What if that insatiable spark between them had fizzled out? What if he wasn't attracted to her any longer? What if—

"Nervous?" the man seated next to her asked.

She shook her head, though yes, she was nervous. She needed to get a grip.

"First time in Portland?"

"I was here a few years ago for a meeting."

"It's a beautiful city. I hope you enjoy yourself."

She flushed. With Brian between her thighs, that was guaranteed. "I hope so, too."

When she exited the ramp onto the concourse, she glanced around for a familiar face. Clad in leather from head to foot, including his floppy fedora, Brian stood at the end of the ramp. She recognized him instantly despite the dark shades he wore to disguise himself. Every concern clouding her mind vanished the instant he smiled at her. He pushed his way through the exiting passengers and captured her in his arms, claiming her mouth in a passionate kiss. Her knees went weak. My God, this man could kiss. He pulled back and raked his eyes over her.

"You look gorgeous," he said, kissing her again.

"You look...mysterious." She tapped the brim of his hat with her fingertips.

"It seems we have a lot of rabid fans in Portland." He chuckled. "I've been dodging them all day. Poor Sed had the shirt ripped off his back this morning."

"Really?"

"Yep."

"So my plan to rip your shirt off isn't very original."

He laughed and kissed her tenderly. "I probably shouldn't say this, but I've had you on my mind nonstop all month. I really missed you."

Her heart thudded. "I missed you, too. I didn't realize how much until I heard your voice."

He stroked a stray hair from her cheek and tucked it behind her ear. "Are you opening up possibilities between us?"

She grinned. "Sexual possibilities."

He smiled and kissed her again. "I'll take what I can get. Should we get your luggage?"

"What luggage?"

"You didn't bring anything?"

"I didn't have time to pack."

He grinned. Smugly. "I see."

"I did bring you a present." She fished the white satin panties out of her pocket and handed them to him. "They got so wet from thinking about you, I took them off on the plane."

He held them up to his nose and inhaled deeply. "Are you trying to kill me?" he murmured. "God, Myrna."

She chuckled.

He whispered in her ear, "Does this mean you aren't wearing any panties under that skirt?"

She grinned at him. "That's what it means."

"Christ, Myrna. You are trying to kill me!"

He took her hand, urging her forward at a run. She had a hard time keeping up with him in her high heels. He found a deserted concourse and tugged her through the door of a men's room.

"Brian? What are you doing?"

"You don't really think I can wait until we get back to the bus, do you?"

He shoved open a stall and pulled her inside, pressing her up against the stall door. His mouth descended on hers. His hands moved down her hips to lift her skirt up around her waist. She shuddered when his fingers found the moist heat between her thighs.

"You really are wet," he said, as if awed by the discovery.

"Did you think I was making up stories for your amusement?"

Her hands moved to the fly of his leather pants, releasing his cock. When she touched him, he drew a shaky breath through his teeth. "Abstinence is so not my thing."

His words didn't have time to register before he lifted her thigh to his hip and plunged into her body. She clung to his shoulders, groaning at the enthusiasm of his strokes.

"Garters under a conservative gray suit, Professor?" he murmured, his fingers running under the straps holding up her stockings. "Do you know how hot that is?"

"I like to keep my smuttiness carefully concealed."

"You're not fooling me," he whispered.

"I'm not trying to, but you're the only one who knows."

"That makes it even hotter."

He held her against the door as he thrust up into her, grinding deeply as he knew she liked it. "Brian. Brian! Oh God, Brian!"

"Shh, someone might come in," he said. "The last thing I need is to be arrested for public indecency."

She tensed. "I'm sorry," she whispered. "I didn't mean to be indecent."

"There is nothing indecent about you, baby." He cupped her jaw and kissed her gently. "You scream my name all you want."

She opened her eyes to look at him and found him still wearing his sunglasses. She took them off and tucked them into his jacket pocket. She wanted to see his eyes. Brown. Intense. Glazed with desire. For her.

He grinned. "Can we change positions? This is pretty hard on my back."

"Are you getting old?"

"Yeah, I must be."

He pulled out and guided her hands to the wall at the back of the stall. He bent her over the toilet, not the most romantic view, and pushed her skirt up around her waist.

He buried his face in her ass and lapped at the liquid heat between her thighs.

"Mmm," he murmured, spreading her labia with his fingers to gain better access. "I missed this, too." As he licked and sucked on her flesh, he ran his hands up and down her thighs, fascinated by the bare flesh above the tops of her stockings. Her breathing became erratic and shaky as she neared orgasm.

He stood and leaned over her, possessing her body with his thick cock again. She cried out as her body shook with release.

She thought she heard a door open but didn't care as she shifted backward to meet his every stroke.

"God, baby, I've missed you. I hear it again."

"The music?"

"Yeah, the music."

The sound of a zipper being released came from the stall next to them. Brian surprised her by increasing his tempo, seeking quick release. "We need to get out of here," he whispered into her ear. "I want to make love to you slowly. With lots of blank paper and pens nearby."

She wriggled her hips and he gasped.

"Do that again."

She complied. Brian groaned.

The guy in the next stall echoed Brian's groan and let a loud fart rip in the toilet.

Myrna covered her mouth with her hand, trying to hold in her laughter.

Another groan, followed by splashes and then...the most horrendous smell.

Myrna gagged.

"Okay, even I can't come under these conditions."

Brian pulled out and forced his rigid cock into his pants. She stood and adjusted her skirt.

"Let's go, sweetheart," he said.

She smiled and nodded, hoping he didn't end up with a huge case of blue balls. Poor guy.

They exited the stall and Brian knocked on the door of the next stall. "Someone's in here," a startled man's voice said.

"Yeah, dude. I heard. You picked a horrible time to take a shit, you know. Have a nice day."

Myrna burst out laughing and ran to the exit, jerking open the door and surprising a young man trying to enter.

"Excuse me," she said.

He looked at the Men's sign on the door and then back at Myrna with a confused expression. Brian came to a halt behind her. The man looked even more confused when he spotted Brian, and then a look of realization dawned on his face.

"No, excuse *me*," the man said and stepped aside so Myrna could exit the men's room. The guy offered Brian a high five as they passed each other in the doorway.

"I don't know what he's high-fiving me about. That didn't go as expected."

"Hey, I came really hard, so I'm not complaining."

He hugged her against his side as they walked toward the parking garage. "If you're not complaining, then I won't either. But you owe me one."

"I'll make it up to you."

He kissed her temple and put his sunglasses back on. "I have no doubt that you will."

Brian led her to the first floor of the parking garage. Beside the stairwell, a large, red Harley-Davidson leaned on its kickstand. He inserted a key into the bike's ignition and handed Myrna a spare helmet.

"A Harley Fat Boy! Sweet. I didn't know you had a bike," she said. "It looks brand-new." She slid the helmet over her head and fastened the chinstrap.

"It's not mine. Jace let me borrow it. He bought it a couple of weeks ago."

"I'll have to thank him. Motorcycles make me hot."

"Is there anything that doesn't make you hot?" He flipped up her visor and kissed her.

She thought for a moment. "Taxes and politics?"

He laughed. "Just tell Jace you rode it without any panties on and that will be all the thanks he'll ever need."

She looked down at her gray, pinstriped suit skirt and three-inch heels. "I'm not exactly dressed for this, am I?"

He took off his leather jacket and handed it to her. "Put this on."

She slid into the jacket and inhaled deeply through her nose. The jacket smelled of leather and Brian—the two biggest turn-ons on Earth. She hoped it wasn't far to the tour bus.

His jacket was several sizes too big and draped over her hands. She could almost wear it as a mini-dress. She zipped it up to her chin.

He smiled at her. "You look adorable." He tapped her nose with his index finger.

Brian crammed her purse in the small compartment under the seat. He took off his floppy leather hat and tried smashing it inside as well. It wouldn't fit.

"Would you mind holding my hat while I drive?" he asked.

"Not at all."

He handed it to her.

"It's a good thing I didn't pack a suitcase," she said.

He laughed and scratched his head as he stared down at the motorcycle's lack of cargo space. "True. I was in such a hurry to get here, I didn't think things through clearly. Jace's bike seemed more manageable than the tour bus."

"This will be fun." She grinned at him and then closed her visor.

Brian put on a helmet and climbed on the bike. God, he looked hot straddling the big machine. The Harley roared to life, rumbling through Myrna's entire body as he revved the engine. He held her hand while she climbed up on the bike behind him. She had to hike her skirt to the top of her thighs to sit. Her garters showed on both sides, but there was nothing she could do about it. Brian's hand gripped the bare skin above her white, lace-trimmed stocking.

"I should have called a cab!" he shouted over the roaring engine.

"No, you should not have! This is great! Let's go!"

"If you say so."

He turned the bike out of the parking spot and, once in the exit lane, took off like a shot. She held on tight, molding herself to his back with a satisfied sigh. Her free hand splayed over his black T-shirt and the hard muscles of his chest underneath. She couldn't think of any place in the world she'd rather be at that moment.

They exited the parking garage and took a ramp to a city street. She assumed he avoided I-5 for her benefit. The sun settled beneath the western horizon as an orange haze. Streetlights flickered on as they traveled a main street through the city.

The blowing breeze made the outsides of Myrna's thighs sting with cold, but Brian's hips between her thighs kept the insides plenty warm. Passing cars slowed to gawk at them. Hanging out the windows of a compact car, a group of young men wolf-whistled at Myrna's exposed garters. When they honked and waved, she waved back.

Passing women glared. She didn't care.

Brian stopped at a stoplight. "It's at least another fifteen miles," he said. "Will you be okay back there? We can stop somewhere and buy you some warmer clothes."

"I'm fine," she said. "How are you?"

"I'm suffering, baby. My balls are starting to ache like you would not believe."

Holding his hat over his lap with one hand, she moved her other hand to his crotch. His cock hardened instantly and his body stiffened. The light turned green. He took off like a shot, the bike rumbling beneath them.

"Don't speed. We might get pulled over!" she shouted. "Then it will take longer to get there."

He slowed down to the speed limit. Her hand continued to stroke him through his leather pants. He took one hand off the handlebars long enough to unfasten his fly and free his cock. Beneath the hat, Myrna's free hand circled his hot, engorged flesh and stroked its length steadily. The smooth skin felt like satin beneath her fingers. She didn't know how he managed to concentrate on driving.

Another red light.

He stopped and put his feet down on the pavement. She could barely hear his groans of pleasure over the roar of the motorcycle as she stroked the head of his cock faster and faster. Faster. Faster. His head fell back and his body stiffened in front of her. Hot cum spurted between her fingers and into his hat. He revved the engine as he cried out hoarsely.

The light turned green. Besides the occasional shudder, Brian didn't move. Someone behind them honked. He took several deep breaths. "Could you put that away for me, Myr?"

"Aw, but it's so fun to play with." She grinned and tucked his slackening cock back into his pants.

"Thanks, baby. I feel much better now."

"Well, I don't. I'm all worked up again. Are we going to sit here all day?"

He glanced up at the green light. It turned yellow. He sped forward, laughing. "That will teach them to honk at me when I'm coming at a red light."

"I think you're going to have to throw this hat away," she said, wiping her fingers on the inner lining.

"Fuck that. I'm framing it and hanging it on the wall. Right next to my gold album."

By the time they reached the stadium, Myrna was shivering. She was grateful that Brian had lent her his jacket. She'd have frozen to death if he hadn't.

Brian circled around to the back of the stadium where a pair of silver and black tour buses were parked. He pulled up to the side of one of the buses, shut off the bike, and closed the fly of his pants.

"You're cold, aren't you?" he asked.

She couldn't lie through chattering teeth.

His warm hand brushed against her ice-cold outer thigh. "You're freezing!"

He helped her off the bike. She tugged her skirt down her thighs. That helped warm her quite a bit. She took off her helmet and handed it to him. He removed her purse from the compartment and stowed the helmet inside. He took his helmet off as well and looked at her apologetically.

"I'm sorry. I'm an idiot. I really should have called a cab."

She smiled and shook her head. "But I had fun. Honest."

"Not half as much as I did." He exchanged her purse for his hat and moved to put it on his head.

"Wait!"

He grinned at her. "Just kidding."

She laughed and swatted him.

"I'll make Eric wear it. Shhhhh…" He held a finger to his lips, looking devious. And gorgeous. She laughed as he drew her against him, holding her close. "You're so much fun, Myrna. Do you know that?"

She shook her head. "I'm an old lady."

"My old lady."

He kissed her, and she forgot to deny that she was his.

The tour bus door opened. "Did you find her?" Jace called from the door.

"Nope," Brian said. "I had to settle for this old lady I found at the airport."

Myrna slugged Brian in the gut. "Hi, Jace. I love your motorcycle."

"You rode it in that?" he asked, eyes wide as he took in her attire.

"She looked hot!" Brian wrapped an arm around her shoulders and led her to the bus.

"But she feels cold."

"We'll take care of that right now," Brian murmured into her ear. He handed his hat to Jace as they passed him. "Give this to Eric."

"Your lucky hat?"

"It's really lucky now."

"I'll keep it." He started to flip it on his head, but Myrna grabbed it.

"You don't want to wear this hat, Jace. Trust me."

"Why not?"

Brian patted Jace's cheek smartly. "Listen to Myrna, Jace. You're a nice kid. Do you have any idea how hard it is to get cum out of a lucky hat?"

His nose wrinkled. "Why is there... Never mind, I don't want to know."

"Brian says telling you I'm not wearing any panties is thanks enough for the ride," Myrna said.

Jace's eyes widened to unnatural proportions.

"But I think I owe you a better thank you." She kissed his cheek. He was at least five years younger than Brian and the rest of the band. She didn't typically go for men who were in kindergarten when she was graduating high school. She hoped her little kiss didn't give him nightmares.

He swallowed hard. "You can borrow it any time, Myrna."

"You're sweet."

Jace chuckled. "That's what all the ladies think. At first."

Brian tugged her toward the bus steps. "Don't fall into his trap, Myrna. You might not survive the experience."

Myrna climbed the steep stairs and entered the bus. The visible common area was quite roomy. And messy. A bachelor pad on wheels.

"Eric," Brian bellowed into the cabin. "You were supposed to clean this place up, loser."

Eric poked his head out of a door near the end of a narrow hallway. "I'm scrubbing the toilet, dude. Is she here already?"

Myrna set her purse on a counter and looked down at Brian's leather jacket, unzipping it with more concentration than required. A warm blush spread up her face. She couldn't bring herself to look at Eric. Would she ever be able to look at him without getting embarrassed? He never mentioned watching Brian make love to her. It probably wasn't a big deal to him, but it was to her. She tugged Brian's jacket off and handed it to him. He tossed it onto the couch.

"She's here!" Eric loped down the hall and grabbed Myrna in an enthusiastic embrace, spinning her around dizzily. "You look gorgeous, Professor Sex." He kissed her cheeks with loud smacking sounds.

She laughed. "You're in a good mood."

He leaned close to her ear and whispered, "We're all happy. Maybe Brian will stop bitching now that you're here. He's been on the rag since you left."

"I heard that, Sticks," Brian said.

Jace closed the door and walked into the room. "Hey, Eric. Brian said you could have his lucky hat for cleaning up the bus."

"Cool!"

Eric squeezed past Myrna and Brian and grabbed the hat out of Jace's hand. He crammed it onto his head and the other three bus occupants burst out laughing.

Eric looked from one person to the next. "What?"

"You look like an ass is all," Brian said.

"You look cool when you wear it, but I look like an ass?"

Brian nodded with his lips pursed. "Yeah, pretty much."

Jace fell onto the sofa, clutching his side as he laughed.

Eric jumped on him and grabbed him in a headlock. "What is so funny?"

Jace choked and struggled as he attempted to get out of Eric's grasp.

"Do you want to die, Little Man?" Eric asked. "What are you laughing about?"

"I'm…not laugh—" Jace gasped. "Laughing at…you."

"You better not be."

Eric released Jace, who sat up on the couch scowling and rubbing his red neck. It must suck to be the youngest and smallest member of this testosterone-laden group. Myrna winked at Jace and he grinned. Behind Eric's back, Jace pointed at the hat repeatedly with a huge smile on his face and his tongue hanging out.

"Where's Sed?" Brian asked.

"He took a couple of chicks to the other bus," Eric said.

"And you aren't filming it?"

"I was scrubbing the toilet."

"Right. Where's Trey?"

"I think he took his boy toy to a tattoo parlor."

"That leaves the bedroom free." Brian took Myrna's hand and tugged her to the back of the bus. "Later, dudes. Do not disturb."

"Don't leave me alone with Sticks!" Jace complained.

Eric grabbed him in a headlock again. "Have fun, kiddies, I'm going to kick Little Man's ass now."

"Eric," Myrna called as Brian opened the door at the end of the hall. "I think that hat looks really good on you. And you know…payback is always a bitch." He'd probably never figure out that she was referring to having cum in his hair as payback to that time he'd jacked off into hers.

"What?" Eric gave her an odd look, but Brian pulled her into the tiny room and closed the door before she could respond.

"Will Jace be okay?" she asked.

"Yeah, he's used to us bustin' his ass."

She scowled. "That's not nice."

"Sed usually keeps Eric in check, but Jace is so grateful for this gig he takes Eric's crap. I think it's because he hasn't been with us since the beginning."

"That shouldn't matter. He's a great bassist." She shook her head. "I don't understand how guys think."

"No one denies that he's an excellent musician, but he has to earn respect as one of the guys. No one is going to hand it to him. Until Jace kicks the shit out of Eric, Eric will torment him. That's just how he is." Brian removed the clip from Myrna's hair, allowing the long locks to tumble free over her shoulders. "Why are we talking about this?"

Hell, she didn't know. She felt protective of Jace for some strange reason.

"We should talk about how cold my legs are instead."

She stared up at him while his fingers unfastened the buttons of her suit jacket. He kissed her temple, jaw, neck, as he brushed her jacket from her shoulders. Her eyes drifted close. She felt warmer already.

Brian stroked her bare arms with his knuckles, his open mouth sucking the flesh under her ear. She tugged his T-shirt out of the waistband of his pants, and he helped her pull it off over his head. She kept her eyes closed as she explored the hard muscles of his chest and arms with her hands. Her arms circled his body. He drew her against him, hands stroking her back soothingly. She rested her ear against his chest, listening to his strong, steady heartbeat. He held her there for a long while, one hand stroking the white satin camisole across her back, the other gently massaging her scalp.

His heart rate picked up beneath her ear. She smiled. "What are you thinking?"

He hugged her closer. "It's emotional. You wouldn't approve."

"Don't be that way. I want to know."

"I'll tell you later." His hand moved to the zipper of her skirt. The garment landed in a puddle at her feet. She kicked it aside.

He drew her camisole over her head, leaving her in her bra, garters, stockings, and high heels. Her panties were still in his pocket. He took her hands and held her arms away from her sides, stepping back so he could get a good look at her.

He grinned deviously. "You do know how to get a man in the mood, Professor. I wondered what you had on under that conservative suit. Even better than I imagined."

She flushed with pleasure. "I always wonder why I buy frilly underwear when no one ever gets to see it but me."

"I'm seeing it. It's very nice. Feminine. Sexy."

He scooped her up into his arms, and she gasped in surprise. Kneeling on the bed, he crawled up the mattress, carrying her along with him. Her shoes tumbled off the end of the bed with a clatter. He gently laid her on top of the comforter and stretched out beside her, brushing the skin of her lower belly with the back of his hand. She shivered.

His finger traced the edge of her white lacy bra. "So no one gets to see your underwear?" He grinned. Smugly.

"Not recently," she said. "Present company being the exception."

He kissed her passionately, his hand cupping her breast over her bra. When his mouth drew away, he whispered, "Let's keep it that way."

When she didn't deny the logic of the idea, he smiled.

"Of course, the rest of your band has seen me naked," she reminded him.

"But it didn't mean anything."

Her legs started to tingle as warmth sank into her flesh. She reached for the edge of the comforter and folded it over herself.

"You're still cold, aren't you?"

She nodded, shivering slightly. He climbed from the bed, removed his boots and pants, and then climbed between the sheets in his boxers and socks. He held the covers up, and she crawled beneath them with him. Brian spooned against her back and draped a leg over hers, cocooning her in his warmth. When she shuddered with cold, he tucked the heavy comforter under her chin.

"You're freezing," he whispered, his nose pressed under her ear.

"I noticed. And you're so warm." She snuggled closer.

His arms tightened around her. "You like me, don't you?"

"What makes you say that?"

"When I called you this afternoon, I thought you'd just hang up on me. Those stupid girls yelling at me to sign their tits the moment I got you on the phone. Great timing, I thought. It took me two weeks to find the balls to call you."

"If I had any sense, I would have hung up on you."

"And now you're here. Willing to drop everything and hop on a plane to see me."

"For entirely selfish reasons. Trust me."

"Willing to freeze half to death and ride on a motorcycle in a skirt to be here."

"Hey, it's a really nice bike."

"You like me. Admit it."

"A little," she said, grinning to herself.

He squeezed her closer. "Wanna go to Vegas and get married?"

She frowned. "No. Why do you keep asking me that?"

"Because I want to marry you, why else?"

"Marriage is not my idea of a good time."

"How would you know?"

"I tried it. Didn't like it."

"You were married?" He leaned away from her. She glanced over her shoulder at him.

"Yeah. I've been divorced for almost five years now. I'd like to keep it that way."

"Well, that explains a few things. He hurt you badly, didn't he?" He stroked her hair from her face and kissed her temple.

"Yeah, actually, he did."

"I'd never hurt you, Myrna."

She snorted derisively. "How many times have I heard that same old song?"

He kissed her cheek tenderly. Her jaw. "Never. No one's heard the songs we make together. We write them as we go. I haven't written more than three notes since the last time we made love."

"Then I think it's time to write another."

"I agree. But I've got a few questions first."

She rolled over to face him. "This sounds serious."

"Now that I know you aren't sleeping with any other men—"

"Well, there is BOB."

His face fell. "Bob?"

"Yeah, but he never actually sleeps with me. Just gives me fantastic orgasms, then I put him back in the drawer. I have to change his double As occasionally, but he's fairly low maintenance."

His brow furrowed. "A vibrator?"

She grinned. "Multi-functional with attachments. BOB. My Battery Operated Boyfriend."

"God, don't tease me like that. You ripped my heart out of my chest for a minute there."

"Aw, I'm sorry." She stroked his longish black hair from his face. "I'm not really sleeping with anyone."

"So you aren't on birth control?"

"I have an IUD. Wait a minute. Is this the it's-time-to-stop-using-condoms conversation?"

"I keep dreaming about coming inside of you."

"You dream about it?"

"All the time. I'm usually awake, but…"

She laughed and kissed him. He looked so hopeful as he gazed into her eyes. "Pregnancy isn't the only thing we have to worry about, Brian. There are STDs—"

He leaned over her body, opened a drawer in a side

table, and pulled out a piece of paper. "I've already been checked. See. All clear." He held up a printout from a clinic.

"But what if I'm not?"

His face fell. "Is that a possibility? I've been inside you more than once without any protection."

"I tested disease free at my last appointment."

"And?"

"And I haven't slept with anyone but you since."

"Awesome." He tossed the printout aside and climbed on top of her. He worked his boxers down his thighs and lowered his head to kiss her throat.

"Brian?"

"Hmm?"

"Did you plan all this? Why did you have your test results in a drawer next to the bed?"

He lifted his head to gaze down at her. "Myrna, you're under my skin. I've been planning for your return since the moment you left me behind in Des Moines. I have several surprises for you, actually."

Intrigued, she lifted an eyebrow at him. "What kind of surprises?"

"If I told you, they wouldn't be surprises."

"That's true."

"So can I come inside you?"

"There's no reason why you can't."

"Yes." Fist clenched in victory, he leaned out of the bed again, retrieving something from the drawer. "Now for one of your surprises."

He opened a small square package with his teeth. It looked suspiciously like a condom. He dumped something into the palm of his hand. She stared at it, perplexed. It wasn't a condom. It was a pink rubber ring about the size of a condom though. On one edge, it had a pill-shaped attachment.

"Is that…"

"A cock ring, with a special part for your enjoyment."

She shook her head. "You don't need it."

He grinned wickedly and crushed the ring in his hand. It started vibrating. "I think you'll like this."

He tossed the covers aside and slid the ring over his cock, all the way to the base. He shuddered. "I like it, too."

"Fine, we'll try it. I just think we're too hot for each other to need toys."

"Are you complaining?" He rolled on top of her, a persistent hum coming from his crotch area.

"No. I just think…"

He slid into her, backing out several times to wet himself with her juices. She forgot about everything but the feel of him inside her. When he buried himself completely, the vibrating attachment on the cock ring brushed against her clit. She jerked. "Whoa." He had the attention of every nerve ending in her body.

"Yeah, that's what I said," he murmured.

He quickly found a rhythm that excited them both.

She was certain his cock was engorged even larger than usual. The Beast stretched her to her limits, and the amazing gadget buzzed against her sensitive clit with each penetrating stroke.

"Oh my," she gasped, shuddering hard against him.

He stayed buried deep while she came, continuing to stimulate her clit until she cried out.

"You like it?" He kissed her jaw as she continued to shudder.

Her body arched off the bed, grinding him deeper still. He pulled back and thrust into her again. She couldn't stop shuddering. The pleasure between her thighs needed to be offset by something. She unhooked the front clasp of her bra and shoved the fabric aside impatiently. Covering her breasts with her hands, she gritted her teeth and pinched her stiff nipples as hard as she could. A little pain balanced the pleasure nicely. She shuddered harder. He pushed one of her hands aside and sucked her nipple into his mouth.

"Ah," she cried.

His fingers stroked her hair gently while he tugged on her breast with his mouth. His hard sucking felt even better than the pain she'd inflicted. She swore his cock was still thickening. Or maybe she was more swollen than normal. Whatever its cause, the head of his dick rubbed against her G-spot with each thrust. She knew of female ejaculation but had never experienced it while making love before. Exploration with a vibrator, yes, she'd achieved it a few times, but a man had never brought her even close to the experience. Until now.

"Brian," she whispered urgently.

He lifted his head from her breast and kissed her lips. He groaned, his teeth clenched, lip curled. "God, this feels fantastic," he murmured. "Skin on skin. Warm, soft velvet all around me. I want to be inside of you forever."

That was the difference. No condom.

"Yes," she agreed. "Oh," she gasped. "Brian. Brian? I think. I think I'm gonna…"

"Just let go, baby. I'll make you come again. You don't have to hold back."

"You don't un-understand. This…"

She bore down on his cock as if trying to pee, and wasn't disappointed. A hard, pulsating orgasm gripped her insides. She cried out. So much different than a clitoral orgasm. Primal in intensity. Every organ in her lower body clenched in hard spasm, relaxed, clenched again. Fucking fantastic.

Her nails dug into his shoulders as her back arched off the bed. He held her back with one hand until the orgasm subsided.

"What happened there?" he whispered.

When her body stopped quaking, she opened her eyes to look at his concerned face.

"That felt different, Myrna. You okay?"

"I'm better than okay." She grinned. "Ever hear of female ejaculation?"

He quirked an eyebrow at her. "I thought that was a myth."

She laughed brokenly, almost maniacally. "Did that feel like a myth to you?"

He grinned. "No, actually…"

"Without a condom, the head of your cock rubs my G-spot every time you pull out and thrust inside me. It's as if we were—"

"Made for each other."

"Yeah." She laughed. "Isn't that the most ridiculous thing you've ever heard?"

He scowled. "I don't think it's ridiculous."

She touched his face. Such a romantic. "Why are you taking a break, Brian? I thought you wanted to come inside me."

"I already did."

"You did?"

He laughed. "No, sweetheart. That was all you. Do you want to be on top for a while? I'm getting light-headed."

On top? When she was on top, she always came twice as often. She didn't know if she could handle his vibrating cock ring in that position. She was willing to endure it for his sake, however.

"Yeah, okay."

He pulled out slowly, wincing when he fell free of her body, and rolled onto his back. She hadn't just been imagining that his cock was thicker than usual. Pulsating. The skin strained over thick veins, its head an angry purple.

"That Beast really is going to tear me in half today. No wonder you're light-headed."

She sucked the head of his cock into her mouth and cradled his nuts in her hand, massaging gently. He groaned. He shifted toward the side table drawer and searched blindly for something. After a moment, he pressed something into her hand. "Put that inside me."

She examined the small object. Black. About the size of her thumb. She released the head of his cock from her mouth and squeezed his balls until he gasped in pain. When she released them, he groaned.

"A butt plug? You are a little kinky, aren't you, Master Sinclair?"

He hesitated and then lifted his head to look at her. "Does it bother you? I can put it away." His hand extended toward her to take it back.

She rolled her eyes at him and stretched out on her belly, her face between his legs. His body jerked when she thrust her tongue into his ass. She licked him eagerly, wetting the area with her saliva until he dripped with the moisture from her mouth.

"Oh God, Myr," he gasped. "My cock is in desperate need of attention."

She squeezed his nuts again but ignored his engorged member as she thrust her tongue in and out of his ass. If she touched his cock, he'd explode, and she'd promised him that he could come inside her—not on his own belly. When his thighs began to tremble, she decided he'd had enough and slid the plug into his ass. He tensed. Groaned. Shuddered. God, she wanted to ride him.

She crawled up his body and straddled his hips, guiding his rock-hard cock inside. She gritted her teeth and sank down, taking him all at once. He arched his back and covered his eyes with the palms of his hands.

"Ah, fuck, Myrna. Fuck."

She slid up his pole.

His back arched more. His entire body trembled. She took him deep again, the vibrating cock ring stimulating her clit. She shuddered, rising and falling faster. She raked her nails down his belly. He convulsed. Chanted her name. Writhed in ecstasy. She'd never seen a guy get off so hard. It excited her beyond anything in her experience. He began to drive himself up into her, lifting his hips up off the mattress, as if he was unable to keep them still. He thrust. Thrust. Thrust up into her like an animal.

Gasps and groans punctuated each thrust as they strained against each other, both close to letting go. When her body shuddered with release, he grabbed her hips and held her down as he came, spurting inside her, his body tense, face contorted with pleasure.

He forgot to breathe.

She couldn't take her eyes off him.

After a long moment, he inhaled deeply and relaxed into the bed, still shuddering. She fell forward, collapsing on top of him. His arm wrapped around her back.

She turned her head so she could look at him.

He panted unevenly to catch his breath, a delirious smile on his face. "That…" he murmured. "That…"

"Was fantastic."

"There are no words."

"Did it live up to your expectations? Coming inside me, I mean."

He opened his eyes. "You have to ask? I think we created our own supernova with that explosion."

She grinned at him. "But you didn't hear any music that time?"

"I heard an entire symphonic orchestra." He laughed. "I'm not sure if I can use it. We'll have to take it down a notch if I'm going to get any writing done for the band."

She lifted her head and pouted down at him. "You don't really mean that, do you?"

"Yeah, I do. I don't think I can stand to come that hard more than once or twice a day."

She sighed. "I guess I'll have to learn to live with it." She ducked her head to hide a grin and kissed his shoulder tenderly.

He rolled her onto her back and removed his hardware, tossing the items back into the drawer. He settled down amongst the pillows and held his arms open. "Come here, baby," he whispered, almost asleep. "I want to hold you."

If she wanted to keep this thing between them solely

about sex, she knew she shouldn't indulge him, but she relented and moved into his arms. He arranged the covers around them. Her legs were definitely warm now, but cuddling up against him warmed more than her body. She sighed and relaxed against his side, her head resting on his shoulder.

He kissed the top of her head and hummed a guitar riff under his breath just as he drifted off to sleep.

She supposed she could tolerate being around this guy and his bandmates for three months. Assuming they wanted her along for the ride.

Chapter 15

BRIAN WATCHED MYRNA BUTTON HER SHIRT, HIDING her sexy, lace bra from his appreciative gaze. The woman should be required to stay naked and in his bed at all times. Covering that body was an abomination. His sleep-muddled thoughts began to clear. Had she really just asked him to call a band meeting?

"Band meeting?" Brian asked.

"Yeah. I have something important to discuss with all of you," she said. "Do you think we can get everyone together for a few minutes? It won't take long. I promise."

He sat up and dangled his legs over the edge of the bed. He rubbed his face vigorously. "What time is it?"

"Seven-ish, I think."

"Seven-ish? As in seven a.m.?" He lay back down and covered himself with the comforter. "Come back to bed, Myrna. I haven't seen seven a.m. in over three years."

"Is it too early?"

"Uh, yeah. It's waaaay too early."

"Go back to sleep then. What time do you all usually wake up?"

"Ten-ish. Or in Jace's case, noon-ish."

"Most of the day will be gone by then." She fastened her skirt and crossed the room to sit on the bed beside him. "I thought we were going to spend today together."

He grinned at her sleepily. "So why are you out of bed and dressed?"

"I was planning on taking you to breakfast, since I'm starving. I was also hoping to pick up a toothbrush and maybe a change of clothes. I'm feeling kind of helpless, trapped here with no provisions."

"Ah, I'm being an insensitive prick. Gotcha."

"I didn't say that."

"I'm up!" He tossed his covers aside and climbed out of bed. He hunted the floor for clothing. He found his boxers under the edge of the bed. He slid into them and stood at the foot of the bed, slapping his face with both palms to wake himself up.

Myrna's arms circled his waist from behind. She pressed her cheek against his back and then sucked a gentle trail of kisses over his skin from one shoulder blade to the other. He paused. Affectionate in the morning? Good to know.

When her hands flattened over his belly, he stiffened, instantly alert. Her kisses trailed down his spine and back up. She then rested her cheek against his back and sighed.

"If you're trying to get me in the mood," he said, "it's working."

"No, I'm not trying to seduce you. Are you awake now?"

"So that was your intention?"

"I'm sorry to have ulterior motives, Brian, but I'm starving." Her stomach rumbled loudly. "All I had for dinner yesterday was a mint on the airplane."

"I invite you here and don't even feed you dinner. I wonder if the roadies stocked the refrigerator with anything but beer."

He tugged her toward the door and out into the corridor. Quiet snores came from the curtained bunks on the left side of the bus. Brian punched Trey in the arm on his way past his bunk. Trey slapped at Brian's head but missed and immediately fell into snores again.

"I've known Trey since fifth grade. It's required that I fuck with him on a regular basis."

She rolled her eyes at him, shaking her head slightly.

He couldn't take his eyes off her. She had a well-fucked look about her. He wondered how she'd talked him into leaving bed. Shouldn't he get the chance to bask in the accomplishment of putting that look on her face?

He forced his attention from her face and opened the small refrigerator. Some leftover take-out containers from God-only-knew when. Cans of beer. Bottles of beer. A half-gallon of no-longer-liquid milk. He closed the refrigerator. "This isn't looking good." He opened a cabinet. An empty box of cereal to go with the solid milk. Cherry suckers. A sock. He closed the cabinet and glanced at her over his shoulder. "Wanna go out to eat?"

"If I want to survive the experience, I think that's probably the best idea."

He hugged her and kissed her temple. "We'll borrow Jace's bike again."

She grinned. "I wonder if Eric is still wearing your lucky hat."

"He probably slept in it. Assuming Jace didn't tell him what was in it. Let's find you some warm clothes. As much as I enjoyed warming you up last night, I'd feel guilty if I made you ride on the back of a bike in a skirt again."

She followed him back to the bedroom and he offered her a pair of Jace's jeans and one of his own band-logo T-shirts. The jeans were loose around her waist but snug on her hips and clung to her ass in a most beguiling fashion.

She slipped into her high-heeled shoes. "I look ridiculous."

"You look gorgeous, as always." He drew her against him and kissed her passionately.

She went limp in his arms, totally submissive to his eager mouth and seeking tongue. He eyed the bed but decided feeding her breakfast was for the best and drew away. "Let's go before I toss you back into bed."

"I wouldn't protest much," she murmured huskily.

Her stomach rumbled. Her eyes widened and she covered her belly with one hand.

"But your stomach would."

He took her hand and they made their way to the front of the bus. He handed her Jace's leather jacket and put on his own before retrieving the spare set of keys from the glove compartment.

He considered a disguise. "Do you think anyone will recognize me?"

Myrna ran her fingers through his hair, looking him over carefully. "You're a mess, Brian. I don't even recognize you."

He glanced into the rearview mirror, stretching the skin on his cheek with his fingers. "Seriously? Did I sleep on my face again?"

She chuckled. "I'm kidding. You are instantly identifiable. Let's just go through the first fast food drive-thru we encounter. We can come back here to eat and avoid your rabid fans altogether."

"Only if I can use your naked belly as my plate and drip my ketchup into your belly button."

She looked at him through half-lowered eyelids. "Let me tell you what I'd rather you drip into my belly button."

His thoughts shifted through various fluids he could introduce to her navel.

He covered her mouth with his hand. "Woman, don't say things like that." Taking her by the arm, he tugged her off the bus. She stumbled on her high heels and he scooped her up into his arms. She laughed, hugging him around the neck as he spun around. She looked spectacular in the early morning sunshine—definitely worth missing three hours of sleep. He deposited her on the back of Jace's motorcycle and started the engine. He handed her a helmet and put on the spare.

Myrna leaned against his back, her arms circling his waist. He covered one of her hands with his and smiled. As much as this woman turned him on, he truly treasured her occasional bouts of tenderness. Her free hand slid down his belly and clutched his belt buckle. His smile broadened. So her bouts of tenderness were extremely occasional. So what?

He drove the bike out of the parking lot and turned left in front of the expo center, sticking to the main road.

When they drove past a super store, Myrna shouted, "Stop here!"

He pulled into the parking lot. "Why here?"

"I can get everything I need here. Drop me off at the door."

"What about breakfast?"

"You can go get breakfast while I pick up a few necessities. It shouldn't take me long."

He pulled to a stop in front of the store's main entrance. "I'll come with you."

"It will be faster if we split up."

"Are you always in such a rush?" he asked.

"I want to get back to the bus and play with ketchup."

That convinced him. Myrna held on to his arm as she climbed from the bike. She lifted her helmet's visor and then ran her hands over her pockets. "Crap, I forgot my purse."

Brian reached for his wallet. "Here."

He pulled out a chunk of cash and tried handing it to her. She shook her head. "I can't take your money."

"Why not?"

"I just can't. You already bought me a plane ticket and..."

She got that "I feel like a whore" look on her face that plagued her on occasion.

"Pay me back later if it will make you feel better, but honestly, Myr, it's not a big deal. I've got plenty."

She snatched the bills out of his hand. "I'll pay you back." She glanced at the money in her hand. "There's over a thousand dollars here! Why do you carry so much cash?"

He shrugged. "I guess when you survive on a hundred bucks a month for several years, you make sure it never happens again."

She started stuffing bills back into his hand. "I don't need this much."

"Take it. Buy anything you want. But hurry up about it. I'll be back with extra ketchup packets in less than half an hour."

She shoved the cash into the pocket of Jace's jeans and lifted the visor on Brian's helmet. Their helmets cracked against each other as they sought each other's mouths. She laughed, kissed her fingertips, and pressed them to his lips.

"I'll hurry," she promised.

She dashed into the store like a woman on a mission. Brian watched her until she was safely inside and then headed for the fast food restaurant down the street. He ordered a lot of food, not sure who would be awake when they returned.

"Can I get some extra ketchup?" he asked the young woman at the window, grateful that the motorcycle visor concealed his face.

"Sure. Like how much?"

"A couple of handfuls."

She fulfilled his request and handed several bags of food out to him. He shifted back on the bike seat to store the food in the compartment beneath it.

After returning to the super store, he parked the bike near the entrance and waited for Myrna to come outside. People eyed him warily as they passed. Brian cracked his knuckles, amused by the wide berth they took around his threatening presence. About ten minutes later, Myrna emerged, carrying two large sacks.

"Have you been waiting long?" she asked breathlessly. "I tried to hurry."

"I just got here." He'd have waited an eternity.

She climbed onto the bike behind him, settling her purchases between their bodies.

As they headed back to the bus, he came to loathe the shopping bags keeping Myrna's body from pressing against his. Once inside the bus, Myrna sped toward the bedroom. Brian tossed a bag of food into Trey's bunk and a second bag into Jace's.

"Too early for this bullshit," Jace grumbled.

Brian thumped him on the head. "I think you mean, thank you for thinking of my bottomless stomach, Brian."

By the time he made it to the back bedroom, Myrna was devouring a sausage and biscuit.

"I couldn't wait any longer," she explained, her mouth full as she talked. "And what's with all the ketchup?" She pointed at the open sack sitting on the long dresser.

He grinned at her crookedly. "I can't eat hash browns without ketchup. Before I get naked, do you want a beer?"

She pointed at her sacks of purchases. "I bought some juice."

Brian would have liked to have a beer, but she didn't drink and it was still pretty early for that indulgence. "Great."

He searched through her purchases and found several bottles of juice and a huge bottle of chocolate syrup.

He held the chocolate syrup out to her, his head cocked to one side. "I don't think that milk in the fridge is drinkable."

She was adorable when she blushed. "I wasn't planning on using it to make chocolate milk."

He grinned. "Ketchup isn't good enough for you?"

She lowered her eyes. He wondered about her sudden shyness. "I prefer chocolate."

"I think you'll like ketchup, too."

He handed her a bottle of juice and searched the take-out bag for a breakfast sandwich. "Why are you still dressed?" he asked. "I thought you were going to be my plate."

She held up one finger, stuffing the last bite of her

sausage and biscuit into her mouth, and then opened her juice to take a long drink.

She fished the money he'd given her out of her pocket and handed it to him. "I owe you a hundred and twenty bucks," she said. He tossed the money onto the dresser.

"Myr, you really don't have to pay me back."

"Why not? You don't think I can afford to?"

He'd never seen her angry before. He liked the way her eyes narrowed and her nostrils flared.

"I don't know," he teased. "You're a teacher. You don't make much money, do you?"

Her mouth fell open in disbelief. "I can't believe you just said that."

"Are you going to hit me?" he asked hopefully.

"You'd like that, wouldn't you, naughty boy."

His eyes dropped to her waist. "Will you use your belt?"

"I thought Jace was the one with the masochism fetish."

He glanced up at her, surprised. "How do you know that?"

"Groupies talk."

"Do they? And what do they say about me?"

She chuckled. "That you're a boring, one-woman man."

He winced.

"I only agree with that second part," she added.

"So I'm not boring?"

"I'm not sure. I've always been the skeptical type, and I can be hard to convince without lots of evidence."

He raised an eyebrow at her. "I see. So I need to prove I'm exciting."

"I think that would be for the best."

He looked down at the sandwich in his hand. "Can I eat first?"

"Please do." She took another long drink of her juice and set it down on the dresser.

She removed her shoes and belt. Jace's jeans slid down low on her hips. She unbuttoned the fly and let them fall to the floor. She tugged off Brian's borrowed T-shirt. He should wear that one onstage tonight to keep her close.

"Do I need to be completely naked to be your plate?" she asked.

He realized he was holding his sandwich in front of his open mouth but hadn't taken a bite.

"Yeah. I've never seen a plate in underwear before."

She unfastened her bra and tossed it aside. She pushed her breasts up with her hands. "You know these things used to be perkier." She looked down at the twin globes of flesh spilling from her palms.

He didn't understand why, but by not trying to act seductive, she was actually turning him on more. "They're perfect."

Her panties joined her jeans on the floor. She glanced over her shoulder, straining her neck to try to see her butt. "I think my ass used to be perkier, too."

Brian bit into his sandwich, chewing slowly.

"Gravity is a woman's worst enemy." She looked up at him uncertainly.

He swallowed. "You're beautiful, Myrna."

"Does it bother you that I'm older than you are?"

"Yeah, like, what, six months older?"

"I'm thirty-five."

He hadn't expected her to be seven years older than him, but frankly, he didn't care how old she was. She was the sexiest woman he'd ever met. "You're in your sexual prime, Myrna. And trust me, that doesn't bother me at all."

"You could have any hot young woman you want—"

"Where's this coming from?"

"Oh my God! Oh my God! It's Master Sinclair!" Myrna squealed and trembled from head to foot with excitement. "Oh my God! Will you sign my tits? Please. Please. You're soooo hot!"

He tossed his sandwich aside, grabbed a handful of ketchup packets from the take-out bag, and tackled her to the bed. He straddled her hips to hold her down.

"Certainly, I'll sign your tits, miss. Anything for a fan." He opened a ketchup packet with his teeth. She laughed uncontrollably, squirming beneath him. "Hold still."

She stopped squirming and looked up at him, her hazel eyes wide. He began to write across her chest in ketchup.

"P-R," he spelled aloud. "O-P." He tossed the empty packet on the floor and reached for another.

"Prop?"

"I'm not finished."

"That tickles." She giggled.

"E-R-T-Y."

"What are you writing?"

He opened another packet and wrote in the middle of her belly. "O-F." He moved to her lower belly. "B-R."

"Property of brrrrrr?"

"Yeah, property of brrrrr. Exactly." He opened another packet of ketchup and finished his name on her belly. "Perfect. Property of Brian. I just need to dot this *i*."

He dabbed a dot of ketchup in the center of her nipple. "Damn, I missed."

He lowered his head and licked the misplaced ketchup off. She laughed, her fingers stealing into his hair.

"Let me try that again." He dripped ketchup on her other nipple. "Damn my terrible aim."

He sucked the tangy ketchup from her nipple, loving the way the rosy peak hardened against his tongue. He stroked the bud vigorously with the center of his tongue until she shuddered and made that maddeningly sexy sound in the back of her throat. His cock hardened instantly.

He was done for. Again.

He lifted his head and dribbled ketchup on her lower lip. Her tongue darted out between her lips.

"Hold it. It's my mess. Only fair that I clean it up." He leaned over her and kissed her deeply.

Her lips tasted spicy, like sausage. Which reminded him. He hadn't finished his breakfast. He broke away from her hungry kiss and looked down at her. "Do you want some hash browns?"

She chuckled. "You know what I want, Brian."

"Hash browns." He climbed from the bed and retrieved the bag of food from the surface of the dresser.

"I think maybe you *are* boring," she teased, watching him from the bed.

He glanced at her, liking the way "Property of Brian" looked written across her body. He wondered if he could talk her into getting a tattoo to make his claim permanent. Climbing back onto the bed with her, he covered the ketchup with chains of small potato rounds. When he had them spread to his satisfaction, he lowered his head and licked one off her body.

"Yeah, hash browns are definitely boring," he said.

She grinned at him. "I think I like being your plate."

He chewed and swallowed his ketchup-coated hash brown. "You don't mind the mess?"

"I assume you're going to clean up after yourself."

"You have a lot of faith in my self-control."

She traced the angle of his jaw with her finger. "I do. I bet you can resist making love to me for at least ten minutes."

He licked another hash brown off her chest. "You have a lot more faith in me than I do." He plucked a hash brown from her chest and popped it in her mouth before slurping several more into his mouth. Ten minutes? He wished he was buried inside her right now. He fed her several hash browns in quick succession and made a pig of himself by eating as fast as he could. Eagerness had gotten the better of him.

She giggled as he licked the food off her belly. "I guess you are hungry."

"Starving!"

After they finished the hash browns, Brian lapped the remaining ketchup from her silky skin with broad strokes of his tongue. She shuddered beneath him and tugged at his hair.

"You're driving me crazy," she gasped, her head tossed back, her back arched.

Encouraged, his tongue moved to her breast, up her shoulder, along her neck to her ear.

He traced the outer edge of her ear with his tongue. She groaned, her fingers tangling in his hair. He settled his body on top of hers, cursing the inventor of clothes, and suckled her earlobe, nibbled it, sucked it again. Her thighs spread for him and he sank between her long, shapely legs. His mouth moved to the pulse point under her ear near her delicate jaw. She shuddered. He brushed his hands along her arms and shoulders, delighting in the feel of her soft breasts pressed against his chest and the heat of her sex permeating the fabric of his jeans.

He kissed his way along her jaw to her chin and finally her mouth. She sucked at his lips, her tongue eager against them. His cock throbbed. He leaned his hips away from hers slightly and unfastened his pants. The Beast, as she called it, sprang free, craving her moist heat. He knew he should take his time with her, work her into a frenzy, make her beg him to possess her, but he could only concentrate on the memory of how it felt to be buried inside her without a rubber.

He took his cock in his hand and probed the hot, moist entrance to heaven. She relaxed beneath him with a sigh. He looked into her eyes as he entered her—languidly filling her with one achingly slow thrust. Her back arched with pleasure, but she didn't look away. They stared at each other, relishing the connection between them. He slid in and out of her slowly, not wanting to find release, just wanting to experience her. To become a physical part of her. To feel her. To know her.

"Myrna," he whispered.

"Brian."

Yeah, Brian. Not Master Sinclair. Brian.

He had everything he wanted. He needed. Right here. This woman. He knew she wouldn't appreciate his sentimental thoughts. She didn't want to hear that he loved her, no matter how clearly he felt it. So he just stared into her eyes while their bodies came together, apart, together, and swallowed his words where they settled as a lump in his throat.

Chapter 16

MYRNA ROLLED OVER, HER ARM LANDING ON BRIAN'S flat stomach. Sheets of paper crinkled beneath her. She smiled. He'd had a very productive day of song writing, and she'd be bow-legged for life. His arm moved to wrap around her back, drawing her closer to his side.

"At this rate, I'll have the entire new album written by next week." He paused. "Except you're leaving in two days."

He didn't sound very happy about the idea. He frowned. She smiled. She hoped the band accepted her as their tag-along. She really did want to spend more time with Brian. He rocked her world in more than one way.

"Do you think the guys are up yet?" she asked.

He tilted his head back to look at a digital clock on the side table. "It's two already?" He sat up. "Yeah, I'd say they're up."

From the bed, he collected the sheets of music he'd composed, peeling one off Myrna's sticky back when she rolled over for him. She needed a shower. And about a liter of water. She'd gotten quite a work-out in the past five hours. Treadmills had nothing on this man.

"I can't wait to show this to Trey." Brian held up one of the scores. The one he'd written while fucking her hard on the floor. "He's going to flip."

"I can't wait to hear it. It sounded fantastic when you were screaming it at me."

He beamed like a kid at Christmas. "Yeah, it's good, I think."

Myrna crawled from the bed, unsteady on her feet. "I still need to talk to the band. Should I wait until after you've gone through all your new music with them?"

"What do you want to talk to them about?"

"You're included in this," she said.

"In what?"

"I want the entire band to make the decision. So when we're talking this over, I don't want you to think of me as your lover."

"Yeah, that's possible." He laughed. "Not!"

He set the sheets of music on the dresser near the door and wandered around the bed. He drew her naked body against his, hand sliding over the curve of her ass. "So tell me what this is about."

She kissed his jaw. "I have to talk to all of you at once," she insisted.

He pouted. "I'm not special?"

"In this case, no."

He sighed. "All right, I'll call this band meeting for you." He found his discarded pants and slid into them, fastening them around his slim hips. "Get dressed. I'll be back."

He picked up his sheets of music and left the room shirtless and barefoot.

Myrna found the bags of items she'd purchased that morning and dressed in her new clothes. Cheap, but functional. Better than a suit. But a suit would have made her seem more professional when she asked the band for this favor. She searched the floor for her discarded suit and held it up, deciding if she should change into it. It was a wrinkly mess. The door opened. Brian peeked in.

"I've got the guys all together. You ready to talk to us?"

She smiled, tossing her suit on the bed. She slipped on the sandals she'd bought and searched for her purse to retrieve her grant acceptance letter. "Have you seen my purse?"

"I think it's by the door."

"Right. Thanks."

She walked past him, dropping a soft kiss at the corner of his mouth. He closed the bedroom door and followed her. Locating her purse on a counter, she pulled the letter from inside. "Where are they?"

Brian stared at her bare throat above the flowing, green tank she wore. "You look hot." A glazed look came to his eyes.

"Earth to Brian," she said. "Your band members. Where are they?"

He closed his eyes and shook his head slightly. "On the other bus."

Guitar music and boisterous conversation came from the open door of the second bus. Myrna climbed the stairs, nervous for some strange reason, and entered the vehicle. A large group of men stood, sat, or perched in a circle around the main room. She saw all the band members and several familiar faces from the show in Chicago. Roadies. Trey had an acoustic guitar in his hands and was strumming notes written across a piece of paper splattered with chocolate syrup.

Trey stilled his guitar strings. Heads turned and all eyes fell on Myrna. She flushed. "Hello."

"Myrna!" Eric said, wrapping an arm around her shoulders. He was still wearing Brian's hat. She bit her lip so she didn't laugh.

Her eyes moved to Sed's face. He sat in a captain's chair watching her. He was undeniably the leader of this band. His presence radiated from his body like a monarch's. If he said no, she was certain the rest of the band would take his side. Sed was the one she'd have to convince.

"You smell like Brian," Eric said in her ear.

Her face hot, she pushed him away. Eric squeezed around her and sat beside Jace on the beige leather sofa.

"So what's this about?" Trey asked, setting his guitar on the floor at his feet. He sat next to Jace on the sofa across from Sed. All the roadies watched her curiously. Brian wrapped an arm around her waist, and she leaned against him for support.

She grasped the letter tighter. Why was she so nervous? She didn't want Sed to tell her no, that's why. She wanted a reason to... She glanced at Brian. He smiled gently, offering encouragement. Maybe it was better if they told her to get lost. She'd have a much easier time not falling for their lead guitarist.

She focused on Sed. "I have a favor to ask of you."

"Anything, Myrna." He seemed sincere.

"I need a million dollars to pay the ransom on my kidnapped poodle," she said.

Sed's jaw dropped.

She laughed. "Kidding."

Brian burst out laughing. "Oh my God, did you see the look on his face?"

"Fuck you, Sinclair," Sed said.

"Sorry, Sed, I couldn't resist," Myrna said. "You looked so serious sitting there."

"I respect you, Myrna," he said. "Or I did."

Every male occupant on the bus stared at Sed with his mouth hanging open. Myrna wasn't sure why his statement shocked them so much, but she pressed on. "In truth, it's for work. My research."

"Which part of me would you like to study?" Sed asked, grinning.

She flushed once again, flustered. The man was all alpha male. She didn't think a woman existed who wouldn't react to him.

"Your groupies."

"I didn't know you swung that way, Myr," Eric said. "Can I watch?"

"You want to study my groupies?" Sed asked.

"Well, not just yours." She glanced at each member of the band in turn. "Trey's, Jace's, Eric's." She looked up at Brian. "Brian's."

"I don't get it," Jace said.

"That's because you don't have any groupies," Eric said, punching him hard in the arm. Jace shoved him. Eric climbed to his feet, his hands balled into fists. Myrna flinched.

"Knock it off, Eric," Sed demanded.

Eric hesitated, glanced at Sed, and then plopped down on the sofa, his jaw flexing as he clenched his teeth together.

"Myr, what are you asking for?" Brian asked. "Specifically. I mean, why do you need our permission to study our groupies? It's not like they're our property."

They were, in a way, but that's one of the things she planned to study. "Well…I was hoping I could go on tour with you for the summer." She forced her eyes from Brian to Sed. "I know I'll be a burden, but I'll try to stay out of your way. The grant includes a stipend for the band for allowing me to travel with you and to cover my expenses— ten thousand dollars. You can have the entire sum."

Sed laughed, his head thrown back, the deep sound rumbling through his broad chest. "You've got to be fucking kidding me."

Her hopes plummeted. She bit her lip and lowered her gaze. Why did her heart feel like a big lump of ice in her chest? It wasn't that big of a deal. She could find another band. A less famous one that could use the money. She turned to leave and ran into Brian's chest.

He wrapped his arms around her and squeezed. "I say she comes with us."

Sed's laughter trailed off. "Well, of course she's coming with us. She's your fucking muse, Brian. I just can't believe this amazing stroke of luck. She's offering to pay us to help you write songs."

She turned her head to look at Sed. "No, you've got it all wrong. I'm not doing this to stay with Brian. This is for work."

Sed grinned. "Like the reason matters. Yeah, I say you're welcome to tour with us. What do the rest of you say?"

Trey blew a huff of air through his lips. "Have you seen these licks Brian's been writing?" He swept a hand toward the stack of music on the table. "I was prepared to kidnap her *and* her little dog. Yeah, she stays. Of course she stays."

"No objection," Jace said.

"I have one condition," Eric said. He lifted a finger into the air.

"Whatever you're going to ask, the answer is no," Brian said.

"Damn." He scowled. "But—"

"No."

"Fine, since you insist, she'll sleep in my bunk with me. The sacrifices I make for this band."

Myrna shook her head at Eric in disbelief.

Brian took her chin between his finger and thumb and lifted her face to look at him. He searched her eyes and then lowered his head to kiss her. The grant letter tumbled from her fingers as she clung to the skin of his bare chest. Three months with Brian? Yeah, she might be able to handle that.

Chapter 17

"IT'S JUST A FEW MORE DAYS, BRIAN," SHE SAID INTO her cell phone as she walked to her car after work. "I have a bunch of things to take care of here first. I do have a life, you know."

"It's just… I'm going crazy with missing you."

She smiled. "I miss you, too. Thanks for the flowers, by the way."

"Flowers?"

"Don't play coy. They were signed, *See You Soon*, so it had to be you. And how did you know gladiolas were my favorite flower?"

"I should have sent you flowers, but I can't take credit. Who would send you flowers?"

"They weren't from you?" She bit her lip. Who would send her flowers? Her parents maybe? Or one of her sisters?

"No, they weren't from me. Is some bozo hitting on you?" He sounded more upset than he should be.

"Nah. Probably from my parents. So, where will you be on Saturday? I should be able to get out of town by then." She unlocked her car and slid her laptop case across the front seat.

"Saturday? That's five days away!"

"Friday night? I might be able to swing that, but it doesn't look good. I need to pack. Get all my obligations in order. The workweek doesn't end until Friday, and final grades are due tomorrow. I'll be up all night grading." She smiled to herself, knowing the reason for her being behind in her grading was on the other end of the line. Every minute spent with that reason was worth missing out on a night of sleep. "Be patient just a little longer. I promise I'll make it up to you."

"I just miss you."

"Brian, we've only been apart for one night."

"I know. I know." He sighed. "Let me check the schedule."

She climbed into the Thunderbird and waited for Brian to speak.

"Friday. Um… We'll be in Nebraska. Looks like Lincoln."

"That's about four hours from here."

"That's not far," he said, an excited edge to his voice.

"What time is your show?"

"We go on at ten. We have three bands opening for us. The actual show starts at six-thirty."

"I'll probably miss it, but I'll try to get there. I will see you afterward. I promise."

"Or we can skip the show, meet in Vegas, and get married."

"No, we cannot."

"Are you sure there isn't some guy making his move on you?"

"Good-bye, Brian."

He sighed. "I'll call you later."

She flipped her phone closed and tossed it into her purse. She backed the car out of her parking space and headed for her apartment on the north side of the city.

Brian was already getting too close. Too clingy. She

didn't do clingy. It made her nervous. And jealous? Jealous led to protective. And protective drove her nuts. She liked him, probably more than she should, but she wasn't prepared to make a long-term commitment. And he kept bringing up this marriage thing. She knew he was joking, but still…

Marriage? Myrna shuddered.

Chapter 18

MYRNA PARKED HER CAR BEHIND THE LIED CENTER in Lincoln, Nebraska. The throbbing sounds of the concert rattled her dashboard. The drive had been long and uneventful, but she was tired. Driving four hours after a full day at work and an insane amount of packing wasn't advisable. She climbed from the car and headed for the end of the barrier fence. She'd just wait for the band on the bus and send a roadie after her luggage.

A security guard in a bright yellow shirt stopped her from entering the area in front of the waiting buses.

"I'm with the band," Myrna told the guard. He had a six-pack stomach. The kind produced by consuming a six-pack of beer every night.

"I've heard that before," he said. "You can't go past the barrier."

"So I'm just supposed to wait here until the band comes out and validates my story."

"That's the only way you're getting past me."

She sighed loudly, too tired to be patient. "Are there any roadies around? They know me."

"Promising roadies favors won't get them to lie for you."

"Ugh! I could strangle you. When does the show end?"

He checked his watch. "Forty minutes or so."

She might as well sit in her car. "When Brian or any of the other guys blow through here, tell him Myrna

Evans is waiting in her car. And she's not very happy about it after driving for four hours."

"You're Myrna?"

"Yeah."

"ID?"

She shuffled through her purse until she found her driver's license. She handed it to him. He inspected it carefully as if she were some fifteen-year-old trying to sneak into a nightclub.

"All right," he said finally, handing her license back to her. "That guitarist guy kept coming out here asking if anyone had seen you before their show started."

She smiled. Eager to see her, was he? The guard shoved the metal fence piece slightly so she could squeeze between two of the barriers. "Thanks for keeping my guys safe." She patted him on the cheek and walked the inside of the barrier toward the building. Several fans milled near the back door, waiting for the band to come outside. Maybe now would be a good time to do a preliminary survey for her research.

Nothing formal. She didn't have her survey questions set yet, but she could do a few informal interviews to get a better idea of how to ask questions. The hardest part about studying psychology was getting the questions worded properly to avoid leading the subject or introducing her personal bias.

She approached a young scantily clad woman.

"Hello," Myrna said to the woman. "Can I talk to you for a few minutes?"

"How did you get on that side?" she asked.

"I'm with the band."

She glanced at the security guard and whispered to Myrna, "Can you get me backstage?"

"No. Sorry. Why do you want to go backstage?"

"So I can meet Trey Mills. Why else?"

"He's a great guy. Incredibly talented," Myrna said. "What do you know about him?"

"Uh, everything. His birthday is June 9th. He has seventeen tats and twelve piercings. His real name is Terrance, which he hates, so he goes by Trey. His middle name is Charles. Trey was born and raised in Los Angeles. His best friend is Brian 'Master' Sinclair, who he met when he was eleven and they started a band called Crysys in eighth grade. He had a dog named Sparky when he was a kid. It got hit by a car. You know their song, 'Good-bye Is Not Forever'? Trey wrote that about his dog. He—"

"Okay, you do seem to know everything about him. Why do you want to meet him?"

"Duh. He's Trey Mills."

"Yes, I know who he is. Why do you want to meet him?"

"I love him. I want him. I need him." She clutched her hands in front of her chest and rolled her eyes for emphasis.

"And what do you hope comes from this meeting?"

She laughed. "A baby. Are you a reporter or something?"

"No, I'm just curious. So you want to have sex with Trey Mills?"

"Yeah, of course. Don't you?"

Myrna laughed uneasily. "I have other interests. Have you had these feelings for any other men? Study their lives in detail, think you know them, profess to love them, and try to have intercourse with them?"

She shrugged. "Just other band members."

"Let's say that Trey isn't interested in you, but Jace Seymour invites you to the tour bus for sex, do you go?"

Her brow furrowed. "Yeah, I'd do Jace. He's hot. He might introduce me to Trey. A win-win situation. You know what would really be awesome? A threesome with Trey and Master Sin—"

Myrna lifted her hand to silence her. "So how do you act toward regular men? Ones who aren't famous."

"What do you mean?"

"Do you regularly engage in promiscuous sex?"

The girl stared at her for a long moment. "Are you asking if I'm easy?"

"Are you?"

"Yeah, I guess." She shrugged. "Is there something wrong with that?"

"As long as you're okay with it, it's fine. Have you ever had sex with a man you've just met?"

She looked puzzled, as if thinking hurt her brain. "On a first date, you mean?"

"No, I mean, some hot guy comes out of that door, walks up to you, and says, 'Let's have sex.' Do you go?"

She scowled. "No, that's sick."

"Let's say Trey Mills comes out of that door, walks up to you, and says, 'Let's have sex.' Do you go?"

"Yeah. I already said I would."

"What's the difference between the first guy and Trey?"

She paused and then shrugged. "I know Trey."

"You know facts about Trey's life, but you don't *know* him. You've never met him, have you?"

"I *do* know him," she spat. "I love Trey. And as soon as he meets me, he'll love me back. Understand?"

"Yeah, I think I'm starting to understand, actually. I really appreciate your talking to me."

"So can you introduce me to him?"

"I'll put in a good word for you."

She smiled. "That would be awesome!" She pulled a tube of lip gloss from her tiny purse and applied several coats.

Myrna talked to several other young women while she waited for Brian to finish his show. A trend emerged among them. They all had similar attitudes. She even found a girl in love with Brian. Talking to her was weird.

"How long have you been in love with Brian?"

"He prefers Master Sinclair, actually." The girl rolled eyes surrounded with far too much blue eyeliner.

Myrna knew for a fact that he didn't, *actually*, but let Fangirl think what she would.

"Um," the girl continued. "I saw him live a couple of years ago, before the band got really famous. Have you seen him onstage?"

"Yeah."

"Isn't he sexy?"

"Yeah. He's definitely sexy."

"And when he fingers his guitar, like…" She wriggled her fingers in rapid succession. "It's like, oh my God, I want him, you know?"

"Yeah. I totally get that. How do you know you're in love with him?"

"I think about him constantly. I have every picture of him ever taken taped to my wall. I watch his videos in slow motion."

Creeped out, Myrna didn't bother suppressing a shudder. "Isn't that obsession, not love?"

"No, it's definitely love. I'd do anything for him."

She couldn't stomach talking about Brian with obsessed fans any longer. "Thanks for talking to me."

"Can you hook me up with Brian?"

Fuck no. She smiled at the girl. "I don't think he's interested, honey."

Maybe she should stick with studying the rest of the band's groupies, but avoid Brian's.

The back door swung open. Brian emerged, steam rising from his skin as the cool evening air hit his sweat-drenched body. He raced toward her and wrapped her in his arms, seeking her mouth for a welcoming kiss. Camera flashes went off. Something slammed into the back of Myrna's head. Hard.

She jerked away from Brian, rubbing her scalp. "Ow."

Brian looked down at her. "What's wrong?"

"Something hit me," she said, her eyes watery with tears. "It really hurt."

He retrieved a black ankle boot from the ground. "Who threw this?" he demanded, scanning the congregated fans.

Only one girl stood beyond the barrier with a matching boot on one foot and nothing on the other. Brian approached the girl and shook the boot in her face. She flinched. It was the same girl who had claimed to be in love with Brian minutes before. "Did you hit my girlfriend with this?"

"Your girlfriend!" she wailed.

"Your girlfriend?" Myrna murmured.

Myrna rubbed the lump on her head, stunned more by his words than being clobbered in the back of the head.

"I'm sorry, Master Sinclair," the fangirl said. "I love you. I love you."

"And you think hitting someone I care about in the back of the head will get positive attention from me?"

"I didn't mean to," the girl cried, tears pouring down her cheeks. "I'm sorry. Please don't be mad at me."

He shoved the boot into the young woman's chest. "Get out of here!"

He looked at the back of Myrna's head, fingering the lump there. She sucked a pained breath through her teeth.

"Are you okay, baby? I think this is bleeding." He looked down at his fingertips for signs of blood.

The rest of the band exited the building then. Sed paused in front of Myrna, who looked up at him, still grimacing in pain.

"What happened?" he asked.

"Some bitch hit her in the back of the head with a boot." Brian touched the lump on the back of her head again. She wished he would stop already.

"What is this?" Brian asked, fingering the back of her head again. "A scar? What—"

She twisted away from him. "It's nothing."

"Come on, let's get out of here," Sed said. They ignored the group of fans who were growing in number by the minute and went directly to the bus. Sed told the girls following him to wait outside.

Brian directed Myrna to a seat at the dining table and treated her scrape with peroxide from a first aid kit. The entire band was looking at her like she'd been in a horrible accident and was expected to die at any moment.

"I'm okay," she insisted.

"You've got to be more careful, Brian," Sed said. "You know what some of these fans are like."

"I wasn't thinking." Brian tossed a wad of wet gauze on the table and kissed Myrna on the back of the head. "I was just happy to see her."

Sed grinned. "Yeah, I get it. But be happy to see her in private. Okay? We don't want her to get any death threats."

"I don't know how you guys deal with some of this stuff," Myrna said.

"What stuff?" Brian asked.

"The fans. They honestly believe they know you. That chick who hit me knew more about you than I do. They say they're in love with you and they mean it. It's pretty twisted. They've never even met you."

"It gets us lots of pussy." Sed grinned.

Myrna chuckled. "I guess so."

"Are you going to party with us, Myr?" Eric asked.

"Not tonight, Eric. I've had a long day. I think I just need to go to bed."

"I agree," Brian said.

"We'll just leave you two lovebirds alone." Trey grabbed Eric by the arm and pulled him out of the bus.

"Take good care of her, Brian," Sed said. Jace nodded. They followed Trey and Eric out. The fans cheered their return.

"I'm really sorry about this, Myrna."

"It's not your fault."

"I shouldn't have kissed you."

"It was worth it. What I really wanted to do was tell that girl you were mine and she better turn her obsessive attention elsewhere."

He smiled broadly. "You did?"

"Yeah. Will you do me a favor?"

"Anything?"

"Go wash off your eyeliner. I want to be with Brian right now. Not Master Sinclair."

"Can Master Sinclair have a kiss first?"

"I'm not sure. I think my *boyfriend* might get jealous."

He smiled and leaned down to kiss her. She clung to his shoulders as he plundered her mouth. When he pulled away to gaze down at her, her heart throbbed with excitement. "You're right, Brian is a little jealous," he said. "But he's stoked that you called him your boyfriend."

She shrugged. "Boyfriend I can handle. It's that m-word I can't tolerate."

"Magical?"

"No, magical is fine. It's that other m-word."

"All right," he said. "Brian promises not to ask for a massage after a show anymore, even though he really, really enjoys it and was hoping you'd indulge him in a few minutes."

"You know what I'm talking about. Why do you keep asking me to marry you? It really bothers me that you joke about it."

"Who's joking?"

Her heart skipped a beat. "I hope you are."

Brian lowered his gaze. "It figures the first woman I ask to marry me thinks I'm joking."

Her breath caught. "The first?"

"Yeah, the first. Only."

He moved away from the table and went into the bathroom. Water splashed into the sink. Myrna took a deep breath and climbed to her feet. She had assumed he was the type to ask every girl he liked to marry him. Was she honestly the first? She still didn't want to get married—not ever—but she knew she should be more sensitive to his feelings. He couldn't understand why she kept turning him down. She should probably explain it to him. She fingered the lump on the back of her head and then the long, thick scar beside it.

She followed Brian and stood in the bathroom door, watching him scrub off his stage makeup.

"I'm sorry," she said.

"What do you have to be sorry about?"

"I didn't mean to hurt you. I thought… I didn't realize you treated me specially."

He looked at her. "Why wouldn't I? You are special."

She snorted. "Brian, you could have any woman you want. There's nothing special about me at all."

He shook his head in disagreement. "You sell yourself short, Myr. You're wonderful. And I don't want just any woman. I want you, but I guess you're totally against the idea of marrying me."

"Brian, I'm not against marrying you. I'm against marrying anyone. Besides, we barely know each other, how could you even contemplate such a crazy idea?"

"Sometimes you just know."

"Know what?"

"You know when it's real. This. You and me. This is real. I've never had anything that felt so real."

"And to me it's not real at all. It's like a fantasy."

He looked down at the sink. "Okay, that hurt."

"I'm sorry."

He looked up at her and smiled sadly. "Don't

apologize for your feelings, Myrna." He approached her in the doorway and touched her cheek. "I think I know what it is. Tell me about your ex-husband."

She flinched and turned away from him. He moved behind her and circled her waist with his arms, drawing her up against his body. She didn't realize she was trembling until his steady strength settled behind her.

"I don't like to talk about it." Her trembling increased as flashes of memories assailed her.

"I've got you," he murmured. "You're safe."

Safe.

Brian did make her feel safe. And for that, she'd tell him a little so he would understand there wasn't anything wrong with him. It was her. "Jeremy was a good man when I married him. He just drank sometimes, and when he was drunk, he became a different person. At first, he got belligerent every couple of months. And then, every couple of weeks. At the end, he was drunk every night. He'd accuse me of things, things I'd never done, never even considered doing. He thought I was having affairs. He was paranoid. Cruel. When I denied it, he'd—" A broken sob cut off her words.

She dashed away her tears. Why was she crying? She hadn't cried over Jeremy in years. She'd left him in her past. He couldn't hurt her anymore. But even she recognized that as a lie. He hurt her every day.

Brian turned her around and held her against his chest.

She wrapped her arms around him, drawing on his strength. "He'd threaten me until I admitted doing whatever he accused me of. Fucking some guy. Touching or flirting with or even looking at some guy with too much interest." Myrna looked up at Brian and his face blurred behind her tears. "You have to believe me, Brian. I never. I would never. I didn't cheat. Not once. I never even considered it." Her fingers curled into his shirt.

Brian's arms tightened around her. "I believe you." He rubbed his lips against the side of her head. "Did he hit you?"

She shook her head. "No, not while we were married. Strange as it sounds, I sometimes wish he had. It would have made it easier to leave. He mostly yelled. Made me doubt myself. Sometimes I can still hear his voice, screaming at me, calling me a whore. If our problems had stayed between us, I might have been able to deal with it, but Jeremy confronted several of my male coworkers and accused them of seducing me. He even got several of their wives involved. I had to leave my first faculty position because of it."

"Why did you stay with him?"

"I was stupid; I kept forgiving him. He'd say, 'I love you, Myrna. I love you. I love you. That's all that matters. I love you.' I believed it for so long. I don't know how many second chances he earned by bastardizing those three words. Hundreds. I can't even stand to hear them now. Those words repulse me. Remind me of my weakness. My stupidity. I think the worst part was, as a psychologist, I knew what he was doing to me—I *knew*—and hated myself for taking him back over and over again, but I couldn't break the cycle. I wanted it to work. But…"

Having already said too much, she bit her lip and fell silent.

His hand brushed over her hair and he kissed her temple. "But you left him, right? So you're not weak. You broke away."

"Yeah, I finally left him, but it didn't matter. If anything, it got worse. He stalked me. I thought he was going to kill me. I got a restraining order. He ignored it. They'd arrest him and he'd be out of jail almost immediately. He was a well-respected man in the community. Wealthy. Old money. Highly educated. Charming. Most people had no idea what he was really like. And those who did were too afraid of his family's affluence to do anything. After I left him, he followed me everywhere for months; his footsteps always echoed mine. I'd often find him standing outside my house. Watching. Leaving little love notes in places he knew I'd find them." She shuddered. "But because he never hurt me physically, they wouldn't do anything. Verbal and emotional harassment don't carry the same weight as physical abuse. I understand why, but it didn't make it easier to live through it."

Brian stroked her back, and her preferred numbness returned. Why was she telling Brian all these things? She'd never told anyone the full extent of her terror.

"The divorce," she whispered. "The divorce was horrible. He refused to sign the divorce papers, so we had to go to court and I relived the entire ordeal in front of a judge. The accusations. The things he said to me. How he humiliated me in front of people I wanted to respect me. Thank God the judge believed me and pushed the divorce through, even though Jeremy contested it. The day I was legally free of him, the day our marriage officially ended, was the best day of my life. I never want to be trapped like that again—by the word love or the institution of marriage."

"So after the divorce he finally left you alone?"

She shook her head. "He refused to accept it. He kept stalking me. Continued to refer to me as his wife. When I started dating again, he snapped. In his mind, I was cheating on him. I'm sure Jeremy slashed my date's tires while we were having dinner. Then one night he broke into my apartment and waited for me to come home. I don't remember much of it, just waking up in the hospital two days later." She took his hand in hers and lifted it to the uneven ridge on the back of her head. "This scar. He gave it to me. Hit me with the fireplace poker, knocked me out cold, beat me within an inch of my life, and then the idiot called an ambulance."

"Jesus Christ." Brian pressed his lips to her temple.

"He confessed to the whole thing and went to jail. I changed my last name, moved, and covered my tracks, so he'd never find me again." That's why she'd been so scared when Brian had found her so easily. She reminded herself that Brian had known to look in Kansas City. Jeremy would not. He couldn't find her. He *couldn't*. He didn't even know her name. But the flowers... Jeremy knew gladiolas were her favorites.

"Thank you for telling me," he said. "I understand a few things about you that were bugging me."

She *bugged* him? "What kind of things?"

He hesitated. "I... Well, I notice you tend to freeze up for a few seconds when we try something a little kinky."

She flushed. "You noticed that, huh?"

"It's like you, the real you, is this uninhibited, open, sexual being, but something makes you feel it's wrong. It's not wrong, Myrna. It's wonderful."

"Somewhere in my head I know that, Brian, but I'm damaged."

He squeezed her. "No. You're perfect." He kissed her temple again. "Perfect."

Her breath came out in a gasp and she tried to pull away, but he tugged her closer. "Please don't make it impossible for me to live up to your expectations, Brian. This is too much. Too soon. I can't handle it. I feel... trapped. Don't..."

Brian tilted her head back and gazed into her eyes. He kissed a stray tear from her cheek. "I'm not that guy, Myrna. I accept you for who you are."

"I know," she whispered.

"I would like to kill that guy, though. Do you have his address?"

She shook her head. "I have no contact with him. I haven't seen him in four years."

He held her quietly for several moments, and she reveled in the feel of his strong arms around her. So safe.

But still scary.

He tugged her back by her shoulders and stared down at her. "So I guess what you need most from me is emotional space."

"Yes."

"And time."

"And patience," she added.

He nodded. "I'll try to give you what you need, but it won't be easy. I'm pretty into you, Myrna."

She smiled, staring into his warm brown eyes. "I'm very much into you, Brian."

"I guess you wouldn't like me to use the l-word then."

"Not unless it's lips." She wrapped her arms around his neck and kissed him hungrily.

"Lips is a very good l-word," he murmured.

"Yeah, so is lust." She pulled his shirt off over his head and flicked her tongue over his nipple. "And lick."

"I'm particularly fond of let's go." He took her hand and tugged her toward the bedroom.

She laughed, following him. "That's two words."

"Semantics."

Chapter 19

MYRNA CRAWLED OUT OF BED, SLID INTO THE discarded white sundress she found on the floor, and stumbled toward the bathroom. They'd been driving two days straight to play a show in Florida. The band would play an hour, and then the crew would break down the set and be back on the road by midnight to head up the Eastern seaboard. She honestly didn't know how these guys maintained their sanity. All they did was ride on a bus all day and night, constantly moving from city to city with no time to enjoy the places they traveled.

After using the bathroom, she contemplated returning to bed but decided Brian would wake up and then she'd spend several hours with his slim hips between her thighs. Not that she ever considered that a bad thing; she just had work to do and found herself entirely too distracted to get anything done.

Myrna shoved a stack of papers to the side of the square dining table, sat in the she-didn't-want-to-know-why-it-was-sticky booth, and booted up her computer. Now that she'd designed an appropriate survey, she spent her evenings interviewing groupies. Her project was moving along beyond her wildest expectations, and she had a huge backlog of data. While she waited for a shoddy Internet connection, she sorted musical score sheets from pages of beer-stained data, pulled a sucker stick off one page, and eyed a mysterious brown spot apprehensively. The guys were slobs and had no respect for her personal belongings. She only tolerated the mess because she didn't feel it was her place to correct them.

She checked her email and answered half a dozen distraught messages from her graduate students. Myrna was working on creating a data spreadsheet when the bus slowed and pulled to a stop. She craned her neck to peek out the heavily tinted window on the other side of the bus. Another fast food restaurant? Gag!

Jake climbed from the driver's seat and stretched, his mouth opening in a wide yawn. He started when he noticed Myrna sitting at the table.

"I didn't know anyone was awake," he said. "Do you want some breakfast?"

"Coffee would be fantastic."

"One coffee coming up. Make that two. I'm about to pass out."

Jake exited the bus, leaving the door open so fresh air could circulate into the cabin. Myrna heard the unmistakable screech of her Thunderbird's tires next to the bus. The roadies were abusing the hell out of her car, and the miles were adding up quickly. As convenient as it was to have a car at their disposal, she was going to have to put it in storage. Driving the extra vehicle disrupted the roadies' sleep rotation, which she recognized as a safety hazard.

The bedroom door opened and Brian emerged. He blinked his eyes in the early morning sunshine and smiled at Myrna when his gaze focused on her. "There you are. I've been waiting for you to come back to bed for over an hour."

He didn't even try to conceal his nakedness or his

rock-hard cock jutting into the space before him. This was exactly why she hadn't returned to bed. He never allowed her time to catch up with her work. His diversions were always spectacular, so it wasn't as if she could say no. She didn't want to say no. Her body was already responding to his on some subconscious, primitive level. She'd expected their mutual delirium to decline now that they were together 24/7, but it intensified with each day. She'd never experienced anything like this. She was hopelessly, madly, deeply in lust.

"I was trying to get some work done," she said.

"Are you finished now?"

"Uh…" She knew she wouldn't be able to concentrate with images of naked Brian burned into her retinas. "I can take a little break. Actually, we need to do something with my car."

His eyebrows lifted and he grinned. "Great idea. Your car. I'll go find some pants."

"Wait, you misunderstood."

He'd already disappeared back in the bedroom, however.

He emerged a few minutes later in jeans and a T-shirt. Her heart thudded in anticipation. She climbed from the booth and went to find shoes while he used the bathroom. At the exit, they waited for Jake to climb the bus steps with two coffees.

"Oh, Brian, you're up. Here, you can have my coffee." Jake tried to hand a cup of coffee to Brian.

"Keep it," Brian said. "Myrna and I are taking the Thunderbird. We'll meet you in Tampa this evening."

"I don't think that's a good idea, Brian. You get lost in your parents' backyard." Jake handed Myrna her coffee.

She took a sip of coffee and made a face. Too strong and black.

"My parents' backyard is huge. But don't worry, we'll get there."

Jake shrugged. "I think Dave has the keys. I saw him get on the other bus a minute ago."

"Thanks, Jake. And dude, you look like shit. Why don't you wake Sed and have him drive for a while?"

"I'm all right. See you in Tampa." Jake chugged his coffee and headed for the bathroom at the back of the bus.

Brian led Myrna to the car, where she waited, sipping her bitter coffee, while Brian retrieved the keys.

Within moments, he climbed in next to her and started the car. "Did I even tell you good morning?"

She shook her head. "You don't think so well when all your blood's in your smaller head."

"Smaller?"

She laughed. "What I actually wanted to do with the car, before you jumped to conclusions, was find a place to store it while I'm on tour with the band."

"So you didn't want to suck my cock while I drive?"

"Well, yeah, now I do, but that's not why I mentioned the car in the first place."

Brian pulled out of the parking lot, leaving the tour buses behind. "It's nice to have the car with us. It's handy for errands and we can get away from the guys for a few minutes. Maybe we can get a trailer and pull it behind the moving van."

She smiled. "That would work perfectly." She slid across the bench seat and kissed him on the cheek. "The roadies will appreciate it, too. They all look like the walking dead."

"They'll get some rest soon. Just ten more days on the road, then we have a week off. You're coming out to Los Angeles with us, right?" He took her cup of coffee from her and took a drink. He winced, took another sip, and returned the cup to her hand.

"Los Angeles?" she said. "I don't think so, Brian. I can get caught up on my work during that time. You've got more tour dates after your week off, don't you?"

"Yeah," he said quietly.

"What's wrong?"

"Nothing. Shot down again." He fashioned his hand into a gun and mimicked shooting himself in the chest.

"Are you pouting because I have to work?"

"I don't pout."

Sure looked like pouting to her. "Are you *whining* because I have to work?"

"No, I'm whining because you'd rather work than spend a week in L.A. with me." Under his breath, he muttered, "Why do I always sound like the chick in this relationship?"

"Won't you be working on the new album anyway?"

"So?"

"So, it will do us both good to have a few days to collect our thoughts and get some work done. I have the damnedest time concentrating when you're near. All this slacking bothers me."

He took her hand and put it on his crotch. "Does that feel slack to you?"

"No one said you were slacking. You've been composing and putting on one awesome show after another." She loved to watch him when his attention was elsewhere. She could ogle him without making her infatuation blatantly obvious. The length of his black lashes fascinated her. When he blinked, her attention shifted to the harsh line of his well-sculpted cheekbone covered with a light shadow of beard.

"You're not slacking," he said. "You've been doing your survey things with the groupies."

"I have," she agreed, "but collecting the data is the tip of the iceberg. I have to analyze the data. Do statistics. Hopefully, find some interesting trends in the results and write journal articles for publication. This project is really important to my future and I have a lot of work to do."

"And I interrupted your work again this morning."

"I wish I could say it annoyed me that you're so distracting." She grinned and squeezed his cock gently with the hand still in his lap. His body tensed. "I'd be lying though."

Myrna placed an open-mouthed kiss under his ear and gently sucked his flesh into her mouth. His growl of approval made her nipples taut.

She unfastened his pants and found him lacking underwear. His cock sprang free, and she wrapped her hand around the base.

"Can you drive?" she asked.

"I am driving."

"With your cock down my throat?"

He grinned at her. "There's only one way to find out."

She kissed the corner of his mouth and lowered her head. She licked the length of him, drawing her tongue over the smooth skin rhythmically and blowing cool breaths across his flesh to draw delighted shivers from his body. He placed a hand on the back of her head, trying to urge her to suck him into her mouth. She resisted, wanting to tease him. She squeezed and relaxed her hand at the base of his cock while she trailed her tongue over his flesh. He grew harder. And harder. Myrna's own excitement began to get the better of her. A shame to waste something this hard in her mouth.

There was a loud honk as one of the tour buses pulled up beside them on the four-lane highway. Myrna sucked Brian into her mouth.

"Ah God," he cried. He hit the brakes.

Myrna jerked her head away so she didn't bite him as he swerved off the road. They drew to a shuddering halt on the shoulder, with two wheels on the pavement and two in the grass. He slammed the gearshift up into park and reached for her. "Turns out that no, I can't drive with my cock down your throat."

He slid across the bench seat and pulled her to straddle his lap. His hand moved under her sundress and pushed the crotch of her panties to one side. He grabbed her hips, shifted her forward, and then filled her body with his. His fingers dug into her hips as he encouraged her to ride him. The elastic of her panties cut into her flesh each time she rose and fell, fueling her excitement.

Cars flew past them at high speed. She wondered if they could see what she and Brian were doing in the middle of the front seat. It might make someone's morning commute a little more interesting.

Brian pushed the straps of her sundress from her shoulders and bared her breasts. He bent his head to suck and lick her nipples, pushing her breasts together as he attempted to get them both in his mouth at once.

"God, you're hot," he growled. He sank his teeth into

her tender nipple, and her body jerked before she shuddered with release. She tightened her vaginal muscles and rose up to excite him with fast, shallow strokes. His head fell back, his breathing erratic.

"Myrna. Myrna. You're going to make me come if you keep that up."

A flash of blue and red lights in the back window caught her attention. "You'd better hurry up about it. We've just been spotted by a cop."

"Shit!"

He rearranged her top to cover her breasts and his rapidly softening cock fell free of her body.

"You could have finished," she said. "He'll have to run the out-of-state plates before he comes to talk to us."

"I couldn't have finished. My balls are now hiding up in my belly."

She laughed and slid off his lap. She rearranged her panties and sat beside him. He slid behind the wheel and fastened his pants.

"It's not funny," he said.

"You're afraid of cops?"

"No, I'm afraid of jail."

"Ah, poor baby," she said, kissing his cheek. "I'd bail you out. Hopefully before Big Bart made you his bitch."

"How kind," he said. "And who would bail you out?"

"I'm sure Sed would bail me out for a favor."

Brian pinned her with an angry glare. "Don't even joke about that."

"A little cranky now, are you? I told you that you can trust me. I have no interest in Sed."

"You know, that's exactly what Angie said. And Kristie. And Jenna. And Bethany. And Samantha. And—"

Myrna's eyes narrowed. "You don't have to flaunt their names. I realize you've fucked a lot of girls."

"What? Are you jealous?"

"Why would I be jealous? This thing between us isn't serious. We're just having a good time."

"Of course." He slammed his fist into the dashboard.

There was a knock on the window.

"What?" Brian yelled at the glass. He took a deep breath and rolled down the window. "Can I help you, Officer?"

The car was still idling, but the trooper said, "Car troubles? Do you need a tow?"

"Everything is fine, sir," Myrna said.

Brian gripped the steering wheel. "Let me handle this," he growled at her. He gazed up at the police officer. "Everything is fine, sir."

The lanky man looked Brian over carefully, his hand resting on the service pistol at his hip. He turned his attention to Myrna, who sat demurely in her innocent-looking white sundress.

"Are you okay, ma'am? I heard some yelling and arguing as I approached."

"I'm fine." She smiled at him reassuringly.

"And why are you parked on the side of the road?"

Myrna glanced at Brian and grinned wickedly. "My companion was having a hard time driving, so he had to pull over."

"Have you been drinking, sir?"

"It's seven o'clock in the morning!"

"Or using?"

"What?" Brian calmed his tone. "No, I haven't been drinking or using drugs. I was having a hard time concentrating for...*other* reasons."

"I see." The officer didn't look convinced. "So you pulled over to switch drivers?"

"Yeah," Brian said. Myrna didn't know Brian was capable of blushing until that moment.

"You should do that at a rest area. It isn't safe to park on the side of the highway."

"Good point," Brian said. "Are we free to go?"

"Let me run your license, registration, and proof of insurance first. Make sure everything checks out."

Brian pulled his wallet from his back pocket and retrieved his driver's license. Myrna found the registration and insurance card in the glove box. She handed them to Brian, who offered the paperwork to the trooper.

"California license. Missouri plates." The officer shook his head and then carried the documents back to his patrol car.

"He thinks I'm a shady character," Brian said.

"You do look suspicious with all those skull and demon tattoos."

"You don't like my tattoos?"

"I didn't say that. I just said—"

"I heard what you said. Tattoos are suspicious."

"No, I said they make you *look* suspicious."

"Same difference."

"It's not the same. At all."

"You sure are bitchy this morning," he muttered.

Myrna's nostrils flared. "Excuse me. Did you just call me a bitch?"

"No, I said you were bitchy this morning."

"Same difference." Realizing she'd mimicked his words, she chuckled.

He grinned at her. "We should argue more often."

"Let me guess. It's turning you on."

"Yeah, my balls have come out of hiding and The Beast is ready to roll."

Her eyebrows rose suggestively. "Can I ride The Beast?"

He put his fingertips against her forehead. "You must be at least this tall to ride The Beast."

"Looks like I qualify."

"Secure your belongings and keep your arms and legs around the ride at all times."

The trooper cleared his throat outside Brian's window. Brian started and then glanced up at the officer as if they'd been discussing the weather.

"Everything checks out fine," the cop said. "You have no outstanding warrants, Mr. Sinclair. And the car hasn't been reported as stolen."

Brian scowled. "You sound surprised."

The officer laughed nervously and handed Brian his license and other papers. "Next time, make sure you do this at a rest area."

"A rest area?" Brian ducked his head to hide his grin. "Okay, next time we'll do it at a rest area."

Myrna laughed, leaning heavily against the passenger door as she clutched her midsection in hysterics.

"Am I missing something?" The cop scratched his head, a puzzled look on his face.

"Nope." Brian returned his license to his wallet. "She forgot to take her meds again."

Myrna slapped at him and wiped tears of mirth from the corners of her eyes. "Thank you for checking on us, sir," she said to the cop.

"Yeah, thanks a lot," Brian said.

Myrna burst out laughing again. The two men stared at her as she struggled to contain her hilarity.

"We'd better switch drivers now," Brian said.

He slid to the center of the seat and Myrna climbed over his lap to settle behind the wheel. She gave his crotch an appreciative squeeze beneath her skirt as they switched places. She waved at the trooper and rolled up the window before shifting the car out of park and easing back into traffic. Brian slid closer and squeezed her thigh.

"Now," Brian said, "let's see how well you can concentrate on driving with my head under your skirt."

She grinned at him and took his wayward hand in hers. "Wait until we get to a rest area. I already know I won't be able to concentrate with any part of you under my skirt." She squeezed his hand. "Not this." She lifted her hand to touch his lips. "Or these." She cupped his package through his pants. "And definitely not this."

"What about these?" He pulled his boot off and wriggled his socked toes at her.

"Hmmmm," she said, keeping one eye on the road. "I'm not sure about those."

Chapter 20

TAMPA 78 MILES. BRIAN SHIFTED HIS GAZE FROM THE green road sign to his watch. Eleven a.m.

"We've got plenty of time before we have to be in Tampa," he said. "Let's take a detour."

Myrna took her eyes off the road long enough to glance at him. "What kind of a detour?"

"I don't know. The spontaneous kind."

"I like spontaneous detours. We have to be careful not to get lost, though. No Master Sinclair means no Sinners show."

"We won't get lost. At your next opportunity, head west."

"That won't take us far. The Gulf of Mexico is west."

"Exactly."

She smiled. "West it is."

Within ten minutes, they were off the main highway and headed west. "It looks like it might rain," she commented, gazing at the western horizon.

Brian scowled at the bank of black clouds rolling in from the distance. It figured the weather wouldn't cooperate on their first real date. He hoped he could manage to keep his hands off her long enough to romance her a little. He had ten days to convince her to stay with him in L.A. In order to get her to comply, he'd need to seduce more than her body.

"Oh wow," she said. "Look at the water. It's gorgeous!"

"Not bad," he said. "California has spectacular beaches."

She glanced at him sidelong. "I suppose you mean in the Los Angeles area."

And she was on to him already. "San Diego is better, but yeah, Los Angeles isn't too shabby."

"Uh huh. I thought the beaches in California were toxic."

"Not all of them. Have you ever been to California?"

She hesitated. "Well, no, but I'm sure I'll get there eventually."

Did that mean she was considering joining him? Doubtful.

They entered a small gulf town. Every sign they passed had some depiction of a clam. Brian's stomach rumbled. "Do you like seafood?"

"It's okay. I'm not a fan of fish, but I love clam chowder."

"Manhattan or New England?"

"New England. The thicker, the better."

"Hungry?" he asked, watching little restaurants pass.

"Starved. As per usual."

"Let's find a place to eat."

"Just no fast food. I think I'd rather die than eat another french fry."

"Park over there." He pointed to the common lot at the end of the block. "We'll walk until we find a good place."

"How will we know?"

"Follow the locals."

"Good plan."

As soon as she pulled into the nearest parking spot, Brian climbed from the car and hurried around to her side to open her door. He watched her try to straighten her hair in the rearview mirror with her fingers. He liked to keep it in that "just took a toss in the hay" style. It suited her. And him.

He opened the door and she looked up at him.

"I look like crap," she said.

"Didn't your mother teach you not to lie?"

"I never lie."

"You just did." He took her hand and helped her out of the car.

"I have eyes, you know."

"They must not work very well. You look gorgeous. You always look gorgeous." He brought her hand to his lips and kissed her knuckles gently.

She surprised him by smiling instead of arguing. "Thank you. You're very good for my ego." She stared at the ground as she walked beside him. "Even if you are blind."

"Are you fishing for compliments, Professor Evans?"

She pointed to her face. "Does this face look fishy to you?"

He shrugged. "It is a little scaly."

Her mouth dropped open. "Oh really?"

"No, not really. I already told you that you were gorgeous. Everyone's going to wonder why you're hanging out with a thug like me."

"I'll tell them I've been kidnapped."

"They'll probably believe it."

She took his hand. He smiled, his heart warming. She could deny it all she wanted, but he knew she cared. "What that trooper said bothered you, didn't it?"

Actually, he hadn't thought about that trooper since his toes had been used in ways they'd never been used before. He shrugged. "Eh, I'm used to it."

She squeezed his hand. "I'm sorry to hear that. No one should have to tolerate being discriminated against based on their looks."

They paused at a street corner and waited for the traffic to thin enough for them to cross. Brian watched the patrons entering the restaurants in the vicinity. A construction crew, several office workers, and three well-dressed executives entered a small eatery in the center of the block. It didn't look fancy, so the food must be good. *Pam's Clams*. Myrna wasn't watching the pedestrian traffic. She was watching him again. He liked it when she couldn't keep her eyes off him. He pretended he didn't notice, but she stared at him a lot.

"Pam's Clams?" he asked.

"Huh?"

"Do you want to eat there?" He tugged her into the street and they hurried across.

"Fine with me."

By the time they were seated, every person in the place had gawked at Brian at least once. It was a small town, apparently not used to men with chains, tattoos, dyed hair, and leather attire. At least he wasn't wearing his stage makeup. Had he been drunk, he probably would have cussed them out, but Myrna's calming presence made it all seem unimportant.

"What sounds good?" Brian examined the small, laminated menu. Beer sounded good to him. Beer and battered fried clams with french fries. Unlike Myrna, he never tired of french fries.

"They have clam chowder in fresh-baked bread bowls." She looked orgasmic with delight.

"Is that what you want?"

"Yeah, and a salad. A huge salad. I miss vegetables."

The waitress appeared. "What can I getcha to drink?"

"Do you have lemonade?" Myrna flipped the menu over to search for their drink selection.

"Yeah." She scribbled on her order pad. "What for you, doll?" she asked, pointing the end of her pen at Brian.

"Corona. And we're ready to order."

He ordered for the both of them, and the waitress collected their menus before heading to the kitchen.

"We should take detours more often." Myrna reached across the table and lightly trailed her fingers over the back of his hand.

He smiled. "The tour bus does get pretty boring."

"I wouldn't know. You never give me the opportunity to get bored."

"That's been my plan from the beginning."

"I'll be in trouble when you finally get tired of me."

"I think you're safe for at least a century." He linked his fingers through hers and rubbed his thumb over the back of her hand.

"Are you always this sweet?"

His eyebrow shot up in question. "Sweet? Now there's something I've never been accused of before."

"Really? I'm surprised. You're so considerate and complimentary and generous."

"Actually, that's not typical of me. It's only because I lo—" He caught himself and shifted his gaze to the red-checkered vinyl tablecloth. "I like to see you smile." He'd almost spoken that forbidden word of hers. Had she noticed? When she didn't speak for a moment, he forced his gaze upward, expecting her eyes to be watery as she thought of that other man. That bastard he despised.

What was his name? *Jeremy*. Myrna wasn't teary-eyed though; she was staring at their joined hands reflectively.

"I do seem to smile a lot when I'm with you," she said, smiling as usual. "I guess that means you're charming, too."

He chuckled. "You forgot virile and sexy."

"No, I didn't."

"Are you saying I'm not—"

She glanced up at him. "I meant that I didn't forget. It's obvious, you know. Goes without saying."

"But you *could* say it."

"I could."

Their waitress returned with their drinks and Myrna's salad. While Brian sipped his beer, he watched her methodically move the cherry tomatoes and red onions to the edge of her plate.

"I thought you missed vegetables."

"I don't like raw tomatoes. And I thought I'd skip the onions so I could make out with the sexiest man alive after lunch without subjecting him to my death breath."

He grinned at her compliment. He was used to girls stroking his ego, but when Myrna did it, it made him happy. She had such an unusual effect on him. He didn't try to fight it. He was ready for this and hoped she'd come around soon. He knew he had to keep a rein on expressing these powerful emotions in front of her. The last thing he wanted to do was scare her away.

"You want it?" She speared a tomato with her fork and offered it to him.

"If you put some dressing on it." Can't have vegetables without dressing.

She dipped the little tomato into her cup of ranch

dressing and held it out to him. He chewed slowly, watching her devour her salad.

"So how much data do you think you need to enter into your computer?" he asked.

She glanced up at him, her fork halfway to her mouth. "Why do you ask?"

He was wondering how much of her time her work was going to take. "Just curious."

"Let's see. I've been doing about twenty interviews a night, each with forty-two questions. And there have been eight concerts, so that's about 6,500 pieces of data I need to enter. Give or take."

"That's a lot!" he sputtered. "You have to enter all that stuff by hand?"

"Well, yeah. I don't have an assistant in my back pocket." She laughed. "It's not the data entry that's hard, anyway. It's the statistical analysis and reporting the results in journal articles that takes so long."

"You're going to be really busy, aren't you?"

"I tried to explain that to you earlier. You seem to think I don't want to go to L.A. with you because I don't want to spend time with you."

He shrugged. Was he that easy to read?

"I don't want to go to L.A. with you because I want to spend *too* much time with you."

When he tried to respond, she popped another tomato in his mouth.

"So I hope you won't make it harder on me by getting all pouty."

He swallowed. "I don't pout. What if you get done with all your work early? Will you come with me then?"

"I'll consider it, but don't get your heart set on it."

"You don't want to meet my parents?"

She paled. "Your parents?"

"You realize who my dad is, don't you? You being a collector of guitar riffs and all."

"Uh." She paused. "I don't know any other guitarists with the last name Sinclair."

"He used a stage name. I can't believe you don't know this." He grinned. "I'll give you three guesses."

Her brow furrowed with concentration. "Is he as good as you are?"

Brian scoffed. "Better. Way better."

She shook her head. "Now I know you're making up stories."

She'd eat those words after she figured it out. Brian had stood in the shadow of a legend his entire career.

"Does he still play professionally?" she asked.

"The occasional reunion tour, but not really."

"Leftie?"

"No."

"Malcolm O'Neil."

"So you did know. I wondered how you didn't know something like that."

She dropped her fork and stared at him in shock. "Malcolm O'Neil is your father? Oh my God!"

If people weren't staring at them before, they were now.

He scowled in puzzlement. "You didn't know."

"I was joking when I said Malcolm O'Neil. He was the only classic rock guitarist I could think of who was better than you are." She grabbed his hand. "No offense." She dropped his hand and pressed her fingers to her forehead. "I mean, I think you're better than he is, but…"

Brian laughed. "Calm down, Myrna. Is that enough incentive to get you to Los Angeles? Well, they actually live in Beverly Hills."

"I couldn't," she said. "I'd make a total ass of myself."

"Like now?" He was teasing, but she glanced around the room and flushed in embarrassment.

Their waitress delivered their lunches. "Can I get you anything else?"

Myrna clutched her chest. "A defibrillator."

The woman's eyes widened. "Are you having a heart attack?"

"She's joking," Brian assured her. "Myrna?"

"I'm joking," she agreed, still breathless. "I can't believe you didn't tell me you were Malcolm O'Neil's son."

"You're Malcolm O'Neil's son?" the waitress asked. "Winged Faith's lead guitarist?"

"Don't be ridiculous," Brian said.

"You do sort of look like him, if you had huge sideburns and a chubbier face," the waitress said. "I saw them at Woodstock. That was right before they made it big. Do you play guitar, too, doll? You have that rock star look about you."

"A little," Brian admitted. He hoped she didn't make a scene. He'd been enjoying his obscurity, even if he had been the object of curious stares.

"I'd love to stay and talk, but I'm so busy," the waitress said. "Do you want another beer?"

He glanced at Myrna, who was cautiously slurping steaming chowder from her soupspoon. "Just water."

When the waitress left, he started eating his fried clams. They were grubbin'. Tender instead of chewy. Fried to a perfect crisp, yet not greasy. Deliciously seasoned. "Try one of these, Myrna." He placed one on her plate next to her bread bowl.

She bit into the fried clam. "That is good." She scooped some chowder on her spoon and leaned across the table. "Careful, it's hot."

Her chowder was good, too. "I know how to pick 'em," he said, grinning to himself.

"Then how do we always end up eating fast food?"

"It's fast."

"Hence, the name." She stole one of his french fries. "Now, that's a french fry."

After lunch, Brian headed for the restroom. On the way back, he cornered their waitress near the kitchen and convinced her to disclose the location of a nice, quiet beach. He left her a nice tip, double the cost of the meal, and escorted his lovely date back to the car.

"I'll drive," he said, opening the passenger door for her.

Myrna reached up and slid her fingers into the hair at the nape of his neck. She rose up on tiptoe to claim his mouth in a searing kiss. His heart skipped a beat when her tongue brushed against his lip. She knew how to get his blood boiling, but he had other things in mind for their romantic beach visit.

"Thanks for lunch," she whispered. "Are we going to Tampa now?"

"Not just yet."

Chapter 21

MYRNA LEANED FORWARD TO GAZE OUT THE windshield. A gorgeous view of the Gulf of Mexico stretched as far as the eye could see. Tall palms punctuated the narrow strip of white sand beyond the grassy dunes. Rough waves sloshed against the shore as the storm clouds in the distance continued to march across the landscape. Brian had driven half an hour into the middle of nowhere, but their venture off the beaten path had been well worth it. Here, she could imagine they were the only two people on earth.

"How did you know about this place?" Myrna asked.

He smiled. Smugly. "I persuaded our waitress to disclose her secrets."

She couldn't explain the pang of jealousy that pierced her chest. "Persuaded? Did it have anything to do with those amazing fingers of yours?"

"Not telling."

She slapped his shoulder and then opened the door. He grabbed her and pulled her across his lap, wedging her between his body and the steering wheel. "I just asked her where I could find the most romantic beach in the area. She called you a lucky girl and pinched my cheek as if she were my great-aunt Stella."

"I am a lucky girl," Myrna whispered. She touched his face, staring deeply into his eyes. She expected him to kiss her, but he didn't. He held her gaze until she had to look away.

"Let's go watch the waves," he said.

She nodded and slid from his lap.

They walked hand in hand to the beach. Brian settled on the sand and urged her to sit between his legs in front of him. He tugged her against his chest and rested his cheek against her hair as they gazed out at the water.

"There's something about the ocean that feels eternal," he murmured, his breath tickling her ear. "I get disconnected when I don't see it for a while."

"I find it soothing," she said. "Being from the Midwest, I haven't seen the ocean many times."

"Then what makes you feel connected to the universe?"

She thought for a moment. "Gazing at the stars at night. You can't really see them well in the city. Whenever I go visit my parents in the summer, I look up at the stars for hours."

His hands stroked her bare arms. "Can I look up at the stars with you sometime?"

"I would like that."

"And meet your parents?"

"I wouldn't like that."

"Are you ashamed of me?"

She could tell by the tone of his voice that he was teasing, but he wasn't far from the truth. She wasn't ashamed of him, but they'd be ashamed of her for dating him. Brian wasn't what they would consider son-in-law material, or even boyfriend material. But they had adored Jeremy, so they obviously were poor judges of character.

"Of course I'm not ashamed of you," she said.

And she didn't want to discuss her parents. She wished he would stop trying to pry into her private life.

She kicked off her sandals and wriggled her toes into the warm sand with a contented sigh. She reached for Brian's left boot. "Take your boots off." He helped her tug it free and then the other one. She pulled his socks off and tucked them into his boots. He drew her close to his chest again and she stroked the tops of his bare feet with her fingertips—tracing the ridges of tendons and toying with the light dusting of hair on the top of his foot.

"Even your feet are sexy," she murmured.

"Is that your favorite part of me?" he asked, his low voice so close to her ear goose bumps rose on her nape.

"You should know my favorite part of you."

"Do you call it The Beast?"

She grinned. She figured that's what he'd think. "No, but The Beast made the top ten."

"Top ten, huh?" He kissed the edge of her ear. A shiver raced down her spine. "Is it my lips?"

She shook her head. "No, but they're also in the top ten."

His tongue brushed against the pulse point beneath her ear. "Tongue?"

"Nope. My top ten seems to be awfully crowded."

He laughed and hugged her. "It's obviously my hands." He held them in front of her and flexed his fingers.

"Wrong again. Good guess, though."

"Okay, I give up," he said.

She turned her head to look at him. "It's your brain."

He covered his surprise with a laugh. "Well, I can honestly say that was the last thing I thought you'd say."

"Why? It controls all your other parts. It's responsible

for your amazing talent, both on the guitar and in bed."
He grinned. She'd never figure out why he needed her
to compliment him when he had groupies screaming his
godliness at the top of their lungs. "It makes you say
things that make me laugh and make me think. And it
gives you that sweet, romantic streak that I try so hard
to resist. Your personality, your talent, heart, soul. What
makes you, you. It's all in that amazing mind of yours.
Don't get me wrong. The body that carries it around is
fabulous, too."

"I think I'm blushing."

She turned to face him, kneeling between his thighs,
and wrapped her arms around his neck. "Is that really all
it takes to make you blush?"

She kissed him tenderly. He kissed her in return but
didn't turn up the heat like he usually did.

When she leaned back to look at him, he smiled and
said, "Let's go for a walk."

"Did you lock the car?"

He sighed. "You're always so practical, Professor."

"You mean boring."

"Yeah, that's what I meant." He rolled his eyes at her
and shook his head. He stood and helped her to her feet.
While she brushed the sand from her skirt, he scooped
his boots and her sandals from the sand and tossed them
into the car before locking the doors. When he returned
to her side, he claimed her hand and led her toward the
angry surf. The cool wind from the approaching storm
blew Myrna's hair against her face, and her skirt tangled
around her legs.

"Great day for a walk!" she called over the crashing
waves. "I think we're going to get caught in a downpour."

Brian glanced up at the sky. "We might."

He kept walking, her hand tucked in his. The wet sand squished between her toes. She curled them under with each step, liking the way it felt. A wave washed across her feet, and she danced sideways. "That's chilly."

"The water's really churning. If you want to go back—"

"A crab!" Myrna bent to snatch a half-dollar-sized crab out of the sand. She held it up by the edge of its shell to show Brian. The creature's legs wriggled as it tried to run away in midair. "Isn't he cute?"

He chuckled. "He's a little small to make a good meal."

"I wouldn't let you eat him." She turned the crab to look it in its stalked eyes. "Isn't that right, Pinchy?"

"You named him?"

She carefully placed the little crab back in the sand and nudged it toward the surf. "Run for your life, Pinchy. I've seen the way this man eats."

"Hey!" Brian grabbed her from behind, his fingers digging into her ribs. She laughed and struggled out of his grasp, taking off at a full sprint along the edge of the water. She could hear Brian's steps just behind her. She slowed slightly so he could catch her. He collided with her back and she stumbled. Her arms shot forward to catch her fall, but Brian rescued her from an impending face-plant and scooped her up into his strong arms.

She laughed, slightly breathless, and gazed up at him.

"I almost bit the dust," she said, "or I guess it would be sand. You rescued me."

"Does this make me your hero?"

"You were already my hero."

He grinned and rolled his eyes. "Yeah, right. I've never met a woman who needed saving less than you do."

"That's not true. You've saved me from loneliness." She kissed him. "And sexual frustration." And she hadn't heard Jeremy's accusations in her head for a while now.

He chuckled. "Then you must be my hero, too."

She kissed him again, her arms stealing around his neck, her fingers intertwining with the long silky hairs at the nape of his neck.

"Don't get me all worked up," he murmured against her lips.

"Why not? We've got the beach all to ourselves."

He groaned into her mouth and hugged her closer. She deepened the kiss. He pulled away. "That's enough of that."

He set her to her feet, and she wobbled unsteadily. He took her hand and started walking again. She walked beside him silently, pondering his reluctance. This wasn't like him. Had she done something wrong?

"Have you worked up the courage to ask yet?" he asked, scooping a piece of driftwood from the beach and flinging it into the waves.

"Huh?"

"Why I'm not rutting around on you in the sand yet?"

"Oh, that. I hadn't noticed."

"We're here to get to know each other better. And I don't mean in the biblical sense of the word. We already know each other that way. I've decided no sex until after the show tonight."

"No sex?"

"That's right."

"And why do you get to decide?"

He grinned. "It's more of a personal challenge. Do you have any interest in getting to know me at all? Personally, I mean."

"Can't I just Google you? Isn't your entire life somewhere online?"

He scowled. "Probably."

She reached up and smoothed his forehead with her fingers. "Don't make that face. Tell me how Sinners was formed."

He glanced at her. "Do you want the real story or the more theatrical, online version?"

"The real story. I can always read the online version later."

He smiled nostalgically. "Trey and I were the outcasts of Beverly Hills."

"You lived in Beverly Hills?"

"Yeah, my dad got rich and famous when I was a kid, and Trey's dad is a plastic surgeon, so we lived in the Hills."

"No shit? I never would have guessed that in a million years."

"We didn't really fit in with the other rich kids, and everyone else on the planet hated us because we were rich. So we stuck together. We played guitar. A lot. In eighth grade, we started a failing band—"

"Crysys."

He chuckled. "I thought you hadn't Googled me."

"One of Trey's groupies mentioned it."

"Ah. Anyway, we got seriously heckled during a party gig in the tenth grade. By Eric Anderson."

"Eric Anderson?"

"He's since changed his last name to Sticks."

Myrna chuckled. "I always thought it was strange that a drummer had the last name Sticks."

"Yeah, he's lame that way and had it legally changed. Anyway, when he heckled us, Trey got so pissed. I honestly don't think he'd ever been that pissed before. He dove off the stage and tore into Eric. Trey was always fighting back then, but this was beyond brutal. Blood everywhere. Shattered Eric's cheekbone. Good thing Trey's dad is a plastic surgeon."

"Trey?" She found that hard to believe. He didn't seem the type to hit someone that hard.

"Yeah, I was always breaking up his fights. I got my ass kicked more than once because of that chip on his shoulder. He's chilled a lot in his old age."

"Yeah, twenty-eight is ancient." Myrna rolled her eyes at him.

"It's a hell of a lot older than sixteen. Anyway, after he and Eric beat each other to a pulp at this chick's birthday party, Trey said something like, 'Yeah, well, if you can do better, why don't you prove it?' And Eric did. He's fucking gifted, you know?"

"He is a great drummer," Myrna agreed.

"That's what he plays now, but he can play guitar, too. Bass. Piano. Sax. Violin. Ukulele. Fuckin' kazoo. You name it, Eric wails on it."

"I didn't know that."

"And he has a fantastic voice. He sang and played bass for Crysys until Sed found us, and then he switched to drums permanently."

Myrna's brow furrowed. "Why did he switch to drums?"

"He's the best drummer in the business. And…Sed gives him an inferiority complex."

"Sed gives everyone an inferiority complex. The man has more self-esteem than fifteen supermodels combined. I think he was a monarch in his past life or something."

"Henry the Eighth, probably." He made a cutting motion across his throat complete with sound effects.

Myrna laughed.

"Sed's always been confident like that," Brian said. "He came up to us after a Crysys gig and insisted he was our new singer. Sixteen years old and he knew his place on the planet. He said he'd been looking for a band to front. Told Eric point blank that he didn't have the star quality or looks to front a band and he should go hide behind the drum kit."

Myrna flinched. "That was harsh."

"He was right. We were going nowhere. If it weren't for Sed, we'd still be playing birthday parties for spoiled rich girls. He had a plan, knew where he wanted to go, how to get there, and he made it work. For all of us. Sed changed the band's name to Sinners and we searched for a bassist to replace Eric."

"Jace."

"Nope, we had a different bassist before Jace. Jace has only been with us for two years. Our first bassist was Jon Mallory—Eric's best friend in high school. Unfortunately, Jon was usually too high to find the stage. If you could swallow it, snort it, smoke it, or shoot it, he'd do it. We tried to help him get through it. He was in rehab half a dozen times, but he almost brought us all down with him, so we had to let him go. It was hard to kick him out of the band. Just making the decision was hard, but watching Sed tell him… Fuck. That was brutal. He was like family, you know, especially to Eric. I feel sorry for Jace at times. He has big shoes to fill, and Eric sure doesn't make it easy for him."

"Drugs and alcohol mess up so many lives." She'd probably still be married to Jeremy if it weren't for his drinking problem. "So how'd you find Jace?"

Brian smiled at her. "He came highly recommended by Trey's older brother." He winked. "Okay, your turn."

"My turn?"

"This isn't a one-way conversation."

"Wait. What do you mean he came *highly* recommended by Trey's older brother? Wink. Wink. Were they lovers or something?"

Brian's shocked expression was quickly replaced by raucous laughter. He stopped walking and wrapped his arms around his belly as he continued to laugh. She thought he'd fall into the sand and start rolling back and forth at any moment.

"What is so funny?"

Brian wiped tears of mirth from his eyes. "Oh God. I needed that laugh."

He hugged her to his side, still chuckling sporadically.

"I still don't understand what's so funny. Trey is gay, isn't he? I mean he doesn't really look or act the part, but…"

Brian tugged her by the shoulders to face him and looked down at her. "Gay? No, not really. Trey is more of an equal opportunity lover. His brother is straighter than an arrow, however. And I think Jace would rather die than be with a man. Just picturing Jace Seymour and Darren Mills together struck me as hilarious."

Darren Mills? Why did that name sound familiar to her?

Brian continued, "What I meant was Jace tried out for

Dare's band and they were going to hire him, but their original bassist decided to stay after all. So when Dare found out that we needed a bassist to replace Jon, he sent Jace our way. We were lucky to get him. I mean, he's good enough to get an audition with Exodus End at the tender age of twenty-one. That's pretty fucking amazing."

Myrna's eyes widened. "Exodus End?" That's where she knew the name Darren Mills. Or rather, Dare Mills. Her lead-guitarist-senses tingled at full throb.

"Please don't tell me you've never heard of Exodus End."

She grabbed him by both arms and gave him a vigorous shake. "Of course I've heard of Exodus End. What planet do you think I'm from? Do you know them? Personally?"

"Uh, yeah. Trey's brother is their lead guitarist."

"No shit? You're teasing me, aren't you?" She didn't know why she'd never connected Trey and Dare Mills. "Holy Toledo!"

"Holy *Toledo*?" He laughed at her sudden bout of fangirlness. "Nope. Not teasing. You know, we're opening for Exodus End at the end of June in Las Vegas. Maybe you'd like to meet him."

Her heart rate accelerated. "Oh my God. I've died and gone to heaven. He's the absolute best guitarist on the planet."

"Hey…"

Brian was pouting again. Myrna patted his cheek affectionately. "I'm sorry, Brian, but he is."

Brian chuckled. "You could at least pretend I'm the best while in my presence. Especially since I have your car keys."

"You know I think you're awesome."

"On second thought, I won't introduce you to him. Not only is he a better guitarist, he's better looking, taller, more famous, richer. He'll steal you away from me."

"Not a chance." She stood on tiptoe to kiss him, a contemplative look sliding into place. "Richer, you say?"

"All right, that does it."

She squeaked in surprise when he lifted her off the ground and tossed her over his shoulder. He gave her ass a playful swat.

"You, Miss Evans, are being very naughty today."

"I'm always naughty."

"True. But today's naughtiness is poking holes in my fragile ego."

Myrna laughed and slid her hand down the back of his pants to toy with the smooth skin on his butt.

"None of that." He pulled her hand out of his pants.

"Since when is your ego fragile?"

"Since I met you."

"So is that the attraction?"

"Huh?"

"Well, I can't help but wonder why you're so interested in me when you can get much better-looking and younger women who jump at your every command."

"There are no better-looking women than you. Though I admit most of my girlfriends have been younger. Okay, all of them have been younger. I didn't know what I was missing."

She slid her hand into the back of his pants again.

"What are you doing?" he asked, pulling her off his shoulder and setting her back to her feet.

"Convincing you to let me down." She grinned up at him mischievously. "It worked."

He shook his head at her. "You never do what I expect you to do."

"Then maybe that's the attraction."

"Is it really so hard for you to believe that I've fallen for you for no reason whatsoever?"

"There has to be a reason."

"It's more like there is no reason for me *not* to fall for you. You're everything I want."

"I don't think I'm cut out to be a rock star's girlfriend." It made her heart ache to say it, but it had been weighing on her mind a lot lately. The more she talked to Brian's groupies, the more jealous she became. She knew he had no real interest in them, but they were so available, and she knew she wasn't there for him emotionally. What if he decided she wasn't fun anymore? That he needed more than she could give him? Would he toss her aside? And why did that thought bother her so much anyway? It wasn't as if they were serious.

He touched her cheek gently. "Then don't be a rock star's girlfriend. Be Brian Sinclair's girlfriend."

"They're one and the same. Your life is so interesting and mine is so ordinary. Boring. I'm an over educated farm girl from the Midwest."

"And I'm a college dropout from the West Coast."

"You went to college?"

"For one semester."

"What did you study?"

"Girls, mostly."

She poked him in the ribs. "Why did you drop out? You could have graduated summa cum laude."

"Sinners signed a record deal."

"Wow, that young? Did your father help you get it? He must have millions of connections in the business."

Brian laughed. "Here's the thing about my dad. He never once encouraged my music career. We cut our first album with a small independent label and went on tour in a piece-of-shit van for eight months. I've never been hungrier in my life. It didn't help that Jon kept stealing our cash to feed his drug habit. When I finally swallowed my pride and asked my dad if he could offer some support, do you know what he said?"

"What?"

"'If you really want to follow this dream, you need to suffer for it so it means something to you if you manage to reach the top.' He wouldn't even buy me new guitar strings. Ever try to play a solo missing your second string? Uh, yeah... Not good."

"Did you hate him for that?"

"Nah, I thought I did, but now I realize he was right. If you don't have to work for something, you just don't appreciate it as much."

Myrna nodded in agreement. "Yeah, I can understand that. That's why I went for my PhD. My parents didn't support me when I went to college. They thought I should get married and have kids. Stay home and raise them like a clone of my mother. So when I was in college, I worked my ass off at odd jobs while most of the traditional students had their tuition and bills paid by their parents. Going it on my own really did make me appreciate it more. I worked harder to get good grades, too. I wanted to prove I could do it."

He hugged her. "See, we do have more in common than great sex."

"Fabulous sex."

"Amazing sex."

"Yeah, let's have some of that right now."

He squeezed her butt. "Not until after the show."

"You know I love a challenge, right?" She closed the gap between them, her hand cupping his half-hard cock through his pants. "I'm very determined to get what I want."

"Something else we have in common." He removed her hand from his crotch. "Will you watch the show tonight instead of interviewing the groupies?"

"Will you make it worth my while?"

"Do you have to ask?"

"Brian, I'm incredibly turned on right now."

He groaned. "You don't plan to make this easy on me, do you?"

"Do you have to ask?"

He stared at her for a moment, worrying his lips with his tongue. He looked ready to pounce on her, and she was more than ready to be pounced on.

"Farmer's daughter, huh? I know nothing about farming," he said. "What's that like?"

She sighed in exasperation. "You really are going to make me wait until tonight, aren't you?"

"Yep."

She turned and started walking back the way they'd come. They must have walked at least a mile down the beach. "Farming is boring," she called over her shoulder. "That's all you need to know."

He jogged to catch up with her. "You're not going to get out of this that easily. Tell me something about yourself."

A rumble of thunder reverberated above. Myrna looked up at the black clouds. "I think we should make a run for it."

"It's too late. We'll never outrun it."

The first fat rain drops splattered across Myrna's upturned face. "We're going to get soaked."

She dashed toward the car at a full run. When she reached the car, she tugged the door handle. Locked. Brian had the keys. She turned to find him sedately walking up the beach.

"Hurry!" The clouds opened wide and drenched her within seconds. "Brian, hurry!"

She could see him grinning to himself as the rain plastered his hair to his head and his shirt to the contours of his chest. He didn't pick up his pace though. She stood there, shivering, waiting for him to open the car. When he finally reached her, he drew her chilled body against his, his strong hands splaying over her back.

"Open the door." She reached behind her to grab the door handle.

"No." His fingers sank into the wet strands of her hair, tilting her head back. He stared into her eyes until she released the door handle and slid her hands up his belly and chest. He lowered his head and kissed her, his fingers easing her dress's zipper down. He brushed the straps of her sundress from her shoulders, exposing her breasts to the elements. Goose bumps rose to the surface of her skin, and her nipples ached as they beaded in the chilly air. Rivulets of rain trickled over her shoulders, between her breasts, down her belly. Brian lowered his head and collected water from her skin with his warm tongue. His mouth burned over her flesh.

Myrna groaned and reached for his fly. If she unleashed The Beast, she knew he would end her torment and possess her body with his. Hopefully right there on the cold, slick hood of her car. Before she could release the button of his jeans, he grabbed her wrists in a steely grip and pinned her arms to her sides.

"No," he said.

He gazed up at her, water dripping from his nose and chin.

"No?"

"That's what I said."

He sucked her beaded nipple into his mouth. His hot tongue rubbed against her sensitive flesh, drawing moans of pleasure from her. She struggled to release her wrists from his grip, wanting to bury her fingers in his hair, but he refused to set her free. She jerked her body away from his devilish tongue, changed her mind, and twisted to offer him her other breast.

When he didn't immediately draw it into his mouth, she looked down at him. His devilish grin made her heart throb.

"Do you want me to suck this one, too?" He stroked her neglected nipple with the tip of his nose.

"Yes."

"Yes?"

"Yes, please."

He drew the flat of his tongue over her offered nipple and she shuddered.

"I think my work here is done." He stood straight and released her wrists.

"Oh no it's not." She threw her body against his, her fingers tangling in the wet strands of his hair, her mouth seeking his in a desperate kiss. He kissed her in return, while drawing the bodice of her dress to cover her breasts and zipping the garment at her back.

He pulled away all too soon. He looked up at the sky, blinking rain from his eyes. "I don't think this rain is going to let up any time soon." He retrieved the keys from his pocket and unlocked the car door. Before she could climb into the warm, dry interior of the car, he asked, "Have you changed your mind about going to L.A. with me yet?"

"Is that what this is about?"

"Nope. I just want you to want me really, really bad."

"Mission accomplished."

Chapter 22

"WE'RE LOST," MYRNA SAID. "PULL OVER AND I'LL get directions."

"We are not lost," Brian said. "We're in Tampa. That does not equal lost."

"But we're not at the stadium and your show starts in an hour."

"I am aware of that."

"Then stop being so stubborn and pull into that gas station. I won't tell them you're lost. I'll nonchalantly ask them how to get to the stadium."

"I'm not lost." He released an exasperated breath and pulled into the gas station. "Just buy a map." He handed her his wallet.

She sighed. She guessed rock stars were still men. Was there a man in existence who would admit he was lost? She hurried into the store, not caring that her hair looked like she'd stuck her tongue in an electrical outlet. While she purchased the map, she asked the clerk for directions.

Within minutes, she was back in the car with Brian. She handed him the map.

He started to unfold it. "What street are we on?" He glanced around as if expecting to find an arrow labeled "you are here" nearby.

"No idea. But the clerk said you should go about eight blocks that way." She pointed down the street.

Brian grinned at her. "See. We weren't too far off."

"Then get on the interstate heading south. Take the third exit."

"Oh…"

"Turn left and follow the signs. It's about twenty minutes from here. Assuming we don't get lost again."

"Shit."

He backed the car up and headed in the direction Myrna had indicated. By the time they found the tour buses behind the stadium, it was nine thirty.

They hurried up the bus steps and were confronted by Sed. "Where the fuck have you two been? The show starts in half an hour."

"Get out of the way. I need a shower. You can yell at me later." Brian shoved Sed aside and peeled his shirt off over his head as he headed for the bathroom.

"Well, hurry up!" Sed called unnecessarily.

Myrna followed Brian into the bathroom. If she was going to watch the performance, she needed a shower, too. She had sand in unimaginable locations and her once-white dress was now a grimy shade of puce. Brian turned on the water in the tiny shower and unfastened his pants.

"Are you going to watch?" he asked.

"I'm going to join you."

"I don't have time for you to join me." Now gloriously naked, he stepped into the shower.

"I need a shower, too. I'm filthy."

Her dress and panties landed in a pile on top of her discarded sandals. She stepped into the shower behind Brian, who was lathering his hair with shampoo. She hadn't planned on touching him, just sharing the flow of water, but when this man was naked and within reach, she couldn't help herself. She kissed his shoulder and his entire body jerked.

"Myrna, please don't. I'm already horny as hell. I don't need to go onstage with a hard-on."

"It's your fault for turning me down on the beach." She pressed a kiss to the center of his back, the unpleasant taste of shampoo in her mouth. "And on the hood of the car." She kissed his other shoulder. "And inside the car." Her hands circled his body to slide up his belly. "And every hotel we passed for seventy miles."

"Can I help it if my girlfriend always wants my body?" She could hear the smile in his voice.

"Like you don't contribute to my uncharacteristic, insatiable appetite."

"What do you mean, *uncharacteristic*?"

"Do you really think I usually need hours of sex every single day? When I have a steady lover, thirty minutes twice a week is sufficient."

"Really?" He turned to rinse his hair, scrubbing with both arms above his head. Her hands moved around him to massage his firm buttocks. She kissed his collarbone.

"So do I not satisfy you, or what?" he asked.

He knew better, but that ego of his needed constant feeding. "You always satisfy me. Now that I know how good it can be, I want you all the time."

He grinned down at her. "I feel exactly the same way." She didn't believe him, but now was not the time to call him on his fib. He had to be onstage in twenty minutes.

They switched places so she could wash her hair while he lathered his body with soap and insisted on rubbing the bar over her breasts and belly. They switched places again so he could rinse his body while she finished washing. Squeaky clean, he kissed her and left her to her own devices.

After hurrying through the rest of her shower, she wrapped a towel around her body and rushed to the bedroom. Brian was already half dressed. She watched him tug a T-shirt on over his head. He reached for a studded belt and laced it through his belt loops.

"What should I wear?" she asked.

"You look damn good in that towel." The slight growl in his voice made her throb between her thighs. They were both worked up to a sexual frenzy. How would she ever get through watching his entire show without pouncing on him in front of a stadium full of fans?

She grinned. "I don't think that's wise."

"Wear a shirt with buttons," he requested. "The rest, I don't care." He sat on the end of the bed to put on his socks.

"Stockings and garters?"

He glanced up. "Yeah. I like those."

"Panties? Or should I not bother?"

With a growl, he grabbed her and tossed her onto the bed. He tugged her towel open and sucked one breast into his mouth. The other he squeezed firmly. The hard bulge in his pants pressed against her thigh.

"Don't you have to be onstage in fifteen minutes?" she asked nonchalantly, though had he taken the time to explore the neglected parts of her body, he'd have found her hot, swollen and wet.

He lifted his head to look down at her. "You're driving me crazy, Myrna."

"You've been driving me crazy all day."

He grinned. "I think my plan worked a little too

well." He moved from the bed, his gaze roaming her body as he stood over her. "I've got to go dry my hair, shave, and put on my stage makeup. Get dressed. And try not to look too sexy. I have to get through the next hour without touching you. If you decide against panties, please don't tell me."

She chuckled and climbed from the bed in search of clothes. She dressed as fast as she could. She wished she hadn't mentioned garters. They took too long to put on. By the time she found Brian in the bathroom, he was ready to go. He wore a red felt replica of his discarded lucky hat instead of going for the messy hairspray-and-gel look he usually sported onstage. He didn't have time to do his hair. The eyeliner he couldn't do without, however. That was signature. She wiped at a smudge under his left eye with her thumb.

"I didn't have time to paint my nails." He gazed at the remnants of chipped black nail polish on his index finger.

She hugged him. He trembled against her with a typical case of preshow jitters. "No one will notice," she said. "I just need to do something with my hair and face. I'll be right out."

"You wore a suit? You know what it does to me when you look prim and proper."

She grinned. "That's why I wore it."

He kissed her on the forehead and trotted toward the bus exit. "Don't be late."

"I wouldn't miss it."

Chapter 23

THE CROWD WAS RESTLESS AND CHANTING, "SINNERS. Sinners. Sinners," at full volume. As Murphy's Law would have it, Brian needn't have rushed so much. There was a problem in one of the video panels behind the drum kit. Their effects technician was working to get it back online as quickly as possible, and the crowd grew louder and more restless with each passing moment. Brian pulled Jace aside to talk to him while they waited for the signal to go onstage.

"Can I borrow your restraints tonight?" Brian asked.

If Brian's request surprised Jace, he didn't show it. "Do you know how to work them? You don't want them too tight or too loose."

"If I can't figure them out, I'll call you."

"The suspension chain should be in the case with them. Make sure her knees can touch the bed or you'll hurt her shoulders."

"I was just going to tie her down, flat on her back."

Jace shrugged. "I guess that's okay, but then you only have one side of her body to work with."

Brian glanced over his shoulder to make sure Myrna hadn't arrived backstage yet. Trey was rocking up and down on the balls of his feet, his energy level sky high. Eric was twirling his sticks and pointing them at people as if he were a gunslinger. Sed looked bored and slightly annoyed by the chick who was hovering around him. No sign of Myrna.

"So I should restrain her arms above her head? I wondered why you put that hook in the ceiling over the bed."

"You'll both get more out of the experience that way. Don't forget to blindfold her."

"Blindfold her? Why?"

"So she really feels what you're doing to her. You've never blindfolded her?"

Brian shook his head.

Jace massaged the silver earring in his left lobe and then the one in his right. "You haven't been working all of her senses then, have you?"

"What? You mean like sight and touch?"

"Yeah. Taste, smell, hearing, pain, hot, cold, vibration, pressure, smooth texture, rough. All the senses."

Brian felt a little strange asking a guy five years his junior for sexual advice, but he wanted tonight to be something Myrna would never forget. "Tell me more."

"I suggest you blindfold her to heighten the senses she doesn't use much. Let her watch you jerk off and come on her, but otherwise keep her eyes covered. And since she creams over your guitar playing, I'd get her some earphones and make her listen to our music the entire time. Then she won't hear what's coming at her either."

Brian decided Jace knew what he was talking about. "What else?"

"Ice and candle wax. Keep her guessing on hot and cold."

Brian felt like he should be taking notes.

"And put the shirt you wore onstage over her nose. Chicks like the scent of their man. I know it sounds weird, but trust me, she'll get off on it. You probably want to bring stuff to put in her mouth. Different flavors. I've got some samples in the case with my restraints, paddles, and stuff, but you'll probably want some extras that are specific to her."

"Do you sit around all day and think up this shit?"

Jace grinned deviously. "Why do you think I'm so quiet all the time?"

The clicking sound of approaching high-heeled shoes drew Brian's attention to Myrna. Ice. Candle wax. Paddles. Blindfolds. He must have looked suspicious, because she looked at him quizzically when she drew to a stop beside him.

"Why are you looking at me like that?" she asked. "And why aren't you onstage yet? I thought I was late."

"Technical difficulties."

"Okay, guys. We've got it fixed," one of the roadies called.

The stadium lights went down. The crowd roared.

"I'll see you soon," he murmured close to Myrna's ear. He adjusted his earbud so he could hear himself and the band play without going deaf in front of the amplifier. He rushed up the stage stairs and trotted across the set to his normal spot: stage left.

His heart thudded as it always did when his feet first touched the stage. Eric started the first song with several taps on his cymbal followed by a drum progression. By the time Jace entered the song with his bass groove and Trey strummed the rhythm riff, Brian's apprehension had vanished. A purple light bathed his body from above and he entered the song with a solo— his guitar a familiar friend. When his solo segued into the lead riff, Sed's voice growled in his ear and the stage lit up all at once. He could hear the crowd roar over the music.

He looked out at the fans but could only see the first few rows due to the stage lighting. A great crowd. Fists in the air, heads banging, mouths voicing the lyrics. When the crowd was pumped up, the band was pumped up and they always gave a better show. Too bad Brian kept getting distracted by Myrna in his peripheral vision. He probably should have let her interview the groupies tonight. As horny as he was, he would have had a hard time concentrating even if she hadn't been standing there. Trey bumped up against him to gain his attention and nodded toward the end of the stage, opposite where Brian normally played.

Brian nodded in agreement. Over there, he couldn't see Myrna, but she'd still be able to see him. He headed across the stage.

When it was time for Brian's solo, Sed turned toward Trey, shook his head in confusion, and located Brian to his right side. He made a gesture as if to say "what the fuck are you doing over there," but shrugged and moved to the back of the stage to stand next to Jace. Trey switched Brian's amp for him with a pedal on the floor and entered the second half of the solo where they dueled. They met in the middle of the stage as they did every show, strumming each other's guitars, which took extreme concentration. Tonight, Brian found himself facing Myrna directly. When she raised her fist in the air and cheered for them excitedly, he missed a long series of notes. Trey laughed at him and shook his head. Shit! Some fan with a video cell phone was sure to post that flub on the Internet.

Brian just had to pretend she wasn't there and he should be able to get through the next nine songs. His plan worked fairly well until the rest of the band left the stage so he could play his recently composed solos. The solos he'd written while making love to Myrna. He usually tried to get the crowd pumped up at this point, but tonight, he decided to just play. They'd either respond on their own or they wouldn't. Selfish of him? Maybe.

He stepped up to Sed's mic in the center of the stage. "I've been writing a lot of new music lately," he said. "I'm going to play a little for you now. You'll be hearing variations of it on the new album." He paused. "Which should be out early next year."

The crowd roared their enthusiasm. Brian closed his eyes and let his fingers find their own way. He allowed his mind to drift back in time to the moment he originally composed this solo. The memory was so distinct, he could feel Myrna's warmth, smell her skin, and hear her uneven breathing in his ear. It wasn't until he reached the end, and Trey appeared at his side, that he heard the crowd.

"Are you trying to steal the show, Master Sinclair?" Trey asked.

Brian put his hand over the microphone. "Actually, I wish it was already over."

Trey grinned at him and pushed his hand aside so he could talk into the mic. "I think Master Sinclair is more worked up than normal, don't you? I mean, where the fuck did that come from? Amazing." Trey paused, his eyes scanning the crowd. "The ladies are looking especially sexy tonight, don't you think so, Sinclair?"

"Lady Sinners are always sexy."

"You know what I think he needs?" Trey said. "A couple dozen bras to work him up even more. What do you say, Lady Sinners? Do you want to help him out?"

"I'm good, thanks." Brian glanced over his shoulder at Myrna. She was laughing as the bras began to fly onto the stage. Within a minute, every size, style, and color of bra imaginable littered the stage at his feet.

Several young women, perched on the shoulders of their boyfriends, lifted their shirts to show off their bare breasts. He hoped Myrna continued to be okay with this. He had to play along now. Brian retrieved a red lace bra from the stage and hung it on the end of his guitar.

Trey picked up a leopard print bra. "Who does this sexy thing belong to?" he asked, dangling it from one finger.

A girl situated several people behind the barrier started to scream excitedly and jump up and down. They couldn't hear her on the stage, but her wild gesticulations made it obvious that the bra was hers.

"Can I borrow this, sweetheart?" Trey asked. He draped it on the end of his guitar. "You can pick it up after the show in person. I'll help you put it back on."

The young woman unexpectedly dipped out of sight. People in the crowd lifted her, now unconscious, and passed her to the front of the crowd over the barrier.

"Damn, Trey, you made her faint."

"Sorry about that. They just can't handle my sex appeal." He smoothed one eyebrow with the side of his finger.

Brian snorted with laughter. "Apparently, they've never seen you passed out with your head in a toilet."

The guys in the audience hollered their approval.

Sed appeared between them and looped an arm around each of their shoulders. "Are you fuckers going to talk all night, or are you going to play some music?"

"I guess we can play our new dueling solo," Brian said. "Do you want to hear it?" he asked the crowd. "It's up to you. We can collect bras all night as far as I'm concerned."

He glanced over his shoulder at Myrna again. She was still smiling at his antics. God, he loved her. Perfect. She was absolutely perfect.

A few more bras landed on the stage. The girls flashing their breasts had the guys in the crowd worked into a frenzy.

Brian leaned closer to Trey to speak to him without the microphone picking up their conversation. "I hope you're ready to play the new dueling solo live."

He shrugged. "I wouldn't want you to be the only one to fuck up in front of ten thousand people tonight."

Brian grinned at him. "Try to keep up."

Sed hung several bras on his mic stand. "I'm saving these for later," he said, and then moved to the side of the stage and stood next to Myrna. Brian saw him wrap an arm around her shoulders and plant a kiss on her temple. He also saw her deliver a well-placed elbow to Sed's ribs. Knowing Myrna could hold her own against Sedric Lionheart's libido, Brian forced his attention back to the task at hand.

He started the solo and paused while Trey echoed him. He repeated the string of notes an octave higher and up-tempo. Trey followed him with no problem. Down an octave and faster. Trey still kept up without missing a note. In reverse and faster still. Every time Trey made it through a segment, the crowd's noise level intensified. Faster and faster they dueled until Trey's echoes were blending with Brian's lead. Trey leaned against his back and instead of dueling, they played in harmony. When the last note rang from the speakers, the crowd erupted into cheers.

"I guess we'll call that a draw," Brian said. First time ever.

"I think you need some practice, Master Sinclair. You usually smoke me in three rounds."

"Maybe we'll have to start calling you Master Mills."

Trey grinned. "I'll beat you one of these days."

Half the crowd was chanting, "Mills. Mills. Mills. Mills." The other half chanted, "Master Sinclair. Master Sinclair."

Eric's pounding bass drum reminded them to get on with the rest of the show. When Jace returned to the stage, he snitched several bras from the floor to decorate the neck of his bass.

Trey had taken Brian's mind off Myrna, but seeing Jace reminded him what he'd be doing in less than thirty minutes. In the future, he'd make sure to make love to her *before* a stage performance, not after. His entire body ached.

Through the next six songs, Brian was glad his fingers knew the music, because his head just wasn't in it. He scarcely moved from a three-by-three foot area of the stage. He crossed the stage occasionally to switch out his amps with the foot pedals on the floor in front of his regular location, but his usual showmanship was nonexistent. Strangely, Jace took up his slack. No hiding out by the drum kit for him tonight. He even talked into the mic at one point. The crowd loved it. Trey and Sed teased him for stepping out of his shell, and he flushed, but Brian just played what he was supposed to.

When the final note of the last song rang out, Brian tossed his pick into the crowd and headed backstage. He handed his guitar to a random roadie, plucked the earbuds from his ears, and grabbed Myrna. She gasped in surprise when he slammed her against the side of a speaker and covered her mouth with his. He filled one hand with her soft, full breast. The other slid under her skirt to find the bare skin of her thigh above her lace-topped stocking. He pressed his cock, hard as stone, against her mound.

"Horny much, Brian?" Trey called as he passed them. "Jesus Christ, dude."

Brian removed his hand from Myrna's thigh long enough to flip off Trey.

Trey pressed up against Brian's back. "Don't offer if you don't plan to put out," he said in his ear and gave its lobe a playful nip.

Brian elbowed Trey in the gut and he backed off. Brian tore his mouth from Myrna's and looked down at her flushed skin. Her glazed eyes. Swollen lips. She looked as turned on as he felt. They needed to get to the bus. Stat.

"Great show, Jace," Eric said as the two of them passed.

Brian glanced over his shoulder. Jace was grinning from ear to ear. "Thanks."

"Someone else seemed to have their head up their ass tonight." Eric swiveled his head to glare at Brian. "Yeah, I mean you."

"I think his head was up something else," Trey

said. "Myrna, you need to escort Master Sinclair to the nearest bedroom before he humiliates himself and comes down his leg in front of his friends."

Myrna grasped the hand Brian had squeezing her thigh and squirmed from between his body and the speaker. "Follow me."

Jace caught his arm. "Should I stop by in about ten minutes?"

Brian nodded slightly and pulled free of Jace's grip to follow Myrna to the tour bus. She ran most of the way. He scarcely got the bedroom door closed before she was against him, kissing him feverishly.

His plans to make love to her evaporated. He could only think of one thing. He had to thrust into her body. Bury his cock in her slick, warm flesh. He couldn't wait. She must have been of the same mind. Her hands were already releasing the fly of his jeans. When his cock sprang free of his pants, she gripped it in one hand and shuddered violently.

"Oh God, Brian. Do me hard. Please."

She didn't need to beg, but he liked it. He backed her into the bed, and she tumbled backward. They both struggled to get her skirt up. He scarcely comprehended that she had opted against panties, and only found himself grateful that it made it easier for him to find her. She spread her legs wide, resting on her elbows to arch her back.

He guided his cock into her body, filling her with one violent, deep thrust. Her entire body spasmed as she came. Hard.

"Oh God. Oh God!" she screamed. She continued to shudder as he began to withdraw and thrust into her as hard as he could. He would follow her to bliss soon. The urgency to spill his seed inside her was already building.

His breath hitched unexpectedly. He was closer than he thought. He didn't have time to delight in his build-up toward release. His body stiffened and he erupted inside her. He rocked against her with a startled cry as he came, and then collapsed on top of her. He trembled uncontrollably for several moments as he attempted to catch his breath.

"Jesus, I'm sorry, Myrna. Was that even thirty seconds?"

She touched his cheek tenderly and kissed him. "You never last long after a show."

"Yeah, but that had to be some kind of world record."

She shook her head. "You lasted longer than I did. I came as soon as you put it in."

He chuckled. "You always make me feel better. Even when I'm terrible."

She knocked his hat off his head and buried her fingers in his hair. "I wouldn't say you were terrible. Just too excited before you started, but you can make it up to me. We'll try it again from the beginning."

Before she could kiss him, there was a timid knock at the door. Jace. Brian smiled.

"I plan to make it up to you all night," he said. "I hope you're ready."

"For what?"

"A special surprise."

He pulled out of her body, tucked his cock in his pants, and fastened his jeans. He admired her exposed thighs for a moment before tugging her skirt down to cover her.

Jace knocked again, and Brian went to answer the

door. Jace carried a huge suitcase into the room, set it on the floor, and opened it. He pulled out a chain.

"I'll set this up for you," Jace said. "It's important to get the length right."

Brian glanced at Myrna. Her eyes were wide as she stretched her neck to peer into the suitcase.

"Don't worry, honey. I don't think he'll use half that stuff," Jace said to her.

Her frightened gaze moved to Brian. "What are you going to do?"

"Ask you to trust me."

"I do trust you."

Jace climbed up on the bed. "Kneel right here, Myrna."

She looked at the chain in Jace's hand. "What are you going to do?"

"Nothing."

She turned her attention back to Brian. "What are *you* going to do, then?"

"It's a surprise," Brian said. "But I promise you'll like it. Jace is just helping me set it up, that's all."

She hesitated, and then went to kneel beside Jace in the center of the bed.

"Lift your hands above your head."

She obeyed.

"A little higher."

Jace fastened the chain to a hook in the ceiling and then whispered something to her that Brian couldn't hear. She looked slightly less pale when she lowered her arms to her sides. Jace hopped off the bed and returned to Brian's side.

From his suitcase, Jace pulled a pair of leather cuffs that were lined with fleece. "Make sure you leave enough room for blood flow, and take her arms down from the hook occasionally or she'll lose circulation to her hands." Brian was surprised by how much experience Jace had with this stuff. Jace retrieved a gag—a leather strap with a rubber ball—from his case of wicked delights. "When she starts crying and begging, you'll probably want to gag her so you don't give in to her pleas."

Brian wasn't going to gag her. "Crying and begging?"

"She'll break eventually and be submissive to you forever."

He glanced at Myrna, who was staring up at the chain and chewing a fingernail. "I like her not submissive."

"Your loss." Jace pulled a candle out of the case and lit it. He set it on the dresser and pulled a second candle from the case. "Make sure you blow it out and let the melted wax cool a little before you pour it on her. You don't want to burn her skin. You should probably avoid the flails. If you don't know what you're doing, you'll draw blood, but there are some paddles in here somewhere." He rummaged around in the case. There were all kinds of things in there that Brian didn't recognize.

"I'm starting to think there's more to this than I realized."

"Don't be afraid to experiment, but be careful not to damage her trust. If she starts freaking out, you should stop what you're doing and do something you know she likes for a while. Push her, but not too hard. You guys haven't been together very long."

Brian took a deep breath and nodded.

"Once you get her bound, blindfolded, and unable to hear anything but the music in her ears..." He pulled an MP3 player out of his pocket and pressed it into Brian's

free hand. "…call for me and I'll show you some tech-
niques. She'll never know I'm there."

"I'll call you if I need you."

Jace winked at him and called to Myrna, "Have fun."

Brian showed Jace to the door, closing it behind him,
and then headed for the bed, hoping Myrna was as open-
minded as he thought she was.

Chapter 24

Wary, Myrna watched Brian approach the bed. Her eyes moved to the camel-colored leather restraints in his hand and then to the chain suspended from the ceiling above her. She'd never been restrained before. She was pretty sure she wasn't going to like it. She was, however, open to new experiences and willing to experiment with Brian.

"Before you start," she said, "I want you to promise me you'll stop if I ask you to."

"Jace said I should gag you when that happens."

Her eyes widened and her heart began to race.

"But I'm not Jace," Brian continued. "I'll stop if you ask me to stop. Do you trust me?"

She hesitated, her eyes dropping to the restraints again. "I think so."

He walked around the edge of the bed and placed the restraints and the MP3 player on the nightstand. Empty handed, he crawled onto the bed with her. They knelt in the center of the mattress, facing each other.

He took her hands in his and stared into her eyes. He still had his stage makeup on, which reminded her how sexy he'd looked wailing on his guitar earlier. He seemed to realize she needed a moment to collect herself. Her heart rate slowly returned to normal as they stared at each other silently. She leaned forward to kiss him. He took it as a signal to begin his latest assault on her senses and turned her chaste kiss into something deep and passionate. Her heart rate picked up again, but not from anxiety.

He unbuttoned her suit jacket and pushed the garment from her shoulders. His fingers worked at the buttons of her blouse, unfastening the first two before he lost patience and ripped it apart at the chest. He squeezed her breasts in his palms and then unfastened her bra's front clasp. His mouth moved to her jaw, her throat, her ear. The fact that he was still so worked up surprised her. He jerked her blouse and bra from her body and tossed the garments aside.

Brian removed her skirt next, followed by her garter belt and stockings. When he had her entirely naked, he reached for the restraints. Her apprehension returned. Maybe this wasn't the best idea. He could do anything to her and she wouldn't be able to fight back.

"Are you okay?" After much fumbling, he got the first cuff fastened. "Is it too tight?"

She shook her head. "Brian, I'm not sure about this."

The fastening of the second cuff didn't take him as long. "About what?"

"Being restrained."

"I thought you trusted me."

"I do."

"And I thought you liked to try new things."

"I do."

"Then what's the problem?"

She took a deep breath and released it slowly. "No problem."

"Good." He pecked her on the lips, then stood and pulled her arms up over her head. He hooked the chain between her wrists to the chain Jace had suspended from the ceiling. Her knees touched the bed, but she couldn't rest her buttocks on her heels. Brian jumped off the bed and stared at her.

"You look really sexy." He reached behind her head and released the clip holding her hair in a loose knot. The long strands were still damp from her earlier shower and felt chilly against her bare shoulders and back. Brian carefully arranged a strand over her shoulder to encircle her breast. When his fingers brushed against her nipple, her hands, suspended far above her head, clenched.

Brian retrieved something from Jace's open case and returned to her side to slide a thick, black mask over her eyes.

She twisted her head to the side, trying to avoid being blindfolded. "Don't."

"Everything will be okay." His face disappeared from view as he slid the blindfold in place. "God, that looks sexy, too. I'm starting to think I'm going to enjoy this as much as you will."

Myrna wasn't sure she was going to enjoy this at all. She didn't like to feel helpless, and that's exactly how being restrained and blindfolded made her feel.

Next, he put something in her ears. The sound of Sinners music filled her head. He pulled one of the earbuds out of her ear. "Is that too loud?"

"No. I like it loud."

He kissed her lovingly. "I won't hurt you." He slapped her bare ass and she flinched. "Much."

He put the earbud back into her ear. She waited, her heart thudding with apprehension. What did he plan to do to her? She couldn't see him or hear him or touch him.

And she had glimpsed some of the instruments of torture in Jace's case.

Something warm and damp draped across her shoulders and around her neck under her chin. The scent of Brian's body assailed her. She groaned and burrowed her nose in his sweat-damp T-shirt. His fingers brushed against her lower back and her body jerked. Deprived of sight, her other senses were heightened. His guitar playing had never sounded so exciting, his scent drove her to distraction, and the gentle brush of his fingers fired a hundred pleasure sensors in her skin. Knowing she couldn't touch him made her want to touch him that much more. Maybe she was going to like this game after all.

Something brushed across the underside of her breast. Soft. Light. A feather? She concentrated on sensation, trying to understand what she felt. The feather brushed along her rib cage, down her belly, and then up the other side. She shuddered, a soft groan erupting from between her lips. Something clamped down hard on her nipple, bordering on pain, but definitely pleasurable. Now the other nipple. Her body trembled as the gentle brush of the feather contrasted with the pinching pain centered at both nipples. Clothespins?

The pinching device on her left nipple was removed, leaving it tender and aroused. Brian soothed the ache with his lips and tongue. She groaned and tugged on the restraints above her head. "Please, the other now."

He moved away and clamped her left nipple again. She gasped in frustration. Something cool and smooth moved across her back between her shoulder blades. A piece of fabric? Satin maybe. The smooth material moved down her spine and over her buttock. A sharp sting assaulted her other ass cheek. She cried out in surprise. He spanked her again. Not with his hand. She decided he had a paddle. She wondered how he was able to remove objects from the case so fast. She started to suspect they weren't alone. But who?

"Jace?" she whispered suspiciously.

Brian moved behind her, the length of his body pressing against hers. She could feel his naked chest against her back and the rough fabric of his jeans against her buttocks. He pulled an earbud out of her ear. "It's just me. Are you still okay?"

"Yeah. This is exciting. Don't stop yet."

"I won't until you tell me to."

He replaced her earbud and released her nipples from their harsh pinching. A few seconds later, something cold and wet brushed against both nipples. Water dripped down the underside of her breasts as the ice melted between his fingers and her skin. He rubbed a frigid trail down her body, circling her navel and then moving farther down. When he brushed the hot swollen flesh between her legs, she shuddered against him. He stimulated her clit only briefly before sliding the ice cube inside her vagina with his fingers. Her thighs clamped over his hand, holding it in place.

A moment later he spanked her with the paddle and, surprised, she released his hand. He left the ice inside her and backed away. Cool water dripped down her inner thigh as the ice melted. Something hot burned a trail over her lower back.

"Ah!" she gasped, twisting away from the heat. It was very hot but didn't burn for long. The smell of paraffin alerted her to his current antics. A second splash of hot wax dripped over her thigh.

The bus rocked forward. They were on the road again. She wondered fleetingly if anyone had found her car, but lost the thought as another piece of ice trailed over her skin, beside the hardening wax on her thigh. Brian's thumb touched her chin. When she opened her mouth, he put something on her tongue. A sweet square of chocolate melted in her mouth. She turned her head to inhale Brian's scent on the T-shirt still draped over her shoulders. One of Brian's best solos now played in her ear.

She protested when he tugged the earbud out of her ear again. She enjoyed being completely immersed in the man's musical genius.

"Are your arms getting tired?" he asked, his low voice next to her ear. His breath stirred the fine hairs resting against her neck and she shuddered.

Actually, she couldn't feel her fingers, but she didn't much care. "If I say yes, will you stop?"

"Do you want me to stop?"

She shook her head vigorously. "Not at all."

His soft chuckle caused goose bumps to rise on her skin. She was so aware of him that everything he did was a turn-on.

"I was just going to take your arms down for a few minutes so you can rest them. I don't plan on stopping until the sun comes up."

"Okay."

He wrapped an arm around her waist and helped her to rise off her knees. The chain suspending her hands above her head came free.

"Lie on your belly."

Disoriented, she felt the mattress in front of her with her

hands so she didn't do a face plant off the end of the bed. When she was lying face down, he pulled her right arm out to the side and fastened it down by the restraint cuff.

"I'm not going anywhere," she said.

He secured her other arm and then clamped something around her ankle. She tried to lift her leg but could scarcely move it. He secured her other leg, so she lay spread eagle on her stomach without an inch of play in any of her restraints.

"Uh, Brian," she said, her heart drumming with a mixture of excitement and fear. "I can't move."

"That's the idea." He returned the earbud to her ear.

He left her like that for what seemed like an eon, her nerves suspended on a knife's edge. She turned her face into his sweaty shirt, still tangled around her neck. She breathed in his scent and wriggled her hips, squirming to try to alleviate the throbbing between her thighs. There was a sharp sting on her buttocks and she went still, panting for no good reason.

The mattress sagged beside her. She could sense him near her left side even though he wasn't touching her.

Something wet trickled down the center of her back.

She tensed.

He spanked her.

She gasped. Forced herself to relax.

His hands moved across her back to spread the liquid into her skin. The heels of his palms massaged her muscles while his fingers gently caressed her. He started at her shoulders and worked his way down slowly. When he reached her lower back, he straddled her thighs. She could feel the crinkly hairs of his legs brush the backs of hers. Was he naked? Did that mean he would take her soon? God, she hoped so. His hands moved lower, over her buttocks. After her spanking, his hands massaging her ass felt amazing. His thumbs brushed against her anus with each circular motion. She could feel the animal-like sounds coming from her throat, but she could scarcely hear them over the music.

She fought her arm restraints, straining toward him, lifting her hips off the bed as high as she could in the hopes that he'd penetrate her. Her muscles felt like warm butter, making the unrelenting ache between her thighs unbearable.

He stopped massaging her. The sting of the paddle on her soothed ass cheek was a total shock to her system. She couldn't take any more of this.

"Please, Brian," she sobbed. "Please take me. Please."

He moved away. The mattress rose beneath her as he left the bed.

"No! Don't leave me like this, you jerk!"

She fought her restraints until she exhausted herself and fell still, breathing hard from her fruitless exertions. He returned to her then, sitting on the backs of her thighs. She could feel his rock-hard cock resting against the crack of her ass. So it turned him on to torture her, did it? See if she ever let him fuck her again after this was over. Or better yet, she'd give him the same treatment and see how he liked it.

Probably not half as much as she did.

She groaned.

His hands trailed lightly over the skin of her back. From what she could decipher, he wore two different gloves. One hand was smooth as satin as it brushed over her skin, the other rougher, more like a loofah sponge.

His dichotomous gloves moved rapidly over her back and sides. A much different stimulation than his soothing massage. Invigorating. Maddening. When his hands dipped under her body to caress her hipbones and belly, she shuddered violently.

"Ah God, you're driving me insane," she said.

She felt his lips against her shoulder and then he began to rub his cock up and down the crack of her ass while he stroked her skin—smooth touch one side, rough on the other. She dug her toes into the mattress and rocked with him, wishing he'd stop teasing her and just thrust into her. She was so hot and wet, she knew she'd come the second he claimed her.

"Put it inside me," she pleaded. "Just for a minute."

He moved away again.

She growled in frustration. A moment later, islands of cold spotted across her back. Ice again. But this time he just set the little cubes in various locations and left them there to melt. He placed them down the backs of her thighs, knees, and calves as well, and then took a cube and ran it down the crack of her ass, rubbed it over her anus, around her vaginal opening, and finally her clit. He slid it inside her, pushing it deep with his finger. He repeated the treatment with a second ice cube, and a third. Those still resting on her skin formed cool pools and dripped water down her sides and the center of her back. The ice inside of her was melting as well and dripping cold liquid over her hot, swollen clit. He unexpectedly shifted between her legs and then filled her with one savage thrust.

She cried out. "Oh God, yes, thank you," she panted. "Thank you."

He thrust into her more shallowly, once, twice, three

times, and then pulled out. A gush of cold water bathed her aching genitals. She shuddered. He thrust into her again and rested his face on her back, rubbing it against her as if trying to control himself. He pulled out again and left the bed.

"Okay, Brian, we can finish now. Let me loose."

She felt one arm restraint come loose from the bed and then the other. She rose up to her knees and reached for him. He surprised her by fastening her wrists together again and stretching them above her head to hook her to the ceiling.

"I said let me loose. You promised you would if I asked."

He put something minty in her mouth and then pulled the blindfold up to her forehead. She blinked against the bright light in the room. She'd had no idea every light in the room was on. When her eyes adjusted, she decided she might climax from just looking at him in his present condition. His eyes were glazed, hair sticking to the side of his face with sweat. He knelt in front of her on the bed, his engorged cock jutting out between them. She spread her legs as much as she could, seeing as they were still restrained to the bed at the ankle. She wrapped her hands around the chain and pulled her knees off the bed. This would be an exciting position. She couldn't wait for him to thrust up inside her.

He filled the palm of his hand with oil and rubbed it over his cock from base to tip. Apparently, he didn't realize she was already dripping wet.

He continued to caress his cock, base to tip, tip to base, base to tip. Faster now. She couldn't stop watching as he stroked himself. The throb between her thighs was painful.

Agonizing. She released the chain and drew her legs closer together, squirming as she tried to stimulate her clit and give herself some much needed relief. It was no use.

Her gaze shifted to his face. His head was tilted back, mouth open, expression taut with impending release. His chest rose and fell with heavy breaths.

His hand moved faster now. Faster over the head of his cock. Faster. He tensed and shuddered as he came — three glorious spurts splashed over her belly and chest. It had to be the hottest thing she'd ever seen in her life. A spasm clenched her insides with a less-than-satisfying orgasm of her own.

Brian sat there for a moment, collecting his breath, and then leaned forward. He licked the cum from her belly and then rose up to kiss her deeply. She licked his tongue, greedy for the taste of him. He lowered her blindfold again.

"Brian?" she whispered when he broke their kiss.

He tugged the earbud out of her ear. "Yeah, baby?"

"If I wanted to restrain you, would you let me?"

He chuckled. "You know I would. Do you want to switch places now?"

She smiled. Jeremy would have never even considered allowing her to have total control. Brian was so different than that frigid bastard. That Brian would be willing to submit to her without any hesitation had her thinking of all sorts of things she wanted to do to him. But for now, she wanted him to continue. She was enjoying this far too much to want it to end just yet. "Maybe tomorrow."

"I'll look forward to it," he growled into her ear and then settled the earbud back in place.

Chapter 25

THE BUS LURCHED TO A SUDDEN HALT, SENDING empty beer cans scuttling over Myrna's sandals. Something thick and gooey spilled from one of the cans and trickled between her toes. She retched and jumped from the bench, slipping with her first step and sticking to the floor on her second. She'd had enough! She stomped over to where the guys sat perched on a pile of dirty clothes playing a video game in the living area. There was a sofa under that mountain of filth somewhere.

Myrna planted her fists on her hips and glanced from one band member to the next. "All right, guys. Some things need to change around here."

Four pairs of eyes turned toward Brian. *Control your chick*, they seemed to say.

She pointed to her foot. "Would someone like to tell me what just dripped out of a beer can onto my foot?"

"A loogie?" Trey guessed.

"As in phlegm?" Myrna sputtered. "Oh. My. God."

Brian tossed her a dirty shirt, which smelled like ass, and she used it to wipe the slimy mess off her foot. It wouldn't surprise her to see one of the guys wearing that very shirt the next day.

"This place is disgusting," she said. "The five of you are going to clean this bus from top to bottom and it's going to stay clean or I'm going to smother every last one of you in your sleep." She kicked a beer can out of her path.

"Myr—" Sed began.

She lifted her hand to silence him. "We're going to start with that disgusting refrigerator. All that moldy takeout food has to go. And then I'm going shopping for some real food. I am sick of fast food."

At the mention of food, the guys' expressions shifted from abject horror to mild interest.

"Real food?" Jace whispered, as if they were speaking a foreign language he'd never heard.

"Yeah, real food. Meat, vegetables, pasta, fruit, *liquid* milk. I don't mind cooking for all of you, and the roadies too, but you guys will clean this bus and keep it clean. I can't live like this anymore."

"Yes, Mommy," Eric said. "Will you spank my tushie if I'm a bad boy?"

He stood, turned around, and presented his butt to her.

"I'll only spank your tushie if you're a *good* boy, Eric Sticks," she said, "which I think is pretty much never."

Eric's lower lip protruded in an exaggerated pout.

She pulled a black garbage bag out of a drawer and tossed it at Jace. He caught it, blinking hard as he always did when something surprised him.

"Everything goes," she said.

"Except the beer," Sed said.

"Put your beer on the other bus. Keep your party pigsty over there. Over here, we'll have a peaceful, clean home."

"This is bullshit," Sed said. He looked at Brian. "Dude…"

"I think it's a good idea," Brian said.

"Me too," said Trey. "Will you spank me if I'm good, Myrna?"

She smiled at him. "You're always good, Trey."

Everyone laughed at her false statement, except Jace. Jace was already braving the refrigerator. Without a hazmat suit. He tossed things in the garbage bag without even looking at them. Sed rescued the beer, setting bottles and cans all along the stained and cluttered counter.

Myrna touched Sed's arm. "I hope you don't mind me bossing your boys around."

He grinned crookedly, showing a dimple. She'd forgotten he had dimples. He didn't smile that broadly often. "They do miss their mommies sometimes. I'd love a home-cooked meal, to be honest."

"Then you get to pick the first one. Assuming I can cook it."

"Pork chops," he said.

"And mashed potatoes!" Trey called, helping Jace empty the refrigerator. He opened the freezer, cringed, and closed it again.

"Asparagus?" Eric asked hopefully.

"Yeah, asparagus sounds excellent," Sed agreed.

"That I can do. I'm going shopping. Who wants to come?"

All five men lined up in front of her. She grinned, deciding they probably just wanted to get out of cleaning. "My car is a coupe, guys. I only have room for one. The rest of you stay here and clean out that refrigerator. Come on, Brian."

"Why does Brian automatically get to go?" Eric complained.

"I'm her boyfriend. Duh."

"We can take my bike," Jace offered. "I'll follow."

"I'll ride with you," Trey said to Jace.

"And Myrna can sit on my lap in the car." Eric snagged her around the waist and tugged her against his side. "I won't mind."

"I'm not fuckin' staying here by myself." Sed slammed the refrigerator door.

The five of them stared at her like puppies at a pound desperate to be adopted. *Pick me. Pick me!*

Like she could say no to any of them. "Fine. We'll find a way to fit, but when we get back, you're cleaning. All of you." Her eyes drifted over her companions. They'd stand out more than usual in this podunk town. "Do you think you all need disguises? Otherwise we'll have to fight off fans."

"We're in The-Middle-of-Nowhere, Wyoming," Trey said.

"This town has like, twelve hundred people," Eric said. "And I think most of them live in the old folks' home."

"What? You don't think the elderly listen to metal?" Myrna asked.

"We'll take a chance," Trey said.

Trey settled on the back of Jace's motorcycle. The rest of the guys crammed themselves into Myrna's little Thunderbird.

With Brian driving, Eric sitting in the middle, and Sed on the passenger side, Myrna was forced to sit partially on Sed and Eric's laps. She spent most of the short drive moving Eric's hands from inappropriate locations. Sed thumped him upside the head on occasion. "Will you leave her alone?"

"I hope we don't get pulled over," Myrna said. "We look like a group of thugs on our way to rob a bank."

Brian laughed. "Yeah. Except our getaway car is frickin' pink and worth more than Sed's dental work."

Sed grinned like a shark to show off his perfect teeth.

They found a family-owned grocery store near the edge of town. Brian pulled into the parking lot and Jace's bike rumbled in after them.

Eric grabbed Myrna in a tight embrace on his lap, while Sed unfolded his six-foot-four frame from the little car. Brian climbed from the driver's seat and offered a hand to Myrna to help her out of the car.

"We're good, thanks," Eric said, squeezing her closer. "See you when you get back."

Myrna slid a hand up Eric's neck into his black hair. He had the craziest haircut she'd ever seen. It was long on one side and down the back, yet shaved to stubble on the other side. A ridge of spikes along the top separated the stubble from the long strands. The finger-thick lock that curled around his throat changed color on occasion. Today it was a deep blue. A week ago, it had been crimson red. His hair suited him, she supposed, but he should sue his hairstylist. As her fingers intertwined in the long strands at the nape of his neck, he glanced down at her, his eyes wide in surprise.

"Yeah, you guys go on ahead," she said, staring up into Eric's pale-blue eyes and running her tongue over her lips. "Eric and I are going to stay in the car and make out."

His grip on her slackened as he lowered his head to—

"Psyche!" She shoved him away before squirming out of his lap.

"Dude," Eric complained. "That was so not cool."

"Yeah," Brian agreed. He helped her to her feet and wrapped an arm around her back. "No one says 'psyche' anymore."

"Well, I'm old," Myrna said. "I can't help my lack of cool."

As soon as they entered the store, a thin, nervous-looking man started following them through the aisles. Myrna supposed rock stars looked like shoplifters. She smiled reassuringly at the little man and he turned to fiddle with the stock on the shelves.

Eric moved to stand next to the store clerk. He stroked his chin as he examined the condiments. "Brian's woman thinks we need to eat better," he said to the guy. "That attractive, normal-looking babe over there. See her?"

The manager glanced at Myrna. He nodded slightly and returned to his unnecessary shelf tidying.

"Anyway," Eric continued. "I'm pretty sure she's going to make us eat salad. Do you like salad?"

"I guess."

Eric clapped him on the shoulder. The man flinched. "Great! I assume you're a salad dressing expert, since you keep rearranging these bottles. So, what dressing would you recommend to a bunch of derelicts like us?" He grabbed the man's name tag and leaned unnecessarily close to read it. "Kevin."

"Eric," Sed said. "Leave the guy alone."

"Why? I assumed *Kevin* wanted to offer some customer service to his customers. That's why you're following us around, right, *Kevin*?"

The man brushed Eric's hand from his shoulder. "Raspberry vinaigrette is good."

"Do we look like the kind of guys who'd eat raspberry vinaigrette salad dressing?" Eric asked.

Kevin glanced from one band member to the next. "Uh…"

Myrna grabbed Eric by the ear. "The answer to that question is: Shut up, Eric."

"Ow!" Eric protested.

"I like raspberry vinaigrette," Trey said. He put a bottle of dressing in the cart. "Do they make anything cherry-flavored?"

Kevin shook his head. "I don't think so."

Trey took his sucker out of his mouth and pointed it at him. "Well, they should."

"Cherry salad dressing? Disgusting," Brian said, his nose wrinkled. "Ranch is best."

Jace selected several bottles of creamy dressing and put them in the cart without a word.

Eric grabbed Myrna's wrist to pull her pinching fingers from his ear. "My point is, *Kevin*," he said, "we don't need a babysitter. Thanks."

Sed was at the end of the aisle looking at spices. "Hey, Myrna, do you know how to make lemon-pepper chicken?"

"Sure do," she called to him. She pulled her arm from Eric's grip and went to help Sed pick out spices. The other guys followed her with Jace pushing the cart. Apparently, Jace had been grocery shopping before. Without any prompting, he added things to the cart that Myrna would have chosen herself.

"Get some jalapeños," Eric said to Jace, who'd just added a jar of dill pickles to the cart. "I'll make us some omelets."

"You'll make yourself an omelet," Brian said. "Your cooking is worse than Trey's."

"Is it my fault you don't like cherries?" Trey said.

"No one likes cherries in stir-fry."

"I do."

Myrna rubbed Trey's head, messing up his hair. "I'll bake you a cherry pie, sweetie. Would you like that?"

He hugged her against his side and kissed her temple. "I love you. Brian, I love your woman."

Brian smiled slightly but didn't look at Myrna when he said, "Don't we all?"

They didn't lose their tail as they wound through the aisles, but Kevin was a little less obvious about following them. He watched them from one aisle over.

The store had an excellent butcher who produced choice cuts of fresh meat. "We'll have to clean out the freezer when we get back," Myrna said. "I can't pass up this meat."

"The freezer is highly toxic," Trey said. "Can't we just throw out the whole refrigerator and get a new one?"

"Yeah, let's do that," Jace agreed. He was tossing T-bones into the cart as if they were having a buy-one-get-ten-free steak sale.

"Sheesh, Jace, are you hungry?" Myrna asked.

"There are fourteen of us."

"Good point. Get ground beef. I'll make chili."

"Do you really want to be trapped on a tour bus with a bunch of guys who've consumed large quantities of chili beans?" Brian asked.

Myrna laughed. "Another good point. Okay, I'll make lasagna instead. Tomorrow."

"Now you're talking." Brian kissed her temple. "I love Italian food."

"Make sure you get enough pork chops, Jace," Sed insisted. "I'll eat like three or seven of them."

They made a second trip through the store for things she'd need for lasagna. By the time they finished, two carts were full to the top.

"I'm not sure all of this will fit in my car," Myrna said. For a small car, the Thunderbird had a good-sized trunk, but their carts looked like they were stocking up to start their own mobile grocery store.

"We'll make it fit," Brian said. "Or load Eric up like a pack mule."

"Uh, no," Eric said.

Jace started unloading the cart onto the conveyer belt. Myrna had a hard time accepting what the groupies said about him. A sadomasochist? He was always such a sweetheart. Quiet. Shy. Gentle. If she hadn't seen what he kept in his suitcase with her own eyes, she'd never have believed it. He didn't even attempt to look like a natural blond. Platinum hair, dark beard stubble, dark brows. It was cute though. Myrna couldn't put her finger on why. With that baby face of his, he looked like the requisite tough guy of a boy band, not a member of a metal band.

Jace must have felt her stare, because he glanced up, his brown eyes inquisitive. "What?"

She shook her head. "Nothing." She handed him a package of Italian sausage. He placed it on the conveyer belt.

"God, I want a cigarette," Trey said, eyeing the locked case behind the counter. He fidgeted with the zipper on his sleeve repeatedly before cleaning out an entire display of cherry suckers and dumping them on the checkout stand.

Myrna squeezed his elbow in encouragement and moved around Jace to the cashier.

"Did you find everything you needed?" the young woman asked as she dragged products over the scanner.

"I think so." Myrna looked at the two cartfuls of groceries being unloaded by an assembly line of rock stars. She smiled to herself. "I hope so."

A bloodcurdling scream emitted from the back of the growing line. Sed's body suddenly careened into Eric's. Brian steadied them.

"Oh my God! Oh my God! Oh my God!" a high-pitched voice squealed from about the level of Sed's belly button. A young girl, no older than thirteen, had almost knocked Sed to the floor with her exuberance. "Oh, Sed, I love you. I love you!"

"So much for the retirement community theory," Jace said as he continued to unload the cart.

Sed glanced at Eric with wide eyes. Eric shrugged.

Sed patted the girl's head uncomfortably. "Hello there. I think you have me confused with someone else."

"I'd know you anywhere," she insisted. "You're Sedric Lionheart. The lead singer of Sinners."

Sed winced. The rest of the people in line started craning their necks, trying to glimpse the rock stars in their midst.

Sed bent and whispered something in the girl's ear. Her face lit up and she nodded. She hugged him and returned to the back of the line, bouncing on the balls of her feet excitedly. Her entire body trembled from head to foot.

"What in the hell did you tell her?" Eric said under his breath. "She's a child, Sed. I hope you didn't—"

Sed punched him in the arm. Hard. "Have some faith in me, fuckhead."

Another line opened, and the very young fangirl rushed to the front of the second line, knocking an elderly lady sideways in her haste. The girl kept her eyes on Sed the entire time the cashier rang up her small purchase. She paid and then rushed out of the store. She stood in front of the glass doors peering in at them from outside.

"What did you say to her?" Brian asked.

"I just told her if she was quiet, I'd autograph my shirt for her outside the store. What kind of sick bastard do you think I am?"

"You don't want me to answer that," Eric said.

"Sticks, you're asking for a serious ass whippin'," Sed said.

Brian presented his stack of cash to pay and they pushed the carts of sacked groceries to the car. Sed's little shadow followed them, chattering excitedly. While the rest of them loaded the trunk, Sed removed his leather jacket and plain white T-shirt. He put his jacket back on and borrowed a pen from Myrna. He signed his shirt before handing it over to the girl. She lifted it to her nose and inhaled, her eyes rolling into the back of her head. Sed ran a hand over his shorn hair, looking very uncomfortable about the entire situation.

"Can I get the band's autographs, too?" the girl asked.

"Of course!" Sed said, taking the shirt back and passing it around until each band member had signed it.

The trunk was full to bursting with groceries, but they managed to get it shut on the third try. After returning to their vehicles, Brian drove out of the parking lot, with Jace following on his bike. The young fan waved good-bye to them, clutching Sed's shirt to her narrow chest.

"Fuck, what a disaster. I'm glad you guys signed the shirt, too. I didn't think of what that would look like when I told her that she could have it. What was I thinking?" Sed said. "I could just picture her daddy showing up outside the tour bus with a shotgun."

"It was completely innocent," Myrna said.

"Yeah, but if your thirteen-year-old daughter comes home with some man's shirt, you wouldn't think it was innocent. You'd want to shoot him in the back."

"I suppose that would look bad," Myrna agreed.

"I guess when you say you'd give your fans the shirt off your back, you aren't exaggerating," Brian said.

They laughed. Sed's body relaxed, though he kept checking the side mirror for signs of an angry daddy with a shotgun.

Brian pulled up beside the tour bus and put the car in park. "Last one out of the car has to do all the laundry."

"I don't do laundry," Sed grumbled. Before the words were out of his mouth, Brian had already leapt from the car and Eric scrambled out after him.

Sed grabbed Myrna around the waist and refused to release her. "I won't be the last one out of this car. I don't do laundry."

"Then get one of your groupies to do it for you. I'm not doing it."

He buried a hand in her hair and tugged her head back to stare down into her eyes. "I'll make it worth your while."

Myrna leaned against the door, which opened

unexpectedly. She clung to Sed's bare chest with her fingertips to keep from tumbling to the asphalt on her head.

Brian's angry face appeared upside down above her. "What the fuck are you two doing?"

Sed's arms wrapped around Myrna's body. "What does it look like?" His lips brushed over her jaw. "Oh yeah, Myrna. Yeah. Don't stop now, baby."

"I can't believe this." Brian tore his gaze from Sed long enough to glare at Myrna. "I leave you two alone for ten seconds and you're already—"

"You think I'm *cheating* on you?" Myrna sputtered.

She crawled over Sed's massive body and out of the car, landing gracelessly on the ground at Brian's feet.

"You've got your hands all over his naked chest, all submissive in his arms, and he's kissing you. What do you expect me to think?"

Myrna scrambled to her feet and shook her head at him. "I can't fucking believe this, Brian. You're just like my ex-husband."

When he reached for her, she shoved him aside and stormed away.

Still reeling from an eyeful he'd thought he'd never have to see again (Sed with his hands all over a woman he cared about), Brian watched Myrna stomp up the bus stairs. He couldn't believe she'd compared him to her psychotic ex-husband. Did she really think he was like that asshole?

Inside the bus Eric called, "Hey, Myrna, Jace said he'll clean the fridge all by himself. So you can get started cooking those pork chops. I rescued my special cinnamon and dill rub from the garbage." A loud crash of cookware followed. "Don't cry. You don't have to use it if you don't want to."

Brian started after Myrna, but Sed grabbed his arm. "Dude, learn to take a joke."

"A joke?"

"Yeah, I was just playing around. Teasing her. Myrna and I weren't doing anything. She's not like those other bimbos you called girlfriends. You can trust her."

"I did trust her. And then you…you were touching her, and looking at her, and your lips, and her hands, and… she wasn't even trying to stop you…" His eyes landed on Sed's bare chest. "Go put on a goddamned shirt, Sed!"

Brian took a deep breath. He knew he had overreacted, but he also knew what Sed was like. He turned good girls bad. But Myrna wasn't a girl. She was a woman. Somewhere inside, he knew she would never betray him with Sed. She *wasn't* like the others. It wasn't her he didn't trust. It was Sed. "Shit. I've got to go talk to her."

Brian found her in the living area with Jace and Eric, stuffing dirty clothes into a garbage bag. She had a streak of mascara under one eye. He hadn't meant to make her cry.

"Myrna, I didn't mean to accuse you—"

"Go help Trey unload the car, Brian. I don't want to talk about this right now." He touched her arm and she flinched away from him. "Don't even *think* about touching me."

"Sed told me there was nothing going on."

"So you'll believe Sed but automatically think the worst of me?"

"No, I just… It looked like… Sed's done this to me so many times, and…" He rubbed his forehead. He couldn't concentrate. The thought of losing her ate the inside of his chest raw.

Eric grabbed Myrna and shoved her against Brian's chest. "Kiss and make up."

"I think he should squirm a little longer," Myrna said, but she didn't move away. Not even when Brian's arms crept up to circle her back. "He knows how much I hate being falsely accused of cheating."

"I never actually accused… But I shouldn't have even thought it. I'm sorry, okay?"

"Okay."

He breathed a sigh of relief. "Okay?"

"Yeah, I overreacted. A little."

Brian kissed her forehead and squeezed her tighter, inching her body toward the bedroom. "Can we go make up now?"

She laughed and hugged him. "We need to go get this laundry done."

"We could always make up on the washing machine at the laundromat."

She leaned back and looked up at him, adventure sparkling in her gorgeous, green-flecked eyes. "Yeah, we could."

God, he loved this woman. If Sed touched her again, he would kill him.

Chapter 26

Myrna shook her head at Brian. "We've been through this a hundred times. I'm not staying in L.A. with you."

"You can get your work done while we're rehearsing and in the recording studio," he said. "And we have a music video shoot in a couple of days. You can use that entire day to work."

Lounging on his back in one of the curtained bunks, Brian trailed his fingers lightly over her bare shoulder, tracing the spaghetti strap of her satin nightgown. She lay on his belly, her folded arms on his chest and her chin resting on her interlaced fingers. She stared up at his face, which was mostly concealed in shadows, contemplating her options. He'd been wearing her down for almost a week, and as much as she wanted to have fun with him, she knew she had to use this opportunity to get caught up on her work.

"You know if I stay, I'll want to watch everything you do. You're too much of a distraction. Besides, it's only a week. It won't kill us to be apart for seven days."

"We've been together almost every moment of every day for three weeks. Seven days apart will feel like an eternity."

"You know what they say. Absence makes the heart grow fonder."

"If my heart grows any fonder, it's going to hop out of my chest and into yours."

She melted. She scooted up his body to kiss him. "That's the sweetest thing anyone's ever said to me."

"It sounds sort of fatal," he murmured.

"Then I don't want your heart to grow any fonder." She kissed him again and rolled toward the wall.

"Don't think just because you're being stubborn you'll get out of meeting my parents," he said. "They'll be at the show tomorrow night."

She sat up, her head inches from crashing into the ceiling. "What?"

"They always come to our show in L.A. Trey's parents. Sed's parents. They'll probably all be there. It's like an elementary school Christmas program all over again."

"Do they know about me?" she asked, her voice uncharacteristically squeaky.

"Yeah, they know. Mom's a great ear when I'm bummed out. And believe me, that entire month I didn't see you after Des Moines qualified."

"What did you tell her?" When he opened his mouth to speak, she covered it with her hand. "Wait. I don't want to know."

She squirmed over his body and dropped out of the bunk. He caught her arm. "Where are you going?"

"I need a drink." She turned and found Eric, Sed, and Jace staring at her from the spotlessly clean living area where they sat watching TV. She instinctively tugged her baby doll nightgown down her thighs to make sure everything was covered and went directly to the refrigerator. Unfortunately, what she wanted was on the other bus.

"Why isn't there any alcohol on this bus?" she yelled and slammed the refrigerator door.

The guys on the sofa laughed at her dilemma.

"I don't know, Myr," Sed called. "Why is that?"

Eric climbed to his feet, swaying slightly as the bus decelerated and then sped back up. He stopped next to her, reached into his leather vest, and withdrew a silver flask. "Tequila?" He opened the flask and extended it toward her. The fumes made her eyes cross.

"You mean To-Kill-Ya?" She snatched the flask out of his hand and took a long drink. She sputtered and coughed, her eyes watering, stomach protesting. She handed the flask back to him, shaking her head with her eyes closed. "That is some nasty stuff."

"The drunker you get, the better it tastes." He took a swig and recapped it.

Brian appeared at her elbow. "You're drinking?"

"So?"

"I really don't get why meeting my parents is such a big deal."

"Brian's mom is a total MILF," Eric said. "And his dad is a living legend. Brian's parents are way cool."

"I'm sure they are, but meeting his parents would suggest Brian and I are pretty serious."

"Yeah, so?" Eric said.

"So that gives the wrong message. Brian and I are—"

"Just having a good time," Brian finished her sentence.

"Exactly," she said. "Thank you."

"If you don't like parents, you can 'just have a good time' with me," Eric said. "I don't have any parents."

"You don't?"

He shook his head. "I'm a product of the fine state of California's foster care program."

She gave Eric a warm hug. He tugged her closer, his jaw resting against her hair. "I love sympathy hugs," he murmured, and then his hands slid over her satin night-gown from her lower back to her ass.

She elbowed her way out of his grip. "Is it possible for you *not* to cop a feel when I'm within reach?"

"I take opportunities when they present themselves."

She glanced at Brian, who was scowling at her.

"Don't get mad at me," she said. "That was him."

"Why do you get to call all the shots in this relationship?" he asked.

"Huh?"

"Because you're pussy-whipped." Eric retreated to the living area before Brian took out his frustration on him.

"I'm always the one compromising what I want," Brian said, his voice raised in anger.

"I compromise."

"That's bullshit, Myrna. Name one thing you've done that you didn't want to do. One compromise you made because I asked you."

"I'm always putting off work I need to do for you."

"I don't ask you to."

"Yes, you do. All the time. As soon as I start working, you show up wanting sex."

"You can say no. I don't force you to do anything you don't want to do."

"And how would you react if I said no?"

"I'm not sure. I've never had to deal with that situation."

Myrna was stunned speechless. Was he insinuating what she thought he was?

"That's because Myrna is dick-whipped." Eric hid behind a sofa pillow.

"Well, what compromises have *you* made?" Myrna

countered, unable to argue his logic. She didn't ever say no to him. She didn't want to.

"This entire relationship is a compromise for me."

Sed increased the volume of the TV.

Brian talked louder. "I want to tell you how I feel. I want this to be serious. I want to introduce you to my parents. I want this to be permanent and about more than sex. I know this is hard for you, but it's hard for me, too. Don't you get that? I'm not sure how much more of this I can take."

"Then don't take it," she said. "Walk away." She flicked her hands at him as if showing him the door.

She never expected him to turn his back and close himself in the bedroom. Her first instinct was to chase after him. That's what she wanted to do, but she knew she couldn't do that. She had to stick to her guns or things *would* get serious between them, and she didn't want that. Right? No, that would be horrible. Then he'd start with the stupid marriage proposals again.

"You really blew it this time, Myr," Eric called over the blaring TV.

"Shut up, Eric." She stood there indecisively for a moment, wondering why she felt like crying. If this "thing" didn't work out between her and Brian, it was for the best. Right? Yeah, for the best.

She dashed a tear from the corner of her eye and settled into the booth around the dining table. She sat on the opposite side she usually did, with her back to the living area and facing the bedroom. She didn't want the distraction of the guys watching TV while she entered her stupid data into her stupid spreadsheet. At least, that's what she told herself as she booted up her stupid computer with one eye on the bedroom door.

Chapter 27

AROUND THREE IN THE MORNING, BRIAN STUMBLED out of the bedroom in search of the bathroom. He hadn't been asleep long. His brain wouldn't shut up long enough for him to drift off, and then Trey kept cuddling up against him, which made for unpleasant sleeping arrangements. He paused in the doorway. Myrna had fallen asleep at her computer, her head resting on a stack of questionnaires. The others on the bus had retired to their bunks. He didn't know why he should care if she was uncomfortable sleeping on her ever-important work. She obviously didn't give a shit about him or *his* feelings. She hadn't even tried to make up with him after their argument. He had to come to terms with the fact that she only wanted him for one thing. And he didn't think he could settle for that anymore.

After he finished in the bathroom, he headed back for bed. His conscience getting the better of him, he went to the booth and drew Myrna toward him. He'd just toss her in the empty bunk so she didn't wake up with a huge crick in her neck.

"No," she groaned, still asleep. "Gotta get this data entered so I can stay with Brian in L.A."

He smiled and kissed her temple. Yeah, she obviously didn't care about him at all. He just had to be patient with her. It was just so hard to have everything he wanted pressed against him but not be able to claim her as his forever.

He lifted Myrna and carried her past the empty bunk and into the bedroom. He laid her on the bed next to Trey and climbed in on her other side.

"Slumber party," Trey murmured and snuggled up against Myrna. Mr. Cuddles was a total bed hog. But was it really necessary for him to massage Myrna's breast like that? Brian thought not. He grabbed Trey's finger and bent it back until he cried out in pain.

Myrna scowled in her sleep.

"Hands off, Mills."

Trey sighed heavily and rolled onto his other side. "Party pooper."

Chapter 28

MYRNA OPENED HER EYES AND BLINKED IN THE bright morning sunshine. When her eyes adjusted to the light, she found Brian sleeping beside her. She wasn't sure how she ended up in bed with him, but she was grateful to find him so close. It made it easier to apologize. She should have done it last night.

She lifted her hand to touch his face.

His eyes fluttered open and he smiled. "Good morning, beautiful."

"Oh, Brian," she murmured, her eyes strangely watery. "I'm sorry about last night. And I'm sorry I'm not more available for you. You're always so good to me, and I just can't bring myself to…" She shook her head. "But I do want to compromise. So if you still want me to stay with you in L.A., I promise to hang around a couple of days and do anything you want before I go home to get caught up on work. How does that sound?"

He kissed her nose and smiled. "Like a compromise."

"I'll try to be better about finding middle ground."

"And I'll try to be more patient."

"That biblical Job guy ain't got nothing on you, sweetie." She stroked his hair from his cheek. "I don't know how you put up with me."

"I think you do," he said, "but I've been forbidden to say it."

Her heart thrummed in her chest, and she covered

his lips with her fingertips before he let that blasted l-word slip.

A hard, warm body plastered itself to Myrna's back. She stiffened and held her breath. They weren't alone? Within seconds, the man had splayed his hand over her belly, intertwined his bare legs with hers and buried his face in her neck.

Brian chuckled. "Mr. Cuddles strikes again."

"Soft," Trey murmured in her ear. He snuggled closer.

Just Trey. She emitted her held breath and relaxed. Trey snuggled closer still.

"Don't let him smother you," Brian advised.

"I don't think I can move."

"Shhhh," Trey murmured, his nose pressed behind her ear. "Sleeping."

Brian chuckled and shook his head. "You might as well go back to sleep. He won't move for a while."

Myrna wasn't sure how anyone could be expected to sleep when sandwiched between two sexy guitarists.

Chapter 29

WHY WAS SHE SO NERVOUS? THEY WERE JUST PARENTS. Yes, one of them was Malcolm O'Neil, but that shouldn't make her tummy flutter or her palms sweat.

"Are you okay?" Brian asked.

"Fine," she squeaked.

"Don't be nervous. They'll love you."

The mood backstage was more sedate than usual, with scarcely a scantily clad woman to be found. Brian opened the dressing room door and ushered Myrna inside. The instant Brian stepped into the room, a stunning woman grabbed him in a crushing hug and kissed him square on the mouth.

"Excuse me," Myrna said crossly.

"Mom," Brian gasped. "Can't breathe."

"I don't see you for two months and you greet me with 'can't breathe'?"

He gave his mom a hug that lifted her feet off the ground. She laughed.

"Put your mother down," a deep voice said behind Myrna.

She turned and looked up at Malcolm O'Neil. Her heart did a somersault in her chest. She'd been afraid of this. She gaped up at him like a fish out of water—her throat trying to produce sounds, her mouth opening and closing sporadically. Brian's arm slid around Myrna's shoulders reassuringly.

"Well, this is her," Brian said. "This is Myrna."

"She looks normal," Malcolm said suspiciously. He looked normal, too, which surprised Myrna for some reason. Shouldn't rock legends glow with greatness?

"Don't mind him," Brian's mom said. "He's forgotten his manners. I'm Claire Sinclair. Yes, you can laugh. I didn't realize how stupid my name would be when I agreed to marry Malcolm. I had no idea his last name wasn't O'Neil until I saw his real name on the marriage license."

"You never asked," Malcolm said.

Myrna didn't dare laugh at Claire's name. The woman intimidated the hell out of her. She had supermodel looks and a star quality that threw Midwestern-farm-girl Myrna for a loop. Claire had to be close to fifty and she looked spectacular. Not a single wrinkle marred her perfect skin, nor was there a gray to be found in her silky brown hair. If Myrna had met her on the street, she'd have thought her thirty-five. Tops. It seemed biologically impossible for her to be Brian's mother. He had her high, sculpted cheekbones, but they looked more like siblings than mother and son.

"Are you adopted?" Myrna sputtered at Brian.

His eyebrows drew together. "Huh?"

"I don't mean that as an insult." Yeah, great thing to say the first time you meet your boyfriend's mother. "I mean, you look amazing, Mrs. Sinclair. It seems impossible that you'd have a twenty-eight-year-old son."

Mrs. Sinclair beamed. "You're a dear for saying so." She took Myrna's elbow and drew her away from her husband and son. "Please, call me Claire. Now, tell me all about yourself. Brian says you're a doctor."

"Well, not a physician. A professor."

"Yes, he told me as much, but he won't tell me what your degree is in. I'm dying to know."

What little respect she'd garnered by being a doctor was about to be thrown to the wayside. "I...er...well... The thing is..."

Brian appeared at her elbow. "I've got to go get ready for the show. Sorry to abandon you. I'll take you both to a late dinner or something. Dad, too."

Myrna used her eyes to plead with him to rescue her, but he just smiled at her, obviously pleased that she got along with his mother.

"We'll be fine, dear," Claire said. "Break a leg or whatever I'm supposed to say to wish you luck."

Myrna watched Brian head for the shower room, longing to follow him. And not because he was about to get naked.

"Well, Myrna?" Claire continued. "Are you going to tell me? What's your degree in?"

Eric magically appeared at Myrna's side. Either that or she had been too distracted to notice his approach. "She's a certified human sexuality professor."

Claire laughed. "Well, that would explain Brian's fascination with her."

Ouch.

"So you're like Doctor Ruth. Only younger, taller, and more attractive," Claire said.

"No, Doctor Ruth is a sex psychiatrist," Myrna clarified. "I don't treat people for sexual dysfunction."

"Well, that's a relief," Malcolm said behind her, his booming voice making her jump. "I thought maybe my boy had some problems he didn't see fit to share."

"No, no problems." Myrna's face flamed.

"And trust her, she would know," Eric said.

He laughed. Claire laughed. Malcolm laughed. But Myrna didn't laugh. She was too busy looking for a rock to crawl under.

"Doctor Myrna's on tour with us because she's studying the sexual behavior of our groupies," Eric added.

Claire stopped laughing. "Ugh," she said. "Groupies. How do you stand them?" She wrapped an arm around her husband's waist and looked up at him. "I hated your groupies."

"They hated you, too," he said and kissed her passionately. She clung to him as if he'd stolen her senses. If he kissed anything like his son did, Myrna was certain Claire had completely lost her senses. Myrna's face flamed even hotter at her errant thoughts. These were Brian's parents. His *parents*.

Mind out of the gutter, Myrna.

When Claire and Malcolm drew apart, Malcolm looked down at Myrna. It was strange to look up at an older, not quite as gorgeous, version of her boyfriend. "So what have you learned about Brian's groupies?"

"They're all madly in love with his stage persona," she said.

"But you're madly in love with the real person," Malcolm said. Myrna felt the blood drain from her face. "That's why I married Claire. She knew the real me and loved me anyway."

Claire grinned up at him mischievously. "What makes you so sure?"

"Excuse me," Myrna said. "I need to…erm…use the restroom."

She fled to the shower room, not realizing how it must look until she'd already entered and found herself in the company of not only naked Brian, but also naked Sed and naked Trey. She caught a glimpse of three very nice, very white asses before she diverted her gaze and scanned the room for a bathroom stall. Urinal? No can do.

"Don't mind me," she said, locating a stall in the corner. She let herself in and locked the door behind her. She stood there trying to collect her scattered wits. What exactly had Brian told his parents about her? *Madly* in love? She'd never been *madly* in love with anyone.

"You okay in there?" Brian asked from the other side of the stall door.

"Did you tell your father I was *madly* in love with you?"

"Uh… No, of course not."

"Don't lie to me, Brian Sinclair." She opened the stall door. He stood there in his towel, water clinging to his skin, looking as irresistible as ever. Madly in *lust*. Yeah, she'd admit to that.

"I'm not lying. Are you hiding?"

She laughed. It sounded false even to her own ears. "Of course I'm not hiding."

"Trying to get a glimpse of the band naked?"

"Yeah, that's what I was doing."

"So, who said what?"

She could tell his patience was wearing thin. "Your father said I was madly in love with you." She rolled her eyes.

"Maybe he was just calling it like he saw it." He put his hands on his hips, a challenge in his eyes.

"What did you tell them?"

"I didn't tell them anything." He sighed, all the fight going out of him. "Because apparently there's nothing to tell." He turned and walked toward the dressing area.

She lifted a hand toward his retreating back. Trey approached, one towel around his waist, another in his hands as he dried his hair. He dropped the second towel around his shoulders. Trey usually had this devil-may-care expression on his face, so Myrna didn't quite know what do when confronted by this serious version of party boy.

"I try to stay out of this because it's none of my business," he said, "but you need to realize a few things, Myrna. Brian won't say anything."

"About what?"

"About his parents."

Her brow arched in question.

"It's hard to understand what it's like for Brian. To grow up in the shadow of a great and be destined for the same career. Brian has always tried to prove himself to his father, and the man scarcely validates him as a musician. I don't think Malcolm realizes how that affects his son. Brian works his ass off to show his father he's worthy of his approval, but it doesn't matter. He'll always fall short in Malcolm's eyes. And Brian's mother?" Trey rolled his eyes. "She's got her plastic surgeon on fuckin' speed dial. I know because my father handles her wrinkle catastrophes. All she cares about is herself and how great she looks."

Myrna shook her head. "She obviously loves her son."

"Yeah, now that he's famous. She completely ignored Brian as a kid. She was too concerned about Kara's blossoming beauty. Do you know who Kara is? Brian's little sister."

"Brian told me she died."

Trey nodded, a deep sadness in his eyes. "When Kara died, Claire's competition for best-looking in the family was gone. I think she was relieved that her daughter would never surpass her in the modeling world. And Malcolm is the same way with Brian. It's strange to watch. And it eats Brian alive. He always makes excuses for the man."

"Aren't parents happy when their children are more successful than they are?"

"These aren't normal parents, Myrna. We're talking about a pair of highly successful people beyond their prime. Now, the reason I'm even bringing up Brian's family baggage, at risk of a serious ass whippin', is because Brian saw fit to introduce you to his parents. That's a big deal for him, you know. He's never opened a relationship to criticism from them. He identified you as being worthy of their approval. Approval even he can't seem to obtain."

"You mean he's never introduced a romantic interest to his parents before?"

He nodded. "Yeah."

"Well, why didn't you just say that?"

"Because if I called you his 'romantic interest,'" he said, using finger quotes, "you'd probably go hide in the bathroom again."

"I wasn't hiding."

"Yeah, uh-huh, okay. Myrna, you really shouldn't blow this thing with Brian. There will come a time when that fortified wall of yours will turn him away. I mean, a guy can only take so much abuse."

She scowled at him.

"Lucky for you, he's a glutton for punishment." Trey grinned. He paused and ran a finger along one eyebrow. "And he doesn't like guys."

Myrna's eyes widened. Was Trey implying what she thought he was implying?

Trey laughed. "I'm kidding, Myrna."

"Trey, you better get dressed," Sed said. He leaned against the stall partition next to Myrna.

"If you tolerated his parents tonight, it would mean a lot to him, Myrna," Trey said.

Myrna nodded. She'd pretend to be Brian's doting girlfriend for his parents' sake, but he'd owe her one. Trey winked at her and headed for the dressing area.

"What were you two discussing?" Sed asked. "Looked serious."

"Parents."

Sed sighed. "Mine didn't show up. Both of them had to work." He leaned closer to her and grinned. "So all those squats I've been doing have really been paying off, huh?"

"What?"

"Don't tell me you didn't check out my ass when I was in the shower. You'd be lying."

She snorted with laughter. "Yeah, Sed. I can't stop thinking about it. Thoughts of your perfect ass will consume my every waking moment, interrupt my dreams, and send me into an insatiable lust even Brian won't be able to satisfy."

"I could offer my assistance." He ran his fingers over her lapel, his eyes trained on her neckline.

"Only if you want to lose some teeth," she said, brandishing a fist at him.

He laughed. "You know it turns me on when you play hard to get."

"Try *impossible* to get." She patted his recently shaved cheek and headed toward the locker room exit, hoping Brian's parents wouldn't notice that she'd just spent twenty minutes in the locker room with their son and two other guys.

She found Claire laughing hysterically with Eric. Claire wiped tears from the corner of her eye and gave Eric a heartfelt squeeze. "I'm going to adopt you one of these days."

"If you adopt me, I can't marry you," he said, grinning ear to ear.

"Hey, wait until I'm dead before you start hitting on her," Malcolm said, drawing his wife away from Eric and against his side.

Claire started when she noticed Myrna standing at her elbow. "Oh, you're back," she said. "So, how did you meet my son?"

Myrna wondered if Brian had already told her. She knew better than to get caught in a lie, but if Brian had already lied about it, then he'd be the one who looked bad. She smiled, deciding to be as vague as possible.

"I met him in a hotel lounge. I was at a conference for work and he…" Why *had* the band been in the hotel that night instead of staying on the tour bus?

"…was staying in the hotel suite the concert venue provided free of charge," Eric supplied. "Nothing better than a long bath after being on the road for a month."

At Eric's mention of the hotel bath, Myrna's lungs stopped functioning.

Claire giggled.

"I hear you," Malcolm said.

Myrna decided it would be better if she asked the questions. "So I assume the two of you have seen Sinners in concert before. They put on a fantastic live show, don't they? The best."

Eric beamed at Myrna's compliment and shifted from Claire's to Myrna's side. Myrna hoped he didn't start with the perpetual fondling. She glanced up at him and found him behaving himself for a change. Claire didn't look too pleased to have lost Eric's undivided attention. Trey obviously understood this woman quite well. Myrna made a note to never look more attractive than Brian's mother while in her presence.

"We've seen them quite a few times," Malcolm said. "They sound a hell of a lot better than they did when they were making noise out in the garage as teenagers."

Claire giggled again and patted her husband's chest. "They were awful, weren't they?"

"And now they're one of the most popular and talented bands out there," Myrna said, still smiling.

Eric touched the small of Myrna's back, as if trying to protect her from impending doom.

"Just because you're popular doesn't mean you're talented," Malcolm said, scowling.

If Myrna had a cotton swab, she would have cleaned out her ears. *He didn't really just say that, did he?* Eric's fingers gripped the back of her jacket. Was he trying to keep her from jumping Brian's father and kicking the shit out of him? Probably a good move on Eric's part.

"They just don't make music like they used to," Malcolm added.

"Thank God," Myrna grumbled.

"I mean Sed doesn't even sing," Malcolm said. "He just screams and growls."

Eric's fingers gripped Myrna's jacket even tighter.

"And Brian solos constantly," Malcolm continued, the furrow in his brow deepening. "He wouldn't know a good riff if it bit him in the ass."

"Malcolm..." Claire said in warning, but she was grinning to herself in agreement.

"And why in the hell do you need three bass drums, Sticks?" Malcolm asked. "You only have two feet. And fourteen cymbals? I mean really. What's the point?"

"Different sounds," Eric said quietly.

"You're a fuckin' drummer. Your job is to keep the beat, not make different *sounds*."

"Eric is the best drummer in the business," Myrna said, her blood pressure sky high. "Sed has a beautiful voice, and Brian's solos are amazing!"

"Yeah, well, it sounds like a bunch of noise. It ain't music."

"What the hell do you know, you washed-up has-been?" Myrna sputtered. "Why don't you step off your self-erected pedestal and offer your son some support? You don't want him to succeed, do you? He thinks you want him to appreciate his success, but in reality, you didn't want him to surpass you. Too late, O'Neil. He already has."

"Did you just call me a 'has-been'?" Malcolm asked.

She doubted he'd heard anything else she'd said. The important stuff about his son had apparently bounced off his overly large ego. Frustrated to the limits of her tolerance, she shoved Eric away and spun on her heel. Sed, who was standing directly behind her, caught her by the shoulders to steady her. And beside Sed stood Trey and…Brian.

Shit!

From Brian's stunned expression, she gathered he'd overheard her tirade.

"I'm sorry." She ducked her head so she didn't have to see his face. What was she thinking? Calling a rock legend—Brian's *father*—a washed-up has-been. To his face. She wouldn't take it back though. She'd meant every word. "We'll talk later, Brian. I'll go wait on the bus." Maybe she could think of the right thing to say in the interim. She was at a complete loss at the moment.

"Why?" Brian asked.

"You heard what she called me," Malcolm bellowed.

"I also heard what you said." Emotion made Brian's voice waver, but Myrna still couldn't garner the courage to look at him. "If you don't want to be here, you should leave."

Malcolm grunted.

"Is it that hard for you to be proud of him?" Trey asked.

"Trey, stay out of this," Brian said. "He doesn't have to support everything I do."

"But he should," Myrna murmured. She wondered how it was possible to produce words with her entire foot in her mouth.

"You don't want to watch the show either?" Brian asked Myrna.

"Of course I want to watch the show."

"I never said I didn't want to be here," Malcolm added.

"It's settled then. Everyone has to suffer through my solos for the next hour."

Myrna reached for Brian's hand, but he threw her off

and stalked out of the dressing room. Before she could start after him, Trey caught her arm. "Thanks for saying something," he whispered. "He'd have kicked my ass for that."

"I should have kept my mouth shut." Now she had to fix things. She didn't want to be remembered as Brian's crazy ex-girlfriend who'd called Malcolm O'Neil a has-been.

Trey grinned. "You just showed how much you care. Brian will be stoked when he cools down and realizes it."

"I don't think he's stoked that I made an ass of myself in front of his parents."

She glanced at Malcolm and Claire, who were talking with their heads close together as they followed Eric out of the dressing room.

"The name-calling was a bit much," Trey said.

"And who instigated the entire thing?" She jabbed Trey in the chest with her finger. "You. I wouldn't have gone off if you hadn't alerted me to the situation."

"I've been wanting to tell off Brian's father for years."

Trey started after the rest of the group, and Myrna followed, her mind racing. "How can I make this up to him?"

"Do you want my honest opinion?" Trey asked.

"No, Trey, I want you to lie to me."

He grinned at her crookedly. "If you can get Malcolm to admit Brian is a great guitarist, I think he'll forgive you."

"That should be easy enough. All he has to do is listen to Brian play."

"Good luck with that."

"Do you think I can talk Malcolm into joining Brian onstage while he's soloing in the middle of the show?"

"Doubtful." Trey paused and took her by the arm, a thoughtful expression on his face. "Unless…"

"Unless what?"

"Maybe if the band plays a tribute to Winged Faith. Malcolm's problem is he's stuck in the seventies. He's an amazing musician but refuses to change, which puts him out of a job."

"That might work. Does the band know any Winged Faith songs?"

Trey's eyebrow arched. "Do you really have to ask? Every band knows every Winged Faith song ever written."

She chuckled. "True." Problem was, she doubted that Malcolm would agree to any suggestion she made. She squared her shoulders. She just wouldn't take no for an answer.

Trey laughed and tugged her into motion again.

She glanced up at him. "What?"

"The look of determination on your face. Papa Sinclair won't know what hit him." He hugged her against his side.

When they entered the backstage area, Myrna and Trey went in opposite directions. She spotted Brian near the stairs behind the stage. He always had preshow jitters, but tonight he looked physically ill.

She considered going to talk to him but figured she'd probably make things worse, and he didn't need the added anxiety right before their set. Trey, now equipped with his yellow and black guitar, approached Brian and pounded him on the back vigorously. He leaned close and said something in Brian's ear. Brian smiled, seeming to relax slightly, and whispered something back.

Trey was so good to Brian. She loved Trey for it and was jealous of him at the same time. She didn't quite understand that jealousy part. Trey had always been there for Brian. She should be happy that he had that kind of friend. And in a way she was. In another way, she wished she was the one Brian depended on.

Brian's eyes met hers across a sea of sound equipment. He sucked his top lip into his mouth and lowered his eyes to inspect his shoes. Her heart twisted and tears prickled her eyes.

He couldn't even look at her.

Was this the end? God, she hoped not.

But even if he never forgave her, she wanted to patch things up between him and his father. She'd put her psychology degree into full operational mode.

She continued around the stage, hurting more than she should. Why did she care if Brian no longer wanted to be with her? She'd never expected him to be a permanent fixture in her life, but this was too soon. She wasn't ready to give him up. Their three months weren't over. She still had six more weeks of data to collect for her project.

Myrna stood next to Malcolm on the floor to the side of the stage. He had his arms crossed over his chest and a look of tried patience on his face. Myrna bit her tongue and turned her attention to the stage. A camera crew stood ready to film a live video the band would be releasing soon. They'd chosen their hometown for the video because the crowd was guaranteed to be pumped up. When the stadium lights went down, the roar of the crowd was so deafening, Myrna covered her ears with both hands.

Knock 'em dead, guys.

The curtain dropped, and blinding white streams of fireworks fell behind the stage. The brilliant light-curtain silhouetted Brian, who stood on a platform behind and above the drum kit wailing on the intro to "Gates of Hell." Myrna's heart thudded with a mixture of pride and anticipation. Claire clapped excitedly. Malcolm didn't move a muscle. The crowd erupted in chaos.

Plumes of fire shot into the air on either side of the drum kit the instant the rest of the band joined Brian. The crowd screamed their approval.

Sed's low growl started to build. Myrna didn't see him at first, but based on their enthusiastic reaction, the fans obviously did. Then she saw what had them so excited. Sed rose from the floor, center stage, the low rumble of his voice increasing in intensity as a platform lifted him. When the platform hit flush with the stage, Sed leapt onto a raised, circular stage section that jutted out toward the crowd. Red and blue fountains of sparks shot up around him on all sides, concealing him in a circle of colorful light. As soon as the display went dark, he started singing the lyrics.

The pyrotechnics display impressed Myrna with its perfect synchronicity to the song. The crew had outdone themselves for the live recording.

"Show-offs," Malcolm grumbled.

Myrna suppressed the urge to kick him in the shins.

As the song's solo approached, Brian worked his way down from the platform behind the drums toward the circular outset at center stage. Sed moved back and Brian took his place. During his solo, a ring of fire surrounded his feet. As if he were playing for the devil himself, the flames licked higher and higher as the music built, until she could only see his silhouette. Myrna's heart squeezed with anxiety. Being surrounded by all those flames must be hot, and if something went wrong…

But the fire died at the end of the solo, and Brian stepped back onto the main stage unharmed.

"Wasn't that cool, baby?" Claire shouted.

Malcolm shrugged.

Myrna suppressed the urge to kick him in the ass.

When the song ended, the crowd yelled their approval.

"Good evening, Los Angeles!" Sed screamed into the mic. "Are you ready to rock?" He held the mic out toward the crowd. When they weren't loud enough to satisfy him, he screamed, "I said, are you ready to motherfuckin' rock?" He punctuated his final words with exaggerated nods of his head and thrust his microphone toward the audience. The crowd responded with greater enthusiasm.

Claire cringed. "Does he have to cuss like that?"

"Small vocabulary," Malcolm commented, grinning to himself.

Myrna suppressed the urge to kick him in the stomach.

Sed continued onstage, "The hometown crowd looks beautiful from where I stand. What do you think, Jace?" He grabbed Jace in a headlock and pulled him to the front of the stage.

"Craziest fuckers on the planet," Jace said quietly into Sed's microphone.

Myrna grinned. He was so damn cute. Some girl in the audience yelled, "I love you, Jace!"

Myrna could see the blush spread up his face from where she stood. "I love you, too."

"Oh, hell no," Sed growled. "I don't get any love?" He spread his arms wide, inviting adulation.

Thousands of women professed their love for Sed at the top of their lungs. He grinned like a shark.

"That's more like it," he said. "As you know, we're filming the concert tonight, so are you going to raise the roof?"

Yeah, they were. He sure knew how to get them pumped up. Myrna covered her ears to protect them from the roar of the crowd.

"Cuz our producer thought we should film this in fuckin' Canada."

Rounds of boos from the audience.

"That's what I said. Now, don't make me look bad. I stuck up for you guys. I said no one knows how to rock harder than L.A. What do you say, Master Sinclair?"

"I don't know, Sed," Brian said into his microphone, stage left. "Remember the last time we were up north? Those fans are pretty fuckin' insane." He paused for the crowd's negative response. "But I think they were just trying to keep warm." He rubbed his arms as if cold and hopped up and down like an overly excited fan. Eric drummed a buh-dum-bumb to accompany Brian's attempt at comedy.

Myrna laughed along with everyone else. Except Malcolm. His jaw twitched as he ground his teeth together.

Myrna suppressed the urge to kick him in the throat.

What in the hell was Malcolm's problem? He seemed to be making an effort to not enjoy himself. Claire had wandered off to chatter with a roadie and the lead singer of one of the opening bands, who obviously didn't real-ize he was hitting on Brian Sinclair's mother. Claire didn't seem to care that her son easily kept ten thousand people entertained with his talent and charm. She paid him no mind.

No wonder Brian desperately needed love and Myrna's constant approval. Stupid parents. Myrna had the strangest desire to just hug Brian. Hold him. Tell him how wonderful he was. How his father's approval didn't matter. He had the approval of hundreds of thousands of fans, but she knew that wouldn't fill that hole in him she hadn't recognized until this evening. Only one thing would fill that.

"You know what you should do," Myrna said to Malcolm as nonchalantly as she could muster. "You should get up there and show these kids where their guitar heroes got their influence."

He glanced at her but quickly covered his look of interest with annoyance. "Why are you talking to me?"

Myrna suppressed the urge to kick him in the teeth.

She shrugged. "Well, if you can't..."

He grunted, the arms crossed over his chest tightening until his biceps strained the sleeves of his T-shirt. "There's a difference between can't and won't."

"The outcome is the same."

The band started the next song. Myrna watched with her usual enthusiasm, pretending to ignore Malcolm, who tapped his toe occasionally and shifted his hands into his pockets during Brian's solo. This might be easier than she thought. He wanted to be up there with Brian. She *knew* he did. So why was he holding back? And why did he find it necessary to belittle not only Brian, but his entire band?

The majority of the crowd was a mosh pit—bodies

ricocheting off each other in chaos. When the song ended, the audience surged toward the barrier as individuals tried to situate themselves closer to the stage.

"Wild crowd tonight," Myrna commented. "Ever had a crowd like this one?"

Malcolm snorted. "Ever heard of Woodstock?"

"Oh yeah, you played there when Winged Faith was first starting out. That was what? Forty years ago?"

He scowled. "Yeah, I guess it has been that long. Best four days of my life."

"I'm betting the days your children were born were right up there with them."

"I was on tour in Cleveland when Brian was born. New Orleans with Kara."

"That must've been hard. Being on the road and missing your children's births."

"Being on the road all the time is hard. I missed a lot. But not being on the road is harder."

"You could get a little taste of that back tonight. I'm sure Brian would love to play a tribute to Winged Faith with you onstage. He said so himself." *Forgive me for lying, Brian.*

Malcolm's brow furrowed with what Myrna hoped was consideration. He glanced at his wife, who had found several more men to add to her entourage. Myrna counted two drummers, a bassist, and a guitarist, in addition to the lead singer and roadie. Malcolm rolled his eyes, removed his hands from his pockets, and crossed his arms again.

She could tell he wanted to be onstage, but apparently he needed more pushing. "I need to apologize to you for calling you a—"

He lifted a hand to silence her. "Do you always talk this much?" he asked. "You must drive Brian insane."

She laughed. "No, I talk a lot when I'm nervous."

He looked at her. *Really* looked at her for the first time. "Why are you nervous?"

"I'm in the presence of one of the original guitar greats. I don't think anyone could make me more nervous. Unless Jimi Hendrix rose from the grave and stood beside me."

"A Jimi Hendrix zombie would make everyone nervous." They laughed, continuing to talk loudly because the next song had started onstage.

"Did you meet Hendrix at Woodstock?"

Malcolm shook his head. "I watched him, though. That man could play."

"Brian's one of a kind, but I hear Hendrix's influence in his sound. And yours."

"Mine? He doesn't play anything like me."

"Sure he does. Listen to him. It's your style with embellishments."

"Lots of embellishments," he said, but he listened. Myrna suspected this was the first time Malcolm had actually *heard* Brian play. She watched Malcolm's expression change from indifference, to disbelief, to interest, and finally pride. "He does sound a lot like me," he murmured. He glanced at Myrna. "With embellishments."

"The fans love his soloing style, but without the sensual undercurrents that he borrowed from you, he'd sound flat."

"Look at him go. I could never keep up with him. He has crazy fast fingers."

Myrna flushed and averted her gaze. "Yeah."

When the song ended after a particularly embellished guitar outro, Malcolm clapped and thrust a fist in the air. "That's the way to play it, Son," he shouted.

Myrna wished she'd gotten that on tape. She almost had him. Just a little more pushing and she knew she could talk Malcolm into joining Brian onstage. She'd better hurry though, because she only had the span of two songs to convince him.

Chapter 30

BRIAN CHUGGED HALF A BOTTLE OF WATER AND returned to the stage. The rest of the band got a ten-minute break in the middle of the show. He was not so lucky. Or perhaps he was the lucky one who got the entire stage and thirty thousand fans all to himself. He approached the microphone on the ego riser at the center of the stage.

"It appears I've been deserted again," he said. He glanced at the side of the stage. The audience that mattered to him had disappeared, too. No Myrna. No Dad. At least his mom was there. She waved at him from the crew of men surrounding her. Nothing new there.

Myrna's absence unsettled him the most. Had he been too hard on her? He should have talked to her before the show. Let her know he wasn't too upset about her calling his father a has-been.

"I was going to play the first riff I ever learned for you tonight, but—"

"He never could play it right," his dad's voice interrupted from backstage.

The unmistakable riff of Winged Faith's hit song "Mystic" blared through the speakers as Malcolm O'Neil headed across the stage in Brian's direction. Dad was playing on Sinners' stage. Too stunned to find his guitar, much less play it, Brian stared at him in disbelief.

"Close your mouth, Son. You'll swallow a fly."

Brian snapped his jaws together, a smile spreading across his face until his cheeks hurt.

"Ladies and gentlemen, our surprise special guest, Malcolm O'Neil of Winged Faith," Sed's voice announced from behind the scenes.

The crowd cheered and Malcolm grinned. "Well, are we going to play them a song, or are we going to stand up here looking stupid all night?"

Brian's answer was to play the intro to "Mystic" with a few dozen extra notes per measure.

"I told you he never played it right," Malcolm said into the mic, but he grinned instead of scowling.

"Just spicing it up a little, old man."

Malcolm laughed.

They played the intro together, Malcolm in the traditional style and Brian with his additions. The crowd ate up every moment. When Eric and Jace joined them after the intro, Brian spun around, startled. Sed sang the opening verse so perfectly, Brian doubted even his father could tell the difference from the original. And then Brian spotted Trey and Myrna standing backstage by the amplifiers. Both of them looked entirely too pleased with themselves, laughing and hugging each other excitedly. So Myrna hadn't deserted him, and he suspected she had something to do with his father's change of heart. He turned back to the crowd, playing beside his father, his heart full to bursting. He wondered if Myrna knew how much this meant to him. Probably, but he'd tell her anyway.

The song ended much too soon. His dad handed his borrowed guitar over to Trey. Before he left the stage, Dad grabbed Brian by both ears and touched his forehead to his. "I'm proud of you, Son. I don't think I've ever told you that."

"I'm proud to be your son, Dad."

Dad grinned and released him. "That woman of yours is relentless."

Brian grinned. "Pretty terrific, isn't she?"

"Don't let her get away."

"Not a chance."

Malcolm took a bow and trotted off the stage. Brian saw his mother launch herself into his dad's arms and kiss him passionately, her entourage of attentive males entirely forgotten.

Brian decided they'd skip those dinner plans he'd made earlier. Mom and Dad looked like they needed some alone time, and God knew he wanted to express his gratitude to Myrna.

Chapter 31

Myrna waited for Brian to unlock the front door of his apartment. She didn't know what to expect when he pushed the door open, but a large, tastefully decorated foyer and expansive, clean, and comfortable living area would not have been her first guess.

"What do you think?" he asked, looking at her with that approval-please expression she'd come to recognize.

"It's great, Brian." She kissed his jaw and crossed the threshold. "I love it. Did you decorate it yourself?"

He laughed. "No. Sed had a thing with an interior decorator for a while. She maxed out his credit card, but we got great digs at his expense. If you think this is nice, you should see his place. It's amazing."

Myrna set her purse on a marble-topped, cherry table next to the front door and ventured farther inside. Brian dropped their suitcases inside the door and locked it behind him. The furniture was heavy and inviting. Neat and masculine. Dark woods contrasted with sage green, taupe, and ivory upholstery. Matching pillows, rugs, and abstract artwork tied everything together. She could picture Brian enjoying the soothing colors, but the décor didn't seem to fit his roommate's style at all. And the place was spotless.

"How do you keep it so clean? Doesn't Trey live here with you?" She was constantly on top of Trey to pick up after himself on the bus. She couldn't imagine his behavior being much different at home.

"Maid service, baby."

"Ah, that explains everything."

She turned to find him standing directly behind her. "Thank you," he murmured, taking both her hands in his and staring into her eyes with sincerity.

"You're welcome," she said, "but what are you thanking me for?"

"For what you did with my dad."

She smiled and squeezed his hands. "I was just trying to make up for insulting him and for hurting you. I don't know why I got so mad when he criticized you and the band."

"I think I know why." He kissed her tenderly.

"I guess I'm just a fangirl, after all."

The front door opened. "Honey, I'm home," Trey called and tossed his keys on the table beside the door.

A tall brunette with big boobs, bigger hair, and an almost nonexistent skirt followed Trey into the apartment. She scowled when her eyes landed on Myrna.

"When you said Brian would be here, you didn't say anything about him having a woman with him," she said to Trey.

"Hey, Carly," Brian murmured. Myrna's head snapped up to look at him. He knew this…this *woman*? Was she an old girlfriend of his? Brian toyed with the button at the top of Myrna's suit jacket, his face red and body tense as he stared at his fiddling fingers.

"I didn't say he *wouldn't* have a woman with him," Trey pointed out.

"I was hoping to be involved in one of your famous threesomes tonight," Carly said, "but everyone knows Brian doesn't cheat."

Famous threesomes? Myrna's eyes widened and her breath caught.

Brian's hands moved to cover Myrna's ears. "Will you get her out of here? We were having a moment," Brian's muffled voice carried through his hands.

Trey said something Myrna couldn't make out. Carly grinned brazenly, grabbed Trey's belt buckle, and led him down the hallway. As soon as the bedroom door closed, Brian dropped his hands.

"Sorry you had to see that."

"Famous threesomes?" she sputtered.

"*Really* sorry you heard that." He turned and headed toward the kitchen off to the side of the main living room. "Are you hungry?"

She trailed after him, stumbling over the edge of an area rug because she wasn't watching where she was going. "Don't change the subject, Brian."

"I'm starved. There should be something in here to eat. Wanda knew we'd be home tonight, and she's always good about stocking up for our return."

He opened the refrigerator and leaned inside.

"Did Carly mean…that you and Trey and…and a…" She swallowed. "…a *woman* have…" She touched her cheeks with cool fingertips. Why was her face so hot? "H-have…?"

"Fucked like maniacs?" He tossed a store-bought package of refrigerated tortellini onto the counter. "Yep, that's what she meant. Red sauce or white?"

Myrna leaned heavily against the breakfast bar. "A *three*some?"

"Myrna, calm down. It was just sex. All in the past. No big deal." He tossed a plastic tub on the counter next to the pasta. "I think red sauce sounds better."

She'd never been involved in anything even remotely as exciting as a threesome. "Have you done that often?" she asked, her voice at least two pitches higher than usual.

Brian shrugged. "Not recently. Trey and I used to share everything. And I do mean everything. We've grown up a lot in the past couple of years."

"Damn," she muttered under her breath.

Brian dropped a pan. It clattered across the floor, but he didn't retrieve it. He gaped at her instead. "Did you just say 'damn'?"

Her eyes widened and she shook her head vigorously. "No." She smoothed her skirt, licked her lips, and lowered her gaze to the floor. "I said pan. You dropped your pan."

"I dropped it after you said damn."

Her flushed face flamed several degrees hotter. "Oh."

His boots entered her line of sight. "Would you be open to something like that?"

Her eyes darted to his face and then back to his boots. "I don't know."

"I'm sure Trey would go for it."

She could scarcely hear him over the blood rushing through her ears.

He touched her chin, and when she found her courage, she looked up at him. "We'd make you feel real good," he murmured. His hands slid over the curve of her ass and he tugged her closer. "Real good."

He seemed as turned on by the idea as she was. And she was at full throttle.

"Wouldn't it make things weird between us?" she asked.

"Between us?"

"Me. You. Trey. All of us?"

"It doesn't have to. Trey never equates sex with

emotion or conquest. He'd think of it as nothing but a good time. Otherwise, I wouldn't let him touch you." He brushed a stray lock of hair behind her ear. "I'll let you think about it. No pressure."

She nodded. She already knew she wanted to do it, but she was afraid that Brian would think poorly of her. God, this would make her the biggest whore on the planet. *I love to fuck you, baby, but if you don't mind, I'd like to fuck your best friend at the same time*.

"I prefer red sauce, too," she said absently.

He burst out laughing, and then bent to pick up the pan he'd dropped. He went to the sink and filled it with water before setting it on the stove. "Talk about subject change. Red sauce it is."

Myrna continued to lean against the counter. She watched Brian burn his fingers several times before she took over the cooking. Seriously, the man couldn't even boil water without causing himself harm. He sat on a stool on the other side of the breakfast bar and watched her cook with a giddy expression.

"Why are you looking at me like that?" she asked him finally.

"You're in my home. Cooking on my stove."

"If you ask me to get barefoot and pregnant and put on a frilly apron, I'm going to clobber you."

"You can wear shoes."

She rolled her eyes at him. "Why, thank you. How generous."

"Vegas is only a four-hour drive from here, you know."

She brandished a slotted spoon at him. "Don't go there, Brian."

"Or you could just move in with me."

"I have this job I'm rather attached to, and I've heard the commute from Los Angeles to Kansas City is a killer."

"You could retire."

"Retire?" She gaped at him. "I'm thirty-five years old. How do you expect me to support myself?"

"I'll support you."

"I told you not to go there, Brian. You're going there."

"Then I'll move in with you. When I'm not on tour or in the recording studio, I'll call Kansas City my home."

"Okay, you totally went there."

"Is it so wrong that I want to be with you?"

No, it was wrong that she was starting to agree with him, which she knew was a huge mistake. "This week apart will do us both good."

He dropped his head to the counter and rubbed his face over its surface. "Don't say that. I already miss you, and you aren't even gone yet."

She sighed and turned off the pan of pasta. Why did he always have to be so sweet to her? He was making it awfully fucking hard for her to keep him at arm's length.

"Do you have a colander?" she asked.

"I have no idea what you're talking about."

"A strainer. To drain the pasta."

"There you go, changing the subject again."

"Would you prefer I leave? I'm feeling very crowded by you at the moment."

He sighed heavily. "In the second drawer, next to the refrigerator."

Silence hung between them as she finished fixing the meal. He eventually climbed from his stool and set two plates and sets of silverware on the breakfast bar.

"Will Trey and Carly join us?" She glanced at him. He was pouting again.

"Doubtful."

When they sat down to eat, she took his hand. "You know my job is important to me, don't you?"

"I just wish *I* was important to you."

Her heart twanged. "I never said you weren't important to me. That's not why I need this week away from you. I have to do well with this research project, Brian. If I don't publish some compelling results by the end of the summer, I'm not going to have a job for much longer."

"What? Why didn't you say something?"

"I'm not proud of the position I'm in. I don't really like doing research in the first place, but I love to teach. I wouldn't trade that part of my job, for anything." She sighed. "The university requires I bring in a certain amount of outside funding to keep my job, and I lost my big grant a couple of months ago. I don't have tenure yet. That means I have to make myself financially valuable to the university or they'll let me go. This summer side project is enough to keep me there for another year, hopefully, but I don't know what I'm going to do after that. I don't want to give this job up. I worked too hard to get where I am to throw in the towel now. That's why as much as I love having fun with you and spending time with you, I've got to get my work done. Do you understand?"

"Yeah, I think I get it. By pressuring you, I'm pushing you away."

"Exactly."

He squeezed her hand and smiled. "I'm glad you told me, Myrna. I feel a little better about you being gone for a whole week."

She released his hand and picked up her fork. It felt good to confide in him. She didn't have anyone in her life to share her worries with. It was nice in an unexpected way. "Maybe I'll get caught up with my work faster than I ever thought possible and come back early."

He grinned hopefully. "Yeah?"

She shrugged and took a bite of her tortellini. "We'll see."

"So do you want to arrange that threesome with Trey before you go or when you return?" He winked at her.

She paused with her fork halfway to her mouth. She wasn't sure how she could be calm when she said, "Surprise me."

Chapter 32

WITH A SLEEPY GRIN, MYRNA STRETCHED HER ARMS over her head and rolled over to spoon against Brian's back. She had to be on a plane in twelve hours, but the last thing she wanted to do this morning was climb out of bed.

She rubbed her hands over his belly, her lips caressing his shoulder. They had a couple of hours to say a proper good-bye, and she was planning to fill every minute with pleasure. He shuddered as her hands trailed up his chest, her fingers bumping over the hoop in his left nipple.

Her eyes flipped open. *Nipple ring?*

"Don't stop now," Trey murmured drowsily. "Feels nice."

Instantly wide awake, Myrna sat up. She jerked up the sheet to cover her bare breasts. "What are you doing here?"

"I invited him," Brian said from the opposite side of the bed.

"Slumber party." Trey's eyes drifted closed.

Myrna scooted closer to Brian, her heart hammering. Brian had her flat on her back beneath him in seconds. "Trey's tired. We'll start without him."

He linked their hands together on either side of her head and kissed her until her rigid body began to relax.

"I'm not that tired." Trey's hand slid across Myrna's

belly, and she tensed again. "Save some of that for me," he murmured.

Soft lips brushed her shoulder.

She tore her mouth from Brian's and looked at Trey. His emerald green eyes met hers unflinchingly.

"You okay?" Brian asked her. "If you've changed your mind, we can stop."

Trey's hand slid up her side, drawing a trail of gooseflesh in its wake. He cupped her breast, his thumb brushing over her pebbled nipple. Her eyes drifted closed with pleasure.

"I don't think it's her who will have a problem with this," Trey said to Brian. "I'm more worried about you. You are not allowed to hate me for this."

"We've done this before, Trey. Did I ever have a problem then?"

"But you really lo—" Trey took a deep breath. "You really care about Myrna."

"And I trust her. I know she won't cheat on me behind my back."

She smiled and reached up to trace his brow with her fingertips. "You're right. I wouldn't."

"But cheating to your face is fine?" Trey asked.

"This isn't cheating," Myrna said. "It's a mutually agreed upon sexual experience. But if you don't want to join us, you can leave."

"Oh, I want to join you. I'm more than willing to fuck your brains out. I just don't want something as meaningless as hot, dirty sex to damage my friendship with Brian."

Brian chuckled. "Told you he was perfect for this kind of thing."

Funny how Trey was the one most concerned about the possible repercussions of their encounter. Myrna would just have to convince him that she wanted this, and Brian wanted this, so it was okay for him to want it, too. She wriggled out from under Brian and tackled Trey to the mattress on his back. She was surprised to find he was wearing his jeans under the covers. He really was reluctant.

She slid her hands up his chest. The glint of metal caught her eye. She lowered her head and sucked his silver nipple ring into her mouth. A sound of tormented protest escaped the back of his throat.

"Myr, what are you doing?" Trey whispered.

She sucked harder, her tongue flicking the ring in her mouth. He drew a breath through his teeth and covered his eyes with his hands. "Please, don't."

The back of her hand scraped against his belly as she reached for his belt buckle. He shuddered and squirmed sideways out of her grasp. He pointed at her for emphasis. "No, Myrna. You don't want to do this."

"Oh, but I do." After unfastening his belt buckle, she unbuttoned his fly and jerked his pants down his thighs. His cock stood at rigid attention. "And apparently, so do you."

Trey looked over at Brian, who was lounging on his side with his head propped up on his hand, watching them.

"Dude, I can't help it," Trey said. "It has a mind of its own."

"Hey, it's completely understandable," Brian said calmly. He wrapped his free hand around his own stiff cock. "I'm hard as a rock just watching her molest you."

Watching her be naughty turned Brian on? How would he react if she sucked Trey's cock?

She slid down Trey's body until the visual evidence of his excitement was at eye level. His shaft was uncommonly long, but lean. She wasn't sure if she could swallow him, but she was willing to try.

"W-wait, Myrna," Trey gasped.

She took him into her mouth, deep into the back of her throat. She swallowed. Trey groaned. She sucked him gently, paying attention to his reactions to determine how he liked to be pleasured. Brian placed a hand on her forehead and eased her back off Trey's cock until he fell free of her mouth. Trey sucked a breath through his teeth.

She looked up at Brian, feeling uncertain of her actions. "Should I not have done that?"

"That's not it. I want some attention, too."

Her gaze shifted to The Beast and she smiled. "I didn't mean to ignore you, big guy." She shifted on the bed and took Brian's thick cock into her mouth. She held the base of his shaft while she sucked him with the rapid technique she knew he liked best. She soon had him gasping in excitement.

She heard the sound of Trey's belt buckle being fastened behind her. He unwrapped a cherry sucker and slurped it into his mouth. The mattress sagged as he moved to leave. Brian grabbed his arm.

"My woman wants you to fuck her, Trey. Are you going to give her what she wants or not?" He sank his fingers into her hair, panting in pleasure as she continued to work the head of his cock with her lips and tongue. "I mean, look at her. Maybe you can say no to her, but I can't. I can't deny her anything."

"You're seriously asking me to bang Myrna?" Trey asked.

Out of the corner of her eye, Myrna caught sight of him clutching his crotch.

"No, not bang her. We're going to make love to her. Together."

"Are you stoned, Brian?" Trey said. "You will never forgive me for this. I know you won't."

"No, I'm not stoned." He leaned close to Trey and whispered something into his ear.

Trey leaned back and stared at Brian for a long moment. He shrugged. "Well, if you're sure." He unfastened his belt buckle again and stripped himself naked.

Caught in a moment of indecision, Myrna's heart thudded with apprehension. Could she really go through with this? She released Brian's cock, and he gasped brokenly. Rising to her knees, she knelt before Trey and stared into his seductive green eyes. The man was sexy, no doubt about it. He removed his sucker from his mouth and rubbed it over her nipple. He then lowered his head to remove the sticky residue with his tongue. Myrna's hands went to his silky hair, simultaneously trying to push him away and hold him to her throbbing breast. Brian spooned up against her back, his hands sliding down her belly and hips, his hard cock pressed firmly into the crack of her ass.

Something harder than a tongue flicked against her nipple. Myrna gasped in surprise. She'd forgotten Trey had his tongue pierced. And God, it felt good.

She relaxed against Brian's body, concentrating on the feel of Trey's eager tongue flicking over her nipple. "Do you have magic fingers like Master Sinclair, Trey?" she asked in a low voice.

Trey glanced up at her with sultry green eyes, part

of his right eye obscured by his long bangs. He grinned crookedly. "Would you like to find out?"

"Brian can make me come in under ten seconds. Let's see what you can do."

"Ten seconds, huh?" Trey said. "With just his fingers?"

"You don't believe her?" Brian asked.

"Ten seconds? No, I don't." He lifted his head and glanced down at his watch. "Go for it. I'll time you."

Brian's hand slid down the middle of her body to the swollen flesh between her thighs. She gripped his thighs and leaned against his shoulder as his fingers sought her clit in the nest of curls.

"Wait a minute," Trey said. "She could be faking."

"I never fake an orgasm."

"So she says." Trey's hand touched the inside of her thigh. "May I?"

She nodded slightly, and Trey slid two fingers inside her. She tensed. Brian kissed her neck. "Relax," he murmured. "It's okay."

It was difficult to relax knowing it was Trey's fingers curled inside her. He twisted his hand and she shuddered.

"You ready?" Brian whispered into her ear.

She bit her lip and nodded. Trey twisted his fingers the other direction. Her mouth fell open and she gasped.

"I think I can make her come by just twisting my fingers," Trey said.

"I wouldn't be surprised," Brian said. "Ten seconds."

Trey looked at his watch again. "Go."

Brian's fingers rubbed her clit with his practiced pressure and rhythm. Within a dozen strokes, Myrna shuddered and cried out, clinging to Brian's thighs. Her pussy convulsed rhythmically around Trey's fingers.

"Jesus. That was like eight seconds," Trey said. He twisted his fingers again, and Myrna's legs buckled. He slid his fingers from her body and added them to his mouth with his sucker. "Mmmmm. Does she always taste this good?"

"Oh yeah."

"No wonder you're always in bed with her. I never realized she was this hot. Sed doesn't know, does he?"

"No and you'd better not tell him."

"I need to lie down," Myrna murmured.

Brian guided her trembling body down until she was lying on her back. She covered her face with her hands. She really was a whore. She'd loved having Trey's fingers up her cunt while Brian stroked her clit until she'd cried out with sexual release. Jeremy had been so right about her. She felt sick to her stomach.

A pair of lips kissed the inside of her thigh. Too soft to be Brian's lips. Trey's? She kept her hands over her face. Could she allow Trey to have his way with her without permanent trauma to her psyche?

The soft lips kissed their way up her thigh until they reached the top of her leg. Something probed her ever-eager hole. Not his fingers or his tongue. His sucker? *Don't,* she thought. He dipped his candy inside her rhythmically and sucked her clit into his mouth. Her fingers curled into her forehead. *I can't do this.* He rubbed her clit with the stud piercing in the flat of his tongue until she began to tremble. *Can't do this.* She gasped. *Oh yes, that's the spot. Lick it, Trey. I want your mouth on me. I like it.* Trey removed his cherry sucker from her pussy and replaced it with his tongue. He wriggled and twirled his tongue, and then thrust it into her deeply.

She'd never been eaten out quite like this before. She shuddered. If Brian had an uncommon talent with his fingers, then Trey's had to be with his tongue.

"God, that feels good," she whimpered.

The mattress sagged beside her. Brian straddled her chest and leaned over her. She moved her hands from her eyes. His cock bounced against her chin. "Suck me?"

She opened her mouth wide, and he slid inside. She sealed her lips around him and he thrust into her throat, holding on to the headboard for support so he didn't choke her. She kept the suction tight and let him carry the rhythm. Her concentration was more on what Trey was doing to every part he could reach between her quivering thighs with his devilish tongue.

Trey stimulated her with his cherry sucker again, and then spread her ass cheeks with both hands and tongued her asshole. She squirmed. God, that felt good, too. Was it possible to have an orgasm just by having your ass licked? Ripples of delight pulsated through her empty pussy. Her clit throbbed with neglect. Maybe just the anticipation could send her over the edge. "Mmmm." She lost concentration and gagged on Brian's cock. Brian pulled back.

"You okay?" Brian asked, stroking her hair.

She nodded. Brian thrust forward again, pulled back, thrust forward deep into her throat. Trey's tongue writhed inside her back entrance. She tensed. She relaxed only when he withdrew his tongue altogether.

"God, you have a tight little ass, Myrna. Can I fuck it?"

She made a sound around Brian's thrusting cock that must have sounded like agreement, though she wasn't sure it was. Trey moved around the bed to a side table drawer that contained Brian's favorite toys. From the corner of her eye, she watched Trey grab a tube of lube and a heavily ridged condom from the collection. Her eyes widened in protest.

Brian pulled out of her mouth and sat on the bed beside her. He urged Myrna onto her stomach and offered his jutting cock to her again. "Like this, sweetheart. Give Trey some room to do his thing."

His *thing*? What thing?

Her heart thudded in her chest.

Just don't think about what Trey is going to do. Concentrate on Brian.

Myrna rested on her elbows, leaned over Brian's lap, and took him deep into her throat. She had better control in this position and could indulge him with other things she knew he liked. Her fingers stroked his asshole, teasing him with promises of penetration. Her head bobbed up and down over the head of his cock. Brian's fingers tangled in the long strands of her hair as he groaned in encouragement.

Trey's hands gripped Myrna's hips and lifted her onto her knees. His thigh eased between her legs, widening her stance. He continued to arrange her body as he wanted it—her knees far apart, her back arched downward. He inserted a slippery finger into her ass, wetting her passage with some sort of warming lubricant. He added another finger, stretching her in various directions in preparation for his penetration. She got the feeling he did this often. More lube. More stretching and probing.

As if she wasn't already nervous enough.

She released Brian from her mouth. "Just put it in already."

Trey slapped her ass. She winced. "I'll put it in when I'm good and ready," he said. Which was apparently that moment. He eased into her body. Heat flooded her core.

"Oh," she whimpered. She experienced no painful burning sensation as he slid deep into her ass. Paused. Pushed deeper. He gave her time to adjust, pressing forward a little at a time. Even when she'd accepted every inch of him and he rotated his hips to open her wider, it didn't hurt at all. Trey's cock wasn't as thick as Brian's, and he obviously had a lot of practice in this technique. His angle of penetration was perfection. She rocked back against him with a groan.

"Do you like that?" Brian asked.

She expected him to start taking notes or something.

Trey pulled back and she shuddered. He took her deep again. *Dear God, yes.* His thrusts became rhythmic, the heavy ribs on the condom further stimulating her throbbing flesh.

"Yeah," she gasped. "He's good at it. Oh."

"That's because he's been done that way himself." Brian chuckled.

Myrna expected Trey to protest Brian's barb, but he said, "Fucked by the best."

Trey's rhythm was constant. Unrelenting. Myrna took Brian's cock back into her mouth and matched Trey's thrusts with the movement of her head and tongue. Trey skimmed his hands up her back, down her back, over her ass, down the backs of her thighs, and then stroked the same path in reverse. She shuddered. His fingertips slid up the fronts of her thighs, the protrusions of her hipbones, her belly, breasts, and back again. The sides of her body next. Returning to her back. Every inch of her skin was alive with stimulation. The light pressure of his fingertips over her flesh never wavered. Each thrust matched his last perfectly. Trey Mills was all about perfection. And when she became accustomed to his perfect synchrony, he slapped her ass again. The unexpected jolt to her system made her tense.

"Ow," Brian protested.

She released him from her mouth. "Did I bite you?"

"Yeah. You've never bitten me before. You're having a hard time concentrating, aren't you?"

She looked up at him. "I'm sorry."

He touched her face. She'd try harder to pay attention to what she was doing. She ran her tongue around the head of his cock and drew him inside her mouth again. She pressed his legs farther apart so she could massage his balls with the palm of her hand and rub his sensitive hole with two fingertips. Brian's head fell back against the headboard with a loud thunk. He grabbed her hair in both fists as she sucked him deep, her tongue working against the underside of his cock all the way down and then all the way back up. She could tell he approved of her renewed concentration by the punctuated gasps coming from the back of his throat.

Trey leaned over her, his sweat dripping over the surface of her back. "You should see his face, Myrna. I think he's about to blow the back of your head off."

Myrna reached between her legs and brushed her fingertips over Trey's sac. He gasped and lost his perfect rhythm altogether. He stayed buried deep so she could reach him. She massaged Trey's balls with one hand

and Brian's with the other. The combined gasps of the two men drove her to distraction. She rubbed her wrist against her clit while she fondled Trey, seeking sexual release. God, she ached. Her pussy was so empty.

"So who's gonna let go first?" Trey asked, biting into his sucker with a loud crunch. "I think I can outlast Brian."

"You aren't even moving anymore. Let her suck you and see how long you last. God, woman! Just put your fingers inside. Quit teasing me."

She complied, sliding two fingers deep. He cried out hoarsely.

"She's doing some amazing stuff with my nuts," Trey said. "If I move, I'm pretty sure she'll stop."

Myrna lifted her head. "What about me?" she whispered. "I want you inside me, Brian. Please. I need your thick cock buried deep…"

Trey pulled out, making Myrna moan. "Let's switch then."

"Do you want to ride me, sweetheart?" Brian asked.

"God, yes." And if that made her a whore, so be it.

Brian slid down the bed to lie flat on his back between her thighs. She grabbed his cock and guided it into her aching pussy, taking him deep and fast. Rubbing that itch deep inside that only he could satisfy. Her head fell back as she pounded into him, vocalizing her pleasure in the back of her throat.

Trey drew a breath between his teeth. "God, that sound she makes…"

"…is so fuckin' hot," Brian finished Trey's sentence.

Trey touched the back of Myrna's head and she opened her eyes to look at him. He was standing on the bed in front of her. He'd removed the condom and his long cock stood at attention, glistening before her.

"Suck him, Myrna," Brian encouraged, looking up at them. "I can see everything from here."

"Did you ever think you'd be lying there looking up at your best friend's sac? How's the view?" Trey chuckled.

Myrna leaned forward and sucked Trey into her mouth. He'd coated his cock with one of Brian's flavored lotions and tasted like sweet coconut. She slurped him deep, and he cursed under his breath.

"That's it, baby. Teach him a lesson for being such a smart-ass," Brian said.

"Yeah, teach me a lesson, Professor."

Brian wrapped his hands around her hips to help her raise and lower herself on his cock. She found it hard to concentrate on pleasuring Trey and herself at the same time. She placed a hand on Trey's sweat-slick belly and pulled away. He grunted in protest as she abandoned him. She lowered her head, resting her forehead against Brian's temple. Her hand ran down Trey's thigh as she whispered into Brian's ear, "Tell me what you want me to do to him. I'll do anything you say."

"Anything?"

She turned her head to look at Brian. He was grinning deviously.

"You're really okay with this?" she asked.

"Why wouldn't I be? It was my idea."

"You don't think I'm a whore?"

He laughed. "Why would I think that? You're a gift from heaven as far as I'm concerned."

Myrna glanced up at Trey. "Yeah, I'll do anything you tell me to," she whispered into Brian's ear.

"What are you two plotting?" Trey asked, grabbing Myrna's hand that was still resting on his thigh. He shifted her hand to his cock and used it to stroke his flesh, twisting her wrist slightly each time her hand rubbed over his swollen head. "Please don't tell me you changed your mind and now you're going to toss me out in the hallway with a horrible case of blue balls."

"You know I wouldn't do that to you, buddy," Brian said and laughed maniacally.

"On second thought…" Trey took a step sideways.

Myrna's hand tightened on Trey's cock, and he stopped. She looked up at him. "Where do you think you're going?"

"Just trying to keep personal injury to a minimum."

"I won't hurt you, Trey," she promised, sitting up.

"Unless I tell her to."

"Huh?" Trey gasped.

"Move him a little to the left," Brian said.

Myrna's hands moved to Trey's hips and she shifted him to the left.

"Wait, I—"

"Put your hand on his chest and shove him against the wall. Don't let him give you any lip," Brian instructed.

Myrna shoved Trey against the wall. He hit his head with a loud thud. "Hey!" he protested.

"Grab his nuts and tell him to shut up."

She grabbed Trey's balls and he cried out in pain.

"Easy," Brian said.

Her grip loosened slightly. "Shut up." She felt like she had a little devil on her shoulder, whispering naughty instructions to her.

"Yes, ma'am," Trey squeaked.

"Lick the head of his dick."

Her tongue darted from between her lips, wrapping around the head of Trey's cock. He shuddered violently.

"Don't give him much. Lick one side along the rim, over and over again. I want you to drive him crazy. Go."

She did exactly as Brian instructed. Trey groaned in protest. Within a minute, Trey was rocking on the balls of his feet, just like he did when the music overtook him onstage.

Brian laughed. "Tell her what you want, Trey."

"Suck me," he growled between clenched teeth. "Please."

She glanced down at Brian for instructions and he shook his head.

"Put two fingers in his ass and do that thing you do to me sometimes."

"What thing?" Trey asked suspiciously.

She grinned. "You're very generous with your friends, sweetheart," she murmured.

She slid her index and middle fingers into Brian's mouth to wet them and then reached between Trey's legs and shoved them inside his body.

Trey gasped brokenly. "Oh yeah. You know I like that."

She searched inside him until she found her target and stroked the swollen gland persistently. Trey grabbed her hair in both fists and directed his cock into her mouth. His cries of ecstasy encouraged her to suck him hard while she continued to stimulate him with her fingers.

Brian grabbed her wrist and eased her fingers from Trey's body. She released his cock as well and glanced down at Brian for further instructions.

"Leave him for a minute," Brian said. "Ride me until you come, and if he's quiet, I'll tell you to suck him off. Maybe."

Still trembling from the pleasure she'd given him, Trey groaned in protest. He wrapped his hand around the head of his cock and flinched.

"If he's quiet," Brian repeated. "And doesn't touch himself."

Trey's brow furrowed. "Fu…" He bit his lip. He shifted both hands to his hips and stood there waiting for Myrna to make her next move.

She grinned down at her devious lover, rising and falling over him now. Brian's fingers worked her clit, driving her mad with desire. Her head fell back as her cries grew louder and louder with each thrust.

"Shit," Trey muttered. "I'm supposed to just stand here and watch you two fuck while I get nothing?"

Myrna lifted her head to glare at Trey. "You already had yours. And you're supposed to be quiet," she said, and shoved him against the wall. "You broke my concentration. Now I have to start over."

Brian gasped in pleasure. She looked down to find him writhing on the brink of orgasm. She slapped him across the face. "Don't you dare let go. Not yet. I'm not finished with you."

. He caught her wrist before she slapped him again. "You're getting awfully bossy." He looked up at Trey and nodded. Trey hopped off the bed.

Brian grabbed her around the waist and rolled their entwined bodies onto their sides. She gasped as his cock rammed into her. He lifted her left leg to rest around his waist. Trey spooned up against her back. She stiffened.

"Relax," Trey whispered into her ear.

He probed her back entrance with the head of his cock and then he was inside her.

Both of them were inside her. Oh. So gloriously filled.

They began to move. Brian thrusting into her, while Trey pulled out. Brian pulled out, while Trey thrust inside. Her senses were so overwhelmed that she couldn't do anything but cling to Brian's chest and gasp for air, her head tilted back and pressing into Trey's shoulder.

"Are you okay?" Brian whispered into her ear.

"Yes," she gasped. "Yes. Yes, oh God, yes! Yes! Fuck me. Fill me. Both of you. I love it. I love it!" She saw stars when she came, but they didn't let her recover. They switched to thrusting into her and pulling out in unison.

Trey's body convulsed behind her. "God, Brian, your cock is driving me crazy."

"Yeah," Brian agreed. "I feel you moving inside her. Feels so good." His breath caught. "Faster, Trey. Stay with me."

Myrna turned her head to look at them. They lay facing each other, staring into each other's eyes over her shoulder. She'd seen this intensity between them onstage before, this *connection*, but was surprised to see it here. Brian closed his eyes. Still matching Brian's thrusts, Trey leaned forward and kissed him on the mouth.

Myrna's eyes widened.

Trey's tongue probed Brian's lips.

Brian opened his mouth and Trey plunged his tongue inside. Trey's hand moved to the back of Brian's head to hold him still as he kissed him. He sucked Brian's lips passionately, his thrusts into Myrna's body growing increasingly vigorous as his excitement got the better of him and he lost their synchronicity. Trey watched Brian the entire time he kissed him, his eyes glistening with unexpected tears. After a moment, he squeezed his eyes shut, his kiss shifting from passionate to desperate.

Myrna lay there, too stunned to do anything but gawk.

Oh my God. Trey loved Brian. She knew it for a certainty. Trey *loved* Brian. Loved him.

The urge to scratch out his eyes overwhelmed her. Did Brian realize this? Myrna didn't think Brian even realized that Trey was kissing him. He'd gone into that muse trance mode that struck him completely unaware on occasion.

After a moment, Brian twisted his head to the side, breaking the kiss. Trey's head dropped to rest against the side of Myrna's face. He cupped Brian's jaw with such tenderness, Myrna's fist clinched. She knew Brian didn't love Trey. Not that way. He couldn't. Brian was hers. Only hers.

Trey panted with exertion, pumped into her deeply twice, and then shuddered with a startled cry as he found release. "Brian," he gasped. "Brian."

Brian hadn't moved for several minutes. He opened his eyes, but they were glazed over with that far-off look he got when he was completely inside his own head. "Do you hear it?" he whispered.

Myrna smiled. She knocked Trey's hand aside and stroked back the strands of hair sticking to Brian's sweaty face. "Yeah, baby. I hear it. Let it come."

Trey lifted his head, listening intently. "I don't hear anything."

"Go get something to write on," she said to Trey. *And leave us alone. He's mine.*

"What? He didn't finish, did he? I wanted to watch him come. He always looks so hot when he lets go."

"He'll be out of it like that for a while. Go get something to write on. Trust me, you're going to want to write this one down."

"Thanks for sharing Brian with me this morning, Myrna. He's been distancing himself from me lately." Trey kissed her temple affectionately and pulled out.

Uh, no. She was *not* sharing Brian with him. As exciting and pleasurable as they had made this encounter for her, she much preferred having Brian all to herself. Brian was hers. Only hers. And she wanted to keep it that way.

Trey searched the room noisily for something to write on, but Myrna scarcely noticed. She was too busy coming to terms with the idea that she wasn't just hopelessly, madly, deeply in *lust* with Brian "Master" Sinclair. She might actually *love* him. An idea that did not sit well with her.

"Why are you looking at me like that?" Brian asked her, much more alert than he'd been a few moments before.

"Like what?"

"Like you have a bad taste in your mouth." Brian licked his lips, his brows drawing together in confusion. "And why do my lips taste like cherry?" He lifted his head to glare at Trey. "Did you kiss me again?"

Again?

Trey chuckled uneasily. "Of course not." He tossed a pen and pad of paper onto the bed and fled the room. The door closed behind him securely. He hadn't even bothered to take his clothes with him.

Brian looked at Myrna. "He kissed me, didn't he?"

"Maybe."

"I'm going to go kick his ass now. Excuse me." He backed away, his cock falling free of her body.

Myrna wrapped her arms around his neck. "I don't want you to go." She nuzzled her face against his neck. She could never remember feeling this emotionally attached to anyone. Why did knowing that someone else loved Brian make her want him for herself even more?

"He knows better."

"Are you and Trey more than friends?" she asked, her heart thudding. *Please say no. Please.*

Brian stopped trying to pull away and went entirely still. "I'm not sure how to answer that question."

"Are you lovers?"

He hesitated for far too long. Myrna felt sick to her stomach. Not because it was Trey that Brian shared an intimate relationship with, but because she and Brian weren't as exclusive as she had led herself to believe.

"I know I'm going to regret telling you this." He took a deep breath and avoided her gaze when he said, "Trey and I experimented with each other in high school."

"High school?" she said breathlessly.

"Yeah. It was only once." He squeezed his eyes shut. "Okay, twice. I fucked him twice. But we got it out of our systems and we never did it again." He buried his face in her neck. "I disgust you now, don't I? I should never have told you."

"I'm not disgusted," she whispered. Relieved. Yes, that's what she was feeling. And happy that he trusted her enough to tell her something that personal.

He lifted his head to look at her, his eyes wide with surprise. "You're not?"

"No. It's fine. It's all in the past. Right?"

"Yeah, of course. I don't even like to think about it." He stared into her eyes for a long moment and then pressed his lips to hers. "I can't believe you're cool with this. You're too good to be true."

He showed his appreciation with deep, all-encompassing kisses and questing hands. She encouraged his attention, knowing that even though Brian was well over his brief attraction to Trey, Trey was in no way ready to give up on Brian.

Chapter 33

MYRNA SET HER STACK OF DATA ON THE COFFEE TABLE between her laptop and cup of chamomile tea and answered her cell phone. Didn't he realize it was eleven o'clock at night in her time zone?

"Hello?"

"I miss you," Brian murmured. "Did I wake you?"

She smiled. She missed him, too, but had been getting a lot of work done since she'd returned home. She was almost caught up. Her guilt trip for abandoning her work to enjoy Brian was starting to wane. Just a little. Maybe she could return to him sooner than she'd imagined. "No, I'm still working. How did the music video shoot go today?"

"I'm in all of five shots. Sed's a total camera hog. The rest of us were bored." She heard the slur in his voice.

"And so you drank all day," she guessed.

"We were bored."

"I'm going to let you go."

"Why?"

"Because I'm working." *And I can't stand the sound of your voice when you're drunk.*

"Is that really why?"

"Call me back tomorrow," she said. "When you're sober."

"Myrna?"

She hung up. She sighed and picked up her data. She'd

only typed in one number when the phone rang again. She considered not answering but finally picked up.

"Brian, I don't want to talk to you right now."

"Who's Brian?"

Myrna's blood turned cold. Her throat closed off. *Jeremy*.

She couldn't breathe, much less speak. How had he gotten her phone number? She'd been careful to keep it unlisted and had given it to very few people.

"Who's Brian?" he repeated.

Her only reply was a gasp. Paralyzed with fear, she couldn't move. Or think.

"Is he the reason you've been away from your apartment for over three weeks?"

How did he know she'd been away? Was he watching her again?

"Are you fucking him?"

"How did you get this number?" she asked around the lump in her throat.

"Are you *fucking* him? I'll kill him. No one touches you but me. Do you understand? You're my wife. You belong to me."

"Jeremy, we're divorced. And in case you forgot, I still have that restraining order."

"Are you going to call the cops? Go ahead. They don't know where I am, but I'll see you real soon, sugar." He disconnected.

Myrna tossed the cell phone across the couch as if it had transformed into a snake. She jumped to her feet, lowered the blinds at all the windows, and jerked the drapes closed. She checked to make sure the front door was locked. Bolted. Chained. She looked in the closets.

Checked under the bed and behind doors. In the kitchen cabinets. The refrigerator. She was alone. Too alone for comfort. She picked up her cell phone and locked herself in the bathroom.

When she closed the door, the shower curtain billowed. Myrna dialed 911 and held her thumb over Send as she approached the bathtub. Heart thudding, she grabbed the curtain and jerked it back.

Empty.

Her shoulders sagged with relief. She sat on the edge of the bathtub with her back against the cold tile wall so she could see the entire room. Jeremy might have learned to teleport since she'd last seen him.

She called Brian.

He answered on the second ring. "Oh, so now you want to talk to me."

She could hear a lot of noise in the background. Loud music. Conversation. Laughter. Clinking glasses. She was scared out of her wits and he was partying like, well, a rock star. The jerk.

"J-Jeremy called," she whispered.

"What? I can't hear you," he shouted.

The noises in the background changed rapidly. He must be on the move toward an exit, or some place a little more quiet.

"Say it again," he said.

"J-Jeremy called." She wiped at an annoying tear with the back of her hand. What did tears get you? Nothing. They sure didn't make a drunk stop accusing you of being a filthy whore.

"Your ex-husband? I thought you had no contact with him. Why did he call you?"

"He wanted to know where I've been for the last three weeks," she whispered. She couldn't seem to talk any louder. As if Jeremy might overhear her.

"He's stalking you again," Brian said with a certainty. "Do you have someone who can stay with you until I get there?"

"No, I didn't call you to get you to come here. He said he was going to kill you."

"He said that? How does he even know about me?"

"Don't come here."

"Then you come here. Immediately."

There was a thump in the apartment next door and Myrna jumped.

It was bad enough that she had to live in fear, but she refused to put Brian at risk. If she went to him, or he came to her, she knew Jeremy would hurt him. She swallowed and took a deep breath, hoping she sounded confident when she said, "Don't be ridiculous. I have a ton of work to do. He's just being a jerk. I'll be fine. I know he won't bother me again. I reminded him that I have a restraining order. If he comes near me, all I have to do is call the police and they'll arrest him."

"Yeah, okay. I'll just sit around here for a week and hope your psychotic stalker of an ex-husband leaves you alone."

"Brian—"

"I'll be there as soon as I can. Do you want me to stay on the phone with you?"

"That's not really necessar— For a little while."

"Tell me about your day," he said. She could hear the bar noises in the background again. "Hey, Phil," he called to someone, "call me a cab, will you?"

"You're leaving already, Brian?" some annoyed-sounding woman said. "We just got this party started."

"You're not telling me about your day," Brian said to Myrna.

"What do you want to know?"

"Everything. Start from the moment you opened your eyes."

"Shouldn't I start from the moment I rolled over in bed and tried to find you, but you weren't there?"

"Yeah, start with that." She could hear the smile in his voice.

She told him all about her day. Every moment, including what Jeremy had said to her on the phone. Brian kept her talking on his cab ride to the airport, while he booked a flight at the ticket counter, and the entire time he waited for his flight. She felt safer just having him on the other end of the line. She eventually let herself out of the bathroom and crawled into bed with her phone. She left all the lights in the apartment on, however. She didn't think she could handle darkness.

"My battery is going dead," he said. "I'll keep talking as long as I can. My plane is boarding soon."

"I'm sorry to be a pest, Brian."

"You're not a pest."

She didn't realize she was on the verge of tears until they started to fall. "I shouldn't have called you. And I shouldn't let you come here," she whispered, and sniffed her nose. "Jeremy might hurt you."

"I can take care of that stupid prick. Don't worry about me. Keep yourself safe until I get there. You know, if you go to sleep now, I'll be there when you wake up."

She nodded as if he could see her. She was exhausted. Mentally drained. "Thank you for being there for me."

"Think nothing of it. You know I lo—"

The phone disconnected. His battery must've died. Not wanting Jeremy to have the opportunity to call her again, she shut off her phone. Tomorrow she'd get the number changed.

But *how?* How had Jeremy found her? She'd been so careful.

Chapter 34

THE SOUND OF THE DOOR BUZZER PULLED MYRNA from a listless sleep. It took her a moment to remember she was home, not on the tour bus.

The buzzer sounded again. A few stray rays of sunshine filtered around the edges of her bedroom curtains. Morning already? Myrna stumbled from bed, still in the clothes she'd worn the day before.

The buzzer sounded again. Several times in a row. Loud knocking followed.

Brian! He'd made it.

"I'm coming," she called as she hurried toward the door.

She unlocked it and pulled it open, a bright smile on her face. It faded instantly.

"Good morning, darling," Jeremy greeted. His bright blue eyes raked over her body from head to toe. "Did you sleep in your clothes last night, sweetheart? You're a mess."

He wasn't. Deeply tanned, blond, tall, athletic, and handsome, he looked like a walking advertisement for a country club. Her mouth worked at producing words but nothing came out. Her entire body had gone numb. She couldn't move.

"Here, I brought you flowers. I know how you like the frivolous things." He shoved a huge bouquet of mixed flowers into her chest. She caught them automatically.

He edged his tall, lithe body into her apartment and closed the door. "I told you I'd see you soon. Why do you look so stunned?"

"Leave!" she managed to bellow.

"You're not happy to see me?"

"Of course I'm not happy to see you. Get out of my apartment!"

He lifted his hand to touch her cheek, and she whimpered in fear.

He dropped his hand, his blond brows drawn together with concern. "I'm not going to hurt you, darling. I don't drink anymore. See? Smell my breath."

The minty scent of his mouthwash bathed her face. She flinched. She couldn't help it. She was terrified of him. "That's not the point, Jeremy. You aren't supposed to come within three hundred yards of me. If you don't leave by the count of three, I'm calling the cops."

"Myrna, just hear me out."

"One."

"I realize what a jerk I was, and I've come to ask for your forgiveness."

"Two."

"I've been through treatment, Myrna. The thought that we can be together again is all the reason I need to stay sober for the rest of my life."

"Three." Myrna tossed the flowers on the floor and turned to search for her phone. She remembered that she'd fallen asleep with it against her chest the night before. She hurried toward her bedroom to retrieve it.

"Wait." Jeremy followed her into the living room. The sound of his footsteps behind her made her heart race. She covered the back of her head with one hand

and walked sideways so she could keep an eye on him. She wouldn't put it past him to clobber her over the head the second she turned her back.

"Just give me a chance. Please, Myrna. Listen to me." His strong fingers gripped her arm.

She froze, trembling uncontrollably. She couldn't catch her breath. "How did you find me, Jeremy?" she said, gasping. "How? I did everything right."

He chuckled. "That part was easy. There aren't many '57 Thunderbirds registered in this state."

Of course. Her car. How could she have been so stupid?

"Why are you shaking? I said I wouldn't hurt you. Don't be afraid."

"Don't be afraid? Don't be *afraid!*" She turned and shoved him with both hands. "You put me in the hospital, you crazy son of a bitch. You almost killed me."

"That wasn't me, baby. It wasn't. I was drunk, and you were cheating on me with that gas station attendant. I lost control. But I won't slip again. I promise. I'll never hurt you again. Never."

Gas station attendant? What the fuck was he talking about? She'd never dated a gas station attendant. She didn't even *know* a gas station attendant.

"I'm not that man anymore. Remember that charming man you fell in love with?" He smiled, and she could almost remember the man she'd married, but she remembered a face twisted in rage and a pair of hard fists much more vividly.

"He's back. I," he continued, pressing a hand to his chest, "I'm back and we can go back, Myrna. Back to the way things were at the beginning. You'd like that, wouldn't you? I never meant to hurt you, sweetheart.

You have to believe me. I'm better now. I've changed. I love you. So much. I do. I love you. You believe that, don't you?"

Her stomach churned at the sound of those three little words slithering from between his lying lips. Nothing had changed. This was exactly like every other time he'd talked her into taking him back. Well, one thing had changed. She had. She knew real love with a good man. Brian had showed her the difference. She shook her head at Jeremy. "Even if I did believe you, and I don't, it wouldn't matter. I don't love you. I have a new boyfriend. One who respects me and treats me well. He doesn't think I'm a whore or falsely accuse me of cheating on him."

Jeremy's eyes hardened and his upper lip curled. A thrill of fear raced down her spine. As she suspected, the darkness in him was carefully veiled behind his lies and attempted manipulations.

After several seconds, Jeremy relaxed and smiled. "Oh, yes. Brian."

"Do I know you?" Brian asked from the open front door.

Chapter 35

BRIAN WAS STILL GROGGY FROM THE LONG FLIGHT, but he didn't think he was hallucinating. There was something intimate between Myrna and this guy who had his hand wrapped around her arm.

The tall man turned and his eyes widened. "This has to be a joke, Myrna. Your new boyfriend is a thug?"

"He's not a thug," she whispered. "He's perfect."

"Am I interrupting something?" Brian asked, his brows raised in question.

Myrna's hands clenched into fists. Her entire body was shaking. He could see it from halfway across the room. Something wasn't right here. Who was this guy? And why was he touching Myrna with such familiarity? Had she actually been in such a hurry to return to Kansas City so she could rendezvous with some secret lover of hers? She'd known he was on his way. Surely she wasn't stupid enough to get caught this easily.

"You can leave, thug. My wife and I are getting back together." The man wrapped an arm around Myrna's shoulders and tucked her against his side. His lips brushed her temple.

Brian's heart slammed into his chest. "Wife?" Brian sputtered.

This was Jeremy? This handsome, clean-cut man was the evil son of a bitch who had damaged Myrna so severely she couldn't stand the sound of the word love?

It couldn't be. Brian was certain Jeremy had curved horns, thick red skin, glowing eyes, and cloven hooves. This guy, who belonged on a Christmas card dressed in a reindeer sweater surrounded by his doting wife, 2.5 kids, and his faithful golden retriever, could *not* be Jeremy. Not possible. Besides, weren't they divorced?

Myrna shook her head and opened her mouth but didn't produce a sound. Brian had never seen her look so pale. He decided she wasn't freaked out because he'd caught her in the act with some good-looking man. She was terrified. But Brian was here now. He wouldn't let this asshole hurt her again. Not physically. Not emotionally. Not psychologically. Brian wouldn't give him the chance.

"So you're Jeremy," Brian said, easing farther into the apartment. No sudden movements. There was no telling what this crazy bastard was capable of.

Jeremy smiled and tossed his blond head with a self-satisfied grin on his perfect face. "She told you about me, did she?"

"Oh yeah, she told me all about you." Brian's rage simmered beneath the surface, but he knew he had to keep it restrained. His first instinct was to pound the shit out of this guy, but he didn't want to scare Myrna. Brian didn't want her to think he was anything like this prick.

Jeremy trailed his fingers up and down Myrna's upper arm as he waited for Brian to make his move. Myrna stood frozen at his side, looking nauseous with anxiety. When Jeremy eased her closer, she whimpered.

Brian's rage erupted. "Get your fucking hands off her." He crossed the room in three strides, his fisted hands raised in threat.

"Whoa, whoa, whoa, whoa, *whoa*!" Jeremy said, backpedaling and shifting Myrna in front of his body for protection. "I know you thugs settle your differences with violence, but civilized men—"

"You're about to find out how violent this *thug* can get, you piece-of-shit pansy. I told you to get your fucking hands off Myrna. I mean *now*."

Jeremy dropped his hands from Myrna's shoulders.

Emitting a gasp of relief, she took a step toward Brian. He opened his arms to draw her near, but Jeremy grabbed her again. She flinched as if he'd struck her.

Brian's heart thudded faster. His eyes narrowed. "I warned you, asshole," he said. "Now I'm going to kick your ass."

Brian advanced on Jeremy, but before he could land a blow, Myrna stepped between them and lifted her hands to stop him. "No, Brian. Don't hit him."

Brian's eyes widened. She was defending him? How could she defend him? Maybe what Jeremy had said about them getting back together had been the truth. He certainly looked the part of her husband—attractive, clean-cut, wealthy, and well-educated. Perfect manners. Perfect face. Perfect body. Everything Myrna deserved in a husband. Certainly a more practical choice than Brian. Even he couldn't deny that reality.

Brian shook his head at his thoughts. No. Jeremy didn't deserve her. He had hurt her in every way imaginable. She didn't need someone who looked proper standing beside her. She needed someone who supported her and let her be herself. She needed Brian, dammit, even if she wouldn't admit it.

"I'm not just going to hit him," Brian said. "I'm going to beat the shit out of him."

"No, please don't."

Brian could not believe that she was *still* trying to protect the jerk. Was she mental? "Why not? He deserves it."

"Because," she said, looking up at him with concern in her pretty, hazel eyes, "you'll hurt your hands." She grabbed a tall crystal vase off a nearby end table and shoved it into his chest. "Use this instead."

Brian grinned and lifted the vase in one hand, testing its weight. "You sure? This is a really nice vase. It's also heavy. Potentially lethal." He glanced at Jeremy, satisfied to see fear in his eyes. Brian shifted his gaze to the flowers littering the floor by the door. "And you have some nice flowers over there that someone—not me, once again—delivered personally…"

Myrna careened into Brian as Jeremy shoved her out of the way. Jeremy sprinted toward the front door, but Brian grabbed him by the collar of his baby blue polo shirt before he could get out into the corridor. "Where do you think you're going?" Brian shut the door with his foot.

"Let me go!"

"I don't think you understand. I have a serious beef with you, dude. And I very much want to cause you permanent harm."

"I'm going to go call the police," Myrna said. "He's not supposed to be anywhere near me."

Brian was glad to see her confidence returning. He'd scarcely recognized her when he first arrived. "Great idea. I'll keep this guy occupied until they get here."

As soon as she disappeared into a room at the back of her apartment, Jeremy took a wild swing at Brian. Brian ducked. In his youth, he had been in more fights than he could count and it was obvious that this wuss had never squared off with a man. No, he was the type of coward who hit women and kicked puppies.

Jeremy struggled against Brian's hold on the back of his collar. "Get your hands off me, you filthy thug. If you so much as scratch me, my father will have you put away for the rest of your life."

"You're going to tell your daddy on me? You're even more pathetic than I realized." Brian jerked him away from the door and shoved him into a wingback chair. "Have a seat while we wait for your handcuffs to be delivered."

When Jeremy tried to get up, Brian put a fist in his face.

"Now listen to me, you son of a bitch, the only thing preventing me from tearing your head off and pissing down your neck hole is realizing what a mess your blood would make on Myrna's carpet. So you just sit there calmly, or I might do something you won't live long enough to regret." Talking trash usually did the trick with this type of coward, but Brian would be more than happy to turn his threats into reality. He would take great pleasure in rearranging this guy's overly handsome face.

"I really don't understand why you have it out for me. If it's because I called you a thug, then I apologize for that."

Jeremy oozed charm from every pore, but Brian wasn't buying it. "I don't care what you think of me, you arrogant ass. You hit a woman. *My* woman. You are on the top of my shit list."

"I don't know where you got your information. I would never hit a woman. Especially not Myrna. I love her." He closed his eyes and shuddered with tormented ecstasy. "Oh God, I love you, Myrna. I love you so much."

Brian's nose wrinkled and the skin on the back of his neck crawled. This guy was five brewskies short of a six-pack. "No wonder she hates that word."

Jeremy opened his eyes, a cold grin spreading across his face. *Creepy*. Make that six brewskies short.

"She's never said it to you, has she?" Jeremy chuckled with an odd merriment. "And she never will. She won't tell you she loves you because she still loves me. I own her heart forever. I made sure of it. She'll always be mine. Eternally. I ruined her for all other men. And I did it on purpose." Jeremy lowered his chin and stared up at Brian with icy blue eyes. "Thug."

Myrna came back into the room with her cell phone in her hand. "They're on their way."

Jeremy launched himself out of his chair and shoved Brian backward with both hands. Brian stumbled, regained his footing, and headed after him. He should never have let his guard down. Jeremy yanked the door open. Brian thrust his arm in front of him to stop his progress. Sneering maliciously, Jeremy slammed the door. On Brian's hand.

"Ow! Fuck." Brian cradled his crushed hand against his chest.

"You idiot," Myrna yelled and jumped on Jeremy's back.

Her knees digging into Jeremy's sides to keep herself clinging to his body, she repeatedly slapped him on the head with both hands. "You stupid, stupid, stupid, stupid—"

"Ow, Myrna, that hurts. Stop it," Jeremy complained.

She continued to slap him, punctuating her blows with, "Stupid, stupid, stupid, stupid, stupid."

Brian watched, strangely amused by her tirade. Jeremy tried to dislodge her from his back, but she had him in a leg lock he had no hope of escaping.

Brian's left hand was already so swollen that he couldn't make a proper fist. He hoped to God it wasn't broken. But seeing Myrna slap the shit out of Jeremy in retaliation? Totally worth it.

Jeremy covered his head with his arms to try to block her continued flat-palmed slaps.

"I hate you," she bellowed. "I hate you. I hate you." When the tears started flowing, Brian couldn't stand there and watch anymore. He touched the center of her back and she hesitated. She turned her head to look at him, tears streaming down her face and dripping off her jaw.

"It's okay, baby," he murmured. "Come here."

She fell into his embrace, wrapping her arms around his neck and her legs around his waist. She sobbed against his shoulder, drenching his shirt in seconds. He stroked her back and rubbed his lips against her hair. "It's okay. I'm here. I've got you. Shh."

Finally free, Jeremy yanked the door open and found two police officers standing on the threshold.

"Are you Jeremy Condaroy?" one of the officers asked.

"No, but thank God you're here. You arrived just in time," Jeremy said. "That's him. Right there." He pointed at Brian.

Chapter 36

MYRNA DIDN'T UNDERSTAND WHAT WAS HAPPENING. Why was she being pulled from Brian's steady and comforting embrace? Why were two police officers wrestling Brian to the floor and handcuffing him? Why had they let Jeremy walk casually out of the apartment?

"What is going on?" she screamed.

"It's okay, ma'am. We've got him," one of the police officers said, and then he started to recite Miranda rights to Brian.

"Why are you arresting my boyfriend?"

The two cops looked at her in confusion.

"I'm not the guy you're looking for," Brian said, still face-down on the floor. "You let him get away."

The officers looked at Myrna as if they didn't believe what Brian was saying and needed her verification to proceed.

"That's Brian Sinclair, not Jeremy Condaroy," Myrna said. "Jeremy is a tall, prudish, blond man."

"Shit!" said one of the officers, and he took off out of the apartment and down the corridor. "Freeze," he yelled, his footsteps carrying down the hall. "I said freeze. I'm going to Taser you if you don't stop."

The younger of the two officers hesitated, looking down at Brian with a giddy sort of expression. "Brian Sinclair. The lead guitarist of Sinners?"

"Be a fanboy later," Myrna said. "That dickhead you

let escape broke Brian's hand. Are you just going to let him get away?"

The officer's eyebrows drew together. "I'll take him down," he said and headed after his partner.

The sound of electrical crackling carried down the hallway, followed by a yelp of pain.

"Heh, I think they got him." Brian smiled. "I hope it fucking hurts, you asshole!" he called.

Myrna helped Brian sit up, but there wasn't anything she could do about the cuffs holding his hands together behind his back.

"I'm so sorry about all this." She knelt in front of him and touched his face.

"No big deal. I've been arrested before."

Her heart skipped a beat. "You have? For what?"

"Fighting. I used to be a hotheaded little snot."

She chuckled. "Somehow I totally believe that." She circled around his body and leaned close to examine his hand. It was horribly bruised and swollen. She couldn't tell if it was broken and didn't want to hurt him by examining it too rigorously. "How's your hand? Do you think it's broken?"

"I can't tell. But it doesn't matter. What's important is that you're safe."

He was so sweet. If Jeremy had caused permanent damage to Brian's hand, Myrna would never forgive herself. "I'll go get you some ice." She started to rise from the floor, but he leaned against her.

"No, stay with me."

She stared unseeingly at his shoulder. "I should never have called you."

"What? You can't be serious, Myrna. I don't even

want to think of what could have happened if you'd been here alone with that guy. He's a total nutcase. How is he out on the streets?"

"Parole. His father has friends in high places."

"Maybe this time they'll keep him locked up. He obviously hasn't learned his lesson."

Myrna rubbed her forehead, a feeling of helplessness washing over her. "I guess I need to change my name again. Move to a new city. Start over. God, I'm sick of this. I'm sick of him controlling my life."

"Fuck him, Myrna."

Myrna stiffened, the very idea filling her with dread. And nausea.

"I don't mean literally." Brian shook his head at her. "He's the one with issues. You shouldn't have to hide in fear because someone beat *him* with a crazy stick."

"Sometimes it's easier to hide."

"Since when are you the kind of person who takes the easy way out?"

She knew she wouldn't be able to explain it in a way that he'd understand. She didn't really understand it herself. Jeremy knew her every button, and he pushed them all repeatedly, without hesitation. "There's just something about him, Brian. He gets to me."

"I know, sweetheart. You do whatever you need to do to feel safe." He shifted so his shoulder pressed against hers. "I'd really like to hug you right now, but I'm sort of stuck."

She wrapped her arms around his waist and rested her head on his shoulder. "I do like you restrained from time to time, but not like this."

"You're going to let me stay here with you in Kansas

City until we go back on tour, aren't you? I obviously can't record with my hand all jacked up."

"I'd rather go back to L.A. with you. I don't know if I can stomach being in this apartment right now." She glanced around. Yeah, Jeremy's presence was fouling up the entire place. Forget finding the focus to work on her research. She'd never be able to sleep, much less concentrate.

"If you're really set on changing your name, you're more than welcome to mine."

She covered his mouth with one hand. "Don't you dare suggest Vegas again."

The younger of the police officers entered the front door. "Well, we have him in custody," he said. "Let me get you out of those handcuffs, Master Sinclair."

Myrna moved aside and the officer squatted behind Brian to unlock his cuffs. As soon as he was free, Brian cradled his left hand against his chest. He tried to disguise his wince of pain with a smile of gratitude, but he wasn't fooling Myrna. His fingers were already black and blue. She needed to get him to the emergency room and have his hand X-rayed.

"I hope there was some police brutality involved in that arrest," Brian said.

The officer winked. "Maybe a little. I feel stupid asking this, but I'm a huge fan of yours. Can I have your autograph?"

"Yeah, no problem." Brian climbed to his feet.

While Brian signed an autograph with his uninjured right hand, the officer talked to Myrna. "We probably have enough to keep your ex-husband incarcerated until he goes back to court—the idiot removed his house arrest ankle bracelet, is hundreds of miles outside his perimeter, and violated a restraining order—but I suggest you press additional charges against him. The more we have against this guy, the easier it will be to keep him locked up."

She glanced at Brian, who was pushing on the knuckles of his injured hand and scowling. "I need to take Brian to the hospital and get his hand checked out. Can I press charges later?"

"Um, yeah. Just go downtown and file a complaint as soon as possible. Sinclair should press charges, too."

"I will definitely press charges," Brian said. "I'm even considering making some shit up."

Chapter 37

A WEEK LATER, SITTING AMONGST A PILE OF DIRTY laundry and empty beer cans on the pigsty bus, Brian entered into a pentatonic scale progression and Trey echoed him two notes behind.

When they reached the end of the riff, Sed said, "Yeah, I like that. Eric, what do you have?"

"It's hard to compose when your drum kit is locked in a truck, dude." He tapped his sticks on the side of the refrigerator beside him. "That's the beat I hear, but without my cymbals and my bass drums and…" He sighed and shook his head.

"We really need to find some studio time," Brian said. "When's our next break?" Because of Brian's injured hand, their last break had been a complete bust. His hand hadn't been broken, but the swelling had kept him from playing for almost a week. All the recording they'd planned to do in the studio had been a complete wash. They hadn't been forced to cancel tour dates, but Brian knew last night's performance had been less than stellar on his part.

"We've got another week on the road, and then two weeks off at the end of June," Sed said. "We'll get some recording done then. For now, we'll just keep writing so we're ready when the time comes."

"As often as Sinclair gets laid, we'll have enough guitar music for ten albums," Trey said around his sucker.

Jace thumped Brian on the back. "You need to start composing bass riffs, too. I can't keep up."

Brian glanced at Jace over his shoulder and smiled. "I'll give it a try."

"Where's your lady love, anyway?" Sed asked.

"She's on the other bus working on her research stuff," Brian said. "She said we're too distracting and she's never going to get it done if she doesn't hide from us for a couple of hours."

"So that's why we're having a session on the pigsty bus. That woman knows how to get exactly what she wants, doesn't she?" Trey chuckled. "No wonder Brian's in love."

Jace thumped Brian on the back again.

"Too bad the feeling isn't mutual," Brian muttered under his breath. He reached for a sheet of music from the stack on the table. This one had splatters of chocolate syrup all over it. Recalling what he'd been doing when this gem had come to him, he grinned to himself.

"What do you mean, it isn't mutual?" Trey asked. "You stormed the castle and saved her from the evil dragon. And no woman would put up with five slobs for five weeks for the sake of research. She loves you, man. She wouldn't be here if she didn't love you."

Brian snorted. "Try convincing her of that. She's just here to work."

"Who cares if she loves him?" Eric said. "She fucks him well, keeps the bus clean, and cooks us meals. As far as I'm concerned, no one loses in this game."

Sed shoved Eric off the counter onto the floor. "Don't talk about Myrna like that, you prick."

Eric climbed to his feet and shoved Sed before

retreating to the other side of the bus and sitting next to Trey at the dining room table. "I don't mean any disrespect. She's a great woman. I just mean, if she doesn't want to admit that she loves Brian, what's the big deal?"

"It's nice to hear it," Sed murmured to the floor. He glanced up at Brian and smiled. "You'd like to hear her say it, wouldn't you?"

Brian shrugged. "Neither one of us has said it."

"You haven't told her?" Trey asked. "Dummy. She's probably one of those chicks who refuses to say it first."

Brian shook his head. "She forbids it. You've heard her. When anyone asks her about us, she just laughs and says it's nothing serious. We're just having a good time."

"No one believes that, Brian," Trey said. "You don't believe it, do you?"

Maybe. "Just drop it, okay?"

"That woman has got you by the balls, Brian," Jace said.

Brian glanced up at him and laughed. "Yeah, but the way she grips them—hard enough to get my attention, but not so hard that I want to get away—feels so good."

Eric commenced to banging his head on the table.

Maybe he did need to tell her how he felt and to hell with her barriers. What's the worst that could happen?

She could leave.

His stomach plummeted.

He'd wait awhile longer.

Brian shook the chocolate-splattered sheet music at Trey. "I think this solo fits well with that last riff."

Trey offered him a sad little smile. "Okay, then. Let's hear it."

Chapter 38

MYRNA ENTERED MORE NUMBERS INTO THE spreadsheet on her computer. Her survey gave consistent, reliable data and showed two strong behavioral trends among the groupies. She had no doubt that this research was going to save her entire career. And if it didn't, it wasn't the end of the world. She'd started working on a proposal for a nonfiction book guaranteed to be a bestseller.

"I hope you're smiling like that because you're thinking about me," Brian said.

She glanced up from the computer screen. She hadn't heard him enter the bus. He kissed her cheek and slid into the booth across from her.

Her smile brightened. "I'm always thinking about you."

There was a clatter near the front of the bus as Trey entered. "Myrna," he said, "look what I've got."

"Cherry suckers?" she guessed.

"Fresh shrimp. One of the roadies bought them. Will you make some shrimp scampi?" He set the bag on the table and gave her his puppy-dog look. The one he knew she couldn't resist. "Pwease."

She smiled at him and nodded. "After I finish entering this data." She started typing in the next row of numbers.

"You mean, after I finish entering you," Brian said.

She glanced up from her computer screen. Brian

gave her that *other* look she couldn't resist. That "get naked immediately" look. She saved her file and closed the laptop, stuffing the stack of papers under the computer. "Sorry, Trey. Brian wins."

"But I'm *starv*ing."

"We'll be finished in an hour or two," Brian said.

"Or four," Myrna said.

"Or four." Brian slid out of the booth and extended his hand toward Myrna.

"Four hours? I'll die by then." He took Brian's vacated seat and peered into the fishy-smelling bag.

"I'm sure you can find something to eat in the fridge." Myrna slid from the booth, took Brian's hand, and glanced back at Trey. "What did you guys do with yourselves before I joined the tour?"

"We were barely alive," Trey said. "Drowning in our own filth. Malnourished. Scrawny. Anemic. On our last limb." He stretched out a hand toward her, his head collapsing on the table as he played dead.

She chuckled. "You poor babies."

Brian tugged her toward the bedroom. "You're too good to us."

"I like taking care of you guys. You've all become important to me over the past month."

"Even Eric?"

She laughed. "Yes, even Eric."

"You're important to all of us, too," he said. "I can't remember the last time we felt so…settled."

Settled? Ugh. "I'm a drag, aren't I?"

Brian tugged her through the bedroom door and pulled her against his body, kissing her hungrily. He kicked the door closed.

"Not a drag," he murmured. "You're wonderful. Like I said, too good for the likes of us."

She kissed the corner of his mouth. "Your lies are good for my ego."

"I'd never lie to you," he whispered, his lips trailing lightly over the skin of her cheek to her ear. He drew her earlobe into his mouth, pressing it against his upper teeth with his tongue. Her breath caught. She forgot about everything but him.

His hands moved to the buttons of her shirt, releasing them one at a time as his tongue rubbed the sensitive spot behind her ear. Her fingers curled into his hard chest as she swayed against him.

He brushed her shirt off her shoulders and moved his mouth to her collarbone, kissing her skin gently. So gently it made her want to cry.

"Brian?" she whispered.

He lifted his head to look at her. "Hmm?"

"You're being tender."

"You don't like it?"

"I didn't say that. I just wondered what brought it on all of a sudden."

He grinned. "Jace needs bass music. I have to slow it down a little."

She placed her hands on his face and rose on tiptoes to kiss his lips. "Is that all? I thought maybe you had something to tell me."

His brows drew together. He swallowed hard and fixed his gaze on her forehead. "Like what?"

"You've thought up something kinky and figured you'd better soften me up before springing your trap."

"You think I have a one-track mind." He sighed

and shook his head slightly. "Sometimes I think this is hopeless."

Her heart thudded painfully in her chest. Ever since they'd returned from Kansas City, he'd been acting strangely. Like he wanted to break up with her or something. And after being so rudely introduced to Myrna's past baggage, who could blame him? But it wasn't something she could change. Jeremy had left a big impact on her life whether Brian liked it or not. "I don't know what you want from me, Brian."

"Yes, you do. That's why it scares you when I'm tender with you."

So this wasn't about her past. This was about their future. "I'm not scared." But she was. Terrified. Mostly because she couldn't picture a future without him in it.

"Can you let me be tender without making it into a joke?"

"I'm not making it into a joke."

He quirked an eyebrow at her. "You're not?"

"I'll be quiet."

"Just stop thinking so much and feel," he said. "And I don't mean your body. I know you feel me with your body. I mean here." He placed three fingertips on her chest over her heart. "I don't think you ever listen to what's going on in here."

"I lis—"

He covered her mouth with his fingertips. "Shhh." Something had changed in him. She could see it in his eyes. He looked…desperate.

"Bri—"

"Shhh."

"But—"

"Shhh."

She nodded. He removed his fingers from her mouth. She bit her lip. He stared down at her, obviously struggling with words. She waited for him to say something, but he lowered his head and kissed her instead. His feelings of desperation came through in his kiss as well.

"Just love me, Myrna," he whispered against her lips. "Please."

She turned her head to break his kiss. "What did you say?"

He stared over her head, swallowing several times. "Make love to me, Myrna. Please."

That's not what he'd said, but she could accept his amended words. She couldn't accept his original plea. The look on his face as he struggled to conceal his emotions made her heart ache. She touched his face and his gaze shifted to hers. "Tenderly. That's what you need, right?"

He nodded slightly. She nodded, too, tears prickling her eyes. She would have given anything to have met Brian before Jeremy. Then it wouldn't be so goddamned hard to uncover what she concealed in her heart and accept what was in his.

They undressed each other slowly until they stood before each other naked, both excited and soothed. Her hands slid over the warm skin of his chest. Her lips followed in their wake.

"This is when you sweep me up into your arms and carry me to bed," he said.

She laughed. "Hey, I'm trying to be serious."

"Who said I wasn't being serious?" He grinned down at her and then gasped as she wrapped her arms around his waist and lifted his feet several inches off the floor. She took a couple of steps and dumped him on the bed. He laughed, covering his eyes with his hands. His laughter warmed her heart. It was one of the many things she loved, erm, *liked* about this man.

"Sorry, I kind of flubbed that one. I need to work out more. Puny biceps." She climbed onto the bed beside him, urging him to scoot up toward the headboard. "And this is the part where I rub rose petals over your skin, right?"

"I think we're fresh out of rose petals."

"Close your eyes." She loosened her hair from the clip holding it in place at the back of her head. He closed his eyes. She leaned over him and trailed her long, thick hair over his belly. "Imagine this is rose petals."

"I like knowing what it really is better. Wrap it around my cock."

"We're being tender, Brian, remember?"

"That's not tender?"

"Tenderness doesn't involve your cock at all and especially not wrapping my hair around it."

His eyes flipped open. "You're kidding!"

She covered his lips with her fingers. "Shhh. Close your eyes."

He hesitated for a moment and then obeyed.

"I'm going to touch every inch of you," she whispered. "Kiss every inch."

He grabbed his half-hard cock and stroked it from base to tip. "All ten? Give me a minute. He's not quite ready yet."

She laughed. "Now who's making jokes?"

He winked at her. "Sorry. I'll behave."

Her featherlight touches began with his left hand. The

bruises had faded and the swelling had gone down, but she would never forget that terrifying wait for his X-ray results. She'd been convinced that he'd never play guitar again and it would have been all her fault.

She trailed her fingers over the palm of his hand, the thick calluses on his fingertips, and back to his palm. His fingers curled involuntarily.

Involving her lips now, she kissed his palm while moving her tender touch to his wrist and up his fore-arm. She sucked his ring finger into her mouth and he groaned. Out of the corner of her eye, she saw his cock twitch in response. She withdrew his finger from her mouth and kissed her way to the inside of his wrist.

Extending her arm, she continued to stroke his skin as she kissed her way up the inside of his forearm to the inner surface of his elbow. Her questing fingers found the crisp hairs surrounding his nipple. She teased the hairs, her middle finger brushing against his nipple as she sucked on the inside of his elbow.

She loved touching him, experiencing his body in slow motion, but soon she was craving his intoxicating touch. She shifted her body so her breast was positioned in his hand. He squeezed gently.

Her nipple strained against his palm, desiring more rigorous attention.

When he relaxed his hold, she moved up his arm again, kissing a trail over his hard biceps toward his shoulder, dragging her hardened nipple over the inside of his forearm. Her belly clenched with need. Being tender with him was really turning her on.

Her hand slid across his chest as her mouth found his throat.

"Brian," she murmured, her kisses becoming less tender, more excited as she worked her way up the side of his neck to his ear. She plunged her tongue into his ear and his body jerked.

He chuckled. "Are you getting worked up already, baby?"

"You do this to me, Brian. Only you." She kissed a trail along the hard angle of his cheekbone and found his mouth. She shifted her body so that his hand was between her thighs. He didn't move his fingers to touch her though he must feel her heat, her moisture, her need.

"Touch me," she panted into his mouth.

When he didn't comply, she tugged her mouth away from his and reached between her legs, guiding his fingers into her body. She rocked her hips against his hand, burying his fingers deeper.

"You're just not very good at this tenderness stuff, are you?"

She looked down at him and cringed. She'd lost her intent in her own excitement. "I'm sorry."

"I'm not going to pretend I don't like that I turn you on so much you shove my fingers inside your body. It's hot." He twisted his hand slightly and she shuddered. He pulled his hand away. "Finish what you were doing. I'll fuck you good and hard when you're finished. That's what you want, isn't it?"

"Yes, hard. And fast. Gentle. Slow. I want it all as long as it involves your neglected cock."

But she couldn't neglect it any longer. She turned and slid down the length of his body, belly to belly but upside down. She took his shaft in her hand and licked its head.

"Mmmmm," he murmured.

He grabbed her hips and lifted his head to rub his chin against her clit. She gasped and sucked him into her mouth. His tongue traced the emptiness at her core, drawing her attention to the vacant feeling inside until she couldn't concentrate on anything else.

She had to have him. Needed what he gave her. What she could never get enough of. Him.

She released his cock from her mouth and slid down his body, straddling his hips. She didn't turn to face him, but guided his cock into her body backward and sank down, driving him deep.

Whore, Jeremy's voice whispered through her thoughts.

She hesitated. Brian gasped and tilted his hips to drive himself deeper still. His fingers ran down the center of her back, and she arched backward, her long hair trailing over his chest.

You like that, don't you, whore?

"Yeah," she whispered. "Feels good."

Brian shifted beneath her, and she glanced over her shoulder to find him propped up on his elbows, gazing down where their bodies were joined. She smiled and reached down to massage his balls gently. She rode him slowly, trying to remember he wanted tenderness from her.

He slid a finger up her ass and she gasped, pausing as he plunged it in and out of her several times. "Oh," she gasped.

"Do you like that?"

"Yeah."

Filthy whore.

She rubbed her ear against her shoulder, hoping to

silence Jeremy's ever-present criticism. Brian pulled his finger out, and she heard the side table drawer open, followed by the hum of a vibrator. He placed a hand on her back to ease her upward and then carefully slid a slender vibrator up her ass. She shuddered.

"Ah," he gasped, his head dropping back to the bed. "I can feel it inside you, vibrating against my cock."

She glanced at him over her shoulder. He was biting his lip, his head tilted back in sensual abandon. "Does it feel good?"

"Oh yeah," he gasped. His belly clenched as his back arched in ecstasy. "Ride me, sweetheart. Oh God, don't sit still."

"I want to watch your face."

His cock fell free of her body as she turned to face him. He grabbed her hips eagerly as she took him inside again. The vibrator drove her crazy. She rode him fast, rubbing his cock up and down the vibration with each penetration. It felt amazing, but watching his response was far more stimulating. He gripped the bedclothes beneath him, writhing in time to her movement.

He grabbed her hips to still her. "God, baby. We have to take that out or I'm going to explode. Like, immediately."

She took his wrists and pinned them to either side of his head. She began to rise and fall over him again, moving fast to drive him over the brink. She cried out as an orgasm shook her unexpectedly.

"Oh wow," she gasped.

She released Brian's wrist and pressed her fingers against her clit to try to calm herself so she could finish him. She rode him even faster, until he was calling her name each time their bodies came together. A muscle in his cheek began to twitch. It always twitched when he was close. *Almost, baby. Just let go.* There was nothing sexier than watching this man come, and though she'd seen it dozens of times, she never tired of it.

He's a whore, too, Jeremy's voice said.

Yeah, he was. And she wouldn't want him any other way.

Brian's head tilted back, eyes squeezed shut, lips parted. He gasped. His face contorted with ecstasy and then his entire body went rigid. He shuddered, crying out hoarsely as his fingers gripped the covers beneath him.

Perfect. The man was perfect. Perfect for her. And she loved him.

She *loved* him.

She did.

How could she not?

She needed to tell him.

Needed to say it. *I love you, Brian.* Her heart stuttered and then raced. Perhaps she'd find the courage to tell him tomorrow.

Or next year.

Brian's body relaxed, but he began to twitch uncontrollably. He lifted her away by her hips. "That's a bit much," he whispered. "I can't stand it."

She giggled and removed the vibrator from her body. "I think you liked it."

"I liked it too much." He reached for a score sheet and jotted down a single line of chords. "Jace will be pleased with our naughtiness." He tossed the music aside and drew her against his body.

"Not as pleased as I am."

"God, that was fucking fantastic, wasn't it?"

She nodded in agreement.

He kissed her tenderly, stroking her bare arm. "Now I'm sleepy," he murmured.

"Take a nap. I'll be here when you wake up. We'll try that tenderness thing again." She smiled. "I'll get it right eventually, though it might take me a few hundred attempts."

He chuckled sleepily and tucked her body against his. "Practice makes perfect, baby."

She lay there listening to him breathe as she blinked languidly.

"I love you, Myrna," he whispered, just before he drifted off to sleep. "I really do...love...you..."

Her breath caught. He *loved* her? Somehow, she knew he did, but until he'd said the words, it hadn't felt real.

Her heart lodged in her throat, Myrna watched Brian sleep for several minutes. She touched his face tenderly and kissed his cheek. Maybe she could say it while he was asleep. Just to try out the words for the first time. "I love you, too," she whispered.

His eyes flipped open.

He was awake? Shit. *Shit!* Now there was no taking it back.

His smile spread ear to ear. He looked as giddy as one of his fangirls. "Did you just say that you love me?"

She opened her mouth to deny it but nodded instead. "I think I've been waiting for you to tell me," she whispered, "and I was too afraid to say it first."

"You've been waiting for *me* to say it?"

"Maybe. I don't know. I just realized..."

He laughed and kissed her gently with tears in his eyes. "I was afraid I'd chase you away by telling you."

"Ten minutes ago, you probably would have. But that was then. This is now."

He hugged her against him. "Ah Myrna, I think I've loved you since I took my first breath." He rubbed his lips against her forehead.

She tried swallowing her emotion, but it did no good. Her throat closed off. "I'm sorry it took me so long to recognize it," she said breathlessly. "To say it."

"If you were really sorry, you'd say it again." He cupped her cheek and leaned back to look her in the eyes. His thumb brushed across her lower lip.

She took a deep breath. "I love you, Brian. Master Sinclair. Brian...I love you." She squeezed her eyes shut and then opened them again, her heart thudding in her chest. "I love you so much it terrifies me."

He leaned forward and kissed her deeply. "Don't be afraid, Myr. I love you more than I could ever put into words, but I won't fail you. I promise. This love, our love, is forever."

Forever with Brian? Yeah, she might be able to handle that.

She smiled, her fears dissipating. She trusted this man with her heart. Completely.

"You know," he said, "we'll be in Nevada for a show next week. Wanna go to Vegas and get married?"

Staring into her future's eyes, she grinned at him. Butterfly wings fluttered around her buoyant heart. "I thought you'd never ask."

Acknowledgments

I honestly can't imagine a world without music, and if such a world exists, I wouldn't want to live there. So I offer heartfelt thanks to the hundreds of musicians who fill my world with magnificent, creative sound. I don't think I could get through a day if I didn't have music to touch my heart and soul in some way.

I'd like to thank my family for being understanding and patient when I'm in "the writing zone" and for never giving up on me or my dream. Their unending support and faith in my ability means more than they'll ever know. Sean, you'll always be my favorite guitar hero.

I'd like to thank my second readers, Sherilyn Winrose, Judi Fennell, and Kat Sheridan, for offering their excellent, professional opinions and advice on this work. How many times did you read this manuscript, Sherilyn? I think you know it better than I do. And Judi, what can I say? You know the craft inside, outside, upside down and are always generous with that knowledge.

Kudos to my online writing group, The Writin' Wombats. It's been fun and sometimes heartbreaking to share our hardships and triumphs as both authors and friends over the years. I wouldn't be where I am today without their knowledge, help, support, and occasional kicks in the pants. I raise a toast to our continued success and offer a virtual hug to any who are struggling.

Major thanks to my agent Jennifer Schober, who gets me through the business side of this and keeps me grounded. Trust me, I need that.

Finally, I'd like to thank my sensational editor Deb Werksman, her ever-helpful associate, Susie Benton, and all the folks at Sourcebooks who believed in a debut writer enough to give her a chance to live her dream.

About the Author

Raised on hard rock music from the cradle, Olivia Cunning attended her first Styx concert at age six and fell instantly in love with live music. She's been known to travel over a thousand miles just to see a favorite band in concert. She discovered her second love, romantic fiction, as a teen—first voraciously reading steamy romance novels and then penning her own. She currently lives in Illinois.